Marius' Mules IV:
Conspiracy of Eagles

by S. J. A. Turney

2nd Edition

*"Marius' Mules: nickname acquired by the legions after the general
Marius made it standard practice for the soldier to carry all of his kit
about his person."*

For my beautiful Callie Sophia, born December 2011, whose haranguing melts my brain, but whose smile melts my heart.

I would like to thank those people instrumental in bringing Marius' Mules 4 to fruition and making it the success it has been, and those who have contributed to the production of the Second Edition, in particular Leni, Jules, Barry, Robin, Kate, Alex, Alun, Nick, two Daves, a Garry and a Paul. Also a special thanks to Ben Kane and Anthony Riches, who have greatly encouraged me towards the improvements in this edition.

Cover photos courtesy of Paul and Garry of the Deva Victrix Legio XX. Visit http://www.romantoursuk.com/ to see their excellent work.

Cover design by Dave Slaney.

Many thanks to all three for their skill and generosity.

All internal maps are copyright the author of this work.

Published in this format 2013 by Victrix Books

Also by S. J. A. Turney:

Continuing the Marius' Mules Series

Marius' Mules I: The Invasion of Gaul (2009)
Marius' Mules II: The Belgae (2010)
Marius' Mules III: Gallia Invicta (2011)
Marius' Mules V: Hades' Gate (2013)
Marius' Mules VI: Caesar's Vow (2014)
Marius' Mules: Prelude to War (2014)
Marius' Mules VII: The Great Revolt (2014)
Marius' Mules VIII: Sons of Taranis (2015)
Marius' Mules IX: Pax Gallica (2016)

The Praetorian Series

The Great Game (2015)
The Price of Treason (2015)
Eagles of Dacia (Autumn 2017)

The Ottoman Cycle

The Thief's Tale (2013)
The Priest's Tale (2013)
The Assassin's Tale (2014)
The Pasha's Tale (2015)

Tales of the Empire

Interregnum (2009)
Ironroot (2010)
Dark Empress (2011)
Insurgency (2016)
Invasion (2017)

Roman Adventures (Children's Roman fiction with Dave Slaney)

Crocodile Legion (2016)

Pirate Legion (Summer 2017)

Short story compilations & contributions:

Tales of Ancient Rome vol. 1 - S.J.A. Turney (2011)
Tortured Hearts vol 1 - Various (2012)
Tortured Hearts vol 2 - Various (2012)
Temporal Tales - Various (2013)
A Year of Ravens - Various (2015)
A Song of War – Various (Oct 2016)

For more information visit http://www.sjaturney.co.uk/
or http://www.facebook.com/SJATurney
or follow Simon on Twitter @SJATurney

Dramatis Personae (List of Principal Characters)

The Command Staff:

Gaius Julius Caesar: Politician, general and governor.
Aulus Ingenuus: Commander of Caesar's Praetorian Cohort.
Cita: Chief quartermaster of the army.
Quintus Atius Varus: Commander of the Cavalry.
Quintus Titurius Sabinus: Senior lieutenant of Caesar.
Lucius Aurunculeius Cotta: Lieutenant of Caesar
Titus Labienus: Senior lieutenant of Caesar.
Mamurra: Famous engineer favoured by Caesar
Gnaeus Vinicius Priscus: Former primus pilus of the Tenth, now camp prefect of the army.

Seventh Legion:

Quintus Tullius Cicero: Legate and brother of the great orator.
Titus Terrasidius: Senior Tribune.
Publius Tertullus: Junior Tribune.
Gaius Pinarius Rusca: Junior Tribune.
Lutorius: Primus pilus of the Seventh
Lucius Fabius: Centurion of the third century, first cohort
Tullus Furius: Centurion of the second century, first cohort

Eighth Legion:

Decimus Brutus: Legate and favourite of Caesar's family.
Titus Balventius: Primus pilus & veteran of several terms.
Aquilius: Training officer, senior centurion and perfectionist.

Ninth Legion:

Publius Sulpicius Rufus: Young Legate of the Ninth.
Marcus Trebius Gallus: Senior Tribune and veteran soldier.
Grattius: primus pilus, once in sole command of the Ninth.

Tenth Legion:

Marcus Falerius Fronto: Legate and confidante of Caesar.
Gaius Tetricus: Military Tribune, expert in military defences.

Crito: Veteran tribune of two years.
Servius Fabricius Carbo: Primus Pilus.
Atenos: Centurion and chief training officer, former Gaulish mercenary
Petrosidius: Chief Signifer of the first cohort.

Eleventh Legion:

Aulus Crispus: Legate, former civil servant in Rome.
Quintus Velanius: Senior Tribune.
Titus Silius: Junior Tribune.
'Felix': Primus Pilus, accounted an unlucky man.

Twelfth Legion:

Servius Galba: Legate.
Gaius Volusenus: Junior Tribune.
Publius Sextius Baculus: Primus pilus. A distinguished veteran.

Thirteenth Legion:

Lucius Roscius: Legate and native of Illyricum.

Fourteenth Legion:

Lucius Munatius Plancus: Legate and former staff officer.
Menenius: Junior tribune
Hortius: Junior tribune
Cantorix: Centurion in the Third cohort.

Other characters:

Quintus Balbus: Former Legate of the Eighth, now retired. Close friend of Fronto.
Faleria the elder: Mother of Fronto and matriarch of the Falerii.
Faleria the younger: sister of Fronto.
Corvinia: Wife of Balbus, legate of the Eighth.
Lucilia: Elder daughter of Balbus.
Balbina: Younger daughter of Balbus.
Galronus: Gaulish officer, commanding auxiliary cavalry.
Publius Clodius Pulcher: Powerful man in Rome, enemy of Caesar and conspirator, responsible for multiple crimes.

The maps of Marius' Mules IV

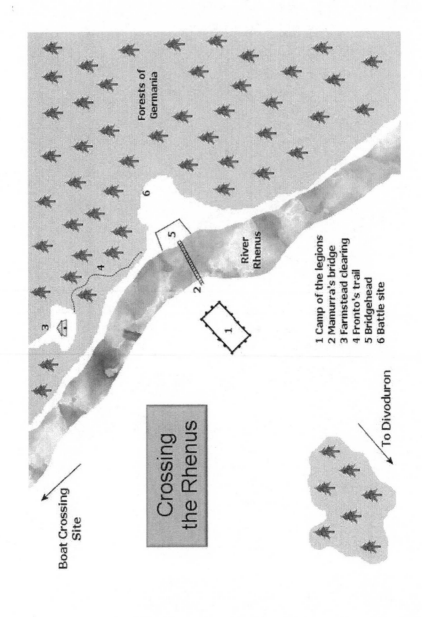

Crossing the Rhenus

Forests of Germania

River Rhenus

Boat Crossing Site

To Divoduron

1 Camp of the legions
2 Mamurra's bridge
3 Farmstead clearing
4 Fronto's trail
5 Bridgehead
6 Battle site

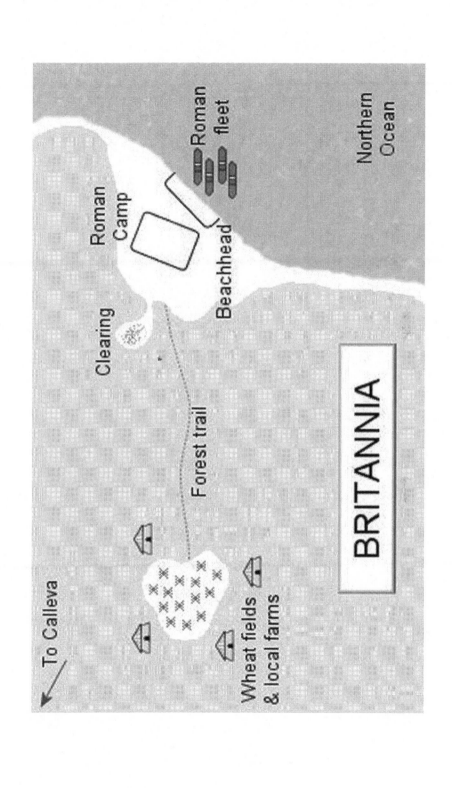

BRITANNIA

House of the Falerii on the Aventine Hill in Rome

Back Street

Main Street

Slaves & Servants' Quarters

Bunk House

Store Room

Bath House

Triclinium (Dining Room)

Cucina (Kitchen)

Stables

Peristyle Garden

with Covered Walkway

Armoury

Store Houses

Exedra

Bunk House

Bed Room

Bunk House

Bed Room

Triclinium (Dining Room)

Tablinum (Office)

Lucilla

Bed Room

Bed Room

Faleria Elder

Atrium

Faleria

Fronto

Faleria

Bed Room

Priscus

Oecus (Salon)

Posco

Master Bedroom

Yard

PART ONE:

GERMANIA

Chapter 1

(Puteoli, near Neapolis, on the Campanian coast)

Marcus Falerius Fronto, confidante of Caesar, legate of the Tenth Equestrian Legion, Roman citizen, Patrician and hero of the Gaulish wars, sulked and dragged his feet.

'Come on or we'll be late for the meal.' Lucilia Balba rolled her eyes as she cast a despairing look at her man. There were times when Fronto appeared not to have passed his seventh year of childhood.

Amid the hum of nature, Fronto gave her a cantankerous frown and glanced over his shoulder as he adjusted the new silken tunic that clung all too tight to his scarred, lean frame and, to his mind, made him look a little too feminine.

The Forum Vulcani loomed almost a mile distant, the ring of jagged rock standing high around a white-yellow crater that jetted and fumed continually with spurts of steam and sprays of hot mud. Despite his almost legendary pragmatism, the Forum Vulcani continued to hold a certain unspoken trepidation for Fronto. He knew the gurgling mud and jets of steam were simply the work of Vulcan's forge beneath the world but in the stories of his youth, told by the elders and menfolk of coastal Campania, the great bubbling, steaming horseshoe was the entrance to Hades. His childhood best friend Laelius had once sworn he saw a great three-headed dog prowling amid the jets. It was impossible to shake off the dread, despite his adult practicality.

And this infuriating woman had brought him here to *lounge in the steam* and slap *stinging hot mud* on his more scarred and ugly patches of skin in the crazed belief that being thoroughly coated with grey-brown sludge was somehow 'healing'. It certainly had not made his bones ache less or removed the burgeoning hangover, though the faint scalding sensation that had reddened much of his flesh had at least taken his mind off the left knee that had started to give these days if he walked up and down hills too often.

'The meal can wait for us. I'm the patriarch of the house, remember?'

'Yes, dear. You're a fine patriarch, but you'll be a fine patriarch with a charred meal and a furious sister if we don't hurry.'

2

Fronto gave the great steaming mountain a suspicious frown – he thought he had seen it move for a moment – and turned back to face the mass of Puteoli ahead and below, not quite in time to avoid treading in a large pile of dung deposited by one of the numerous trade caravans that had come here from the other great port nearby, at Neapolis.

'Shit!'

'Indeed, my love. Horse shit, I fear.'

Fronto grumbled and hoisted the leather bag with their wet clothes higher onto his shoulder so that he could concentrate on wiping his rough military-issue sandals on the kerb to remove the worst of the ordure.

Lucilia gave him an odd smile and then turned away, humming a happy little tune as she picked up the pace a little, strolling down the hill toward the expansion work on the small amphitheatre – pride of the council of Puteoli.

Briefly, Fronto cast a longing gaze down the slope. Spring had come to Puteoli, bringing a bounteous spray of flora, whose scent almost managed to mask the salt tang of the sea. Bees buzzed and cicadas chirruped, birds sang and unidentified wildlife rustled all along both sides of the road that led from Neapolis to Puteoli via the Forum Vulcani. But it was not the bounty of nature or the sheer joy of spring that drew his hungry gaze.

Somewhere, down beyond the oval amphitheatre and past the various baths and temples, right down toward the port, looking out over the water to the distant hump of Baia and the mound of Misenum on the far side of the bay, stood the small building that drew his thoughts. The 'Leaping Dolphin' was a tavern that served wine of questionable quality, allowed some of the more unsavoury types to abuse its hospitality, hosted theoretically-fair dice games, and showcased some of the cheaper exotic women in the region.

That tavern had drained his purse every winter since he had been of age to join the military. And yet this year, he had not put a foot across its threshold.

Regretfully, he tore his gaze from the glorious landscape and the lowbrow establishment hidden somewhere at its centre and turned off on the side road, following Lucilia.

Despite some regret that resided at a deep level and was chiselled into his heart, he had to admit that he had not really missed the carousing until he had actually had cause to think on it - not in the company he had kept over the winter.

It had been nice. It had been an… adjustment, but it had certainly been nice. He had found himself a number of times over the colder months wishing that the young lady who had apparently captured him without the use of net or spear could have helped warm his bed rather than sleeping in a resolutely virginal chamber on the far side of the villa, adjacent to Faleria's room 'just in case'.

The nights after his wine intake had been higher and less watered than met Faleria's approval had been particularly difficult.

He watched Lucilia's figure sway alluringly down the gravelled road toward the complex of villa buildings that clung to the hillside, overlooking the azure sea and the ships arriving from every corner of the world. It was almost hypnotic.

He winced as he remembered that night after the Saturnalia celebrations when the sway of those hips had taunted him just too much and he had found himself, insulated by a thick layer of wine, standing in just his underwear and trying to lift the latch to Lucilia's room with a paring knife. His hands had slipped repeatedly from the target in a pleasant haze, carving furrows in the surrounding wood and leaving scratches on the iron plate.

He had spent almost a quarter of an hour trying and had finally drawn a deep breath ready to call to the room's intoxicating occupant when he had become aware of his sister, standing outside her own door, watching him with an expression that would have split a block of marble or sent a thousand Gallic horse galloping for the hills.

He had dropped the paring knife in alarm and it had punctured his foot. Just another reminder of how far his influence as patriarch really stretched when Faleria was in residence. His mother had ruled the family with an iron fist after his father's death, until the death of Verginius in Hispania had left Faleria preparing for a wedding with a deceased man. The girl had hardened that day into a classic Roman matron and had immediately surpassed their mother in her rigid and humourless control of the house for all too many years.

He shook his head again.

But Faleria had changed again since he had been away campaigning in Gaul. She had softened once more to something resembling the Faleria of his youth. Certainly the addition of Lucilia to the household seemed to have had a powerful effect on her.

'Softened', but not 'weakened'.

Fronto sighed. It had taken him only a few weeks to realise that in signing away his soul to this girl, he had simply added a third headstrong female to the list of those who thought they could rule and control him. Sadly, it appeared that they were correct in that assumption. Caesar, Pompey and Crassus could learn a thing or two from the three women commanding the house of the Falerii these days.

'I've been thinking…'

Lucilia turned slightly to regard him curiously as they closed on the villa.

'You should watch that, Marcus. Such activity rarely leads to good things.'

Another deep sigh.

'I wonder whether it's time to start edging Faleria toward…' he swallowed nervously. This was like addressing the senate and asking for a favour. 'Toward perhaps looking at a new match?'

Lucilia shook her head.

'She says she's too old.'

'You've *discussed it with her*?' Fronto was seriously taken aback. He had been trying to work out a way to broach the subject for two years now.

'At some length. I tried to persuade her that thirty is still an acceptable age and that she has a few years to bear children yet.'

'You said *what*?'

'Faleria is, I think, happy with her station. I think she will never love another like her lost husband, and so she is happy not to try. She knows that at her age, with the lineage and value of the Falerii, she will likely only attract leery old men or greedy young nobodies hungry for power and station. Given that it is now more than possible that you will be able to continue the line, your mother is happy to leave Faleria to her own devices.'

Fronto stopped in a squelch of horse dung and dropped the sack of wet clothes with a similar noise.

'You even spoke to *mother* about this?'

'Oh calm down. You'll do yourself an injury. Women talk, Marcus. I'm sure you're aware of this. What did you think we did while you and your pet servants went down to the races or sat in the cellar playing Latrunculi, draining your father's carefully stocked wines?'

Fronto stared at her as something she had said clicked in his head.

''Continue the line'?'

'Children, Marcus' she said, rolling her eyes as she stooped to lift the bag of clothes and throw it over her shoulder. 'I'm sure you've heard of them. Small people who cry a lot and fall over regularly.'

She set off along the road again, leaving Fronto standing, baffled, until he shook his head and ran after her.

'Don't you think you're getting a little ahead of things there? We've yet to even ask your father if he'll agree to the match. You may think your mother will persuade him, but I'm not so sure. And then there's Caesar. The Agonia Martialis is already passed and the legions will be starting to move in Gaul. If I don't hear from the general by the end of Aprilis I shall have to ride to Rome and prepare for the coming season. I'll only be around for another month or so. Caesar has a plan, I think, to expand his horizons ever further. I will be gone for the whole campaigning season, probably for years yet.'

This time it was Lucilia who stopped dead and it took Fronto another five flustered steps to realise and draw himself to a halt.

'You don't *need* to serve, if you don't wish to' she said, quietly, but with a dangerous edge.

Fronto shook his head.

'Caesar is our patron. My family and yours, both. And I am one of his senior officers. If he needs me then I shall have to...'

'Tripe. Drivel. My father supports Caesar and maintains his patronage out of loyalty. He owes nothing to the man. And you? If I understand what your mother tells me, it is Caesar who theoretically owes the Falerii a small sum, and not the other way round. You run at his beckon because you live for the legions. That will change.'

Fronto thrust an angry finger toward her, but she smiled and walked past him once more on her way to the villa.

'Come on. We'll be late for the meal.'

Fronto stood amid the buzz of bees and the chatter of birds, the hazy blue of the bay providing a strange background to the seething, roiling churn of emotions that held him fast. After a few moments he realised how foolish he must look – standing and angrily gesturing to the open air – checked for any passing observers and, finding none, hurried after the beautiful Lucilia.

* * * * *

Two days later, Fronto hurried out into the courtyard before the villa, taking no time to breathe in the joyous warm evening air, with a scent of jasmine and roses. His sandals flapped around him, the straps loose and untied, threatening to trip him with every step.

'What bloody time do you call this?'

Galronus, noble of the Remi tribe, beloved of Lug and Taranis, lord among the fierce Belgae, dismounted easily from his roan mare and alighted smoothly, dusting himself down as he released the reins. Fronto looked him up and down with an unabashed grin of happiness.

A second winter in Rome had wrung even more changes to the rough figure of Galronus the Gaul. Though he still wore the traditional moustaches of his people, his long hair, once wild and untamed, now had that lustrous sheen and smoothness that only comes with regular attention from an expensive barber and was plaited down before one ear and tied back at the nape of his neck. His skin had that clean smooth look of a man who had managed at least three visits a day to the baths. His sole concessions to his native dress seemed to be the continued wearing of the braccae – the Gallic trousers that bulged at the thigh and reached to the ankles – and a torc around his neck, although even that had an unmistakable look of Roman metalwork.

'Marcus!' The big Gaul left his reins hanging and ran across the courtyard to enfold the dishevelled Roman in a great bear hug. Fronto issued an involuntary squeak at the pressure, but grinned as Galronus let him go. The Belgic nobleman even smelled of scented bath oils. Good job there'd be no chance for him to attend such grand bathhouses back in Gaul; else his tribe would tear him to pieces for womanliness.

'You have spent the winter in a comfortable villa with your own baths and slaves and servants?' Galronus enquired with a furrowed brow.

Fronto nodded as one of those slaves hurried across to take the reins of the visitor's horse.

'Why then does your hair stand up like this and why do you smell like old amphorae, and why is your tunic stained and creased?'

Fronto rolled his eyes.

7

'I think I miss the Galronus who had never even heard of a heated bath. Come on.'

Grasping his shoulder, Fronto guided him toward the door that led into the decorative atrium.

'What draws you away from the delights of Rome?'

Galronus shrugged off the leather bag that hung over one arm and stopped in the atrium as it dropped to the marble floor with a thud. Stooping, he rummaged in it for a moment and then straightened, holding out a wooden writing tablet.

'This.'

Fronto took the item, frowning, and snapped it open. His brow rose as he recognised the handwriting.

'Caesar gave you this? It's not sealed or anything.'

Galronus shrugged.

'Perhaps he trusts me.'

Fronto eyed him askance. 'Or perhaps you broke the seal and had a good read before you left Rome.'

Galronus blinked his innocence, his face devoid of expression, and Fronto shook his head as he snapped it shut.

'I'll read it when we're settled. For now, it's late. We've had an evening repast, but I daresay we can rustle you something up. And I've just broken the seal on some nice Sicilian wine. How's the house?'

Galronus had taken up residence during autumn in the burned out shell of the townhouse of the Falerii on the Aventine hill, keeping the place occupied as the workmen continued to return it to a liveable state after the fights and fires of the previous year.

'Less than half complete, I'd say. There was more structural fire damage than originally anticipated, and the winter weather has made it difficult for the workmen. It may be another year before it resembles your home again.'

Fronto nodded. It came as no surprise to him. At least the family could spend the year in Puteoli and not worry about it yet.

A sudden flurry of activity announced the arrival of the girls and Fronto glanced over his shoulder before raising his eyes skywards again.

'Brace yourself.'

Stepping aside, he watched with some satisfaction as Faleria and Lucilia mobbed the large Gaul, almost knocking him from his feet and chattering their pleasure at his arrival. Turning his attention from the spectacle, Fronto snapped open the wooden tablet again and ran his eyes down the message within.

Caesar's handwriting had always been tight, small and economic, though gifted with an almost oratorical turn of phrase even in such short form.

> *To M Falerius Fronto from C Iulius Caesar, Proconsul of Gaul,*
> *Felicitations.*
> *Having received tidings of your joyous situation, it is with regret that I now send news of the opening of the campaigning season.*

Fronto frowned. How in the name of the seven whores of Capernum had the general heard of his predicament?

> *It had been my intention to travel late to Gaul, perhaps even during Maius, since there have been no signs of renewed insurrection or hostility to the Roman state and the missives from my subordinates have assured me that the process of drawing Gaul into the fold proceeds apace.*

Again, Fronto frowned. The letter had been clearly written carefully in case it should fall into the wrong hands, or perhaps Caesar had even expected Galronus to open it en route? Fronto remembered clearly his last conversation with the general, when the man had avowed his intent to take the Pax Romana and stuff it down the throat of the next Celtic nation he found.

> *However, it would appear that a number of Germanic tribes, driven from their own lands by a vast eastern tribe of even more unyielding barbarians, have crossed the Rhenus and settled in the lands of our Belgae subjects, defending their presence with extreme violence. While it has never been the intention of Rome or this proconsulate to bring war to those tribes beyond that great river,*

Fronto rolled his eyes at the line and shook his head.

9

it is now clearly necessary to mobilize the legions in northern Gaul to repel these invaders and support our Belgic people. To this end, I am summoning all of my officers to return to their commands at their earliest convenience. A trireme under my command is docked at Ostia, and has begun to make the journey to and from Massilia as required in order to ferry said officers to the nearest port.

Our Graeco-Gallic allies in Massilia have agreed to provide a place in their agora for a staging post for us. From there, you will be required to travel north along the Rhodanus, past the allied townships of Vienna and Vesontio, with which you will be familiar. The army will be encamped close to the oppidum of Divoduron in the lands of the Mediomatrici some one hundred and fifty miles to the north of Vesontio.

I trust you will be able to reach your command by the Kalends of Maius.

In the name of the senate and people of Rome.
Your friend,
Caius.

Fronto looked up from the note to see that the clamorous reunion between his friend and the women of the household seemed to have died down. Galronus was looking at him over the heads of the two women, a question in his eyes. Fronto nodded silently.

'Come on ladies. Let our guest at least recover a little from his journey before you bombard him with questions. We'll come and meet you in the triclinium within the hour.'

Lucilia flashed him a hard look that he prudently ignored, but Faleria caught his eye and must have recognised something, for she nodded and clasped Lucilia's hand.

'Come on. Let the boys play for a while. They have such little time to act like children.'

Lucilia frowned and the two women made for the doorway to the triclinium, while Fronto collected Galronus' bag and led him off toward the far end of the villa, where he was wont to pass the time.

'You read the message?'

'I did. He moves earlier than I expected.'

From across the room, a sharp female voice snapped out.

'*What?*'

Fronto turned in surprise and realised that the two ladies had not yet fully left the room, pausing instead to chat in the doorway. He cursed inwardly for having spoken openly and too soon.

'Nothing, Lucilia. We'll be along shortly.'

But the dark haired girl had already torn herself from Faleria's grasp and was storming across the atrium so resolutely Fronto feared she would walk straight through the impluvium pool in the centre without noticing.

'Lucilia…'

'No! You're *leaving*? It's too early. You said you wouldn't go until the end of Aprilis. My father is going to Rome in a few weeks. I was going to take you there to meet him. We need to speak to him.'

Fronto quailed and stepped back as the whirlwind of furious womanhood approached.

'It's just a few more months, Lucilia. I'll be back before winter, and then…'

'No. I will not spend a whole extra summer as a guest with no formal ties to the house. You persuaded me not to travel in winter, else we'd have seen father sooner. You'll not delay our betrothal any further.'

'Lucilia, I *have* to go. I have been summoned to my post by the Proconsul of Gaul. It's only half a year. I've waited this long, after all…' he regretted the words almost before they had left his tongue and the colour draining from the face of the young lady threatened a violent disagreement and likely some thrown crockery.

Galronus opened his mouth and took a pace forward, but Lucilia held a hand up, palm facing him.

'No. You find somewhere to make yourself comfortable. Marcus and I are going to have a talk.'

Fronto cast one desperate, pleading look at Galronus as Lucilia grabbed his arm and, yanking, turned him back to the door before dragging him through it. The large Gaul carefully avoided meeting his gaze and then turned back to the atrium, wondering whether it would be possible to follow them and ask for his travelling bag. Prudence won out and he decided against it.

'Galronus, it has been too long.'

He smiled at Faleria and stepped around the small pool toward her.

'Have they been like this all winter?'

Faleria nodded. 'I think he missed male company. You should have come earlier.'

Galronus cast an embarrassed eye down to the floor. 'I had... other pursuits. The games; the racing; I even watched one of your plays, although it lacks the power of the storytellers among my people. The masks are funny, though. And some of the singing made me laugh,'

Faleria nodded encouragingly. She daren't ask what play he had attended; she was almost certain it would have been a tragedy. Certainly with Galronus in the audience laughing like a gurgling drain.

'How long will you be here? Are you taking him straight away?'

Galronus shrugged. 'I think we can squeeze a few days out. The traders in Rome say that the sea is remarkably calm even for the time of year, so we will make good time, especially if we take a ship straight from Neapolis or Puteoli, rather than riding back to Rome.'

Faleria smiled wickedly. 'Marcus does so love to travel by sea. I think we can defuse the situation between the two young lovebirds. If you travel to Gaul by ship, you will make landfall at Massilia. Lucilia and I will accompany you thus far, where we can meet with Balbus, her father, and sort this mess out.'

'You will come too?'

Faleria smiled benignly. 'Would you seriously expect Marcus to cope with all the betrothal arrangements himself? No, I think I should accompany you to straighten it all out.'

* * * * *

'I do *not* wear socks!'

Lucilia glared at Fronto and snatched the woollen garments from his hand, stuffing them back into his pack.

'Yes you do. You'll be traipsing through soggy swamps above the roof of the world. Do you really want your toes to rot and fall off? Because I do not.'

'I don't *need* socks because I wear boots that are perfectly sized and shaped to my feet. They're closed boots and nice and dry and there's no room in them for both socks and my feet.'

'You're not taking your old boots.'

Fronto blinked and straightened.

'Now listen...'

'You cannot take your boots, Marcus. I threw them out last week.'

Fronto tried to say something but it came out only as indignant splutters.

'I saw the manufacturer's mark on them, Marcus. Those boots were nearly as old as me. And they smelled of stale urine.'

'Of course! That's how you shape them to your feet. It took me nearly a year's pissing to make them comfortable enough for a thirty mile march.'

Lucilia shook her head calmly.

'You're a senior officer from a patrician family and currently the legatus of a legion. You ride; you don't need to march.'

Fronto stared at her.

'Besides, you have a thoroughbred horse of unsurpassed quality. It would be wasteful not to run him. Now try on the boots over there. They're light leather with a fleece inner to help you in the harsh climates of Gaul.'

Fronto's gaze snapped back and forth between the boots on the chair and the woman pointing at them.

'Is there any chance that at some point in the past *you* have commanded a legion, too?'

Lucilia said nothing, but simply gestured impatiently at the boots.

With a sigh, he capitulated.

* * * * *

Fronto staggered along the deck and reached an empty stretch of rail almost in time to vomit copiously over the side without splattering the deck. His face had been a pale grey for the past two days, with only a brief return of colour during the overnight stop at Antium.

'Did you use the embrocation the nice Greek gave you?'

Fronto spat into the water and tried not to concentrate on the way it moved, undulated, wobbled, oscillated…

After another copious session of dry heaving, Fronto wiped his mouth again and look across at Lucilia at the rail nearby; neatly keeping her sandaled feet out of the mess he had left.

'No I didn't. It smells like feet. I hadn't thrown up until I opened the jar and smelled it. That's what set this whole thing off.'

13

'Rubbish. And I expect you've not had any of the ginger root?'

'It makes me hiccup.'

'And vomiting is preferable to hiccupping, is it?'

'Just leave me alone.'

Fronto draped himself over the rail for just a moment until the additional pressure and movement threatened a whole new session of agony. Hauling himself back upright, he focused his eyes and frowned.

'That's Ostia.'

'Yes.'

'Why did nobody say we were almost there?'

Lucilia smiled like a patient parent.

'If you'd looked up any time in the past hour you'd have seen it. And everyone on board has been talking about landfall. You've just been too wrapped up in your own embrocation-and-ginger-free misery to notice.'

'I hate ships.'

'Of this I am acutely aware, Marcus.'

'When I was a boy, my father took me out fishing in the bay below the villa. I was sick in his lunch basket. He never took me again. Should they even be sailing in this weather? Shouldn't they wait for a good day, and then I'd have had a better journey.'

Lucilia rolled her eyes as she took in the cloudless blue sky, the slight heat haze that made the approaching dockside of Ostia shimmer, the glassy, reflective surface of the water, broken only by the lowest, friendliest of waves and the wake of various mercantile vessels ploughing back and forth from the dockside.

'It *is* a dreadful day, I have to admit. I wonder whether Neptune is furious at you for ignoring your medically-prescribed embrocation?'

Fronto glared at her before turning his attention back to the busy town before them, as they approached at speed, a wide dockside presenting a spacious opening for them. More than a hundred merchants, slaves, fishermen and sailors went about their chores on the dock: hauling crates, coiling ropes, arguing and haggling over lists. Beggars and children cut purses, touted their flesh to passing trade, or just called out desperately for a spare coin.

It was chaos but, as they watched, it was clearly a very organised chaos. Ostia was rapidly becoming a more common offloading point for goods bound for Rome than the older ports at Puteoli or Neapolis.

Fronto held his breath as the merchant vessel began to slew sideways toward the concrete and the waiting dockhand. That first bump often knocked him from his feet, with his knees as feeble as they were after a day of being sick over a rail.

His attention, however, was distracted by a sudden glint of blinding light. Squinting, he tried to look past it and suddenly the dazzling beam was gone, leaving the source: a burnished cuirass of golden bronze that had reflected the glorious sun.

'Who are they?' a quiet voice enquired.

Fronto turned to see that Faleria had joined them at his other side. He spun back and examined the small group of men on the dock, trying to get a better view of their faces. It quickly became apparent that the five soldiers on the dockside constituted two separate groups, rather than one large one.

'I don't know the two centurions, but they're veterans. You can tell that just from the look of them. I think...'

Fronto's knuckles whitened as his grip on the rail tightened.

'Their shields! They'd do well to keep the covers on' he growled.

'What is it?' Lucilia asked, her eyes narrowing as she tried in vain to see whatever Fronto had spotted.

'Their shields are still painted in the designs of the 2nd Italic; one of Lucullus' legions.'

'So?'

Fronto turned to look at Lucilia as if she were an idiot, an expression he could not hide, despite the warning signs it drew in her eyes.

'That means they served under Pompey in the east against Mithridates. Hell, they might even have been the mutineers that the scheming little prick Clodius paid off, and who nearly screwed up the whole campaign. If they're waiting to join Caesar's trireme, I may have to have strong words with the general.'

'But that campaign was what? Ten years ago? They've probably been civilians for years in between.'

'Once a shitbag, always a shitbag, Lucilia.'

'Who are the others, then?' Faleria asked, trying to calm her brother.

Fronto tried not to look at the two veterans; heavy set men with bristly faces and iron grey hair and traitorous shields. Instead, he fixed his gaze on the three more senior officers, clad in burnished cuirasses, crimson cloaks, plumed helms and bronze greaves. Their tunics and pteruges were spotless white. They could have been posing for a heroic statue in the forum. They quite clearly had the military bearing of a huddle of lame ostriches.

'The two at the far side I vaguely recognise. Menenius, I think. Can't remember the other's name. They've been on staff since the Belgae revolted two years ago. Tribunes that were attached to the Eleventh or Twelfth. Possibly both.' He shook his head. 'Eleventh. Must be. Only one of the tribunes of the Twelfth survived Octodurus last year.'

The two junior tribunes were chattering away like the mindless, excited youths that so often filled the role. Only one junior tribune in every ten posted to the army had even the faintest idea which end of a sword to grip and which end to poke into the enemy. As he watched, one of the two reared back his head and issued a squawking laugh that grated on Fronto's nerves and ran right down his spine. His spirits sank at the thought of a three day voyage to Massilia in the company of that laugh. Fops and morons. It said much of their effectiveness and involvement that in two years of service Fronto could not actually remember seeing or hearing of them, except in briefings.

'They're about as useful as a parchment shield. And about as welcome as a turd in a bath house.'

'And the other one?'

Fronto squinted again.

'Don't know him. Tall. Obviously patrician. Could do with a little bit more chin and a lot less forehead. He should get on very well with those other two donkeys. He's got a broad stripe on his tunic, though. He's going to be a senior tribune.'

He spun from the rail.

'If that ostrich gets assigned to me, I shall take great pleasure in giving him a shield and standing him in the front row when we meet a bunch of screaming Celts.'

Faleria shook her head with a slight smile.

'Steady, Marcus.'

'I'll have you know that I…' he began angrily, and then lost his footing and slipped in his own outpouring as the ship bounced briefly off the dock before connecting once again and scraping woodenly along the sheer face.

'I told you to be steady' Faleria said with insufferable smugness.

16

'Ladies?'

Fronto, whose grip on the rail had been the only thing that had prevented him from slamming down to the deck, backside first, twisted to see Galronus standing tall and proud, steady as a rock, and an irritatingly healthy colour for a member of a land-locked tribe.

The big Gaul gestured for Faleria and she laid her hand on the bulging muscles of his forearm, allowing him to escort her across the slippery deck to where the plank was being slid out to the dock. Two of the sailors nearby chuckled as Fronto mirrored the chivalrous act, reaching out and grasping Lucilia's forearm to steady himself as he weakly staggered across the deck to the plank, moving like a man twenty years his senior.

Lucilia grinned at him as she helped him onto the plank, and watched with glee as he skittered down it and narrowly avoided collapsing onto the quay.

The four of them recovered their land gait quickly, stamping their feet and walking back and forth, and then made their way along the quay toward the five soldiers in crisp uniform. Fronto could not help but issue a groan as he saw the trireme drawing closer along the Tiber from the direction of Rome.

'It's here already!'

Faleria smiled and patted him on the arm.

'Don't worry, dear brother. We stay in Ostia tonight and sail with the morning tide. Save your retching for tomorrow.'

The five officers had begun to move. Fronto had assumed they were waiting to board a ship, but it appeared that, in fact, they had recently alighted in much the same fashion as his own party and were making for accommodation in the town.

Both groups converged on the main street leading to the forum and the heart of the town: a narrow thoroughfare compared with the great streets at the centre of Rome. At the entrance of the street, a one-legged veteran stood by the corner, supported on a crude crutch, proffering a wooden bowl for spare coins. Opposite him, a bony, raddled woman with a very visible ribcage touted her wares through a gauzy white garment. Even the poorer classes funnelled into the centre to avoid being accosted by either.

'What are you doing?' Lucilia frowned as Fronto picked up a sudden burst of speed and made for the street, dragging his companions with him.

17

'I've stayed in Ostia. There's only a limited supply of insect-free beds. I'm not losing out to two traitorous centurions, two ostriches and a man who's left his chin behind. Come on.'

Unable to hold their friend back, the other three hurried along in Fronto's wake, converging with the people of Ostia and the small group of soldiers as they made for the street entrance.

Suddenly, almost as if choreographed, the general population opened up and made a space around the mouth of the street. Men in senior military uniform had a way of opening such spaces, regardless of their true value. The only people who failed to melt out of the way were the crippled soldier, whose uniped nature made it difficult, and the whore, who saw an opportunity and bared her chest at them, grinning with all nine teeth.

And Fronto.

Into the sudden open space, Fronto almost dragged Lucilia, with Galronus and Faleria at his heel.

'Hold!' called a reedy voice high enough to be a woman, but that issued from the mouth above the receding chin. Fronto was so taken aback by the voice that he actually stumbled to a halt, blocking the access to the street, Galronus ambling to a stop next to him.

The two bristly centurions who had been behind the senior officers came round the side, slapping their vine staves meaningfully against their greaves.

'In thivilithed thothiety, peathenth and barbarianth thtep out of the way of their theniorth!' snapped chinless in a feminine register.

Fronto grinned and opened his mouth, a thousand insults fighting for prominence on his tongue, but no sound made it out, thanks to a breath-stealing rabbit-punch to the kidney from Galronus.

'Ahem...' said a high, calm voice, with a hint of smugness. Fronto recovered quickly, straightening with a glare at Galronus, to see Menenius step forward to address Chinless.

'With respect, my lord, the 'barbarian' is one of your blessed uncle's senior cavalry commanders and the...' the tribune smiled unpleasantly '... the one that looks like a vagrant would be Marcus Falerius Fronto, staff officer and current commander of the Tenth Equestrian Legion.'

The junior tribune's faultless moment was ruined slightly as he finished his words with a girlish titter that he tried to hide behind his hand, failing dismally. Fronto frowned, but noticed with some satisfaction the two centurions straighten, their staves dropping to their sides.

'His uncle?' Fronto said, narrowing his eyes.

'Of course, Fronto, you overgrown poppet' said the other junior tribune in a squeaky tone. 'This is Publius Pinarius Posca, the son of Julia the elder, nephew of the general. He comes to take a tribunate in Gaul.'

Fronto sighed as the chinless one opened his mouth again.

'Are you thure thath who he ith? He lookth half dead, and dretheth like a… I don't know. I've never theen anyone drethed like that.'

Menenius smiled. 'And the ladies, I fancy, would be the lovely sister of master Fronto, and his paramour?'

Fronto's sour look turned on the speaker before returning to Galronus and the girls.

'Come on. This is making me feel sicker than the ship.'

Chapter 2

(Massilia, an allied former Greek colony on the coast south of Gaul)

The *Glory of Venus* bucked once on a particularly violent wave as it passed the mole and entered the harbour, settling almost instantly on the millpond water within.

Fronto had long since given up any hope of feeling well as long as he lived. During the stop at Vado Sabatia, a helpful wag among the oarsmen had carved a commemorative inscription on the wooden rail where Fronto habitually stood to vomit over the side, since when he had deliberately avoided the spot.

At last, though, the journey was coming to an end. He had wondered briefly if his stomach had actually turned inside out the day before. Certainly even the *name* of foodstuffs was now enough to set him off, let alone the sight or smell of them.

His gaze briefly left the churning waters that so mirrored his own gut and played across the heads of those aboard who were not bent over the oars.

Galronus, Faleria and Lucilia stood at the bow, their gaze locked on the great port ahead. Lucilia had gradually become more animated and excited as she neared her family, and the feeling had rubbed off on her companions. Somewhere on the hills a couple of miles back from the city – nominally within the Roman province of Narbonensis but close enough to allied Massilia to spit a peach stone at – stood the villa of Balbus; former legate of the Eighth Legion, future father in law to the grey, shaking figure leaning on the rail.

The two tribunes, who Fronto had now discovered were named Menenius and Hortius, were apparently being reassigned to serve on the staff of the Fourteenth, which Caesar still treated more as an auxiliary unit than a full legion and which he believed needed bringing up to scratch. Fronto had met a number of the men and centurions of the Fourteenth now and his own opinion was of a powerful legion, strong in body and spirit, carrying both the efficiency of the Roman officers who had trained them and the sheer battle-sense of the Gauls who had supplied the bulk of the manpower. What the great, bluff, hairy monsters of the Fourteenth would make of the two fops who actually called one another 'darling' in front of the sailors and hurried off in a panic if their tunic was dirtied, he simply could not imagine.

Even the clerks would eat those two alive.

The only person on board who Fronto feared for more was Caesar's nephew, Pinarius. The man was clearly too weak in both mind and physique to competently direct a music recital, let alone a battle. The elegantly inscribed rail where Fronto had spent much of the journey had been specifically chosen as the place with a flat leaning surface and standing space that was furthest from Pinarius' grating lisp and nasal laugh as it was possible to be without walking on water. It was no surprise to find that Caesar had granted a commission to his sister's son, but Fronto could only picture the general trying to deal with this chinless moron. Hopefully he would only be there for one campaigning season and then gone to ruin the economy in Rome.

Morons like those three almost made him miss Crassus, who was now ensconced in his new position in Rome, regularly attending meetings of the senate and guiding the future of the republic.

Almost... but not quite.

Very much the other side of the coin – a coin now probably authorised to mint by the very same Crassus – was the centurions. Furius and Fabius had spoken to their fellow passengers precisely as much as the courtesy due their social highers and military superiors demanded, and no more. The two men claimed to hold Caesar in very high regard both as an officer and as a tactician, and neither made mention of Pompey or their former commissions. Fronto had planned to turn the conversation around enough to pry into their past, but the constant illness and battering of his senses had made it practically impossible, and so Furius and Fabius remained somewhat mysterious.

One thing was certain: he would trust an oak-bark-sucking druid before he would let one of those two stand behind him with a knife.

Furius and Fabius had remained quiet and apart for most of the journey, talking among themselves and eying the three fops, Fronto and Galronus with equal distain.

Fronto watched with a surly temper as the dockside of Massilia closed on them. Hopefully the other five passengers would be in a hurry to travel north and he would not be forced to accompany them on the journey. Caesar had apparently already disembarked in Massilia on the previous trip of the *Glory of Venus*, and most of his officers would now be converging on the army in preparation. Fronto and Galronus would not be far behind, but there was something that had to be done first.

Despite the best efforts of the port officials of Massilia, there was simply so much traffic that the great trireme commissioned by Caesar had to sit in the glassy waters of the harbour for almost two hours before enough mercantile traffic had unloaded their wares and cleared the queues and jetties to make room for a warship.

In a Roman port, the simple appearance of a military vessel and the name of Caesar would be enough to ensure priority and the dispersal of mercantile traffic. But Massilia was still nominally independent and, at this point, Rome still obeyed her harbour rules.

The sun was already sliding into the western horizon, leaving a fiery shimmer across the water and casting the hills and mountains to the north and east in a deep purple tone when the trireme finally began its approach to the jetty.

Fronto braced himself for the first bounce and yet still lunged at the rail like a novice when it happened, recovering as quickly as he could and hurrying off down to the boarding ramp that was being run out, converging with the ladies and their Gaulish escort. The other centurions and officers had politely stepped aside to allow the ladies to disembark first, and Fronto took advantage, leaping in front of them and hurrying down after his three companions.

Alighting on the solid stone of land, Fronto resisted the urge to crouch and kiss it, concentrating instead on stopping the unmanly wobble in his legs. As he and his companions stood in a small knot on the dock in the rapidly emptying port, the others disembarked behind them, setting foot on the pier and moving away.

Pinarius wore an expression of happy and vacant excitement that immediately annoyed Fronto again.

'Ith tho much more thivilithed than I ecthpected. Thereth a monument near the agora that commemorateth the great ecthplorer Pytheath, you know? He came from thith plath, and ecthplored ath far north ath a thip can go without freething tholid. Mutht we go north in the morning? Can we not thtay a day to thee the plath?'

Fronto winced as his brain tried to add a few solid consonants to the question.

'I think it would be unwise, my dear' replied tribune Hortius with a sad face that resembled one of the theatre masks for Greek tragedies. 'Your beloved uncle wants us all with the army as soon as we can be there.'

Fronto kept his opinion of how desperately Caesar sought the company of his nephew in the privacy of his head. 'Gods, please don't let him be assigned to the Tenth!' He resolved to be extra nice to the general on arrival, just in case.

Furius and Fabius alighted with the steady gait of men used to the sea, adjusting their stride easily to the dock and marching off into the town without a word to any of their former fellow passengers.

Fronto watched them go with lowered brows and grunted something under his breath.

'What was that?'

He turned to his sister.

'Pompeian turds' he repeated. 'I think they were with Pompey when he led the navy too. Experienced marines, they are. What the hell is Caesar playing at?'

Galronus patted him comfortingly on the shoulder.

'You've lost a lot of centurions in the past two years, Marcus. The general can't keep shuffling the ones you have left up each time and bringing in newly-raised officers at the bottom, or there'll soon be no experienced centurions left. He has to bring in veteran officers if they become available, no matter their past.'

Fronto muttered something again in inaudible grunts.

'What?'

'Nothing. Look, the crew can unload the horses and baggage and send them on to the staging post. Let's get up and see Balbus. My stomach seems to have flipped back over and is demanding wine and meat.'

'It's a strenuous walk, Marcus' Lucilia reminded him. 'Are you sure we shouldn't wait for the horses?'

'My legs need the workout. They feel like knotted string at the moment.'

Behind them, the men of Caesar's ship were already unloading the beasts and chests to the dock, where the port workers were consulting their orders, roping chains of beasts together and loading bags and crates onto carts, ready to deliver to their destinations. The cacophony of Latin voices from the ship, Greek tones from the dock, and Gaulish shouts from the immigrant workers rose and fell like the waves of the Mare Nostrum, threatening to make Fronto's gorge rise again.

Turning his back on the havoc just as Fronto's magnificent black horse Bucephalus was walked slowly and carefully ashore, he led the small group up the street and out of the port. As they passed into the city itself, Lucilia was suddenly next to him and then past, as though drawn inexorably by the ever-nearing presence of her family. Sharing a glance, Fronto, Galronus and Faleria picked up their pace and hurried along behind. A local she may be, but no girl in her right mind travelled the streets of a port city on her own.

The journey was a tough one; exhausting, in fact. A mile through the rising streets of Massilia, back northeast away from the port, and then two more turning north on roads that led toward the villa district, rising through the hills behind the shore all the time. Barely half a mile from the edge of the great trade city, a solid, stable road of Roman construction ran along a carefully levelled terrace, stretching from Cisalpine Gaul in the east across to Narbo Martius in the west. A milestone claimed the road as Roman territory and marked the point where the local road from Massilia joined the republican highway.

The small group of travellers moved onto the strangely empty main road and walked some half a mile northwest until they found the familiar track that led off to the villas of the Roman nobles who had chosen to settle on the hills above Massilia.

And finally, their hungry eyes lit upon their destination.

The villa of Balbus had thrived since Fronto's last visit. The garden and building itself were as neat as ever, but the complex also showed signs of growth. Four new buildings had risen to one side, including two bunkhouses for servants or slaves. Ordered rows of newly-planted vines, barely reaching above the soil, marched off down the slope toward the sea, their green tips catching the last of the light.

A slave rushed around the yard and the gardens, lighting lamps and torches where they would be most needed, as labourers returned wearily from the estate beyond, baskets and tools on their shoulders. Fronto smiled.

'Looks like your father's turning into a farmer. Or a vintner.'

Lucilia grinned back at him. '*That's* probably just to cater for your visits, my love. Come on.'

With Galronus looking around appreciatively, perhaps seeing for the first time the possibilities raised by the marriage of Gallic agriculture and Roman organisation, the four stepped into the garden.

Newly acquired benches, arbours and a decorative dolphin fountain graced the frontage of the villa, and the walls had been freshly painted with red and white following the winter depredations.

Fronto frowned at the door, which stood open as slaves and servants rushed back and forth, settling everything for the night. He felt sure someone would have informed the villa's master that a trireme had been seen docking in the port.

'Marcus, you look positively grey!'

Despite himself, Fronto jumped a little at the sudden words that issued from close behind him. Turning, he saw Quintus Lucilius Balbus, former commander of the Eighth Legion, lounging on a curved stone bench under a pergola, his arms folded and a sly grin on his face.

Fronto drank in the sight of his old friend. Balbus had aged more than he should have in half a year, but strangely it did not sit badly on him. While he looked a little older, he looked a great deal healthier and happier than he had last time they had met. He had bulked out a little and achieved the rosy complexion of a compulsive gardener. Laughter lines creased his face and he wore a straw hat that had seen better days and a tunic and breeches that, while cut to military pattern, were covered with the stains of fruit and soil.

'You become a farmer, Quintus?'

The older man laughed, a deep rich sound, and then stood and enfolded Fronto in a crushing hug, releasing him only when he realised that Lucilia was waiting impatiently.

'Daughter. You've seen fit to pay a quick visit to your father, then?'

His eyebrow arched in mock anger, but he could not hold the expression for long as Lucilia rushed into the gap left by Fronto and threw her arms round his nicely-padded ribcage.

'Father, I wish we'd come sooner, but...'

'I know. You had trouble keeping this one out of the taverns long enough?'

Fronto shot him a sour glance, which set the older man laughing again.

'Come on inside. I'm sure we have a great deal to discuss.'

* * * * *

Fronto sank back into the comfortable couch, allowing the cushions to enfold him and take the edge off the ache of his creaking bones and clicking joints. Closing his eyes, he savoured the sip of wine and then opened them at a gurgling sound, only to find Lucilia adding a healthy dose of water to his beaker. Glaring at her, he caught the mirth on Balbus' face across the room and sighed, sipping the now-respectfully-watered wine as he reached to the plate of cheeses on the small table next to him.

'Can you afford a layover?'

Fronto gave a noncommittal shrug.

'A short one. You know the general. Doesn't do to keep him waiting too long, but we've been quite quick so far. Perhaps a couple of days? There's an office in the agora apparently staffed by a couple of ex-legionaries assigned by Priscus. They're organising all the transport of men and goods to the army. It looks like the new camp prefect has taken half the responsibilities of the chief quartermaster from him.'

Balbus grinned. 'I'm sure Cita will just love that. Have you reported to them yet?'

'No. I thought I'd leave it for now.'

'I will go in the morning' said Galronus quietly from his seat at the room's end. He had seemed thoughtful and quiet since he arrived, though Fronto put it down to the awful sea voyage. The five of them sat in a rough circle.

Balbus shook his head. 'Stay and relax, friend Galronus. I'll send one of my lads down tomorrow morning to start organising things for you. That way they can just meet you here in two days and pick you up at the villa with your beasts and goods.'

A brief frown of regret passed Fronto's face as he pictured all the dockside taverns and their owners reaching out to take his coin. It was quickly replaced by a genuine smile. Time later for that. For now: other things were required.

'Are Corvinia or Balbina joining us?'

'Corvinia is preparing a repast that will double your weight and Balbina is helping her. I think Balbina's sulking a little as I told her the adults had to talk before she could see you.'

'Yes' Fronto said quietly. 'There are things we have to discuss, Quintus.'

He glanced sidelong at Lucilia and waggled his eyebrows.

Balbus burst out laughing, almost choking on his own wine. 'Lucilia, my dear, I suspect that my dear friend Marcus would like you to step out and occupy yourself while we menfolk talk.'

Fronto carefully avoided Lucilia's glare. He shot a quick glance at Faleria too, but she simply smiled sweetly and called out 'I'll be along shortly, Lucilia.'

Lucilia nodded once, curtly, at her father, shot a warning glance full of daggers at Fronto, and trotted daintily from the room, her stola swishing about her knees with that hypnotic sway that Fronto was resolutely ignoring right now.

Once she had left, Fronto waited for the door to close and opened his mouth to speak, but Balbus held up a cautionary finger and waited a while in silence. Finally, somewhat muffled by the door, they heard Lucilia 'harrumph' and patter off across the marble. Balbus smiled. 'She reminds me so much of her mother at times.'

Fronto coughed uncomfortably.

'You have something important to say?' Balbus nudged.

'Erm... yes. Sort of.'

'Something that involves Lucilia?'

'Well... erm. Sort of, yes.'

'Has she done something disgraceful?'

'No. No. Not that. Sort of... erm...'

Fronto collapsed into an uncomfortable silence, horribly aware that a pink stain had risen to replace the pallid grey of his cheeks.

'For the love of Venus, Marcus, he's playing with you!' came a muffled voice from beyond the door. Balbus roared with laughter, and Fronto glared at the wooden portal, wishing he was somewhere on a battlefield, up to the knees in gore, facing a thousand screaming Gauls; even on a ship! Anywhere instead of this.

Settling from his laugh, Balbus took on a more serious face and turned to address the door.

'If you do not go and find your mother and leave us to this, Lucilia, the conversation might never happen.'

A huffy noise rose from behind the door, and footsteps pattered away again. Fronto narrowed his eyes. 'Is she...?'

'She's gone. Now calm down, pretend you're ordering a general advance with cavalry on the wings and auxiliary support, and *talk* to me, Marcus.'

'Nothing untoward has happened, Quintus. I'll state that for the record. And I didn't try to drive a wedge between her and the Caecilius boy.'

Balbus nodded sagely. 'She has been writing to her mother, who has in turn been abusing my ears and straining my patience. I am painfully aware of how headstrong the women of my family are. Am I to believe then that Lucilia has succeeded in her quest to entrap you?'

Fronto sighed and, with an apologetic face, tipped the heavily-watered wine from his beaker into a houseplant next to him and replaced it with neat red liquid, taking a sip.

'I was sort of hoping to move things along nice and slowly, but the girl seemed Hades-bent to get me signed up, hog-tied and becoming a father before I can even shave again.'

'It's in the nature of girls, Marcus.'

'It's a difficult situation. You're my friend, Quintus. I know there's an age difference between us – frighteningly, not as wide as the one between Lucilia and myself – but I never saw you as a father figure. It would be... weird.'

Balbus smiled expansively.

'Don't forget that Caesar and Pompey are almost the same age and related in the same manner, and yet there's no discomfort in their relationship.'

Fronto shook his head. He would not have said that, though he understood the point his friend was trying to make.

'I just don't want you to have to say yes to anything you don't approve of, just because we're friends. Family is family, and she's your daughter, after all.'

Balbus smiled and looked down. When he raised his head again, his eyes sparkled. 'To be honest, Marcus, I'm more than happy with the match. I was more worried that you'd been forced into something you didn't want. Feel free to tell me now if Lucilia has pushed you into this.'

Fronto laughed weakly.

'Well she *certainly* pushed me into it, but that doesn't mean I'm unhappy with it. Are *you* sure about this, Quintus? You know I'm career military. A career soldier is a poor prospect for a husband.'

Balbus shook his head. 'Mars would melt and Fortuna pluck out her eyes before they let anything happen to you on the battlefield, Marcus. The match is approved if you wish it.'

Fronto swallowed. His throat had suddenly gone dry. This felt like handing over his sword to the executioner.

'I do, Quintus. A betrothal of... what? A year, for decency?'

Galronus frowned and leaned forward. 'Why delay? Among the Remi, we marry when we find the right match. There is no need for a time to show the people of the tribe first.'

Fronto glared at him.

'If I remember rightly, the Remi don't even pause to remove their breeches, if you get my drift.'

Galronus shrugged. 'When the match is right, the match is right.'

'Let's say less than a year' interjected Faleria from her couch nearby. 'We'll have to organise everything so that we can fit it in during the winter break between campaigns?'

Fronto suddenly felt his stomach flip again as it had on the ship.

'Errrr... alright then.'

Faleria gave him an encouraging smile, and then turned to Balbus.

'Can I suggest, Quintus, that you and I work out the details later: the ring, the gifts, the money and so on. And, of course, the date, the location, informing those who need to know and all the other minutiae?'

Balbus frowned. 'Do you not think that Marcus should have a...' he caught the helpless panic on his friend's face and nodded instead. 'Very well, let's take all the trouble out of his hands. I'm sure Corvinia and Lucilia will want to involve themselves, of course.'

'Of course.'

'Erm...?' began Fronto, looking slightly wild-eyed.

'Don't worry about it, Marcus. We'll sort it all out' Balbus smiled. 'Trust your old friend. I'll see you right, even in the face of all this womanhood!'

Fronto nodded unhappily.

'So' smiled Balbus 'I think that we should settle for a relaxing night of catching up for now. I'll send word to the trireme's captain to remain in port for a couple of days. Once you're safely packed off to the north, I will take the ladies and the girls back to Rome for the summer to organise everything. I was planning on a trip anyway, and besides, after last year's events, I suspect it would be good if someone were to keep an eye on our interests in the city?'

Fronto nodded.

'Shall we send someone to let Lucilia know she can come back? And it's time I saw Corvinia and Balbina. And tried some of Corvinia's pastries again. *Those* I have missed.'

Faleria rose slowly. 'I shall go and find the ladies and bring them here. I may be a few moments. The evening is warm and the honeysuckle on your veranda smells delightful. I could do with a few moments of air before we close ourselves in and gorge.'

Fronto frowned at her as though she must have some ulterior motive.

'Don't wander too far' he said irritably.

Galronus smiled and stretched. 'If it is permitted, I shall accompany you. The night air reminds me of my lands and my people. Sometimes it is nice to remember I am Belgae and born to this sky.'

Fronto moved his frown to his friend. 'I notice your Gaulish nature gets neatly sealed away when there's a racing circuit and a bookmaker anywhere in the vicinity!'

Galronus smiled infuriatingly and walked out of the room, leaving just Fronto and Balbus alone. Almost as if they had requested it, Galronus closed the door with a click as he left.

Balbus leaned forward conspiratorially and Fronto frowned.

'What?'

'Have you had a visitor, Marcus?'

The frown deepened. 'What are you talking about?'

'Vatia?'

'Eh?'

'Publius Servilius Vatia?'

Still no change in the frown. Balbus took a deep preparatory breath.

'How do you not know Vatia? His father's the censor who wiped the pirates out at Isauria? The lad's serving as quaestor for Narbonensis and he paid me a visit a couple of months ago. He expressed an interest in you and I wondered if he'd pursued it?'

Fronto pinched the bridge of his nose. 'You're circling an important point and trying not to make it, Quintus.'

Balbus had the grace to look a little uncomfortable.

'Servilius is making a few enquiries on behalf of his father... enquiries of those who are known to have disputed Caesar's command or are clear of ties to him.'

'Quintus…' Fronto said quietly. 'You're talking about something very dangerous there. What's his interest in it?'

'He never said; just sort of… sounded me out. But I thought long and hard about it, and I seem to remember that his father served as admiral of the Euxine fleet under Pompey in the east, so it's not hard to put the pieces together.'

Fronto shook his head. 'If he *had* come to me, he'd have left with a broken nose. Quintus, you shouldn't even be *talking* to these people!'

Balbus shrugged. 'As far as I'm aware this is still a republic and not a kingdom. Dangerous it may be, but I do have the right to at least listen to every side in a debate. It's what a good Roman does.'

Fronto's eyes flared. 'Quintus, don't tell me things I really don't want to hear!'

'Relax, Marcus. I'm still a client of Caesar's and a friend of yours. But don't tell me you've never even contemplated whether you're doing the right thing hoisting Caesar's banner, because I know you have. I know that you're too bright not to question the general.'

'Quintus' Fronto hissed, 'that's quite enough. You've always been Caesar's man!'

'And I still am… for now. But look at it: Gaul is pacified. He's pushed his remit beyond breaking point and stretched Rome to the very edge, but he's managed it. Gaul is tamed and everything can settle again. Now, he should be back in Illyricum or Cisalpine Gaul, making laws and skimming money off the taxes like a good governor. He doesn't need eight legions to hold on to a peaceful Gaul. He should be settling veterans. And what is he doing?'

Fronto shook his head, vehemently.

'What is he doing, Marcus?' demanded Balbus quietly.

'Preparing for campaign.'

'Against who? For what?'

'Germania. He says they're threatening the Belgae.'

Balbus nodded.

'Good. Then he will push back the Germanic tribes across their river, settle the veterans there to make sure it doesn't happen again, and then he'll return to his gubernatorial duties, I presume.'

'Quintus, I don't like what you're suggesting.'

'Only because you know I'm right, Marcus. Watch what happens. What I just suggested is all that's required, and you know

31

that. But if the general settles veterans and returns to political life after he's saved the Belgae, I'll eat my own cuirass.'

Fronto opened his mouth to argue again, but the door opened suddenly and Corvinia entered with a warm smile, followed by a grinning Balbina and a veritable army of slaves bearing steaming platters.

Corvinia greeted him warmly and Fronto cast one last warning glance at Balbus before, pushing his fears and dismay deep down into his chest, he stood and put on a smile that he hoped would look genuine.

* * * * *

Two days at Massilia had passed in strained pleasantry. Despite their longstanding friendship, the conversation Fronto and Balbus had shared alone that first night had soured the visit and nothing seemed able to dislodge the dark cloud from Fronto's thoughts.

The betrothal arrangements had been made around him and despite of him, largely by Corvinia, Lucilia and Faleria, while Fronto nodded and smiled and made his best attempt at small talk: a thing he had never truly got the hang of. Lucilia had noticed that something was different, as had Faleria, despite his smiles, though both had had the sense and tact not to enquire as to the cause.

The morning he had said goodbye to Lucilia, Faleria and the family had been an unexpected wrench for him, despite the fact that his feet had been itching to hit the trail north as soon as the mood had turned. He was never a man to avoid confrontation in the line of duty, but a confrontation with a good friend was a different proposal.

He and Galronus had checked over their horses as the slaves of the villa and the soldier from the staging post in the agora fussed around their pack animals and the many bags. Fronto had flatly refused a baggage cart due to the interminably slow pace it would set, and had purchased two strong pack beasts for the journey.

With just a few muted last hugs and kisses, he had mounted up, tipped a nod at Galronus, and the pair had been on the road while the sun was still young and cool.

The journey along the valley of the Rhodanus was peaceful and could have been pleasant, had Fronto been in a better mood. Galronus had watched him from time to time with something like concern but, fortunately, the big Gaul seemed to have something else on his mind and did not push the conversation at any point. The worst thing that had risen from his repeated replaying of that conversation in his head was the fact that he could not shake off the feeling that Balbus might be right.

After six days of almost silent travel, they arrived at the settlement of Vienna; last town on their journey north through the province of Narbonensis, before they entered the less well-trodden paths of newly-conquered Gaul. An overgrown Gallic oppidum with signs of Romanised settlement, Vienna was reckoned by many the last civilised place before further Gaul. The signs of recent settlement by the veterans of Caesar's legions were everywhere, from the construction style of the new houses to the foundations of a new theatre and a temple to Venus and Roma in the centre.

Fronto and Galronus made for the mansio off the 'forum'. The Sweeping Eagle was part local tavern, inn or guest house, and part military staging post. It was owned and operated by a former signaller for the Eighth Legion who had retired to the town after the Helvetii campaign three years ago and had opened this business with his severance pay.

The 'Eagle' appeared to be thriving, not only with the traffic directed to it by the Roman officers who used it as a convenient stopping off point, the supply trains that came through here on the way to and from the army and the Roman merchants who used it as a base to ply their wares to the newly-accepting Gauls; but also, apparently, as a watering hole of choice for locals from every sector of society.

The last time Fronto had seen the place, it had been a sizeable, square, two-storey building with a courtyard surrounded by outhouses and stables behind.

Silvanus seemed to have done well in this past season. A whole new wing sprouted off from the near wall, and an extension seemed to be underway on the far side, though currently the roof there consisted of a huge leather sheet apparently constructed from old legionary tent sections. Somewhere a quartermaster would be having a fit, and a legionary mule driver would be swinging a heavy purse.

Dismounting at the entrance to the rear courtyard, Fronto and Galronus enquired as to a room, confirming that there was a double billet available in the new extension so long as they did not mind sleeping under a temporary roof – for a discount, of course.

The groom took their mounts while they removed the bags they would need and hauled them onto their shoulders, making for the tavern door in the failing light.

Within a few moments they were ensconced at a heavy oak table, scratched and decorated with the names of passing soldiers and their units, as well as a number of dubious comments about the physical characteristics of their friends and some anatomically unlikely suggestions.

The man at the bar – a local with a shiny pate and bulging moustaches – caught Fronto's eye and nodded, bringing over a dusty bottle of wine and two earthenware cups; travellers in Roman garb never asked for the local beer. Fronto and Galronus studiously examined the scratchings as the barman unstoppered the wine and gave the cups a quick wipe with his cloth. The man narrowed his eyes as he spotted the officer's tunic with the pteruges that Fronto wore beneath his heavy cloak, and scurried away. Fronto rolled his eyes.

'See? Even he doesn't trust a man of the legions, and this place has been at least nominally Roman since my grandfather was a twinkle in *his* father's eye.'

Galronus looked up and met his gaze. It was the first hint of normal conversation they had shared in days.

'Of course,' Fronto added, 'this far from the sea, I expect they hardly ever saw a citizen until Caesar marched up here.'

'Fronto…'

He frowned as he took in the strange expression on Galronus' face.

'Are you alright?'

Galronus smiled.

'I'm thinking of taking your sister to marriage, Marcus.'

Fronto's cup dropped to the table, splashing cheap, vinegary wine across both him and the wooden surface. His lips moved curiously.

'According to custom, I will need your agreement' the Gaul continued. 'I'm not sure how it all works when we cross our customs, but your agreement is a factor in every way as far as I can see. That and gifts, though I'm a little confused as to whether I should be giving you gifts or receiving them; or possibly both.'

Fronto, his jaw slack, shuffled his chair backward and used his bare hand to sweep the spilled drink from the side of the table where it dribbled and spattered to the floor. His eyes narrowing, he refilled the cup and drank the contents in one open-gulletted mouthful.

'You *what*?'

'You do not agree?'

Fronto shook his head. 'I didn't say that. I just… When…? Why hasn't Faleria mentioned this to me?'

Galronus shrugged nonchalantly. 'I haven't told her yet.'

Fronto dropped his cup again, but caught it this time before the worst of the spillage.

'Listen, Galronus: Faleria might not be interested. She's had a bit of a… past. She…'

'I've seen the way she looks at me. She's interested.'

Fronto shook his head again, not so much in disagreement, as in astonishment. 'Well, I don't know…'

He suddenly became aware of a shadow falling across the table and looked up sharply.

'What?' he snapped at the two men standing above him. The Gallic barman looked nervous and apologetic, but that was hardly a surprise. The surprise was that the expression was mirrored in the face of Lucius Silvanus, former cornicen of the Eighth Legion and proprietor of the establishment. The burly veteran leaned forward.

'You're senior officers, right, sir?'

Fronto frowned and flashed a glance at Galronus. 'We'll pick up on that little problem again later.' Turning back to the innkeeper, he pursed his lips and nodded.

'I'm the legate of the Tenth, and this is Galronus, commander of the Belgic cavalry contingent. What's the problem?'

Silvanus looked around conspiratorially.

'Can I ask you to come with me for a few moments, sir?'

Fronto shared a look with Galronus and the pair shrugged, standing and gathering their packs. Silvanus gave a small, hurried salute and, beckoning, scurried off toward the side door. Curious, the pair followed him out into the courtyard again, where he approached a set of cellar doors in the floor near the inn's back wall. Crouching, he removed a heavy key and unlocked the doors, revealing a sloping ramp for beer casks, down which he trod carefully.

Fronto put his hand on the pommel of the gladius at his side as he glanced once at Galronus and then shuffled down into the dark space beneath the inn. The big Gaul followed. With the deep cerulean sky of late evening behind them, they could see very little within and it came as a surprise when they touched level floor again. A moment later there was a spark and Silvanus lit a small oil lamp, passing it to Fronto before lighting another and holding it high to illuminate the cellar.

Carefully, picking his way around the goods stored in the room, the innkeeper led them round a corner to where the other half of the cellar was divided into three parts with partition walls. Two doors remained closed, but the left hand side, with a wide stable-style door, stood open, revealing a log store, the chunks of heavy, seasoned wood casting strange shadows as the lamplight danced across them.

'We found it yesterday. I didn't know who to tell until you arrived.'

Fronto frowned and stepped in through the low door, ducking his head. Galronus was behind him again instantly.

The legate straightened in shock, cracking his head on the beam above the door and cursing sharply, rubbing his head.

'You see, sir? Not something to shout about.'

Fronto nodded, his eyes wide as he crouched over the body of Publius Pinarius Posca, senior tribune and nephew to Julius Caesar. There were contusions everywhere, caused by his hasty burial beneath the heavy, sharp logs, but it was clearly him. Even without the uniform tunic, Fronto would have recognised the high forehead and receded chin. His heart racing, he turned over the body. A dark stain of dried blood bloomed on his back around a wound, half way down the ribcage, slightly left of the spine.

'Murder. Plain and simple. No accident and not a fair fight.' Handing the lamp to Galronus, he used both hands to tear the crusted, hard tunic and open up a bare patch of pale, almost translucent skin beneath. The wound was neat; narrow and flat, expertly placed and professionally executed. Reaching down to his belt, Fronto slid his military-issue pugio dagger from the sheath and laid it next to the wound for comparison.

'I'd say that's pretty convincing. And he's been dead... three days, I reckon? Two at least, and not more than four.'

Fronto stood again and shared a look with Galronus.

'Travelling with the tribunes you think?'

The big Gaul nodded and Fronto turned to the innkeeper. 'Best get him seen to by the priests in town and then arrange for him to be shipped back to Massilia and then Rome. I'll leave you coin to cover the whole thing. We're going to go up and have enough wine to float a trireme, but if I were you, I'd have a couple of your slaves dig through that log pile and just make sure there aren't two effeminate junior tribunes in there too. Pinarius couldn't have been travelling alone.'

The innkeeper nodded. 'Normally I would remember senior officers passing, but there have just been so many on their way to the army that it's been a bit of a blur.'

Fronto glanced once more at the body and then shivered.

'Come on. I need a drink.'

Galronus helped him out of the log store and the pair made their way back through the cellar and up the shallow slope to the courtyard above. Before they entered the busy main room again, Galronus grasped Fronto's shoulder and pulled him up short.

'You think the same as me, I suspect?'

Fronto nodded.

'Two new centurions, eh? Caesar's not going to be happy at this.'

Chapter 3

(Divoduron, in the land of the Mediomatrici)

Fronto could not help but wonder what it said about him in that he felt profound relief that the brutal murder of a Roman officer had at least changed the subject of their sparse conversations from the subject of marriage and Faleria. Had he become so jaded with his own society that even needless violence was a preferable alternative to the social niceties?

He felt sure Faleria would say yes.

But in answer to what?

Shaking his head in irritation, Fronto glanced across at Galronus, sitting astride his horse with a serene and even happy face. It seemed that he could not even keep off the subject within the seclusion of his own skull.

His eyes drifted back ahead to the tribal capital of the Mediomatrici that loomed ahead of them. Having spent most of the preceding hours riding across a refreshingly flat plain, Divoduron showed the signs of having been founded by a man with an eye for tactical advantage. Curved like a misshapen horseshoe, the huge oppidum occupied the heights of a small range of high, wooded hills that rose like a barrier, crossing the great plain. The only clear pass in view from left to right marched directly through the huge fortified settlement. The Mediomatrici controlled the gateway to the flat lands on either side; a powerful position.

The Roman officers who had brought the army here from winter quarters as an assembly point had wisely avoided the crown of hills and settled for the flat land below for their numerous temporary camps. But the presence of eight legions and their endless support units, supply trains, cavalry corrals and suchlike seemed to have sparked this powerful oppidum into a frenzy of mercantile activity. The winding road that snaked up the pass to the Gallic settlement was dotted with small groups of pack animals – trade caravans taking advantage of the demand created by so many thousands of men. Here and there, a glittering, silvery glint betrayed the presence of Roman troops moving up and down the hill. Clearly Caesar had been magnanimous and allowed his men the luxury of utilising the oppidum's stores, taverns and women of low repute during their off-duty time.

From above it must look like an ant's nest.

Galronus' face blossomed into a curious smile. Slowly, inexorably, they were drawing closer to the lands of the Remi, his tribe. Fronto wondered if they would even recognise him now.

Galronus as a brother in law? It was not that he objected at all. And he liked to think of himself as a very accepting and understanding man. And yet, Fronto had found a small but insistent voice deep down in his soul that screamed denial at the idea of Gaulish blood running in a Roman family. Suppress the thought as much as he could, he still could not kill it, and this strangely intolerant deep-seated fear worried him more than anything else.

He suddenly realised that Galronus was watching him with a questioning brow and wondered what expression he had been wearing in his musings.

Forcing a thoughtful smile back on to his face, he concentrated on the approaching fortified camps. The nearest palisade held no vexillum, and the few men patrolling the rampart were clearly Gallic. The presence of corrals of hundreds of horses confirmed that the camp belonged to the allied Gallic cavalry. Beyond, the next two nearest bore the crimson standards of the legions, followed along the road by another group of horse pens and palisaded enclosures.

'This your bunch?' Fronto asked quietly, nodding at the nearest gate. There seemed to be no way to identify which auxiliary unit was which, there being so many allied Gallic horsemen compared to the few Roman cavalry, and it was only when Galronus nodded and pointed out a small group of pole-arms bearing stylised bronze boars that he could see a difference.

'We present ourselves to Caesar first, though, Marcus. It is fitting for a commander, and we must speak to the general of his nephew.'

Fronto nodded unhappily. That was a conversation he was hardly looking forward to. They had stayed in Vienna only long enough to make sure that Pinarius made it onto a proper funeral pyre and that an appropriate urn had been purchased, then had left instructions with the priest of Jupiter as the only official to whom Fronto felt he could entrust the task. The task of placing a coin in the mouth of the deceased had fallen to Fronto and he had carefully selected a nice, shiny denarius for the journey.

'The general's waited weeks for us. He can wait an hour longer. I want to find Priscus and Carbo first. I like to go into any briefing fully aware of everything going on first, and Priscus will know everything down to whose cloak the rats are nesting in.'

Galronus looked doubtful for a moment but then, acquiescing to the will of his friend, they rode on past the cavalry encampment, toward the central fort, larger than the others, and bearing the great gold and red Taurus flag that indicated the presence of the general.

The central camp bore also the standards of the Eighth, Ninth and Tenth legions – apart from the notable absence of the Seventh, the core of Caesar's force; the veteran legions. The guards at the gate moved to block the entrance at the approach of two riders, despite the military tunics they wore. Fronto prepared himself and took a deep breath to announce their ranks as the transverse crest of a centurion appeared over the parapet above the gate, the shining bronze of the helmet slightly duller than the shiny pink of the chubby face.

'Open the gate for Legate Fronto of the Tenth!' he bellowed before descending the turf rampart, disappearing from sight.

The legionaries at the gate stepped back into position, throwing out a salute to the two officers, and Fronto nodded at them as he passed within, wondering if they were men of the Tenth, given the presence of their primus pilus.

Carbo, remarkably neat and polished, appeared around the gate side and came to attention with a salute and a half-smile.

'Legate. All officers are required to attend the general upon arrival.' Turning to the gate guard, he gestured with his vine staff. 'It's a bloody shambles. Get that walkway cleared of crap and clean out oven number two. I shall be having a word with your officer. Any more of this slovenliness and I'll be reducing pay at such an alarming rate that *you'll* be paying *me* by October!'

By the time he turned back to Fronto and Galronus, who were dismounting, he wore a happy grin.

'Gotta keep 'em on their toes sir, eh?'

A harassed-looking legionary hurried over and took their reins for them, others grasping for their pack animals behind.

'Come on, sirs' Carbo said loudly and gestured up the main thoroughfare to the gathering of large tents at the centre, dotted about with the general's horse guard. As soon as they were out of sight of the gate, the centurion wiped his brow. I expect you'll be wanting to check in with myself after the general, yes, sir?'

Fronto nodded. 'I will, Carbo, but first I want to go find Priscus. Any idea where he might be?'

Carbo pointed to one of the tents ahead. 'That's his tent there, sir. He's just finished morning inspection of the camps, so he'll be there. It's astounding how many things he can find wrong, legate.'

Fronto smiled for the first time that day.

'Giving you a hard time, eh? He has to, Carbo. Having come from the Tenth, he can't be seen to be showing favouritism.'

'Don't I know it, sir? He was never this tough when he was my commander. I shall be at the Tenth's principia tent when you require me.'

Fronto nodded as the man strode off toward his own command.

'See who lurks nearby' Galronus muttered, leaning close. Fronto followed his gaze and narrowed his eyes. Centurion Fabius leaned against a tethering post close to the command section, idly picking his teeth with a splinter from a stick.

'I think we can afford another moment's detour.' Fronto smiled unpleasantly, and angled toward the officer. Fabius, a dour-looking man with dark stubble reaching almost from eyes to collar, turned a pale ice-blue, piercing gaze on Fronto and straightened with an almost deliberately insolent slowness, throwing out a salute. He was unarmoured and unarmed apart from his vine staff, his tousled iron grey hair waving in the gentle breeze.

'Fabius?'

'Legate Fronto. I trust you had a good journey?'

Fronto nodded. He had seen the attitude before: borderline insolent, full of hidden disdain, with a faint sneer. It was an expression career soldiers, and centurions in particular, reserved for the noble classes who liked to play commander without any real hint of military sense. Fabius could hardly be expected to view Fronto any differently, but it did little to prevent Fronto's dislike of the dark officer growing to almost boiling point.

'Been in camp long, Fabius?'

'Four days, sir. Made good time. Left our luggage to come on later with the supply train and just brought a saddlebag, sir. Like you, apparently.'

'Did you travel alone then?'

'Yessir. For speed.'

'Dangerous, given the unsettled nature of Gaul.' The centurion shrugged as if to suggest that he found more dangerous things than barbarian Gaul in his boot. 'And the tribunes you were with at Massilia?'

Fabius shrugged nonchalantly. 'The two junior tribunes got a message at the staging post in Massilia and rushed off ahead even of us. I think they were authorised to use courier horses and change mounts. They had been here for days when we arrived. I think the senior tribune bloke was going to knock around in Massilia for a bit before he set off. Didn't seem too inclined to rush.'

Fronto frowned and wished Priscus was with him. His former chief centurion claimed to be able to identify lies, and the results of dice games with him suggested it was true. Though Fronto would be prepared to put a month's wage on there being an untruth or half-truth there, he could not confirm it.

'Anything else, sir?'

Fronto glared at that smug smile, wondering momentarily whether he could legitimately get away with wiping it away with a right hook. The glare sliding into a sullen frown, he folded his arms and straightened.

'No. If you see Menenius and his ferret-brained friend can you ask them to come and find me.'

The man's parting salute carried, if anything, even more insolence and spite than his opening one, but Fronto ignored it and turned back, gesturing to Galronus as the pair strode on to the camp prefect's tent ahead.

Two of Aulus Ingenuus' praetorian cavalry guard stood outside Priscus' tent, rigid and armed for war, their crimson plumes whipping in the breeze. Their spears crossed as the two men approached, barring the way. Fronto came to a halt and nodded at them.

'Marcus Falerius Fronto, legate of the Tenth, and Galronus, commander of the allied Gallic horse to see the camp prefect.'

'The prefect's left orders he is not to be disturbed, legate, I'm afraid.'

Fronto glared at the man and cleared his throat.

'Priscus!' he bellowed. There was a sudden crash and a thud in the tent as of something heavy toppling over.

'Fronto?' came a slightly muffled voice.

'Let us in!'

A moment passed before the tent door was heaved aside and Priscus' face appeared in the gap. His eyes were underlined with dark circles, his face pale and unhealthy, and his hair knotted and uncombed.

'You took your bloody time. Get in here.'

Fronto shared a look with Galronus as the camp prefect disappeared inside once more and the two guards saluted and straightened, removing the obstacle from their path.

* * * * *

Priscus had returned to a large desk and was busy trying to gather a pile of wooden writing tablets that had fallen to the floor, though they kept slipping from his grasp in comedic fashion. Fronto and Galronus stood in the tent's entrance and took in the sight.

Priscus had the look of a man extremely short on sleep and bothered. Somehow it was extremely odd seeing their old friend dressed in the leather tunic and pteruges of a senior officer, his burnished cuirass and helmet standing on one of a number of wooden cabinets around the tent.

'You need a hand, Gnaeus?'

'Just sit down and let me get these put away' Priscus snapped, returning to grumbling under his breath as he replaced the tablets on the table, then rearranged them half a dozen times until he was satisfied that they were in the correct order. His gaze then strayed up from them to his visitors and he slapped his hands down on the oak surface, leaning heavily.

'Paetus may have been trouble, but the man must have had a mind like a damn librarian. How he kept all this straight, I have no idea. I'd just about got things set over the winter quarters, then we move here and it starts all over again. It's a never-ending bloody task. The last time I slept we had different consuls, I'm sure.'

Fronto smiled benignly. 'I suspect you're taking on more than you need to. I understand you've been interfering in the quartermaster's duties too?'

'I *had* to' Priscus snapped irritably. 'You have no idea how damn disorganised it all was. Whatever I needed was always 'on the way' or 'snagged up in transport at Massilia' or 'not available until next month'. Cita's organisation is a pissing joke! Caesar's trying to foist a number of assistants on me to play camp prefect for each legion; says that's what Pompey always did. But that just means I have eight more disorganised idiots to tidy up after, so I've set them all to counting things just to piss off Cita and his assistants.'

Fronto could not stifle his short laugh and Galronus was starting to smile now.

'Can you give me a quick rundown on what's happening before I go see Caesar?'

Priscus narrowed his eyes. 'You haven't been yet?'

Fronto shook his head, and Priscus scratched his chin and then slumped into a seat. 'You'd best hurry then; he'll be twitching for you to turn up.'

'Fine. Just give me a quick list, then. Note form if you need to.'

Priscus leaned back and scratched his head.

'Well you'll see that all eight legions are here, along with the cavalry, though they're all a bit depleted since Caesar settled his veterans and almost half the Gallic horse have disbanded now that the uprisings have been quashed. Their contract to the general was complete and Caesar thought it politic to let them return to their tribes.'

'Aye, we've seen the forces. And I know there's some trouble with the Germanic tribes. Go on.'

'Well, there's the Seventh. At Caesar's behest, I've spent the entire winter trying to identify any soldier that has any Pompeian connection or uncertain history and transferring them all to the Seventh. Appropriately, most of the veterans and solid men of the Seventh have now been moved out and dispersed among the other legions. It's been a bureaucratic nightmare.'

'Who has been given command of this rotten legion, then?' asked Galronus quietly.

'Who else? Cicero. With his ties to the knobs in Rome who're speaking out against the general, he was an obvious choice.'

'I thought Cicero was bound for the Eighth since Balbus left?'

'Young Brutus has managed to secure the Eighth. Spent half the winter badgering the general by letter, I gather, and started in person as soon as Caesar arrived. They seem quite happy with him. The Seventh is a bit restive, mind.'

'Not surprised. They'll have plenty of chances to prove their loyalty, I suspect. I'm guessing that two new centurions by the name of Furius and Fabius are now in the Seventh? Anything else? What about the Tenth?'

Priscus shrugged. 'Tenth are as good as they're ever going to be without me sticking a vine staff up their arse on morning parade. Carbo's a good man. I've got him terrorising the worst layabouts. And yes, there's two new veteran centurions with the Seventh, as well as a few optios and legionaries. You met them then?'

'The pair travelled with us a way. I'd trust them about as far as I could reasonably spit a donkey. Pompeians through and through.'

Priscus nodded. 'Pompeians they may be, but those two centurions have a hell of an impressive record. Might be just what the Seventh need if they're going to prove themselves.'

'Anything else?'

'Nothing you won't hear when the Gauls arrive to speak to the general – I expect he'll tell you about that. Anyway, I am busy, so you'd best go present yourselves before Caesar starts to get angry. I'll be along shortly.'

Fronto glanced at Galronus as Priscus turned back to his bureaucracy, acutely aware that they had just been summarily dismissed by a theoretically inferior officer. The two men shrugged and, ignored by the camp prefect, strode out of the office and turned to make for the large command tent nearby, guarded by six of Ingenuus' cavalrymen.

The men to either side of the door straightened and crossed their spears again as the two men approached and Fronto drew in a deep breath to announce himself just as the familiar, tight and strained voice of the general issued from the tent.

'Fronto? Get in here.'

Galronus smiled at him as the two guardsmen straightened and removed the impediment, allowing them to enter the slightly dim, spacious interior. The general was clearly in his element. Always invigorated by the commencement of a military campaign, and animated in his planning of such, Caesar moved energetically to the desk, his eyes bright, and leaned his back against it, crossing his arms. His hair seemed to have receded a little further over the winter, but otherwise he appeared as young and vital as ever he had.

'I was starting to think about sending out scouts to try and find you, Marcus.' His sole concession to Galronus' presence was a respectful nod in his direction.

'We came with good speed, Caesar, barring a two day layover at Massilia to visit Balbus.'

'And how is Quintus? Well, I hope? In truth I had hoped to pay him a visit myself on my journey north, though events beyond my control required me to reach the army with all speed.' His face took on a sly smile. 'But then, I suspect you had a more pressing need to speak to him than I. How is the lovely Lucilia?'

Fronto felt the colour rise to his face and once more damned his own blood for it.

'She's good Caesar. Look, I'm sorry about this, but there's some bad news we have to deliver before anything else happens.'

Caesar nodded. 'Best get on with it then.'

Fronto looked at Galronus, who shrugged uncertainly. Turning back to the general, he clenched his fists by his side.

'It's about your nephew, Caesar.'

'Young Pinarius? I'd assumed he'd come with you. Don't tell me the half-wit's got himself waylaid.'

'I'm sorry, Caesar, but it's worse than that. I'm afraid he's dead.'

'Dead?' The general never even flinched. His eyebrow arched slightly, but the only other sign that the news was of import was a slight whitening of the knuckles as he gripped his own elbows. 'How?'

'He was found in a tavern cellar in Vienna, general. He had been stabbed deliberately. I saw the body myself. I'd put good money on the murder weapon being a standard issue pugio, the blow delivered by a professional hand, and I have some theories as to the reason. Galronus and I have been mulling it over as we travelled. There's these two centurions...'

'It's damned inconvenient.'

Fronto blinked. 'Caesar?'

The general unfolded his arms and tapped his chin with two fingers thoughtfully.

'Very inconvenient. Oh, not for you, of course. I'm sure you'll be happier without a senior tribune for the Tenth. And Priscus will be happy not to have to deal with him. But I'll have to write to his mother and his wife. Young Domitia will be beside herself. Pinarius may have been a waste of good skin and bone, but she loved him for some reason, and he gave her a son. Inconvenient.'

''*Inconvenient*'?' Fronto said with a dangerous edge to his tone.

'Indeed. Oh Fronto, stop looking so offended. You've barely met the man. I doubt he'd have lasted very long out here anyway. Julia pushed me into giving him a term in command, and my sister usually gets what she wants in the end. Now perhaps I'll get no more family members foisted on me.'

Fronto felt the old familiar anger rising and it was with some difficulty that he forced his abhorrence at the general's off-hand, casual dismissal of the matter down into his deep, seething soul, where it could fester until the next time he had cause to explode at the republic's favourite son. It would only be a matter of time, after all.

'Do you wish an investigation into the matter?' he asked tightly.

'If you want to, be my guest, Marcus, but don't let it interfere with more important matters. Great things are afoot. The Germanic tribes are moving and threatening our hard-won peace. I'm interested to see what the Gallic noblemen have to say to me before we consider repeating our chastisement of Ariovistus, however.'

Fronto's hard gaze remained on the general. 'What is the current situation then, Caesar? Are we to move out shortly? I've not seen signs of decamping.'

The general shook his head and folded his arms again.

'The Gallic tribes near the Rhenus have a large force of Germanic tribesmen encamped in their lands. Mostly they are bulk infantry of the type we have encountered before, though apparently, these tribes...' he closed his eyes in a moment of recall 'the Ubii, the Usipetes and the Tencteri – also have a form of cavalry. I am led to believe that they do not use their horse the same as us, but dismount for the fight. I enquired of my sources as to how effective that could possibly be, but I am given to understand that they are fearsome indeed.'

Fronto nodded. 'So what are the local Gauls doing about them?'

'Mostly cowering in their huts' Caesar said, surprisingly without a sneer. 'These trans-Rhenal tribes have a dangerous reputation, Marcus. They have been preying on the more peaceful tribes for centuries. I understand that their people divide into two groups and alternate annually between breeding horses and feed animals, and raiding and fighting. Essentially, their tribes have not seen a peaceful season in a hundred generations.'

Galronus, next to Fronto, nodded.

'The Tencteri I am particularly familiar with, general. They are bred for war. They live for war and pillage. They have learned these ways from the Suevi, a tribe that lives in the wastes beyond, to the east, and whom you should pray to your gods that you never meet. I have heard tales in Rome that the Germanic tribes are all six feet tall or more, with the bodies of Vulcan, flame red hair, and are weaned on the blood of their enemies. Not so for many tribes, but the Suevi are the source of those tales. Among the Belgae they are the ghouls of childhood tales.'

Caesar nodded thoughtfully. 'Fortunate for us, then, that we face only these other three tribes. What do you think of them, master Galronus?'

'The Tencteri are dangerous and warlike, and the Usipetes almost the same. The Ubii are more civilised. They have traded with the Belgae for many decades, and have often shown restraint. However, if they have crossed the Rhenus, it is because the Suevi forced them, and that will mean they are desperate. And desperate men are unpredictable and dangerous.'

Fronto tried to take it all in but, as was often the case in briefings such as this, the names battered at his skull, refusing to sink into the brain matter within. His soldier's brain distilled it for him in the moment's silence that followed.

'So you're telling me that the Suevi are essentially monsters from nightmare, and they have pushed three tribes that are lesser-nightmare-monsters across the river, where they've frightened the locals enough that they hide? Is that the upshot?'

Caesar smiled benevolently.

'Succinct as ever, Marcus. But furthermore, I received visitors from those tribes on whose lands they settled. Two days ago, men came to seek our help.'

The general's smile was the old wolf grin that Fronto recognised instantly. It was that satisfied smile Caesar wore when everything he had pushed for and hoped for had fallen into place, giving him exactly what he wanted.

'They asked you to go to war with these Uspi-thingies and their friends?'

'They had sent their own ambassadors, offering the invaders chattels, food, weapons, warriors, herds and much more just to return across the Rhenus; a cowardly offer, of course. These tribes are unwilling to return to their own lands, as their nightmare enemies from the east await them there. But even should they not be, why would they leave the lands of men so weak as to try and buy their absence? No, the Ubii and their allies simply accepted such weakness for what it was, and expanded the area of land they were depredating to take in more Gallic tribes.'

'We've pacified Gaul and thus left it open to new predators' Fronto said quietly. 'We've killed off or conscripted so many of their warriors they no longer have the strength to defend themselves from other tribes. It is not weakness that drove them to it, Caesar. It was our conquest that did that.'

A tiny flash of flint passed across Caesar's eyes, but his smile, cold though it was, was quick to come.

'You have a way with words, Fronto. If only you could dress them up a little, what an orator you would make in the senate. But your words I accept as a possibility. I would then urge you to question why, when our conquest was complete and all rebellion had ended, I continued to keep all eight legions wintered in the north of Gaul? We must hold on to the peace with a warlike hand, Marcus.'

Fronto nodded wearily. He had wished he could have thought of that when discussing the motives of the general with Balbus. It made so much sense when the general said it.

'So what's next, Caesar? We march on them?'

Caesar shook his head. 'Not yet, Marcus. I have sent out couriers to summon the Gallic council to Divoduron. Gaul is under Roman protection,' his eyes flicked uncertainly to Galronus for a moment and then back, 'but it is still important for the kings and chieftains of Gaul to make the decisions about their lands and people. We can help, advise, support and protect, but, within the aegis of the Roman Republic, these people still rule themselves. The Gallic council must decide what to do about the invaders and make a formal request of myself as the proconsul. Only then can we legitimately move.'

Fronto frowned at the general even as he nodded. Caesar had to satisfy the senate that he was still working within their remit, in order to stem the troubles being stirred constantly in Rome, but how much of such courtesy was spoken for the benefit of Galronus as a prince of the Remi? What might Caesar have been inclined to say had the Gallic officer not been present?

Caesar smiled.

'And our army is a little depleted by years of campaigning, settling veterans, and releasing our allied cavalry from their duties. I have had some success with recruitment, despite the limits continually imposed upon me by the senate, but if the council does wish us to go to war for them, I will have to request that they supply me with further cavalry forces. I'm sure Galronus will appreciate a bolstering of his forces?'

The Remi noble nodded silently, and Fronto tried unsuccessfully to look behind those unreadable eyes to see what lay within.

'Very well, Marcus. I suspect you have a few weeks before the council arrive, despite my asking that they come with all speed. I suggest that you reacquaint yourself with your command during that time. And possibly experience the scrape of the razor once again. You are starting to look Germanic.'

* * * * *

Fronto and Galronus stepped out of the command tent into the bright sunshine, blinking, grateful to breathe the relatively fresh air of the camp.

'You coming for a drink?'

The Remi officer shook his head 'I'll return to my cavalry. There will be much to oversee and discuss. Perhaps I shall find you later.'

Fronto watched his friend stroll off toward the south gate once more, marvelling yet again at just how well the man fitted in among the Roman forces. His Latin was now fluent, even with a hint of an Oscan twang that had probably come from hanging around with Fronto so much. He was, admittedly, much neater and cleaner-shaven than Fronto himself.

With a small smile, he turned and strode down toward the camp of the Tenth. The sound of Carbo venting spleen at some misplaced piece of equipment rose from somewhere among the tents, but really the Tenth was as perfectly organised and efficient as ever. Fronto began to wonder, as he moved along the neat lines of tents, whether Priscus was perhaps leaning a little too heavily on the Tenth, even given the situation.

Rounding a corner and reaching the area of the command section, he was both surprised and pleased as one of the tribunes' tent flaps swung open and the young, energetic figure of Tetricus emerged, almost stumbling into his commander.

'Fron... sir!' Tetricus pulled himself up straight into a salute.

'Gaius' Fronto grinned. 'Good to see you. You busy?'

Tetricus' eyes flashed back and forth conspiratorially. 'With respect sir, it doesn't do to be anything *other than* busy. Even for a tribune. Priscus has eyes everywhere and if anyone sits down for a rest, they acquire a new job in moments.'

Fronto sighed and grinned. 'I think I'm going to have to have a word with the new camp prefect. Paetus knew how to do his job without impeding the legates and senior officers of a legion. Priscus seems to be trying to be the primus pilus of all eight legions and the support forces.'

He laughed. 'Anyway. Here's a new job for you: go find the usual reprobates and ask them to come join me for a catch-up and a drink. You too; and Priscus, if he can walk this far with that stick up his arse.'

Tetricus smiled with relief. 'Varus and Brutus in particular have been waiting for you to get here, Marcus. I'll bring everyone along shortly.'

Fronto nodded as Tetricus threw him another quick salute and ran off in search of their various friends. Shaking his head in exasperation at the effect Priscus' promotion seemed to be having on the army, Fronto turned and strode between the tribunes' tents to his own, where he was surprised to find four men standing in quiet conversation outside.

Labienus had changed little, though his face was a little more drawn and a haunted shadow seemed to flick around his eyes. His smile as he spotted Fronto was as friendly as ever, though. The man beside him was faintly familiar, though Fronto could not say from where, and his eyes lingered on the man only long enough to realise that, despite his Roman officer's mode of dress and clean-shaven face, his hair was braided in the Gallic fashion, and the telltale bulge of a neck torc showed beneath his tunic. One of the cavalry, most likely, and doubtless an officer if Fronto recognised him.

The bigger surprise for a moment was the presence of the tribunes from the Fourteenth, Menenius and Hortius. They stood in easy conversation, hands on hips as though in friendly banter, and it took a moment for Fronto to remember that he had asked them to come.

Labienus stepped out of the group, somewhat rudely interrupting Menenius, who appeared to be extolling the virtues of some sculptor or other.

'Marcus. By Mercury's wings, it's good to see you. I had word that you'd returned.'

Fronto noticed the way the Gallic officer beside him stepped forward like a shadow imitation of Labienus and wondered whether it was a move informed by desire to stay close to the staff officer whom he obviously knew, or more by the need to stay away from the mindless chatter of the two tribunes who seemed to be quietly discussing something that made the pair of them giggle like girls at a bawdy house.

'Titus' he smiled at the senior officer. 'Good to see you too. Would you like to step inside and I'll join you in a moment. I've not been in yet, but if Carbo's following his standing orders, there'll be a dozen cups and two amphorae of good Latin wine.'

Labienus raised a questioning eyebrow, his eyes flicking momentarily to the two tribunes, and then he nodded, his gaze searching out the meaning in Fronto's dour expression and finding none.

'Come, Piso. Let us avail ourselves of Fronto's wine. He always has an excellent stock. Hopefully he's got water for it too, though you can never be too sure with Fronto.'

With a smile and a last curious glance, Labienus escorted Piso inside.

Fronto waited until the two tribunes finally noticed he was watching, and then beckoned them with a crooked finger and turned, walking toward Tetricus' tent nearby. Lifting the flap, he motioned for the two fops to enter and then followed them in, allowing the flap to drop behind them.

Tetricus' tent was exactly as Fronto would have expected. The engineer's logical, analytical mind was reflected perfectly in his surroundings: every item in the interior placed with precision and nothing out of place. A wooden cabinet stood to one side with half a dozen drawers. A rack for two dozen scrolls stood on top and it crossed Fronto's mind for a moment to pry, before he forced the urge away.

The two tribunes stood, looking somewhat befuddled, in the centre of the tent, almost lost in the dim light.

Fronto walked round them in a circle, looking them up and down. He was not sure exactly what he expected to find, but he needed to be sure that these two men had nothing to do with Pinarius' death. The two tribunes watched him move like a prospective buyer at the slave market, probably wondering if he was going to open their mouths to examine their teeth.

Both men wore white leather tunics with white pteruges hanging in two rows from both waist and shoulders, each strip edged with gold and ending in a gilded fringe; ostentatious in the extreme. Though they wore no cuirass, helm or greaves, their boots were enclosed, soft leather efforts, a fleece lining poking from the top. Under normal circumstances, they would have attracted the same disparaging mental comments as the tunics in Fronto's mind, but he was also painfully aware of their similarity to the boots he currently wore, courtesy of Lucilia's mania for renovating him. Perhaps he could acquire a new pair of boots from Cita and start pissing them into shape over this summer? He made a mental note to do so.

He frowned as he sniffed. Rose petals and camphor? It was a cloying scent. He wondered for a moment why the two men stood together wearing scents that combined to such appalling effect until he realised that, in fact, both men wore the combination individually. His eyes watering, he stepped back and faced them.

'Tell me about your journey.'

The two tribunes exchanged a slightly baffled look, and then Hortius smiled.

'I had a piebald mare. I called her Aphrodite, because she was so sleek and beautiful. I used to have a horse like her on the estate at Alba Fucens, only I called her Hector, because I was initially confused about sex, and...'

Fronto pinched the bridge of his nose and held up his hand to stop the tribune, who may well still be a little confused about sex as far as Fronto was concerned.

'Too much background detail, Hortius. Tell me about Massilia to Divoduron.'

Menenius smiled. 'He cannot help it, legate. He likes horses. We were rather swift actually. I went into Massilia, but not to the military staging post. You see my uncle, who was a praetor two years ago, retired to a villa above Massilia and he has enormous influence with both the Greek council there and the local officials at Arelate. I managed to secure us a constant change of horses at the courier stations until we passed Vienna, where we purchased several fast horses and just gave the tired ones to some poor sad-looking local each time we changed mounts thereafter. It's amazing what a little money and influence can achieve.'

Fronto held his tongue, his own opinion of nepotistic and monied influence being unlikely to sit well with these two.

'So you were here before any of us.'

'I would imagine so.'

'And you travelled alone, through Gaul? With no escort?'

Menenius frowned in incomprehension. 'Yes. Gaul is conquered, and no uneducated barbarian would interfere with a Roman officer on official duty. You took an escort?'

Fronto blinked. 'Well, no. But I had a Gaul with me, and anyway, we're more...' his voice tailed off as he could find no way of saying what sprang to mind without levelling an insult or two at the pair. 'Fair enough. What of Publius Pinarius Posca?'

Hortius' brow furrowed. 'Pinarius? Did he not travel with those two burly brutes of centurions? He stayed in Massilia to see the sights; wouldn't accept our offer of relay horses. I think, to be quite honest, that he's not quite the man we all are, eh, legate? Cannot imagine young Pinarius riding a horse. Probably had a silk-lined wagon.'

The two men burst into an annoying cacophony of snorts and giggles at the idea of Caesar's wet nephew riding a courier horse. Fronto rolled his eyes, fighting the urge to complain about being lumped in with them as 'men' almost as heavily as the urge to try and beat some sense of military decorum into them..

'Thank you. That's all I wanted to know.'

The two men slowly recovered from their humour and shrugged.

'Any time, legate, my lovely.'

Fronto managed to leave the tent somehow, miraculously, without laying a hand on either of them. He found himself simply grateful that they were not assigned to the Tenth, else he would have buried them both up to their necks in a latrine trench before they ever got as far as war.

The two men exited behind him and moved across the camp, giggling like idiots while Fronto, still breathing deeply in annoyance, strolled back toward his tent.

Throwing the flap aside, he found Labienus and his friend sitting in camp chairs beside his table, with cups of wine, a third poured ready for him. With a nod of thanks, he sank gratefully onto his bunk, undoing his boots and letting them drop to the floor. Labienus shuffled his chair a few feet further away, his eyes quickly beginning to water.

'New boots, Marcus?'

'Bloody women' was his sole reply as he let the other fall, peeled off the now-greyed woollen socks and wiggled his toes, releasing a fresh waft of four-day stink.

'There's a bath tub in a bathing tent in the command section for senior officers, Marcus, and there's always heated water ready.'

'How nice.'

'So if you'd like to scrub off your journey first…?'

'No, you're alright, Titus. I need to rest and have a few cups first.'

Labienus glanced across at his friend, who had also moved his chair a few feet further away.

'I'd like you to meet Piso, Marcus. He's a chieftain among the Aquitani and now one of the senior cavalry commanders along with Varus and Galronus. They'll command a wing each, with Varus in overall charge, of course.'

Fronto nodded his greeting, scratching his toes and rubbing his feet with a free hand while consuming the prepared wine with the other, noting with distaste how Labienus had already watered it for him.

'I thought I'd best introduce you. There are still a great number of blinkered officers in this army who will not consider a non-Roman officer worthy of their attention, but I know you're not one of them. Galronus, after all…'

Fronto nodded as he placed the cup on the table and stretched back on his bunk.

'Pleased to meet you, Piso. You seem, like Galronus, to be a man fond of our custom?'

Piso shrugged. 'In weaponry, art and devotion to the gods, the Aquitani will always be paramount, but I am not beyond being able to see the advantage of a comfortable tunic and a clean-shaven neck. It is my staunch belief that both Roman and Gaul have much to learn from one another.'

Fronto smiled appreciatively and nodded toward Labienus.

'A seductive viewpoint that our officer friend here has propounded to me before.'

'Marcus, there's a particular reason I wanted you to meet Piso. Beyond being an embodiment of what I see for the future of Gaul.'

Something in Labienus' tone made Fronto sit up straight. The staff officer looked nervous; pensive.

'What is it, Titus?'

55

'Did you know that Caesar continues to draw more levies from the tribes of Gaul, Marcus?'

'Well, yes. He needs them to push the Germanic tribes back out.'

'Fronto, Caesar could deal with those invaders with two legions and a single cavalry wing. Do you not think it's time to put the future of Gaul back in the hands of the Gauls?'

Fronto frowned. 'That's what he's *doing*. He's summoned the Gallic council so they can decide whether to ask for our help.'

'Marcus, don't be so blind. Listen to yourself. Caesar has 'summoned' the kings of Gaul. Only a despot can do that. Caesar places himself above those kings. He only panders to them because he is not yet strong enough to oppose the senate!'

Fronto's stomach knotted and he felt a sudden cold shiver run down his spine. This conversation was starting to sound disturbingly familiar.

'Have you been listening to Cicero and his brother? This is a dangerous path to walk, Titus, and I don't want to hear anything more about it.'

Labienus shook his head and poured Fronto another cup of wine. 'I'm not advocating mutiny or anything like that, Marcus, but I think we need to start questioning the general on his motives and actions and perhaps try to persuade him toward the path of reason. We need to bring him back into concord with the senate before things turn ugly.'

'Enough, Titus. You're one of the general's most senior lieutenants. Don't say anything else you might learn to regret.'

'But Marcus...'

'*Enough*, Titus! I think the pair of you had best leave now before the others get here.'

Labienus rose slowly from his chair, alongside Piso. Before exiting the tent, he paused and turned back, pointing a finger at Fronto. 'Think on it, Marcus.'

Before Fronto could shout angrily at him, the two slipped out, leaving Fronto seething and uncertain. What was this damned army he had come back to? It barely resembled the one he had left last autumn.

ROME

Quintus Lucilius Balbus sat on the steps of the wide stairway that led up from the forum to the Arx, from which the grand temple of Juno dominated the skyline. The ancient temple of Concordia's featureless and high north wall cast a deep shadow on the stairway, bringing blessed relief from the sizzling sun that already, even in the mid-morning, was unseasonably hot.

His eyes had been straying across the numerous structures that formed the nucleus of the city and the heart of the republic. It had been some time since he had made a trip to Rome, where he had spent so much of his youth and his early adulthood. The shape and form of the conurbation had changed even in those few years, with ever more grand buildings rising to display the wealth and generosity of various power-seeking benefactors, and each one was accompanied elsewhere by another towering brick hovel; a monstrosity of living quarters that would shame a slave, and yet were clamoured for by the poor of the republic.

And the forum had never been so alive in his youth, or so it probably seemed through the eyes of age. Men, women and children of every colour and every social status rubbed elbows as though they were equal in the press of people buying goods, haranguing public speakers, making for the law courts, picking purses, or any of the myriad of diversions the forum provided.

He and his family, along with Fronto's sister, who had formed a worrying alliance with Corvinia that boded ill for his future, had arrived by ship from Massilia last night and made their way to Balbus' townhouse on the Cispian hill. Faleria had been determined to return to her own home but, with it still undergoing renovation, Balbus had had to insist that she join them as their guest.

His townhouse had remained unoccupied for more than two years, with only a small skeleton staff of servants to keep it clean and intact, and the provisions within were woeful. After an evening of scraping up whatever they could for a meal, sending the servants out to find the few remaining late-night food stalls still open, the womenfolk had decided that the next morning would be a full resupply shop that would require at least half a dozen servants for porterage, and Balbus himself, in case male choices had to be made, or the family coffers had to be opened to pay the enormous bills.

It had taken a quarter of an hour of struggling through the throngs of people, trying to keep up with the four women who moved like a pack of wolves through the crowd, for Balbus to decide he'd had enough. Stating flatly that he had more intention of joining a theatre troupe than contemplating another moment's shopping, he had arranged to meet them here.

Here, because a short walk to the north, along the Clivus Argentarius, stood a nice little tavern that would be a good place for the women to take stock of their purchases and for Balbus to silently, and with wine, bemoan his fate among this group of Amazons.

In the meantime, it was rather nice sitting in the shade. His hand dipped into the pack of honeyed dates he had managed to purchase during the fray and the sweet, sticky treats brought on such a thirst that he had to reach for the skin of grape juice that he had also bought.

Taking a deep pull, his gaze passed over the top of the skin and locked on the curia building below and to the left, where the senate was in heated debate. At less than seventy paces distance, it was almost possible to hear the subject matter from the steps; almost but not quite. But still, occasionally, the debate would rise in pitch, tone and volume and words would carry this far. The third time he heard Caesar's name shouted in the building and the roar of assent that followed, he had decided that this situation needed more attention, and had paid an urchin to go stand near the doors and listen in. After all, it didn't do for a man of stature to lurk outside the senate doors like an eavesdropper. Besides, the stairs were so much more comfortable.

Whatever they had been discussing in there for the past hour, Caesar had apparently been at the very crux of the matter. Other words had risen from the cacophony, each one as expected as the next: Gaul, Pompey, Consul, Glory, Triumph, Cost. Cost. Cost seemed to be an important matter for debate, too.

It was not hard to piece together the arguments from those snatches he had heard, though the urchin would help later, in return for the three copper coins promised from Balbus' purse.

His attention was suddenly drawn to the front of the building as the senate house's doors swung open, releasing the roar of angry and excited politicians into the city. Balbus was less than surprised to recognise the first figure to emerge.

Cicero had his hands raised in triumph as he stepped into the light, beaming at the crowd that had assembled outside, hoping to set eyes on the men who controlled their republic. The great orator had the look of a victorious gladiator, playing to the people. The senators who followed him closely, though Balbus knew perhaps half of the faces at most, were clearly Cicero's supporters and pets, cheering him on.

The chorus of 'Summons for Caesar' was still being echoed around the curia's interior, and Balbus frowned. Had Cicero already managed to press for such a drastic move in the general's absence? But the more he listened, the more it sounded like a demand than an announcement.

Cicero had paused on the steps and dropped into conversation with two senators at his side and Balbus' eyes strayed across the scene until he locked onto the wretch who was dutifully eavesdropping for him. The boy had managed to get himself remarkably close to the city's most honoured and respected orator. That conversation alone would be well worth the three copper coins.

Balbus started and shrank instinctively back into the shade as his eyes lit upon the small group behind the boy; five men in the drab brown tunics of the Roman poor. They would blend into any crowd with ease. But Balbus had served with the legions for more years than he cared to remember and the stance of a soldier was unmistakable, no matter what he wore. His gaze played across the men, taking in the long sleeves on their tunics, unfashionable, but long enough to cover any marks of military service and the bulges in the tunics at their waists that spoke of hidden daggers.

Cicero and his two favourite pets left the stairs and began to walk across the forum. Balbus felt his heart jump as the boy scurried out of the way and began to jog toward the stairs where he sat, while the five lurking men moved across the open space formed by the crowd parting for the senators, shadowing them. A sinking feeling settled like a river stone in his gut.

His eyes darted back and forth until he spotted Corvinia at a stall behind the shrine of Venus Cloacina. They might be finished any moment, but if he waited, he would lose any hope of finding out what was going on.

Biting his tongue, he gathered up the punnet of dates and the skin of juice in the sweep of his large hand and began to descend the steps three at a time. By the time he reached the paving of the forum and his young, scruffy accomplice had converged on him, he had already dug a number of small coins from his purse. Pausing, he dropped the collection into the young lad's waiting hands. It was perhaps the cost of a couple of good cups of wine, but represented a clear fortune to the boy. His eyes widened.

'I have to go for now' he said, his breath coming heavily. He was not built for this sort of exercise these days, since his illness in Gaul. 'Stay here and wait for me with your information and I'll double that when I get back.'

The boy's face split into a wide grin as he nodded vigorously. Balbus smiled at him and, scanning the crowd until he spotted Cicero and his friends, ran on, pushing his way through protesting women and men, priests and traders. A pickpocket hoping to make an easy target received an elbow in the face for his mistake, and Balbus was suddenly bursting through the crowds only a few paces behind the five soldiers in their dreary kit.

As Cicero rounded the side of the arcade of shops known as the tabernae vetae, he paused, sharing a few quick words and a smile with the senators before they departed. The two lapdogs moved off, still chatting together, along the Vicus Tuscus, toward the cattle market and the Tiber, while Cicero turned, making his way past the temple of Castor and along the Via Nova. Unnoticed behind them, their stalkers also split, three of their number following the senators toward the river, the other two climbing the hill after Cicero.

Balbus fumed for a moment, his head snapping back and forth between the two streets and finally settled on Cicero as the more important of the two groups. Stepping into the shadow of the great temple, Balbus attempted to melt into the background – no mean feat for an overweight ex-soldier with a gleaming pate and a pristine white toga. As the shadowing soldiers crested the first rise, following their prey with little subtlety, Balbus moved like a panther along the side of the quiet road.

Ahead, Cicero paused in the street and, adjusting his toga, strode toward a large townhouse at the southern edge, a bakery built into its frontage. Balbus nodded to himself in confirmation as he spotted the name of the bakery: 'Pistrinum Ciceronia'. The orator had simply returned home from his deliberations. As Cicero disappeared into the house's interior, the door clicking shut behind him, Balbus stepped back into an angle between two buildings and watched as the two men following him huddled together in deep conversation and then broke up and hurried away along the street.

Again, Balbus dithered, torn between following the men, returning to the corner to see if the other senators were still in sight, and heading back to the forum to try and meet up with his young informant and the ladies.

Wishing he had not started all of this, the ageing ex-officer strolled on along the street after the two men who had previously been shadowing Cicero. Given their clandestine nature, the men seemed to be somewhat lax in their awareness, only occasionally glancing around and not paying even enough attention to spot the portly man lurking in the shadows.

Up the Via Nova they strode, calmly, unaware of anyone following them, turning right and climbing the slopes of the Palatine, passing through the ruined piers of the Mugonian gate and cresting the hill to the area of the city occupied by the spacious houses and villas of the city's wealthier and more important folk.

Balbus frowned at their presence in such a rich area, and followed them with deepening interest and suspicion as they passed across an open square, turning down an alley to the right and disappearing through a small gate in the back wall of a sizeable property.

Balbus stood for a moment, still frowning, and then strode across to a low bench beneath an apple tree at the far side of the square, where he could just see the closed gate and high wall of the expensive residence into which the dubious men had passed.

For a while he sat, contemplating what to do next, starting suddenly as a click resounded just behind him. Craning his head around urgently, he saw a middle aged and well-to-do matron and her house slave leaving a gate just such as the one he watched. The woman looked at him with something between surprise and suspicion but, taking in his age, weight, and togate attire, her brain labelled him equestrian class at the least and therefore unlikely a threat to house and person. Nodding a greeting, she turned to head for the forum.

Balbus narrowed his eyes and cleared his throat.

'Excuse me, good lady?'

The woman paused and turned with an elegantly sculpted eyebrow raised.

'Sir?'

Balbus gestured toward the gate in the wall that he faced.

'Do you happen to know who resides at that villa?'

The woman's face took on a look dark and disapproving enough that Balbus wondered whether he should apologise for asking.

'That, sir, is the house of Atia Balba Prima, daughter of...' she actually looked as though she might spit as her mouth formed a name with distaste, 'Julia Caesaris.'

Without further ado, the woman gathered her stola around her and strode off toward the forum, her slave at her heel, leaving Balbus staring at the gate in consternation.

Atia? Niece of Caesar. What the hell was the general up to now?

Wishing there was another urchin around to set to watching the door, Balbus stood, stretched, and turned back to locate the busily shopping women somewhere back down in the forum and the boy with his overheard senatorial musings.

Clearly he was going to have to pay attention in Rome.

Something was afoot.

Chapter 4

(Divoduron, in the land of the Mediomatrici)

The most powerful men in Gaul sat on low benches around three
sides of the tent, the legs of the seats deliberately shortened, forcing
them to look up at the general and his officers who occupied the
fourth. Periodically one would stand as though he were a Roman
patrician addressing the senate, and make some salient point or other
to which Fronto paid no attention whatsoever.

The assembly of the chiefs of Gaul had been in progress for over
an hour now and Fronto had retained precisely zero words that had
been spoken in that time. To pay attention and contribute was not
why the officers were here; they were here as a reminder of the pomp
and sheer power that Rome and Caesar had at their disposal. They
were here to help make the Gauls feel small, just like the shortened
seat legs, the captured Gallic standards that hung on the leather wall
behind the officers and the centurions and men who stood erect
behind the Gauls as though guarding them.

It was an assembly of the Gallic rulers about as much as it was
an orgy of the gods. It was, in fact, Caesar once more playing the
Gauls for his own benefit. Indeed, he had even feigned ignorance
over the very existence of Germanic tribes this side of the great river,
just to allow the Gauls to plead, demand, and urge Caesar to come to
their aid.

Showmanship.

Fronto felt uncomfortable with the whole pretence, all the more
so since Labienus kept catching his eye and raising his eyebrows,
nodding toward the general. He knew why it was all happening, of
course. The senate continued to bemoan Caesar's pushing beyond
the limits of his granted powers, and the pleas of the allied Gallic
chiefs would legitimise his campaign. But still it reeked to Fronto.

Another Gallic chieftain stood, his silvery braids whipping
around his neck as he rose, his moustaches all but obscuring his
mouth as he refused to grant Caesar any more levies for his cavalry.
Fronto rolled his eyes and mouthed along with Caesar's somewhat
predictable reply.

'Without adequate cavalry support, I cannot see any way in
which we can reasonably challenge your Germanic aggressors.'

63

He had heard Caesar use the same line three times already. It was a stalemate situation at the moment. The Gauls were all in favour of Rome coming north in force and driving out the new invaders, but many of their husbands, fathers and sons had finally been released to return to their tribes after two or three years of serving with the Romans. Their tribes were beginning to recover, the returning manpower allowing them to raise their farming and manufacturing to the levels they had achieved before Caesar had first enlisted their cavalry. Only three tribes had so far relented and agreed to provide new men for Caesar's horse army and those were tribes that had only recently become allies and had lost few men to the campaigns.

It was all about attrition. Caesar had them in the palm of his hand. The Gauls needed him to get rid of the invaders, lacking the strength to do so themselves, and everyone there knew it. They simply jostled to get the best deal from the situation for the fewest losses. By the time the meeting was over, Caesar would have his cavalry, of that there could be no doubt. But it was extremely wearing to be a part of.

Fronto glanced across and accidentally caught Labienus' eye once more. The staff officer was watching him intently, damn him.

Fronto's eyes strayed to the other figure in the room whose presence offered something of an interesting alternative to the stony-faced Roman officers and wheedling, supposedly-noble Gauls.

Centurion Furius was in position at the rear of the tent, next to the entrance, casting unmoved, superior looks at the gathered chiefs. Fronto had watched him for a lot of the last hour, drinking in every detail about the man. Here was a soldier he would trust as far as he could throw a ballista.

Furius was marginally shorter than Fronto, perhaps five feet four or five, but his body mass was clearly higher. The man had shoulders like Atlas, broad and strong, a dimension betrayed by the fact that his mail shirt showed signs of having been altered to give extra shoulder room, the shinier newer links standing out against the dulled old ones. The lower half of his face was covered with grey bristles that reached from the collar of his armour almost to his eyes, covering his neck and even his cheekbones. It gave him a deeply animalistic appearance that seemed in Fronto's opinion to suit him. One thing had particularly interested him, though: a shiny white scar on his tanned skin followed the line of his collar bone, and just above it.

There were a number of ways a man could receive such a wound, of course, but Fronto could not help remembering stories of the men who had worked for Clodius Pulcher and instigated mutiny in the eastern legions being executed by Lucullus' officer with a single downward thrust into their hearts.

He shook his head to bat away such fanciful thoughts. No man would survive such a blow.

As he watched, he realised Furius had straightened and come to attention.

His mind focusing once more, Fronto glanced around. Caesar was gesturing at the centurion.

'Bring me the records of our cavalry numbers.'

Furius saluted again and turned. Fronto frowned for a moment as an opportunity struck him to escape this gloomy proceeding. Turning to the general, he cleared his throat.

'If I might be excused, general, I will bring Galronus. He has just completed a full inspection of one of the three cavalry wings and could probably provide useful information for you.'

Caesar frowned for a moment at the breach of protocol, though hardly unexpected, given the perpetrator, and then nodded.

'Be quick.'

Fronto bowed slightly and shuffled out behind the line of officers, making his way around the tent and out of the entrance. The arguing began once more before he had even made it out of earshot.

He knew exactly where Galronus would be: in Fronto's tent, helping himself to whatever tasty vittles he could find. Fronto had arranged to meet him after the meeting. Almost certainly Priscus would be there, too, and Priscus would be the man with the cavalry records.

Centurion Furius was busy striding across the command compound toward the camp prefect's tent. With a tight smile, Fronto jogged off after him. As they approached the large tent, Furius came to a halt outside and barked out a request for entry, his voice deep and gravelly.

Fronto slowed and sauntered up alongside him.

'He won't be in there, centurion.'

Furius turned and glowered at the legate.

'Sir?'

'Priscus. He won't be there. He'll be at my tent.'

The centurion nodded his thanks, showing no sign of real gratitude in the movement. As he turned and strode off toward the Tenth's ranks, Fronto fell in alongside and walked with him.

'You served with Pompey? Or Lucullus?'

Furius cast him a suspicious look.

'Both, legate.'

'Lucullus was an extraordinary general. Never met him, but I wish I had. My father spoke highly of him.'

The centurion nodded. Fronto waited. Clearly conversation was not one of Furius' strong points.

'And Pompey, eh?'

Another nod.

'And now you serve with Caesar. You're making a career of soldiering for some great generals. Did you not think of signing up to go east with Crassus?'

Furius' step faltered and he slowed, turning to Fronto and casting a withering glance that took the legate by surprise.

'Well, I mean' Fronto said almost defensively, 'you've served in the east before with Lucullus and Pompey. You know the lands and peoples. You'll be used to the heat and the dryness, and it's no secret even in Rome that Crassus is mounting a campaign against Parthia. I imagine at least half of the veterans of Pompey and Lucullus' legions will be signing on to march with him.'

The withering stare was making him extremely uncomfortable. With the almost bestial features of the man, he could not escape the impression that Furius was eyeing him in much the same way as a bear might eye its next prospective meal.

'I'm just interested in what brings a veteran of the eastern campaigns out to soggy, cold Gaul when he has the option of returning to the east.'

They were approaching the Tenth's command tents now as Furius turned to face front again. The centurion made a strange nasal noise and cleared his throat.

'Caesar is a great general. Even Pompey thinks so. Crassus is a rich moron with the military expertise of a gutter whore. Those who go east with Crassus are signing on for a parched journey into the jaws of Cerberus. I choose life and glory.'

As they came to a halt at the tent, Furius turned to him again.

'It has been obvious since Ostia that you neither like nor trust me, legate Fronto. And from what I've heard of you, I believe you're a dangerously unpredictable drunkard to have in a position of command; insolent and disobedient. You wouldn't last an hour in the centurionate before you were beaten to death for the things you say and do. I think we can both agree that we dislike each other intensely and that we're both grateful we serve in different legions, and whatever you're hoping to get out of this conversation, I hope you've got it now, because the conversation is over. I will not breach protocol by entering the tent of a senior officer unbidden and I have no desire to lay eyes on the debauchery that I hear goes on. Would you be so kind as to send the camp prefect out to speak to me?'

Fronto stood still for a long moment, staring at the centurion. The man had just insulted him at a very personal level as well as a professional one and, in theory, Fronto could have the man broken for speaking to him like that. And yet he found that no words would spring to his lips for his throat had run as dry as the Parthian sands.

Trying to communicate his anger with only his expression, Fronto turned away and entered his tent.

Priscus sat on his bunk, shaking two dice in a leather cup, while Galronus, Brutus and Varus sat on cushions on the floor with cups of well watered wine.

'Gnaeus? There's a self-righteous arsehole of a centurion outside who needs accurate cavalry figures for Caesar.'

Priscus nodded, making to rise.

'Slow down, my friend. I would take it as a very great personal favour if you took your time getting him them. Perhaps you could struggle to find the tablets with the figures on?'

Priscus gave him a half-smile. 'I won't need to fake that. Finding anything in that mess is like trying to find a virgin at the Bacchanalia. Bit childish, though? Making him look bad like that?'

Fronto glared at him. 'I've already been called insolent, disobedient, drunken and debauched in the last few moments. I could do without you adding childish to the list.'

Priscus grinned. 'But they're almost all your most endearing traits!'

A ripple of laughter ran through the men on the floor and Fronto shared his glare with them all.

'Just do it, Gnaeus.'

Priscus nodded and made for the tent's exit. Fronto turned his attention to the rest of them.

'Varus? Galronus? Just how detailed is your knowledge of your commands?'

Varus smiled, immediately latching on to Fronto's point. 'Good enough, I'd say. Let's just stop off and pick up Piso on the way. He's with the quartermaster.'

Fronto smiled. It *was* petty. It was childish in the most pathetic way, to sidetrack Furius and delay him, while he himself supplied Caesar with the information directly from the commanders of the three cavalry units. And yet it gave him a little thrill of happiness to drop the obstinate centurion in the dung heap.

* * * * *

Two weeks passed in drudgery at the Divoduron camps. Spring began to blossom into early summer with a brief play of storms that cleared the air and brought a fresh blue-skied world to northern Gaul. The cavalry had mounted patrols that ranged over the few miles around the encampment and across the ridge onto the far plain, though the Germanic aggressors remained steadfastly out of reach toward the Rhenus.

The legions champed at the bit each and every day, feeling the need to move and exercise their sword arms as opposed to sitting in camp digging latrines and carrying out routine guard duties. The men asked of their centurions and optios when the army would move, and those officers in turn asked their legates and tribunes when the march would begin. And inevitably, since few dared question the permanently-busy general, most senior officers asked the same question of the camp prefect.

Priscus pushed aside the flap of the tent without asking for admittance or preamble of any sort, ignoring the surprised look from Fronto who stood shaving with a specially sharpened knife in front of a bronze disc. As the legate turned at the unexpected and unorthodox interruption, Priscus unfastened his helmet as he crossed the large tent and flung it angrily at the wall, where it hit, bounced, and rolled under the bed.

'Come in.'

The prefect turned a glare on Fronto that carried so much raw irritation that the legate accidentally jumped a little and nicked a neat red line above his throat apple.

'Don't start with me, Marcus. Your tent was the nearest place I knew I could drown my sorrows.'

'Bad day again?'

'I'd never have accepted this commission if I'd known what it involved. Morons, donkey-brains, thieves, wastrels, layabouts and flatheads all badgering me day and night for details I don't have, supplies I can't get, tasks that no one will do and shite-knows what else. I swear the next person who asks me when the army marches is going to be visiting the medicus with a gladius hanging out of his arse, only probably hilt-upwards.'

Fronto grinned. 'So when...'

'Knob off. Get the wine out and don't bother with the water. I'll go down your route today.'

Fronto looked at the patchy bristles on his face in the bronze disc, shrugged and, turning, collected two cups and a wine jug from the table by the bed – a location for keeping wine that had practical benefits of which his sister wholeheartedly disapproved. He had even joked about digging a personal latrine on the other side, too, so he would not need to get out of bed until he was called for.

'So what's especially troubling you today?'

Priscus sighed as he gratefully accepted a proffered cup. 'The simple answer is that the army will be moving in the next few days, and every hour it gets closer brings more work and more idiots.'

He gestured expansively with his free arm, sloshing the wine over the edge of his cup onto Fronto's bed, the legate noted with dismay.

'We currently have in supply enough grain to keep the entire force in the field for four weeks. Caesar seems to think that the amount is ample and that, if the campaign stretches more than a month, we can start foraging and rely on the supply train reaching us from Vesontio and beyond.'

'And we can't?'

'One thing I've learned in this job is that quartermasters are disorganised and lazy and that Cita is the biggest, fattest, laziest blob of grease that ever wore a helmet. We'd probably be better relying on buying it from local tribes if it weren't for the fact that the local tribes won't have any because of the bloody stinking Germanics!'

Fronto opened his mouth, but Priscus was in full flow. 'And we've got several thousand new cavalry coming in later today, which will stretch those supplies slightly thinner too. Plus for some unknown reason it's become my job to organise the redistribution of the cavalry between Varus, Piso and Galronus. As if they couldn't do it themselves.'

Fronto grunted and let his friend barrage on.

'I've decided on the quick answer to that anyway. Galronus' lot will be split to bolster the other existing units and our Remi friend can have all the new raw cavalry for his own.'

'That's hardly fair on Galronus.'

'Varus will argue against having them and take it to Caesar, and Piso has a good rep, but I don't know him well enough yet. At least Galronus can mould them into a unit and I don't have to do any splitting up and moving about.'

Fronto smiled and took a quick pull of the wine, the last jar of good stuff that he had brought in his personal baggage. After this it was a matter of relying on whatever Cita had in stock.

'Well at least you'll be able to relax once we're on the move.'

'It doesn't bloody work like that, Marcus. When we move, I just have to start working on the next night's camp.'

'You'll just have to train up some of the men Caesar gave you and then...'

His helpful suggestion tailed off as the door flap swept open once again and Carbo ducked in through the door.

'Sir?'

'Does nobody in this camp knock anymore?'

Carbo, the primus pilus of the Tenth, held his helmet beneath his arm, the feathery transverse crest tickling his armpit as he gestured breathlessly with his vine staff.

'Sorry, legate... no time.' He gulped in a deep breath. 'Need help, sort of urgent-ish!'

Fronto framed his question, but Carbo had already ducked back outside the tent. The legate and the camp prefect shared a confused and concerned frown. Carbo was not a man to rush or be jumpy for paltry things. Grateful he had already strapped on his boots, Fronto stood, dropping the cup to the table and grasping the hilt of his gladius. If something had made Carbo jumpy, he wanted to be prepared.

Priscus was at his shoulder as he stepped outside to find Carbo waiting impatiently on the main roadway, his usual pink features flushed to an almost beetroot colour.

'What the hell is it?'

Carbo gestured down the road and started to jog with the gait of a man who has just sprinted to his own speed record and needs a breather. As he ran, the two senior officers keeping pace with him, he spoke in brief staccato bursts between heaving breaths.

'Centurion in... the Seventh. He's... he's sentenced a man... to death.'

Fronto and Priscus shared a surprised glance again. It was an unpleasant thing, but hardly unknown, and nothing to do with anyone outside the Seventh.

'Carbo, what is the actual problem?'

The centurion realised they had stopped and pulled up short, heaving in a huge breath.

'Man fell out of step during drill. Now he's to be beaten to death!'

Fronto's eyes widened. 'That's insane!'

Carbo, his breath spent, simply nodded and pointed onwards, in the direction of the distant camp of the Seventh.

Priscus narrowed his eyes. 'But this is the province of their legate. Where's Cicero. You should have gone to him first.'

Carbo shook his head wildly. 'Legate Cicero is in with Caesar and not to be disturbed, like most of the seniors. One of their lesser centurions found me and asked me to help. He was one of ours 'til he got reassigned over winter.'

Fronto and Priscus began to run.

'I have a sinking feeling. The centurion who's in charge of the punishment. Would it be a certain Furius by any chance?'

Carbo shook his head. 'Name's Fabius.'

'That would have been my second guess, yes.'

Fronto blinked as if realising something for the first time. 'You do realise that I have no authority over the Seventh, Carbo? I can strongly advise, but I can't stop it.'

Carbo looked a little abashed. 'Respectfully, sir, it was the camp prefect here that I came to get. He can override any centurion's decision.'

Fronto blinked again as he glanced across at Priscus, who was nodding with a serious and thoughtful look. A position that theoretically had seniority over every centurion in the army. In some very important ways, Priscus now outranked him. For some irritating reason, deep in the darkest part of his heart, that annoyed him, though he was disgusted to realise it. He was only just beginning to understand the responsibility and power that Priscus now commanded.

The three men held their talk, concentrating all their energy into running through the camp, much to the surprise of the men they passed, who struggled to salute before they were past and gone. The guards at the gate, through which Carbo had entered a few moments earlier, had held it open for him and glanced with interest at the sweating, ruddy-faced trio of senior officers as they passed beneath.

A short run later they reached the gate of the Seventh's camp, jogging across the causeway that traversed the twin ditches and up to the closed wooden portal.

'Open up.'

'What's the password?'

'I don't have your legion's password' Fronto snapped angrily, pointing at the pteruge-fringed tunic that denoted his status as an officer. To his surprise, Priscus, next to him, cleared his throat.

'Persepolis. Now open the damn gate.'

The huge timber construction swung ponderously open before them and the three men were through it while the gap was still widening. Without pause they ran along the decumanus toward the small parade ground in front of the headquarters and officers' tents that Priscus had set as a standard camp requirement.

The deathly silence that hung over the camp was almost deafening in itself and Fronto frowned as he ran. Had he been one of the men, he would be vocal right now over the harsh punishment decision.

Within moments, they drew close to the open, gravelled ground, surrounded by the men of the Seventh legion. The crowd, some six deep, blocked all access to the parade ground, from which the sound of hollow hammering issued.

'Move!' bellowed Fronto, startling the men around him so that they quickly melted out of the way of the three breathless officers.

Pushing their way into the open ground at the centre, Fronto took in the scene in a disgusted instant.

Centurion Fabius stood in full uniform, his face bristly and reminding Fronto of the other former Pompeian who had insulted him. His iron grey hair glistened in the sun, as his helm was cradled in his left arm, his right gesturing with his vine staff. Taller than Furius, he was narrower as well, with a wiry look that suggested to Fronto that he was probably fast and dangerous in a fight.

In front of the centurion, two men hammered a stake into the ground, matching one that already stood proud, at just the right distance to string a man between them with his arms outstretched. The accused was easy to identify. A young clearly recent recruit knelt on the floor, his wrists bound behind him, while two legionaries stood over him, pila pointed at his neck. The man's entire century were lined up in rows of four, each wielding a wooden practice sword, weighing considerably more than a real gladius and more than capable of breaking bones.

Carbo had stopped. Here, he had no authority at all, and had deferred, falling behind the two senior officers.

Fronto opened his mouth, bursting into a racking cough from the run. Priscus glanced at him. 'Jove you're unfit for a career soldier.' Ignoring the look on Fronto's face, Priscus turned back to the scene where the hammering had paused at the interruption.

'Prefect.' Fabius came to attention, making no mention of Fronto at all.

'What is the meaning of this, centurion?' Priscus demanded in a low, dangerous voice.

'Punishment detail, sir. Fustuarium. This man endangered his century and therefore his cohort, his legion and the entire army.'

Priscus shook his head. 'I understand he fell out of step in a drill?'

Fabius narrowed his eyes and flicked a quick cold glance at Fronto and Carbo.

'I can't help what you're led to understand, sir, but the punishment is in line with current guidelines. The drill was a three sided defensive wall in battle formation and held under battle conditions with real weapons. Standing orders are that under battle conditions, everything is to be treated as if it were live and not a drill. Moreover, the man did not just fall out of step. He slipped and lost control of his pilum.'

He turned to the column of waiting men.

'Passus?'

A legionary limped out of the column and saluted with difficulty, using his pilum to lean on and support a leg that had suffered a vicious calf wound. Blood blossomed on both sides of the dressing, indicating that the weapon had fully impaled him. Fabius turned back and raised his eyebrow challengingly.

'Passus? Do you think the punishment harsh?'

A dark, angry look passed across the man as he shook his head.

'Step back into position.' Turning back to the three officers, Fabius tapped his greave absently with his stick.

'Sir?'

Fronto turned to look at Priscus and was astounded to see a look of uncertainty on his face.

'What are you doing? Stop this!'

Priscus pursed his lips. 'He's right though legate. I set the orders myself. The man's incompetence caused the grave wounding of a fellow soldier and I would guess upset the entire defensive formation. In a battle, they might have lost the whole cohort because of him. I'm loathe to interfere.'

Fronto glanced angrily between him and Fabius, who wore a look that struck Fronto as far too smug to countenance.

The quiet voice of Carbo piped up behind them, little more than a whisper. 'Commute the sentence?'

Priscus glanced once at Fronto's angry face and nodded, turning back to Fabius.

'In principle I agree with you, centurion. However, the army is about to march, and I think both troop numbers and morale could be better served with a lesser punishment in this case. A non-fatal beating should be enough to make the lad more careful next time.'

Fabius' face betrayed no sign of irritation. He simply nodded and turned to the century of men.

'Lines two and four, you may retire. Lines one and three, you will continue to administer your punishment, with a single pass.'

Fronto leaned close to Priscus. 'That's still forty blows from practice swords. The lad might just die anyway.'

Priscus nodded. 'Then we'd best go pour some more of your wine on that little altar to Fortuna – that I know you carry with you – in the lad's name eh?'

Fronto glared at him for a moment, and finally nodded unhappily. The three men turned away as the victim was lifted and tied to the posts. Even halfway back down the decumanus on their way to the gate they heard the screams of the first few blows. Fronto ground his teeth as they left.

'That centurion's more of a bastard than any Germanic warrior we're going to meet.'

Carbo looked uncertain, but Priscus shook his head. 'I think you're letting your personal feelings about those two centurions get the better of you. His decision was harsh, but entirely appropriate. I might have done the same thing.'

Fronto glared at him.

'You've turning into a hard hearted man, Gnaeus.'

* * * * *

Fronto eyed the column ahead with mixed feelings. He had always liked Cicero, for all his minor faults and leanings, and it went against the grain of every soldierly fibre in his being to see a legion singled out as dispensable. And yet, with the Seventh legion in the van, at least Fabius and Furius were as far away from Fronto as they could be, and that suited him just fine.

The column stretched out both ahead and behind and he had a fairly clear view of the whole affair from the back of the glorious ebony-coated Bucephalus – following the customary quarter hour argument with Carbo about the benefits of an officer who marched with his men.

Of course, with advance scouts, the Seventh would theoretically have time to deploy should any aggressors be discovered up ahead, but Caesar had sent Piso with one wing of the Gallic cavalry ahead to scout the lie of the land and, to both Caesar and Fronto, Piso was still something of an unknown. He seemed in every way the perfect man for the job; thoroughly Romanised – as far as an Aquitanian could hope to be, clever, brave, strong, and quick-witted. It seemed that his men had taken an almost instant shine to him too, calling him 'Camulos' – apparently the name of a war god from these parts. And yet, while Caesar sent this trusted man forward, Fronto remembered Piso only from his association with Labienus during that conversation upon his arrival at camp. Just how far could any man be trusted these days?

Just like the republic, the army seemed to be decaying, riddled with tumours and cancers, falling apart and in need of surgery. His attention was suddenly caught by a single rider making to intercept the army.

Varus' cavalry had the task of patrolling alongside the column as outriders, while Galronus and his men kept a rearguard with the wagons and the Fourteenth. The lone rider was one of Varus' men; one of the few Roman cavalrymen among the hordes of auxiliary Gauls.

Fronto calculated the man's rough trajectory and, nodding to Carbo to keep the men moving, dropped out of the line and turned Bucephalus to walk back along the line of the Tenth to where the senior commanders rode between Fronto's legion and the Eighth. The crimson cloak of the general and the glinting cuirasses of the senior commanders rose from the cloud of grey dust that marked the passage of so many thousand feet, and Fronto converged with them just as the general, having spotted the rider, rode out to the side from the line of march with his top men.

The Roman cavalryman came to a halt a few paces away, reining in expertly and throwing a salute.

'Soldier?'

'General, commander Varus begs to report that a small group of what appear to be Germanic riders approached from the northeast. There are only a score or so of them and they're demanding to speak with you. What are your orders, Caesar?'

The general gave a half-smile and raised his eyebrow.

'Shall we see what they have to say, gentlemen?'

As the small party of officers turned their horses and rode off at a tangent from the column, toward the bank of the fast flowing Mosella River that ran some quarter of a mile to the southeast, Fronto fell in alongside them and Varus' man, a frown etched into his forehead. He had no doubts at all about Varus or his veteran riders, but having a vanguard out there made up of Piso's horse and Cicero's legion made him very nervous.

Regardless of the lack of obvious danger, Fronto's spine was tingling in the same way as it had a couple of years ago when he had first had bad feelings about the brutal Belgic campaign. Something about what awaited them to the northeast felt wrong and dangerous.

He suddenly realised he was rubbing between the fingers of his free hand the amulet of Fortuna he had taken to wearing on a thong around his neck. Irritated, he pulled it away, though apparently not before Caesar saw.

'Something wrong, Marcus? You look nervous.'

Fronto muttered something under his breath.

'Marcus?'

'Nothing. Got a bad feeling about what's coming.'

Caesar smiled benignly. 'It's rather unusual for you to be jumpy and superstitious.'

'Just a feeling, Caesar. It feels like I'm riding a wolf into combat against a bear. I don't know which one's going to snap at me first.'

Something in Fronto's voice pulled a serious expression across Caesar's face. 'Anything you want to tell me, Marcus?'

Fronto forced himself to look the general in the eye, trying not to note the hard, accusatory glance Labienus was levelling at him from the general's other side.

'Nothing concrete, general. Just a feeling of danger and unease. Let's make sure we keep Varus' men close by.'

'Of course.'

A quarter of an hour passed for Fronto in a sense of nervous agitation that deepened and sharpened with every passing step. Caesar and the others continued to pass the time in small talk, but Fronto declined to take part in the light-hearted banter.

Finally, on a small hillock rising from the north bank of the Mosella, the group spotted a small knot of horsemen and, as they closed on them, Fronto was surprised to see that very few of them appeared to have any kind of rich adornment. Indeed, most of them bared their torsos, their only covering the baldrics that hung across them, supporting the heavy Germanic swords, and the long beards that in many cases hung down to below their collar bones, oft braided or tied in a knot. Their hair, almost uniformly wheat-coloured, was wild and tied in a knot atop their heads. Their weapons were, however, sheathed. The men who sat ahorse behind these visible front men appeared to be almost entirely naked apart from their wild hair and a loincloth, their spears pointing at the heavens.

Caesar smiled happily, and the men with whom he had been chatting seemed to find the appearance of their visitors amusing.

Not so Fronto. The first thought that entered his head was how suicidally brave a score of mostly naked men would have to be to ride up to the Roman cavalry and demand to speak to their commander. After all, word must have spread to them by now of the Gaulish council's decision and Caesar' approach.

These were the sort of men who would try and outstare a crocodile.

'Let's be patient and courteous, gentlemen' Caesar said quietly as they slowed on the approach.

'Good greet Caesar' intoned one of the lead tribesmen as the general reined in and turned his horse to face the visitors with the expert knee control of a cavalryman. Fronto, less sure and practiced, simply hauled on the reins until Bucephalus complied.

'Good day' replied Caesar. To whom do I have the pleasure of speaking?'

There was a brief silence, and then a huddle of confused murmuring.

'Who are you' simplified the general.

'We not here to fight Roman.'

'Clearly not, with only twenty men' the general smiled. The visitors frowned in incomprehension. Finally someone seemed to grasp the point.

'We – all tribe – we not cross Renos to fight Roman.'

'I can imagine.'

The man narrowed his eyes, a strange move that, given his wild hair and huge beard, almost entirely removed his face from the picture.

'But if Roman want fight, we not run.'

'How kind. It would certainly save us some energy and legwork.'

A chortle broke out among the officers and again the tribesmen conferred until they reached a consensus about what had actually been said.

'Tribes never turn from war. Ancestors fight; we fight. On to tomorrow. Never we talk 'stead of fight. Is Roman way, yes?'

'I would invite you to put that to the test' smiled Caesar coldly, causing another confab.

'But this time different. Tribes here because we pushed across Renos.'

'Indeed.'

'So we talk. You leave us land we take, we support Roman. We make many strong horse warrior for you. Is good trade.'

Labienus nodded thoughtfully. 'It's not a bad option, Caesar. I'm sure we could talk the council around.'

Caesar glanced at him once and Fronto could not see the general's expression, but the staff officer lowered his gaze deferentially. When he turned back to the visitors, Caesar's face had taken on the hard military look that Fronto knew only too well. Impervious, imperious and immovable.

'I'm afraid, gentlemen, that I have already given my word to the chieftains of Gaul, who we now call ally. There can be no alliance with an aggressor into their territory. There is no land available for you here. I believe that one of the tribes you represent is the Ubii who straddle both banks of the Rhenus? If that is the case, I urge you to settle in their lands on this side of the river. To this I will turn a blind eye, but to nowhere else.'

There was a long pause as the barbarians conferred again and Fronto watched them, curiously. Something was very odd about all of this. The man's Latin was not wonderful, for sure, but he knew words like 'ancestor' and could form, admittedly broken, sentences. They should not be having so much trouble understanding the general's words.

Frowning, he wondered why they appeared to be labouring over this more than need be.

'Caesar – you give three day. We deliver term and come with reply. Good, yes?'

Fronto frowned. Three days now too? He wished there were some way to speak to the general alone. Suspicions were forming like dark clouds around his brain and he felt a storm coming. A flash of inspiration struck him and he dug deep into his mind for the words.

'I expect they will have great trouble understanding this' he said loudly to the general, in rusty Greek.

Caesar turned to frown at him and then, seeing the urgent look on his face, turned back to the small group. A new sense of worry and confusion had fallen on them, as though everything that had happened had been their own plan, but this new and incomprehensible development was a serious problem.

'I didn't even realise you knew the tongue, Marcus,' Caesar replied in fluent Greek with a marked Illyrian accent. 'Go on. I think we're mentally alone.'

'Caesar' Fronto said, again in Greek, 'they're just trying to delay us all. I don't know what their game is but they've been deliberately faffing and now they're asking for more time.'

Caesar nodded, wrinkling his lip.

'I fear they are trying to buy time to bring home the huge amount of horse I understand they sent raiding to the south a few days ago. Without them, they will be at a disadvantage against us.'

'Would that it were that, Caesar, but I think it's more important than that. The Ubii at least are supposed to be reasonably civilised, or so Galronus said. They trade with Rome. If they were going to send ambassadors, they would be noblemen with fluent Latin, dressed like rich men and would act like them.'

Caesar frowned.

'Not ambassadors?'

Fronto shook his head. 'I think what they are is decoys, sent to keep the bulk of the army busy. Something's about to happen, or it's happening already.'

Caesar nodded slowly, a worried shadow in his eyes. Turning to Varus' cavalry, he scanned the ranks until he spotted the commander himself.

'Varus. Take some good men and ride for Piso's vanguard. Make sure all is as it should be and order them to pull back to the main column.'

Varus saluted and started shouting out orders, but Fronto saw a few snarling lips and wrinkling brows among the enemy. Caesar had switched back to Latin to give the order. In moments, as Fronto drew breath to get Caesar's attention, the Germanic riders were already turning and racing off down the far side of the hill.

'Caesar!'

The general glanced at the sudden explosion of movement and nodded.

'Let them go. I won't push any more men out from the column to catch them. They're too light and fast; they'll easily outrun our heavy-equipped cavalry.'

As Varus trotted past the group of officers, a turma of regular cavalry forming up behind him, Fronto reached past and tapped him on the arm.

'If you value the cavalry, ride like Pegasus himself and get Piso and his men back here.'

Somewhere away to the northeast a single flash of lightning rent the sky.

'Great' Fronto muttered as his left hand rose involuntarily to the Fortuna pendant.

Chapter 5

(Border of Treveri & Ubii lands close to the Rhine & Moselle Rivers)

Varus and his turma of cavalry raced up the gentle incline across open swathes of grass between the forested low hills that covered the landscape here, hiding fertile valleys and the ruined shells of small, peaceful settlements that had fallen victim to the Germanic invaders.

The small force had paused at one, despite the urgency of their mission, to confirm their worst fears. Varus very much wished he had not entered the hut and seen what the Tencteri raiders had done to the Belgic farmer and his wife and daughters, almost certainly both before and after their deaths. Since that first encounter, they had warily avoided stopping at any of the other two dozen villages and isolated farmsteads they had passed.

Half an hour they had been riding now, the later half of which they had followed the unmistakable trail left by Piso's cavalry wing, some five thousand men and mounts.

Across the low saddle they rode, almost three dozen men pounding the earth in their haste to reach the vanguard as fast as possible. Crossing easily into a wide, shallow depression surrounded by forested hillocks and ridges, they espied a deeper and narrower valley across to the west, flattening where it met the river to the east.

Full of milling horsemen.

Piso's cavalry had come to a halt in the valley. Their direction of travel so far, following the north-easterly course set by the general, would lead them directly over the highest hills ahead, with the deepest, most tangled forests. Since clearly the army could not pass that way, the cavalry commander had paused, sending scout units out to locate the best route, whether it be along the Mosella River or further up the valley. Varus nodded as he slowed his mount at the crest. He would have done exactly the same. Of the force of five thousand cavalry, perhaps three thousand remained in the centre of the wide valley, the rest split into units of three hundred, each under its own officers, dispersed around the valley, probing each low saddle or side valley for the best route onwards.

At least they were intact. Nothing untoward had befallen them.

'Sir!'

Varus turned to the man who had addressed him, a regular cavalryman, holding his shield and reins in one hand, while jabbing his spear out toward the valley.

'Hmm?'

'I saw movement on the hill opposite. Above the tree line.'

Varus did not even bother to look. His men were good. The first turma in his command was made up of veterans, each of whom had served since the first push against the Helvetii, and many even in Hispania before that. Each man in this small unit knew Gaul backward and inside out now. Each one of them was as alert and trustworthy as a soldier could be. If Afranius said there was movement, then there was movement.

And the Roman forces in the valley were scattered over more than a mile of open land in small groups.

'Form up!' Varus bellowed, already kicking his bay mare into activity and urging her down the slope into the wide depression.

By the time he had picked up to a canter and then a gallop, the turma had formed on him and kept to a tight knot as they descended toward the large force of auxiliary cavalry – Gauls, Belgae, Aquitanians, and the occasional Roman officer amid the spread out mass.

By the time they were half way down the valley side, Piso and his officers had spotted them, a standard bearer gesturing in their direction with his silver wolf standard, other men pointing and many horses turning to face them.

Varus' gaze took them all in, and then rose above them, tracking across the fields and past the burned shell of a small farm, to the tree line opposite, from which shapes were now detaching. Enemy cavalry; lightly armed and clothed men – a number of them naked he assumed from the fleshy tint – were leaving the shadows of the wood and pouring down the hillsides toward the large force.

A quick glance showed the same thing happening up and down the valley. There were not a vast number of enemy riders, but they had been well positioned in groups, each small force falling upon one section of the separated Roman cavalry.

Finally, Piso's men had noted the enemy coming at them and horns rang out with half a dozen contradictory orders. Varus cringed at the cacophony. He was watching a potential disaster. Piso was a new commander and, for all his vaunted abilities, he was as yet unused to leading a force like this in such a campaign. Many of his men had served together before, but the mixing in of the former forces of Galronus had destroyed a lot of the units' cohesion from the previous year, and the result was chaos.

As the enemy appeared, some of the more mixed or greener units panicked, turning and racing for the river or up the inland valley, abandoning their comrades. Others tried to form a small defensive shape but, with only a month or so to practice together so far, they were less than successful as often as not.

Piso's standard bearer was waving his silver wolf, directing the units while, Piso having calmed the conflicting orders, had his own musician blow the recall on his horn, summoning all the distributed units to his side. Still, the mass of cavalry at the centre were only just beginning to realise the danger they were in. Varus kicked his mount in urgency as the small Roman turma reached the valley bottom and raced past a few groups of allied horsemen milling about in confusion.

Piso waved him over.

A few hundred paces down the valley, the first casualties occurred. A group of three hundred men – one of the few who had managed to form into a solid square with spears at the ready, began to succumb to a hail of small stones that rained down on them from the trees.

'They're using slings!' Varus exclaimed as he finally reached Piso in the press. 'I thought they supposedly consider missiles a dishonourable way to fight?'

Piso nodded, wheeling his horse.

'Doesn't stop them using them. Just the noble warriors won't touch them – they leave them to peasants. Half the damn forces in the valley haven't heard the recall, Varus!'

The senior commander nodded.

'I'll get them rounded up. You martial the main force here.' His eyes rose to take in the forces pouring from the hillsides. 'There aren't many of them, really. Not more than a thousand, I reckon. They're only a danger while we're spread out. In a centralised force we can take them.'

Piso smiled and began to bellow orders to his standard bearer and musician, who called out individual unit commands, drawing the main force together to stand in open ground.

Varus returned to his turma and gestured for his three decurions to step out front.

83

'Take eight men apiece and ride to each of the forces in the valley who seem to be having trouble. Get them pulled back and rallying on Piso's standard. Afranius and Callus, you head up the valley, one on each side. Petro, you head toward the river on this side. I'll take the spare men and follow on the far side of the valley. As soon as you run out of men to herd, get back here, and try not to engage the enemy in the meantime. We'll crush them here.'

Petro frowned.

'What if there are too many of them sir?'

'There aren't. We outnumber them about four to one and they won't have infantry. This is a running ambush, so they'll want to be able to get out quickly too.'

'What about the slingers?'

'Peasants. They don't consider them warriors; they'll probably leave them to die. They certainly won't come down from the trees.'

Without waiting for further questions, Varus called out two men from each of the Decurions' commands and drew them together before heading off across the valley.

Not far away, three groups of horsemen had managed to join together to form a consolidated force of almost a thousand men and were in a good defensive formation, having pulled themselves far enough back from the forest's edge to be out of the range of the hidden slingers.

The large unit had formed up close to a small cluster of charred and blackened farm buildings, the animals stolen and butchered by the Germanic invaders, the occupants slain and left in a pile in the farmyard, with a large dog impaled on a spear standing like some grisly banner above the corpse-heap.

Sickened, Varus moved past the farm and tried to spot the officers in the large group. Some five hundred enemy cavalry were descending the slope toward them, though they had slowed from a charge and were advancing with a menacing slowness. Even though they faced odds of two-to-one, the Germanic riders grinned their rictus war masks. Their blood boiled now with the urge to kill.

In the ordered ranks of Gallic cavalry, Varus could just see a dragon head standard with a coloured streamer tapering from behind. Even as he watched, that dragon head dipped and then circled, the air filling the conical taper and whistling through it with a shudder-inducing scream. Suddenly it dipped again, signalling an advance.

Even as he and his six companions closed on the ordered mass, the ranks began to step forward, spears lowered.

'Belay that order!' Varus bellowed. A number of men turned in their saddles in surprise, and frowned. Even the non-Latin-speaking Gallic auxiliaries had had certain commands and a few choice phrases drilled into them, in order to serve under Roman officers. Many of them clearly understood what he had said, though no man paused. To break formation would be unthinkable for most of them.

Biting his tongue, Varus raced along the side of the unit, repeating his order, until he could see the commanders. Three Gallic nobles conferred together as they moved slowly forward, their status only marked out, to Varus' eye, by the quality of their armour and helms and the gold that adorned them. In his own allied cavalry unit, he had assigned Roman mail shirts and green cloaks to the officers, as well as green feathers for their helms, so that he could easily identify them. But Piso was Aquitanian and was bred to the culture. Spotting their commanders would be a simple thing for him.

Taking a deep breath, he broke out into the open space between the two slowly advancing forces. Any moment now, the Germanic force would break into a charge. They were not, reputedly, a people to move carefully and slowly into battle. Only the fact that their prey had consolidated into a large, well-ordered unit seemed to have thrown them and made their advance a cautious one.

'Who's in charge here?'

All three noblemen turned at his voice. 'Commander Varus?'

'Break off your attack and rally to Piso.'

'Are you sure, sir? We've got them at two-to-one here.'

Varus nodded. 'And if we get everyone back to Piso we'll have them at five-to-one. Better odds. Now pull back.'

Commands were issued in the complex language of the Gauls and the dragon standard dipped and waved again, howling its horrible cry. In good order, the nine hundred men turned their mounts and rode away toward Piso's banner. The enemy cavalry seemed to take it as a move of cowardice and jeered as they picked up the pace, pursuing the retreating Gauls. Varus watched them for only a moment as he and his half dozen riders reached open space at the valley centre again, and then ignored them, concentrating on where to head next. The large unit was well-ordered and well-commanded and would easily regroup with Piso. The pursuing enemy would break off early rather than face the whole mass together.

His eyes ranged around the valley. Two groups of three hundred at the far side of the valley were already making for Piso's standard, Germanic aggressors shouting insults at their retreating backs as they followed them cautiously.

Varus frowned.

Why were the enemy being so cautious? It seemed so unlike the Germanic tribes of which he had heard.

There was only one group of men left on this side of the valley and it took a long moment for Varus to spot them. A single turma of thirty men had been separated from a unit and were beleaguered by twice their number of enemy horsemen pressing in on them.

Again, his mind raced. Sixty or so Germanics advancing slowly on half that number of Gauls, their pace menacing. What was going on?

Waving to his men, Varus rose to a canter, bearing down on the unit. The enemy was not pressing for a fight. Why were they advancing slowly and not charging?

The answer struck him in a series of flashing images from around the valley. They were being herded. The enemy was not *allowing* them to regroup at Piso's standard, they were actively *herding* them there. But why? They would be outnumbered five-to-one. What possible benefit could that be to them?

But something was going wrong here. The turma of Gauls were backing up to yet another small burned out farm building which, along with the fence and irrigation ditch, would hamper them and prevent them retreating any further. The retreating Gauls trapped, the enemy would have no option but to attack. Varus gestured to the men with him as he broke into a gallop.

'We've got less than a hundred count before those barbarians have no choice but to smash our lads. Come on. Let's break the attack.'

The seven men hurtled through the lush grass of the meadow, toward the shell of the charred wooden building, on the far side on which he could just see the Gauls in good order, unable to retreat any further, preparing to meet the inevitable charge.

'Let's put the shits up them' Varus grinned as he urged every ounce of speed out of his fast-wearying mount. Across the field he raced, the other six close behind. The fence – a stout construction some four feet high, constructed of rough-sawn timber and treated against the weather, was too much of an obstacle to the Gauls, who had retreated there at a walk.

Not for galloping horsemen, though. With a single command, augmented by rein-and-knee activity, Varus urged his steed into a jump, clearing the fence easily and coming down on the far side, releasing his reins to draw the long cavalry sword as he did so.

The trapped Gauls first became aware of their allies' arrival reflected in the faces of the enemy, who stared in mixed surprise and confusion at the small party of red and silver heavily-armed cavalry leaping the fence into the fray.

Perfectly-trained, Varus' regular cavalrymen cast their spears almost the instant their hooves touched the turf on the far side of the fence, three of the six missiles flying true and plunging into the advancing Germanic riders and their steeds. Two horses collapsed, screaming, thrashing and foaming, snapped spear shafts protruding from them. The third impaled a rider, who toppled from his mount, the beast trotting away.

The blows drove the enemy into the almost expected rage. The Germanic warriors, not a people to flee a fight, felt the final uncontrollable surge of blood into their brains and roared, leaping from their horses and running forward, brandishing their weapons and shields or, more often, two weapons.

Varus almost pulled up in surprise. Why had they dismounted? What in Juno's name were they doing?

Off to the right, the Gallic cavalry had realised what was happening and the thirty men, with their decurions leading them, broke into a run, levelling their spears at the invaders and trying to join up with Varus' men in a line.

And then everything exploded into chaos.

Perhaps half a dozen of the dismounted enemy fell victim to the levelled spears in the initial flurry, and Varus learned the hard way the reason for the strange tactic of leaving their horses behind and running into battle.

Three men made directly for him, likely seeing him as the man to kill for the most glory, his kit marking him out as a senior officer. Even as he tried to imagine what they hoped to achieve, Varus had already fallen into the rhythmic actions of the Roman cavalryman, his sword swooping out and low and shearing off half the man's head at the bridge of the nose, pulping both eyes and sending a hairy cap of bone sailing through the air as the rest of the body slumped to the ground, brain matter falling out to mingle with the soil.

Even as the blow was made, his left arm had reacted to a sign of danger out of the corner of his eye, slamming down his shield so that he broke a reaching arm with the bronze rim.

The third attacker had disappeared. In the sudden flurry, Varus turned this way and that. Now, riders and their dismounted opponents were locked in individual combat all across the field. The body of his sword victim lay to his right, and a man on his left howled as he clung to an arm that was bent impossibly out of shape.

No sign of the third man, though.

Suddenly, Varus' world turned upside down. The third warrior, who had made himself small with a crouch, had ducked amazingly between the front legs of Varus' horse and had then reached up with a wide, sharp knife and jammed it into the horse's soft underside, driving it deep and raking it this way and that.

The horse screamed in impossible pain at the gruesome task being performed on its belly, and bucked. The man, his work done, took the opportunity to step out and away before the beast came back down, with Varus tumbling away from the stricken mount.

The commander hit the ground heavily, making his best attempt to roll and come up into a crouch as training dictated, but realising that something was wrong. It took a moment of utter confusion to realise that his horse's flailing hoof had caught his helmet a glancing blow and, as he reached up to unfasten the strap and let the painful, dented helm fall to the ground, releasing his throbbing head, he also became aware that only one of his arms had obeyed his brain.

A glance at his other arm showed a gleam of sharp white amid the crimson mess that was his forearm.

A landing his old riding tutor would have beaten him for. Appalling!

His brain was starting to swim with the pain-killing euphoria of battle – often the only thing that saved a soldier's life when badly wounded and in a sticky situation.

He was suddenly aware that the barbarian who had gutted his horse from underneath was now approaching him, blade held forward, coated to the waist in the slick of horse's blood that had sluiced down over him. Varus felt a terrible rage infecting his mind though, unlike these crazed barbarians, he knew battle-rage for the double edged gift it was and his sheer will channelled it into a hard, cold urge to make this man pay for the death of his lovely mare.

No sword. He had lost both sword and shield during the fall. The shield, of course, would have been what broke his arm as he landed. He should have let it go. But the sword he had simply dropped.

A quick glance and he could see his expensive, carved and etched cavalry blade lying in the blood-soaked grass some ten feet away. Too far.

The barbarian was on him. The blade flashed out, quick as a snake striking: once... twice... thrice.

On the third lunge, Varus stepped calmly forward into the blow, coming alongside the man's arm, and brought his elbow down on the man's wrist, numbing the barbarian's joint with a blow that sent waves up Varus' own arm. The barbarian's horse-gutting knife fell to the grass and the man stared in surprise at this Roman who had appeared on the verge of death and totally helpless and unarmed a moment ago.

With a growl, Varus' good arm reached out and grasped the barbarian by the throat, his grip squeezing instantly with all the strength of a man who has spent twenty years using that fist to cling on to the reins of a startled mount or swing a heavy sword from horseback.

The man's gristle, cartilage, muscle, bone and soft tissue crunched and ground into a pulp in Varus' tightening grip. His eyes bulged and his face turned purple and then grey, his head flopping at an angle, indicating that he had kicked his last and that the jerks Varus could feel were those that came in death.

Calmly, with steely eyes, Varus let go and the dead thing dropped to the ground before him.

'That's for Hyrpina. I raised her from a foal.'

Turning slowly, he took in the situation. Despite the loss of a number of horses due to the unpleasant tactic of the enemy, the Gauls and Romans were winning out. Few of the enemy remained and at a shout they disengaged and ran to their beasts. One of the decurions called an order to chase them down, but it went unheeded in the chaos. No one had the urge or the energy to follow.

As Varus watched, the Germanic warriors remounted in a smooth jump and, gathering the reins of the unmanned beasts, left the scene with every horse they had brought. Varus looked at the remaining twenty-odd men. He had lost two Romans and about fifteen Gauls.

With a cry of the sheerest agony, he yanked loose his neck scarf and pushed his broken arm into it, forming a temporary sling. His eyes streamed with the pain and he had to bite down on his lip with every movement that rubbed the raw wound on the rusty-coloured wool. With a wince and held breath, he retrieved his fallen sword and gestured with it.

'Mount up and move – two to a horse if you have to. Let's get back to Piso.'

As one of the Roman riders closed, he reached down and helped haul Varus onto the back of his steed, trying not to jostle his bad arm in the process.

Perhaps Fronto and his bleak mood had been right about today.

* * * * *

Piso had done a sterling job of consolidating the Gallic forces as they converged on his wolf standard. Each bolstering unit of three hundred horses and riders had joined the massed ranks, sitting in ordered rows, the front lines with their spears levelled and ready, the rest with the tips raised safely.

Varus watched as he hurtled across the grass with his small battered unit, twenty two men sharing only fifteen horses. The Germanic tactics had been brutal and horribly effective. What it said about tribes that were supposed to hold the honour of individual combat in the highest esteem, he could not say. It was apparently dishonourable to release an arrow at an enemy, or sling a stone, but to gut his horse from under him and then pick off the downed rider seemed perfectly acceptable.

The ranks of near five thousand horsemen were drawn up in their alae of three hundreds, with only a little manoeuvring room between the units. Piso had carefully withdrawn from his original position to the most open area of fields with no fences or ruined buildings to hamper his cavalry. It was a sensible, safe tactic.

The Germanic attackers had abandoned their missile troops somewhere above the tree line, where the sling-wielding peasants were probably already running for their tribes' camps. Now, the barbarian horsemen had drawn up in groups to three sides of the Roman forces.

Varus' initial estimate had been roughly accurate. There could not be more than a thousand of them. And they had herded the Roman forces back into a group at the centre, but left open a side for the cavalry to escape?

Clearly they did not expect to crush the overwhelming superior forces, then. So what? Frighten them? Do enough damage to make Caesar stop and consider their offer? Anything was possible with these crazed people.

Even as they rode, putting pressure on the tired horses with the extra riders, Varus watched the barbarians sweep forward and realised what they had done.

As the Germanic warriors reached some hundred paces distant from the Gallic spear tips, they vaulted smoothly from their moving horses like athletic dancers on a Greek vase, landing lightly and already running, their heavy swords in one hand and their now free hands going to their belt to withdraw their horse-gutting knives.

The slaughter was going to be appalling. The barbarians had driven the Roman cavalry to withdraw into their tight ranks. It was a standard tactic against enemy cavalry, but once the enemy warriors got in among the press of men, they could merrily move about gutting anything above them and the Gauls would hardly have room to plunge down with a spear or swing a sword within their own massed ranks.

Piso clearly did not know what to do, and Varus felt for the man. What could a commander do against such a strange tactic, and Piso had not seen it happen yet; had no idea what was to come. He was simply stunned by the strangeness of cavalry dismounting and running at him. Ridiculously, the cavalry would have been better off in a traditional Gallic grouping, rather than the ordered ranks of Roman organisation that would turn the lines into a slaughterhouse.

In a desperate move, the Aquitanian chieftain shouted an order in Gaulish and then Latin, which was relayed by the man with the horn and by the dipping and waving of the silvered wolf standard.

The front ranks of Piso's cavalry charged, their spears lowered and ready to thrust, or raised overhand, ready to throw. Shields were gripped tight. Shafts were launched almost instantly, as soon as the front rank broke; the enemy had already got too close to make any sort of charge effective. The cast spears came down haphazardly, only one or two finding a useful target, their throwers already drawing their long blades ready to swing from horseback.

But the Germanic warriors had no intention of meeting the charge.

As the Romano-Gallic cavalry reached them, the enemy warriors hurled themselves to one side, rolling and coming up running, or ducking beneath swings. A few met the spear points or blades of Piso's men, but far more slipped between the charging horses, more lithe than any hairy barbarian had any right to be. And suddenly Piso was faced with perhaps eight hundred warriors closing on his ranks of horse from three sides, his charges foundering as the riders tried to turn their mounts to follow the attackers back to their own lines.

Varus was closing on the chaos as he watched the true horror and carnage unfold.

Just as he had predicted, as soon as the enemy managed to get into the tight mass of horses in the Gallic lines, their work became the simple, brutal job of slaughtermen. It was not a fight – it was a massacre; and he had been wrong about the numbers. In quarter of an hour or so, the eight hundred or so remaining enemy warriors could gut the entire Gallic force, finishing off the stricken riders at their leisure.

Something had to be done.

Turning to Afranius, riding the horse next to him, Varus pointed and raised his voice to be heard over the approaching din.

'We need to get them out of here. Get to the standard bearer and musician and have them sound the call. We'll form a wedge to push through.'

Afranius nodded and turned, relaying the orders to the other men of Varus' small band, just as they reached the press of men. The scene was horrendous. The turf had lost every blade of grass, churned to mud that sucked at hooves and feet, coloured a rusty red by the gallons of blood that had been mixed in.

Horses bucked and thrashed, their flailing hooves breaking the legs of others and smashing the skulls of men who floundered in the mud trying to pull themselves upright. Screaming Gauls lay trapped under convulsing horses. And among it all – the stamping and thrashing legs, the screaming and bucking – moved the enemy warriors like some sort of crimson demons, coated to the waist in blood, seemingly uncaring whether they lived or died.

Varus and his men pushed into the mass, the commander jumping from the back of the horse he had shared and gripping his sword in his good arm. As he landed a jolt ran up his body, forcing him to clench his teeth as the agony from his shattered arm roared like white fire up to his brain. Around him, the extra riders who had hitched a lift across the valley dropped from horseback and ran alongside, swords at the ready. The small force of dismounted men stayed in close support of the horsemen, preventing the underhanded Germanic tactics from destroying their small attack with their gruesome tactic.

Here and there in the press, as Varus and his dismounted men clambered over bodies both wounded and dead, beast and man, they found one of the enemy warriors gouging a fallen Gaul or shredding a horse's belly to stop it rising again. Individually, in a straight fight, these barbarians were no match for Varus' regulars and fell like wheat before their blades.

But it was slow going.

Clambering across a horse whose blood had run so dry that it lay helpless and heaving ragged final breaths, Varus paused to take stock of the situation. Despite the apparent carnage, a great number of Gallic cavalry remained intact, pressed in the tight formation and unable to do anything about the swathe of destruction moving slowly and inexorably their way.

The standard wavered in an unpredictable manner, clearly random while its bearer fought off one of the enemy, rather than in the regular motions of a command being given. Since the standard would likely denote the position of the commanders too, that suggested that the enemy warriors had cut a line through the cavalry directly toward Piso, where they were currently embroiled. If the commander and his signallers went down, there would be precious little chance of pulling anyone out of this mess.

With a single, economical motion of his sword arm, Varus indicated to his men the wavering standard. Afranius and Petro nodded, taking his meaning, the former turning his horse and the latter clambering over a body behind him.

Like a force of avenging spirits in steel and crimson, the twenty two men hacked and stomped their way through the mess without pause or comment.

The slogging through a mire of mud, blood and entrails seemed endless – the destruction left by the Germanic warriors making every step wearying and hazardous. And then suddenly, almost unexpectedly, Varus hauled himself painfully across the stilled body of a large piebald mare to find that he had reached the scene of current fighting. The press of men and horses blocked every inch of his vision and he could no longer identify the wavering standard. Taking a deep breath, he bellowed 'Piso!'

The clamour and din surrounded them, and Varus, his arm burning with pain, strained to see. 'Piso? It's Varus!'

'Varus?' came a distant, desperate voice.

And then Varus' world turned crimson.

A dozen or more blood-soaked, crimson painted barbarians, each easily a head taller than Varus, hurtled out of the mass, hamstrung a horse as they passed, and launched at him. Varus lurched back, trying to get a swing in with his sword, but there was simply not enough room. Two blows came at him simultaneously and he managed to turn one aside at the last moment with his own blade, but only the timely intervention of an unseen soldier behind him prevented him being spitted through the face by the other.

More and more demonic, blood-slicked enemy warriors were appearing from the thong of horses now, attracted by the Latin shout. Identified by the language as officers, Varus and his men had suddenly become the prize targets in the fight, and every barbarian there wanted their heads.

In mere moments the carnage had turned their way. In a heartbeat, his twenty two men had become two thirds that number. In another heartbeat and a gaggle of screams they had dropped to a half, the throng of Germanic warriors around them never dropping in number. No matter how many they killed, fresh demons appeared from the welter of blood and legs to plug the gaps.

Varus who, in the space of ten breaths, had taken two minor slashes to his wounded shoulder and a nasty lunging knife wound in his left hip, was struggling simply to stay alive now. His men – the cream of the corps and the best Caesar's army had to offer, fought by his side and at his back, trying with their every move to stop the blows coming at their commander as well as those striking directly at each of them.

Varus knew he was costing his own men their lives through their desire to protect him, and guilt riddled him even as he collapsed with a shriek, a fresh strike having cut the scarf/sling, allowing his broken arm to swing agonisingly loose. His vision swam with the agony and his head felt tremendously light. He was close to passing out from the pain and he knew that when he did, it would be the end of him.

Desperately, he tried to raise his sword to block a descending blow and almost turned it away, feeling the blade shear off the tip of his ear. He probably screamed, but then he was sure he had been screaming almost nonstop for the last few moments, so it did not seem to matter.

Somewhere in the depth of the pain, fug and confusion, he felt sure he had heard his name called. Blinking away sweat, blood and grime, Varus squinted upwards. The blades had stopped coming down at him. With a genuine and unbelievable sense of relief, Varus recognised Piso swinging left and right in his saddle, slicing, hacking and carving the barbarians that a moment ago were getting ready to take his head.

Varus looked around in wonder. Maybe half a dozen of his own men remained, mostly wounded. Piso and his personal guard had arrived just in time. The standard waved silvery in the air behind the commander and Varus could see the musician, horn in his right hand, smashing the boss of his circular shield into the face of a barbarian.

'Piso!'

'Come on!' cried the other commander in reply.

Varus struggled to his feet, wincing and shaking, having to lean on his sword to steady himself. His legs failed and he slumped again. 'We have to get back to the column before we lose everyone.'

Piso nodded and turned to the signallers behind him.

'The commander's safe. Sound the retreat!'

The horn, put to the signaller's lips, rang out with the five note call, the order confirmed by the circling of the silver wolf, high above the heads of even the mounted men.

Piso smiled.

'Been a bit of a shitty morning, all told!'

Varus shook his head with relief and then looked up just in time to see a crimson-slicked warrior burst out of the crowd, a long, broad bladed sword in his hands. Even as Varus tried to form the warning, the man swung a wide, two-handed blow with the sword, hacking with ease through both of Piso's mount's front legs.

With a scream, Piso's black steed collapsed forward, the Aquitanian commander pitched from the saddle and thrown some five or six paces ahead, where he slumped to the ground in a heap, his mail shirt dulled with mud and blood.

Helpless, unable to stand without aid, Varus watched as Piso staggered to his feet and drew his sword, barbarians closing around him in a circle. Varus lost sight of the man behind the grey and crimson bodies apart from the occasional flash of a golden helmet or glint of a sword. Two of Varus' men pushed past him, running to help Piso, while the other four, too seriously wounded to do much else, helped Varus up.

Somewhere close by came a shout in Gaulish. Varus looked round in surprise to see the signaller push his wolf standard into the hands of the musician before leaping from his horse and drawing his sword on the run. Behind him more and more of the Gallic horse guards followed.

Piso was dead before the standard bearer and the two Roman riders could reach him. Still swinging his sword desperately, he was on his knees in the mud. Most of his assailants had turned away, leaving him for dead to face the new threat, and Varus could see him clearly as the remaining three barbarians toyed with the kneeling man. Piso had taken a crippling lower back wound that had rendered his legs useless. He was covered in blossoms of crimson and gobbets of blood poured from his mouth alongside shouts of defiance in two languages.

His final swing was weary as the strength left him, one of the barbarians knocking it aside, and then the three men were on the commander, holding him up as they sawed off his head.

Varus turned away.

They never lived to treasure their grisly prize as moments later the standard bearer, two Roman cavalrymen and half a dozen of Piso's guards reached the spot and dispatched them. But Varus could not stop staring at the headless figure kneeling on the ground.

Someone's hands grasped Varus by the chin and turned his head away.

'Commander?'

The Roman officer focused as much as he was able. The pain was so intense that he could hardly focus or think. The only image that he could see, despite having been forcibly turned away, was the headless body of Piso kneeling in the mud, covered in blood, his sword lying discarded beside him.

'Commander?'

Better focus. One of the Roman cavalrymen was holding him up and staring into his eyes.

'What?'

'Can you ride, sir?'

Varus shook his head. He could barely stand, let alone ride. The soldier conferred with someone out of Varus' line of sight.

'We haven't got time for a litter. I'll throw him over the back of my horse and have to hope he survives with his arm intact.'

'Be quick. We're in full retreat.'

The last thing Varus remembered was the heaving nausea as his world spun upside down and the shock of unspeakable pain as his arm swung to and fro from the back of the horse upon which he was unceremoniously draped. The image that burned itself into his retinas as he bounced painfully away from both battlefield and consciousness was the body of his rescuer, Piso, still miraculously kneeling in the mud.

ROME

The villa of Atia Balba Prima, like most of the houses of the wealthier families on the Palatine hill had a very austere façade, plain brick walls coated with plaster, with few apertures and even those high up.

Balbus frowned from the shadow of the apple tree.

'I still do not like this.'

Faleria, the sister of Fronto, was proving to Balbus to be every bit as headstrong and troublesome as her brother and probably more so. The well-dressed lady in her lemon-coloured stola and mustard-toned shawl smiled.

'Quintus, we are quite all right, you know. This is a social call; nothing more. Now run along and we'll meet you back at the house in a couple of hours.'

Balbus' gaze slipped back and forth between Faleria and his daughter Lucilia, bedecked in a midnight blue stola and looking far too adult and mature for his liking.

'I'd tell you to look after each other, but I do worry you're each as bad. Be careful.'

Lucilia smiled and patted him on the cheek as they turned and strode across the square, passing a family of the equestrian class and an apple seller who apparently had not cottoned on to the abundance of the fruit going for free in the square. Balbus watched them until they got to the door and then turned with a nervous swallow and returned to the three litters that had brought them from the Cispian.

Faleria arched a perfect eyebrow at her companion.

'Are you really comfortable with this? I've met Atia. She's shrewd and very used to being steeped in the politics of the city.'

Lucilia smiled.

'I'm fine, Faleria. Come on.'

Reaching up, she tugged the bell-pull by the featureless door. A few long moments passed before they heard the muffled flapping of sandals on marble from the far side and, after a couple of clunks and rattles, the door opened.

A short, bald man with an olive complexion and a neat, short beard squinted at them.

'Mistresses?'

Faleria allowed her most imperious expression to fall across her face, her voice matching it perfectly.

98

'Please inform your mistress that the ladies Faleria and Lucilia have come to pay their respects to the gracious niece of the great Caesar.'

The slave gestured to them, inviting them into the atrium, and then shuffled off. A murmur of conversation drifted back from the tablinum nearby, while the two visitors cast their glance around the room.

Close to the door stood the altar to the household and family gods, with its small statuettes and a mass of flower heads in the dipped surface, soaked in Falernian wine as an offering. A similar sight stood inside most households, though more surprising was the small altar to Venus that stood nearby with a tray of sweetmeats in the offering bowl. It was said that Caesar could trace his family line back to the Goddess herself and Atia clearly bought into the idea.

The fountain in the impluvium pool, a bronze statue of a dancing nymph, sprayed a jet into the air that tinkled down to the water with a calming splatter.

'The domina will see you now, ladies. Please follow me.'

Lucilia and Faleria smiled at the slave who had appeared from around a corner and followed him back and into the tablinum. Atia Balba Prima lounged on a golden couch while two slave girls anointed her feet and tended her toenails. Absently, she plucked a grape from the bowl next to her and popped it into her mouth.

Lady Atia could hardly look any more different from her uncle. Rather than being tall and lean, she was diminutive and voluptuous, her nose small and button-like, her hair lustrous and coppery, falling in carefully-curled waves to her shoulders. Her face was pale – presumably with white lead – her lips crimson and her eyes kohl-darkened.

'Noble names. The widow of the Falerii, sister of my uncle's favourite soldier, and the daughter of the erstwhile commander of one of his legions. And keeping company together in the city. To what do I owe the pleasure?'

Faleria nodded – a gesture that suggested an equality between them that surprised Lucilia.

'A social call only. As friends of your family, it seemed polite to make your acquaintance again. We met a few years ago, of course, but Lucilia is new to the circles of Rome.'

Atia smiled and a shudder ran through Lucilia. That face suddenly reminded her of nothing so much as a crocodile.

'Of course; of course. Do come and sit. I will have food and drink brought for you. Wine or fruit juice?'

Lucilia smiled nervously. 'Fruit juice will be fine for me, thank you my lady.' Faleria nodded. 'For me too.'

Atia gestured to the spare couches and snapped her fingers.

'Agorion? Play something sweet for our guests.'

A thin, ebony-skinned man in a loincloth plucked a lyre from beside a pillar and stepped to the side of the room, beginning to pick out a light melody with seeming ease.

'So you have decided to spend the summer in Rome while the men are off playing soldier with the barbarian. Very sensible, I should say. Sadly, you missed one of the great social engagements of the spring, when lady Sepunia held her orgy. It was quite a party, I can tell you. Some juicy scandal and some delicious slaves from Tingis.'

Lucilia sat gingerly on the couch to one side and raised her feet, removing her sandals. Faleria mirrored her opposite with a sigh of relief.

'Thank you, Atia. I don't know about you, but I find litters to be less comfort than walking. The bones are shaken up with every step.'

'Indeed, though it would not do for ladies to walk so far unescorted, of course.'

'Of course.'

The opening pleasantries over, Atia turned to Lucilia with a smile.

'Your father has a villa near to Massilia, I understand, where the family resides much of the time?'

'Very true, lady Atia.'

'Do you not find yourselves overcome with the tedium? Do you not miss the spectacle of Rome?'

Lucilia shrugged.

'I have not spent a great deal of my time here, my lady. Much of my youth I lived in the provinces with father and mother. I have only ever spent short stints in the city.'

'Then we shall have to train you up in the manner of a lady of the city, my darling Lucilia. Why I shall make it my personal task to introduce you to every important face and every delight the city has to offer.'

Faleria switched off. Lucilia was handling herself well, and something that had attracted Faleria's interest since she had first entered nagged at her. Over the general hubbub of the house, the chattering of the lady and her slaves in this room, there had been the barely-discernible sound of male voices in deep discussion somewhere in the house. Now, as she concentrated, trying to filter out the lyre music and the inane chat, she could hear them more clearly.

Because they were becoming louder.

She realised suddenly that the sources of the noise were approaching.

With the pretence of sorting an errant coil in her hair, she draped the falling locks like a curtain, hiding her face from the door, while being able to look between the coils and strands.

Half a dozen men passed the doorway on the way to the front entrance without even a glance in at the lady who owned the building: an unthinkable breach in etiquette that it seemed odd for Atia to ignore.

Faleria squinted through the hair curtain. The men were rough thugs dressed in dirty tunics and leather, at least one bearing the mark of a former legionary on his upper arm. All were armed with knives or stout sticks.

She was peering intently when the face of Publius Clodius Pulcher appeared at the end of the small group of men, his sharp gaze snapping around to the room and Atia's visitors. He was dressed in a toga, yet even he carried a knife. Faleria's heart raced at the sight of the loathsome man. Here was the villain who had burned down their house and tried to kill her family.

So casually that it almost pained her, she turned her face to Atia, away from the door, her pulse thudding, hoping that the man had somehow not recognised her.

'We must away for the afternoon my lady' Clodius said pleasantly. 'Business to attend to; you known how it is.'

Atia waved dismissively at him.

'Just don't disturb my guests and I when you return.'

There was an unpleasant laugh.

'I wouldn't dream of it. Though the lady Faleria and I are old friends, are we not?'

Faleria winced, but he clearly did not expect an answer as he strode out laughing lightly, following his men to the door.

'Horrible man, but he does have his uses' said Atia, apologetically.

Faleria murmured platitudes and made a small deal of the matter, turning the conversation back to Lucilia as her mind raced. Clodius leading thugs from the house of Caesar's niece and following Cicero and other senators. One thing was certain: if Clodius was involved, those senators were far from safe.

It was time to write to Fronto.

Chapter 6

(Border of Treveri & Ubii lands close to the Rhine & Moselle Rivers)

Caesar's fist slammed down on the table surface, causing the cup of water and the wooden writing tablets to jump and clatter back to the oak top.

'How many?'

'We don't have full figures yet' Fronto said quietly. 'But Varus estimated over a thousand horses and at least five hundred riders.'

Labienus leaned forward from the line of officers. 'How is the commander?'

'Lucky to be alive. The medicus says he'll be out of commission for weeks and he may lose the use of his left arm and some movement in his hip. Varus is of a different opinion. He reckons that if his arm's splinted up properly he'll be back in his saddle tomorrow. The truth's probably somewhere in between.'

The two officers were suddenly aware that Caesar was glaring at them for this change of subject. Fronto cleared his throat.

'Caesar, we've been marching boldly toward these invaders on the assumption we were going to meet them in pitched battle in the field, as usual. The fact is that they've taken us by surprise and completely battered the cavalry in the first engagement. We can't afford to go strutting forward now. We need to be cautious or we could lose half the army to tricky ambushes before we can even bring them to a fight.'

Caesar narrowed his eyes at Fronto.

'I have no intention of treading lightly because of a simple setback, Fronto.'

Another throat was cleared and Labienus stepped from the ranks.

'Caesar? Might I suggest that now would be a good time to reconsider a diplomatic solution?'

The general's head whipped around to turn his withering glare on his most senior officer. '*Diplomacy*, Labienus?'

'With respect, Caesar, we are endangering the army and costing both the republic and your esteemed person a great deal of money by keeping this large army marching against a foe who seems to have the measure of us and a good idea of how to whittle down our numbers. Those same foes have offered us the hand of peace and even service in your army for a small allotment of land this side of the Rhenus. It could be considered vainglorious and even prideful to continue this push, considering the alternatives available.'

A small chorus of agreement rose from one corner of the tent, where Cicero was nodding emphatically, his face a picture of suspicion. Fronto's eyes slipped from Cicero to the applauding figures of the two foppish tribunes: Menenius and Hortius. No shock that those two would rather see a negotiation table than a battlefield.

Caesar's face was a mask of cold composition, expressionless and severe. Fronto knew as well as any other long-serving officer in the tent what that meant. Beneath that cold face, the general's blood was rising to boiling point. Fury contained in a stony case.

'There will be no negotiation with these animals. Their diplomacy has already been clearly revealed as trickery and deceit. They used the peace table to distract us while they gutted our cavalry. Should they be stupid enough to send any further emissaries, they will be taken in, executed and sent back to their people from the neck-up. Do I make myself clear?'

Cicero stepped out to join Labienus. Fronto was a little taken aback and distinctly unimpressed to see the centurions Furius and Fabius at his shoulders. It appeared that the bad apples were all congregating in a pile.

'Caesar, it is not seemly or tactically sound to launch into further violent activity simply as an angry response to trickery. I implore you to think on the matter before making your decision.'

Caesar's eyes flashed dangerously and Fronto diplomatically stepped between the two men, obscuring their view of one another.

'You know me, Cicero. You know that I don't back down from a fight, but you also know that I'm not one to waste the lives of my men in unnecessary battle. Whatever we might have done to begin with, we have given our word to the council of Gaul and our ultimatum to the Germanic tribes who crossed the river. Given their treacherous sneak attack in addition to that, we are no longer in a position to back down. Caesar is not acting impulsively through anger or pride, but through expediency and necessity. We must now beat some sense into the invaders and shove their hairy arses back over the river for good.'

A much louder roar of agreement sounded around the tent. Beneath the tumult, Caesar's quiet voice caught Fronto's ear.

'I am not a child that needs defending, Marcus. I can speak for myself.'

Barely moving his lips and without turning his head, Fronto replied 'coming from someone else, it diffuses their argument over vainglory, Caesar.'

Labienus folded his arms.

'Marcus, you know I respect you, but can you not see the waste of an opportunity here? Are you yourself so committed to slaughter that you cannot find it in yourself to consider the alternatives?'

As a general hubbub rose, Fronto's face coloured with irritation and, as he straightened to reply, Menenius and Hortius sniggered and his eyes shot toward them. He had distinctly heard his name in their whispered conversation alongside the word 'donkey'.

Before he could turn his invective against the pair, his own senior tribune, Tetricus, leaned close to them from where he stood nearby. Fronto could not hear what he said to them, but they went very pale and stopped smirking.

Cicero smiled unpleasantly.

'I see now that, unable to make your point convincingly, Fronto, you fall back on having your tribune threaten people. How diplomatic.'

A low growl began to rise in Fronto's throat and he noted with growing ire that Furius and Fabius, still at Cicero's shoulders, were now glaring at Tetricus with barely-concealed contempt.

'At least I can say I'm here with honour to serve the general!' he snapped angrily.

A roar of angry comments rose around the tent. As the noise increased and filled the dim space with deafening malice, Fronto's eyes locked on Cicero and the two centurions. Labienus was busy arguing with Brutus, both men gesturing angrily with their hands. Menenius and Hortius had retreated to the shadows at the rear, though Tetricus had moved to stand near them again, his expression dangerous.

Fronto folded his arms amid the chaos, locked in a silent battle of wills with Cicero.

'Enough!'

The tent snapped to silent attention at Caesar's bellowed command. The general had his sword aloft and, as all eyes turned to him, many arms still pointing at one another accusingly, Caesar turned his hand a half circle and brought the gladius down hard, driving it deep, point first into the table, tearing through a carefully drawn map.

'This is *not* a public market! This is *not* an academy for philosophers! This is *not even* the house of the old women we call a senate! This is *MY COMMAND TENT* and I *WILL HAVE ORDER!*'

Fronto and Cicero, the only two men in the tent who had not turned to the general, finally unlocked their baleful gazes from one another and turned.

'This is not a matter for debate. This is *my* army, *my* province, and *my* command. *I* give the orders and *you* follow them to the best of your ability. That is how things work, gentlemen. Tomorrow we will leave a detachment to guard the baggage train and siege engines as they follow on, while the army will move at the fastest speed we can manage to engage the enemy.'

The general's gaze flitted to Labienus and Cicero.

'If anyone here is discontented with their role and wishes to resign their commission, lose my patronage and return to Rome, then they may do so. But bear in mind that I have a very long reach and an even longer memory.'

Labienus lowered his eyes deferentially, though Cicero met the general's gaze staunchly for a moment before he nodded.

'Apologies Caesar' Labienus said quietly. 'We spoke out of place.'

'You did. Let this be an end to it. What do we know or suspect of the enemy camp?'

Fronto, glancing briefly at Cicero, turned to the general again.

'Nothing concrete, general. Varus suspects it's close. When the cavalry were attacked, the enemy horse were fresh, and they had peasants with them who would have travelled by foot. They wouldn't have spent the night there waiting for us; with that many horses, they most likely came straight from their main camp at dawn. That all suggests that the enemy is encamped not more than, say, twenty miles away, at an educated guess.'

Tetricus cleared his throat.

'With respect, Caesar, I think we will find the enemy encamped close to the Mosella, if not directly on its bank. They will need fresh water and only that river is large enough to supply such a force in this area. Also, they must have some method of crossing the flow. Quite apart from having come from the far side of the Rhenus in the first place, we know that they sent their cavalry out a few days ago to raid south of the Mosella, so they must have rafts at or near their camp in enough size and quantity to transfer a large cavalry force across the river.'

Fronto nodded thoughtfully.

'Also, if they've been there long enough to send out long-range raiding parties, then that camp is at least semi-permanent. I'm guessing it could be fortified.'

Caesar leaned on the table again, his decorative, sharp blade still standing proud from it as a reminder to the more argumentative in the room.

'We must hit them hard enough to break their will, and it would be to our advantage to attack them before their cavalry return from the south. Each legion will leave their Tenth cohort with the baggage train, along with all their standard kit. The army will travel light and fast and equipped only to fight.'

He turned to Fronto.

'I recognise your concerns about the possibilities of them laying traps and ambushes on the route, but we cannot afford to risk their cavalry returning because we are slow and cautious. We will have to rely on scouts out in force to identify any trouble spots before we run into them.'

Standing straight again, Caesar's gaze passed around the assembled officers.

'Return to your units and prepare to march, gentlemen.'

* * * * *

'You won't bloody believe it, Gantus!'

The legionary on the far end of the four-hole wooden latrine seat that covered the stinking pit frowned at the man who had just pushed his head round the rough-hewn timber doorway. Another innovation of Priscus as camp prefect was to do away with the latrine tents that some units favoured and to close in the open trenches that others preferred, surrounding each latrine with a simple slat-wood wall that provided a measure of privacy, prevented the wind blowing the smell across the camp at ground level, and yet allowed air to circulate within and keep the gag-inducing stench a little more subdued.

Fronto looked up from his seat at the opposite end, where he had been sitting, casually reading the medicus' injury and sickness figures for the Tenth. Curiously, despite his popularity that had always made him 'almost-one-of-the-men', legionaries still deferentially used the latrine seat furthest away from him.

That, or possibly it was the spiced lamb he'd had last night was having a more powerful effect than he realised. Raising a leg to flatulate more comfortably, he watched the man's face as he realised there was a senior officer present and saluted.

'At ease. All men are equal in the shitter.'

'What's up?' Gantus asked from the far end, reaching for the sponge on a stick in its water tub and eyeing it suspiciously. 'Wish some people would make more effort to clean the sponge afterwards. I'll be more shitty after this than I was before.'

Fronto smiled and reached to the small bucket next to him, removing his personal stick-sponge and proffering it along the bench.

'I want it so clean afterwards you'd stir your soup with it. Understand?'

'Thanks sir' Gantus smiled and went to work, arcing a questioning eyebrow at his visitor.

'The barbarians have sent more ambassadors. The gate guard didn't know what to do with them, but the duty centurion had them disarmed and taken to the stockade.'

Fronto frowned.

'After yesterday, they'd dare try and talk to us again? Caesar'll be pleased as punch.'

At the far end of the seat, Gantus hurriedly cleaned himself up and then very thoroughly washed out the sponge before returning it to Fronto's bucket.

'Thanks again, sir.'

Fronto waved a hand dismissively and then stood, snapping shut the tablet and rapidly cleaning himself before pulling up his breeches and following the two legionaries out of the latrine.

Though the legate had not yet seen the stockade in the latest camp, it was not hard to locate, the roar of jeering soldiers drawing his attention. As he walked swiftly out to the main thoroughfare, he could see Caesar, Labienus, Brutus and Priscus striding toward the scene. Pausing, he fell in alongside.

'You've heard the news then?' Priscus asked.

'Yes. I find it somewhat hard to believe, though. Are they crazed?'

'Let us find out' Caesar said with a cold, malicious smile.

The stockade was a simple palisade of twelve foot stakes, with a door held closed by a heavy bar. There was room within to contain a dozen men comfortably or a century in cramped conditions. The eight man contubernium guarding the stockade stood to attention, as alert as could be, keeping the gathered crowd of soldiers back largely by the force of their challenging glares.

Fronto's eyes played across the shouting, jeering crowd. It came as little surprise to him that only perhaps a quarter of them were legionaries, the rest being Gallic cavalrymen, many with some small wound marking them as soldiers who had survived the massacre the previous day. Their anger was entirely justified and the joint hatred of these Germanic invaders seemed to have bound the regular legionaries and their auxiliary Gaulish counterparts together in a camaraderie that had not previously been evident.

The duty centurion and a contubernium of his men stood nearby, watching the scene carefully.

'If you really want to take it out on these ambassadors' Fronto muttered to Caesar, 'all you have to do is open the doors and let those cavalrymen in. They'll tear them to shreds by hand.'

Caesar nodded.

'I cannot deny it is tempting. But I want to speak to them first.'

As they arrived, the duty centurion bellowed a command that opened up a path through the crowd. Caesar and his party of officers strode through. Labienus' face, Fronto noted, showed a personal battle raging within, conflicting emotions fighting for control of him. The man was the army's greatest advocate for peaceful solutions these days.

Fronto had asked him about it one night in camp and Labienus' eyes had taken on a haunted look. 'Back when we fought the Belgae, Marcus' he had replied. 'Women and children. Old men. So many. So needless. Just so that they couldn't be enslaved. You never saw the piles of babies. It... it changes a man.'

Fronto had tactfully pressed no further, but something that had happened to Labienus two years ago seemed to have knocked from him the will to conquer. In its place it had left a man who Fronto – truth be told – much preferred. The Labienus who served Caesar now was a thoughtful, peaceful and calm man. He would be a man Fronto would value as a friend in Puteoli. But to an army on campaign, all it did was make him less effective and possibly even dangerous to have along. Even now he fought his own demons at every turn.

Labienus seemed to come to some decision and his face took on a stony impassiveness.

At a word from Caesar, the man on each side of the gate set his pilum point-down in the turf and heaved the bar to one side, freeing the gate. Two other men immediately moved in with their pila, keeping them levelled as the gate ground slowly open. The caution turned out to be somewhat unnecessary, given that the dozen prisoners sat at the far side of the enclosure, their arms encircling their knees.

After the group of low-status warriors and peasants that had masqueraded as ambassadors yesterday to keep the officers busy, these men were clearly the real thing. Their weapons and armour had been stripped by the duty officer and his men upon their arrival, but their clothes were reminiscent of the high quality woollen garments worn by the Belgic nobles, and they were adorned with gold and bronze arm rings, torcs and finger rings.

As Caesar strode first into the enclosure, waving aside the worried protests of the guards, the enemy ambassadors stood and bowed surprisingly deeply and deferentially.

'Great Caesar.'

The general said nothing, merely coming to a halt in the centre of the stockade, with his officers fanning out to either side.

'Caesar, we have come to denounce a traitor in our own tribe and publically distance ourselves from the man who led an unauthorised attack on your army yesterday. If you will agree to hear us out and open talks with us, we are authorised to deliver this man to you for punishment.'

An unpleasant, feral smile curved Caesar's lip.

'Fronto is right. You are relaxed and vital. You have not been in the saddle more than a few hours. I think your camp is less than twenty miles away; perhaps even ten.'

The ambassadors frowned at the strange turn of conversation.

Caesar turned to the duty centurion who had moved in with his men to join them. 'Your sword please, centurion.'

The officer obliged, withdrawing a well-tended and wickedly-sharp gladius with a personalised hilt bearing images of the Dioscuri carved in bone. Caesar reached across and took the handle with an appreciative gaze. 'A nice weapon, centurion. I shall be careful not to damage it.'

Everyone in the party accompanying the general had a fair idea of what was about to happen next. Labienus, Fronto noted, turned his face away.

Caesar stepped forward, the sword hanging by his side, coming to a halt an arm's-length away from the vocal diplomat. Without preamble or explanation, he lanced out with the blade, driving the point into the man's stomach. The barbarian's eyes widened in shock, but Caesar calmly turned the sword slightly and ripped it across to the other side of the man's stomach, tearing the steel free at the furthest extent and raising it to look at the crimson blade.

'It may, however, need a good clean, centurion.'

The officer shrugged. 'I have a man for that, general.'

The barbarian stared down at the wide slash in his belly, his eyes wide with shock, fresh waves of horror and nausea assaulting him as he watched the first purple and pale coils of his intestines slipping out of the hole. Desperately, he grasped the loops and tried to prevent their escape, stuffing his own insides back through the jagged rent. Caesar watched with an interested frown as the man gradually went pale with the pain and effort and sank to his knees in tears, trying to contain his innards.

The other eleven ambassadors had moved sharply forward at the attack, but the centurion's men had stepped to meet them, pila and swords levelled threateningly.

'What is the meaning of this?' demanded one of the nobles in very strong Latin, though thick with some barbaric accent.

Caesar glanced down at the man and then the blade in his hand, flexing his arm muscles as though preparing for another strike.

'Sometimes' he said quietly, 'people can assume that threats are merely empty, hollow things that are used to bargain with. I wanted you to be very well aware of the realism and accuracy of any threat I might level. I hope that this has made very clear just how little your very existence means to me and to what levels I am prepared to sink to achieve my aims.'

There was a silence that spoke of frightened understanding.

'Good. We have fallen foul of your trickery once and our cavalry paid a heavy price.'

He stepped toward the man who had challenged his strike. The man backed a step away, but Caesar followed a pace and the man suddenly became aware that other soldiers had entered the stockade and lined the walls, surrounding them all.

'Now' Caesar said calmly, 'tell me the precise location of your camp.'

The man frowned. 'We are camped by the river near here.'

'Not precise enough.' Caesar's blade lanced out, cutting a slice from the man's arm. The ambassador cried out in pain.

'Oh shut up, man. I've suffered worse myself. Now tell me the precise location of your camp.'

One of the other barbarians stepped forward. 'Three hours ride at an easy pace, general Caesar. Follow the river and you will find the going easiest.'

'And the traps most numerous, no doubt.' Caesar replied.

'Traps, Caesar?'

With a lightning-quick move, Caesar's sword arm jerked up. The sharp tip of the blade sliced through the lightly-wounded ambassador's neck just below his jawline, up through his mouth, shattering teeth, the point appearing through the man's tongue as he opened his mouth to scream.

'I want to know about the ambushes and traps you have set between here and there. You!' he barked at the man who had volunteered the information, ripping the blade out from his latest victim's throat. 'And you' he pointed the gore-slicked sword at a man who had cowered from the outset, shrinking back away from the violence. 'You two will go with this man' he gestured at Priscus 'and you will tell him everything he wishes to know. The prefect is an astute man and will know instinctively if you lie to him. If he is satisfied that you have answered everything truthfully, he will return your mounts to you and you will be free to return to your people. That is the limit of my mercy.'

The two men's eyes took on a hungry desperation as Priscus gestured to them, four of the legionaries stepping out to join him in escorting them away. Caesar waited until they had left, watching the life draining with infinite slowness from the man who sat cross legged on the floor, whimpering and burbling to his own intestines. Gut wounds could linger for days.

Slowly he looked up at the nine men who remained standing, one of whom was clutching his neck as blood ran between his fingers and soaked into his woollen tunic.

'Two of you get to live, for now.' He gestured apparently at random to two of the ambassadors, though Fronto knew damn well that nothing Caesar did was random and that the two men he had picked out were those who had remained as far apart from the rest as possible. Cowards? Or at least men with some sense of self-preservation.

With a gesture to the duty centurion, Caesar stepped back. The centurion and his men rough-handled the two prisoners away. Caesar gestured to him as he left and handed back the crimson sword. The seven remaining ambassadors watched with leaden faces as Caesar stepped back from the circle, gesturing for his senior officers to join him. As they reached the gate, Caesar issued a further command and the legionaries who had lined the inner face of the stockade filed slowly out. The ambassadors stood in confusion in the centre as the circular space emptied around them. Outside, the guards made to close the door but Caesar stayed their hands with an order.

With a gleam of vengeance in his eye, he turned to the assembled mass of angry Gallic auxiliaries.

'Inside are seven of the leaders responsible for your fight yesterday. Do as you will with them, but I want their heads at least vaguely recognisable afterwards.'

A roar of approval went up among the angry Gauls and Fronto swallowed, his mouth dry at the thought of what was about to happen within that stockade. Dozens and dozens of cavalrymen pushed and jostled to get to the entrance and have a first go at the prisoners.

Caesar glanced around and his gaze fell on a regular cavalry decurion in the crowd. He gestured with a crooked finger and the man strode over, saluting.

'Once it's over, have their heads removed, cleaned and bagged up for the journey.'

The soldier saluted again. Fronto looked across at Caesar as they started to walk away.

'What of the two you had removed at the end there?'

Caesar shrugged. 'Priscus will probably get everything we need from the first two, but I thought it prudent to have two men spare for him to question afterwards.'

'And will they be released afterwards as well?'

Caesar flashed a genuine frown of incomprehension at him.

'As well?' Realisation struck him. 'Oh you expect me to release the first two after interrogation? Marcus, if everything goes the way I expect there will not be enough of them left to ride a horse afterwards. There are times, Marcus,' he added with a curious smile 'when you are almost deliciously naïve.'

* * * * *

Fronto glanced over his shoulder, trying to keep his mind on the mundanities of legion command, the ordered lines of soldiers marching through the dust behind him, kicking up clouds of grey, the standards glinting in the sunlight, the crimson flags that stood out blood-red against the blue and green of the summer's day...

But the problem was that even they were too reminiscent and drew his gaze back around to settle on the grisly sight at the front of the army.

Twelve bearded, top-knotted, grisly severed heads bounced up and down on the tips of spears, bobbing along to the gait of the walking horses beneath them. Caesar's cavalry guard had been given the 'honour' of carrying the trophies, and Aulus Ingenuus had selected a dozen of his toughest and most loyal men to carry out the unpleasant task. Flies buzzed in clouds around them where they rode, at the 'head' of the army, as Priscus had put it in a moment of attempted light relief.

It was yet another display of ruthlessness from the general that jarred his sensibilities, and yet Fronto could not help but think that the fault really lay with himself. Somehow, despite having served for over a decade with Caesar, in two different theatres of war, deep down Fronto still expected Caesar to live up to the expectations that he'd had all those years ago when he disembarked in Hispania to take up his post. The fact that Caesar consistently failed to live up to them was more likely a problem with his own expectations being too high than with Caesar being less than he could be.

Irritated with the general for his shortcomings, himself for his naivety and the Germanic invaders for being stupid enough to cross the Rhenus and push the matter, Fronto clicked his tongue angrily and glared at the bobbing heads.

'Do you approve?'

The voice was so close and unexpected that Fronto actually jumped a little in the saddle. Turning, his heart sank at the sight of Labienus, pulling alongside with his dappled grey mare. The staff officer was pointing at the heads.

'Do you like the new standards the general has raised for the army? Are you proud that the Tenth get to march at the front behind them?'

'Leave it, Titus.'

'Do you approve of the execution of men of diplomacy to create a symbol of Roman implacability?'

'Titus...'snapped Fronto, turning a warning glare on him. Labienus blithely ignored it.

'Is this the man you came to Gaul to serve with? 'Cause I know for certain that this is not the man *I* followed.'

'Just leave it, Titus.' Fronto's face darkened further and Labienus searched his companion's eyes, feeling that he had scored a point somewhere – touched a nerve; perhaps there was a chance here...

'Why did you defend the general in the command tent? There was the chance of a peaceful solution. It only took a little more support; a few more of us to stand before Caesar and nudge him to a diplomatic answer. But you defended him. Even though you knew Cicero and I were right. And you *did* know that, didn't you?'

Fronto raised a warning hand.

'Why?' Labienus pressed. 'Why defend him? You've always stood up to him and argued when you thought he'd crossed the line. You're renowned for it. It's what makes most of the officers respect you. I know that I've changed over the past four years, but so have you, Marcus. I may have begun to understand something beyond the simple discharge of duty, but you? You've hardened. Half the time now, when the general is crossing a line, you're crossing it with him! Why?'

Fronto turned in the saddle and something in his eyes made Labienus shrink back. Perhaps he had misjudged the legate.

'Don't stir up things you don't understand, Titus.'

'Fronto...'

'Could it be that there are things you don't know? Could it be that I feel I have a duty to defend and support the man who saved Faleria and my mother from murder by the mob in Rome? Could it be that without Caesar my entire family might have died when thugs and gladiators set fire to my father's house and came to carve Faleria to pieces? That Caesar fought side by side and back to back with me to defend my family? That only he and his veterans stood with us?'

Labienus blinked. He had been in winter quarters with the legions much of the past two years and the troubles in Rome had reached him as mostly rumour, notes and fragments from people like

Cicero. He opened his mouth to speak, but Fronto was almost snarling, spittle at the corner of his mouth.

'Do you think I serve Caesar because of his *patronage*? The only thing I ever got from him was my first military post in Hispania all those years ago, and I've paid him back for that a hundred times over. Patronage? I'm Caesar's client because I choose to be, not because I'm beholden to him. Do you think that every sestertius Caesar borrowed to put himself at the top came from Crassus? Of course not, but I've written off every last coin that changed hands between us because of what that man has done for my family. It's nothing to do with money or power or position. You know me well enough, Titus, to know I don't give a rat's shit about that. But a man who will stand in front of a blade for my sister's sake?'

Labienus shook his head. 'I didn't know, Marcus.'

'You!' Fronto snapped, jabbing a finger into Labienus' chest. '*You* owe him nothing. I know that. You're no client of Caesar's. You came on the staff as an equal; a friend and a colleague. *You* could walk away at any time, so don't push me to do what you won't yourself.'

'Fronto, I have to stay. Someone has to be here to try and temper the worst excesses of this endless war. To gainsay Caesar when he steps across that line. Fair enough if that person cannot be you anymore, and I do understand what you say. I can see the point. But *someone* has to be here. Where else would I be able to make a difference?'

Fronto withdrew his jabbing finger and fell into a sullen silence. Labienus took a deep breath, dangerously aware that he was about to poke a bear with a sharp stick.

'But even with what you say and your personal bond with the general, surely you can still see the wrongness of that.' He pointed at the bobbing heads. 'He broke his word. He murdered them all, or allowed it to happen. Twelve men of peace and diplomacy hacked to bits in interrogation or torn to pieces by angry Gauls, despite the fact that he'd promised clemency to at least four of them. An oathbreaker is a man to watch, and you know it.'

When Fronto turned back to him, there was a glassy deadness to his stare.

'It worked. It may not have been the gentlemanly thing to do, and it sure as shit was not the nicest. But look at the results. Three ambushes we might have fallen prey to, and each one dealt with efficiently and quickly by scouts and advance parties just because we knew where to look. Not a man escaped to tell the tale, either. As far as the enemy is concerned, they don't even know we're on the way. All because of what happened to those ambassadors. And the very fact that there *were* such ambushes tells you just how diplomatic those men were planning on being.'

He gestured with a sweep of his arm. 'And look at the army. Look at the Gaulish auxiliaries and the men of the legions. Those heads don't make *them* question the general. Those heads have focused the mind of every man here. The cavalry were beaten, angry and humiliated by their defeat. Now, they're hungry. They strain at the leash. They're caged lions waiting to be freed and pointed at the enemy.'

He turned to face the front again.

'You can call it barbaric or wrong and you may be correct in doing so. But it served a purpose, as Caesar intended. He never does anything without thinking it through.'

Labienus nodded sadly.

'I can see that you truly believe that, Marcus. I hope that the day when you realise he's gone too far is not the day you realise that *you've* gone too far as well. Sooner or later the general's going to cross the line permanently.'

But the taciturn legate remained facing resolutely away, his silence a powerful statement about his mood. Labienus rode alongside for another few moments and finally shrugged, hauling on the reins and drawing his mount out of the column. His eyes narrowed suddenly and he turned back, keeping pace with the column once more as the dusty scout on his fast Gallic horse converged with the column. His eyes rising beyond the man, Labienus could distinctly see half a dozen other scouts pulling back to the column. Another ambush? There should not be any more according to the information Priscus had torn from the captives.

'Ho! Over here.'

The scout, tracking the call, spotted the armour and plume of a senior officer and veered toward him. Moments later, the man came alongside and slowed his sweating horse to match the column's sedate pace, saluting somewhat half-heartedly, as the irregular scouts were wont to do.

'Commander. I report finding enemy camp.'

Labienus nodded seriously, his eyes slipping sideways to see Fronto turn and pay sudden attention.

'What have you found? Details. Were they prepared? Were you spotted?'

'Enemy not know we come. Busy with meal. No defences; just picket. Not see us. Caesar get easy fight.'

Labienus nodded with satisfaction. Fronto could not help his lip curling a little contemptuously. It was all well and good to condemn the general's tactics in favour of a peaceful solution, yet the senior commander could not help but nod appreciatively at the prospect of taking the enemy unawares, regardless.

'You'd best get back to the general. He'll want to pass out the orders.'

'What about you, Fronto? You need to be there too.'

Fronto, shaking his head, pointed back along the line. 'Everyone else has some manoeuvring to do. Not the Tenth. We stay at the front.'

As Labienus moved off toward the command section, beyond the first three legions where Caesar and his staff rode, Fronto watched the scouts converging on the column.

Riding quietly, his mood dark, Fronto heard the distinctive and purposeful clearing of the throat behind him only on the third time it happened.

'What?' he snapped quietly, not even turning.

'That was a somewhat unprofessional exchange, if you don't mind me saying, sir.' Carbo murmured quietly from behind.

'I find it difficult to care right now.'

There was an uncomfortable silence which, Fronto knew, denoted Carbo taking a mental pause before saying something his commander did not want to hear.

'I fell the men back out of earshot as soon as I realised you weren't going to stop, sir, but you have to remember not to show divisions between those in command in front of the men, and not to talk about them as though they're sheep whose attitude can be manipulated with a few stinking barbarian heads.'

'But they can, Carbo.'

'Yes sir. I know that and you know that, and in all likelihood a lot of them know that, but there are some things you just don't say in front of the men.'

Fronto, his anger beginning to boil over, turned to his chief centurion, but the open sincerity and utmost concern in the man's pink, shiny, bald face was so utterly disarming that he found himself deflating and calming down before he even realised it.

'You're absolutely right, of course, Carbo. Thank you as always. For watching my back, I mean.'

'My pleasure sir. Wait 'til you get your sword stuck into a few stinking naked tribesmen. It'll all be alright then.'

Fronto could not help but smile. It was quite astounding how easily Carbo and Atenos, the new training officer, had managed to fill the gaping hole left by the transfer of Priscus and the death of Velius over a year ago. Already he was not at all sure what he would do without the good natured pink face of Carbo interfering in his affairs.

By the time his mood had risen enough to pay attention once more to the world around him, Fronto could see the army moving into position as per Caesar's pre-arranged orders. The bulk of the cavalry had fallen back to protect the baggage train, their tactics being less useful in an assault on a camp than in a pitched field battle. Only the blooded and vengeful cavalry of Piso, currently serving under a promoted prefect, would be given a direct hand in the fight. The Tenth remained in central position at the front, while the Eighth moved into position on their left and the Fourteenth on their right.

Three columns of legions, with the Seventh, Ninth and Thirteenth following on behind and the Eleventh and Twelfth, along with the vengeful cavalry alae, in the third wave that would seal the trap and prevent escapes.

Fronto squinted into the distance, wishing he could already see the enemy. But they would be in view soon enough. Wishing he could dismount and send his horse back to the commanders, he plodded forward for a while until the command section's buccinae began to blare out the order to pick up to double speed.

Time to run.

Time to fight.

Chapter 7

(Camp of the Germanic invaders by the Moselle River)

The scout had been accurate about the state of the enemy camp – that much was obvious as the Eighth, Tenth and Fourteenth legions crossed the brow of a low hill at a double speed march and caught their first view of the enemy encampment splayed out before them.

The camp of the invading tribes took the form of a misshapen oval, the shorter arc at the southeast eaten into by the course of the wide, fast Mosella River. The only concession to defence was a low embankment at roughly thigh height, spotted periodically with watchfires that still burned in the daylight, doubling as cooking fires, throwing numerous columns of dark smoke into the sky. Clearly the barbarians had no fear of attack. More fool them.

As the first ranks crossed the hill, the pace of the attack changed from being set by the command section to the leading officers and, as Fronto bellowed out the order for the charge, relayed by standard bearers and musicians, he could hear the same commands being echoed among the other two legions.

The pace doubled again, the legions settling into a uniform, organised run. They were already half way down the gentle incline to the barbarian camp when the first cries of alarm went up among the tents, wagons and cooking fires.

Fronto smiled in grim satisfaction. Even the legions, the most organised and efficient fighting force in the world, would stand no chance of mounting a concerted defence in the time they had. Disorganised barbarians were simply doomed.

To their credit, a number of bulky, muscular warriors managed to grasp spears or swords from somewhere and clamber up onto the mound in time to meet the advancing legions, but as a defensive force they would be as effective as wheat to the scythe.

Fronto, his horse keeping pace with the front ranks of the legion, was suddenly aware of the drum of other hooves and glanced round to see that two of the tribunes of the legion had moved forward to accompany him. Tetricus had served with the Tenth since the first days in Gaul – a very unusual choice for a junior tribune, who would usually serve the one season and then return to climb the cursus honorum in Rome. But then Tetricus was, like Fronto, a born soldier and a genius engineer – a fact that had led to Fronto promoting him to the position of senior tribune this spring in the absence of Caesar's unfortunate nephew. Crito, next to him, had now served two seasons, declining the chance to return home last year. They were two good men to have with you in a fight.

Carbo was bellowing encouraging phrases, each more graphic and belligerent than the last, firing his men's blood. Atenos, one of the senior centurions and the Tenth's chief training officer, had his teeth bared like some wild animal moving in for the kill.

Pride.

That was what Fronto always felt going into battle with the Tenth. He personally disliked riding into combat while his men marched, but Carbo's constant badgering about how an officer should act in front of his men had finally begun to take its toll. Besides, Fronto reminded himself as the legions surged across the last few paces to the rampart, he was not getting any younger. Priscus took every opportunity to remind him that he was now the oldest serving officer after Caesar himself.

Suddenly the time for thought was past.

The legions reached the camp of the Ubii, the Usipetes and the Tencteri like a swarm of glinting steel locusts, flowing over the feeble defensive embankment with barely a drop in the pace. Fronto hauled on Bucephalus' reins and kicked, launching the beast into the air and clearing the rampart with the two tribunes at his back.

The ranks of armoured men poured through the camp, all pretence of formation and order thrown to the wind as they tore along open grass between the multi-hued tents, hacking down fleeing barbarians. Some men pushed their way into the tents as they passed, many finding the occupants still struggling to pull on boots or draw weapons.

It was slaughter, pure and simple.

Fronto and his tribunes pushed on toward the centre, occasionally swiping out with their swords and maiming or dispatching a warrior – some of whom struggled to face them while others ran, having clearly abandoned all hope of defending the camp.

Endless moments of battle passed in bloody carnage before Fronto found himself somewhere deep in the heart of the Germanic camp, spying the enemy's baggage that stood in disordered piles among carts and grazing beasts. Legionaries surged through the camp to his left and right, some bearing the standards of the Tenth, some of the Eighth or Fourteenth, with other legions close behind them.

The first the legate realised of the trouble he was in was when Bucephalus reared in pain, a neat red line sliced across his shoulder. Fronto, never the most capable horseman, struggled for only a moment before losing his grip on the reins. The four-horned saddle held him tight for a moment, bruising his hips and smashing the breath from him as he jerked this way and that.

Bucephalus was rearing and bucking, smashing out with his powerful hooves at the three men making a concerted effort to put spears into the Roman officer before them. Another spear point jabbed into Bucephalus' neck – far from a killing blow; more an accidental strike – and the great black horse bucked once more, finally sending Fronto flying from the beast's back as one of the wood and leather saddle horns gave under the pressure and broke.

The world blurred blue, green, red and silver in a nauseating and repetitive sequence as Fronto hit the ground hard and managed to curl into a roll at the last moment, his sword thrust out to one side to prevent accidental wounding.

His head spun as he finally came to rest on his back, the breath knocked from him and a headache that felt like a four-day hangover already slamming at the inside of his skull. Blinking repeatedly to try and clear the painful, dizzying semi-blindness, Fronto just caught sight of the large shadowy shape of Bucephalus hurtling back through the alarmed crowds of legionaries. Even in the depth of battle and the fug of confusion he found time to be grateful to Fortuna that the steed, gifted to him three years ago by Longinus, had fled the scene more or less intact.

Suddenly a shadow was above him, lunging down with a spear. Desperately, he rolled to his left as the spear slammed into the turf where he had just been. In a panic he brought his sword round to try and deal with the man but, even as he did, a pilum punched through the man's chest, hurling him back out of sight, flailing and screaming.

Then legionaries were swarming past and across him, swords out, shield bosses punching into unprotected faces. A familiar huge and muscular figure in a harness of medal discs appeared above him, a grin splitting that wide face beneath the bulky blond moustaches. Atenos reached down with his free hand and grasped Fronto's wrist, hauling him up from the floor with as little effort as a man lifting a child's wooden doll.

'Trouble, sir?'

Fronto reached up and gingerly touched the back of his head, concerned that he might find a sizeable hole there leaking brains, but found only an intact skull with a little blood matting the hair.

'Screw Carbo. Next time I do this, I do it on foot. That bloody horse is more dangerous than a thousand barbarians.'

Atenos grinned at him again and patted him on the back with enough force to make him stagger a little.

'We've got them on the run anyway, sir. Looks like they're mounting a bit more of a defence in the other half of the camp, though.'

'Everything running smoothly?' Fronto asked quietly as he moved his arm in circles, wincing at the muscles pulled during his fall.

'Mostly. Haven't seen the other tribunes since the three of you passed us just inside the defences, though.'

Fronto peered into the chaos around him. Shouts, crashes and the clang of steel on iron rang out from the north-eastern end of the camp. The legionaries now swarming through this area bore the standards of the Ninth and Seventh. Of mounted tribunes there was no sign.

'You'd best get back to your century, Atenos. I'm going to try and find Tetricus and Crito. They were with me a moment ago, so they can't be far.'

Atenos shook his head. 'My men are already in the thick of it with the rest. My optio can keep them in line, and you're in no state to go staggering through an enemy camp alone.'

As if to prove his point, the towering Gaul let go of Fronto's shoulder that he had been clasping for the last few moments and Fronto lurched to the side and almost fell. With a wide smile, Atenos grasped him again and held him steady until the legate nodded.

'Come on.'

The baggage area of the enemy camp had seen some of the fiercer combat through the slaughter and, though the barbarians were being constantly pushed back and were offering little in the way of resistance, the bodies here had mounted up to create piles three deep in places.

The site of the tribunes' last position was not hard to spot.

Tetricus' white mare lay amid the bodies, a broken spear shaft protruding from her neck. Crito's bay steed lay still only a few paces further on. Try as he might, with a lump rising in his throat, Fronto could not see a sign of an officer's armour or uniform among the bodies, and they should be easy enough to spot, given the scarcity of Roman corpses among the dead.

'Over here' Atenos shouted, beckoning to Fronto. His heart pounding, Fronto stepped through the gore and scattered bodies to where the large Gallic centurion stood pointing down into the murk.

Amid the churned turf and mud, slick with blood, lay a body face down and splayed out. Fronto reached down gingerly to the figure in the crimson tunic and the burnished cuirass and gently hauled on him, turning him over.

Crito.

A powerful blow from an axe had punched through the bronze armour and deep into the chest, leaving a long, jagged rent in the metal through which mangled insides oozed in recent death. The officer's head lolled at an uncomfortable angle, his neck likely broken as he fell.

Fronto felt a surge of relief that the body was Crito and not that of Tetricus, and berated himself silently for such an unworthy thought.

'Fronto?'

His head snapped round at the mention of his name and it took the legate a long moment to spot the source of the sound.

Tetricus' short, curly hair appeared from the shadow beneath a wagon, a face that was paler than it should be beneath the mass of dark curls, looking up at him with obvious relief. Fronto felt a weight fall away from his shoulders as he stepped forward.

'If I have to tell Caesar that I found you hiding under a cart, he'll send you home, you know that?' he said with a grin. Next to him, Atenos was frowning and, as Fronto noticed, he squinted into the shadows to see what had caused the centurion such concern.

Tetricus was hauling himself along the ground out from the shadow of the wagon with the pale, taut face of someone in great pain. Again, Fronto felt his heart lurch as he stepped forward urgently. Atenos joined him and they reached out to help Tetricus from his hiding place.

As the large centurion helped the man up, Fronto saw the wash of blood that poured down the tribune's leg from a vicious thigh wound, the hilt of a bloody knife still protruding from it; saw the limp left arm and the jagged, blood-coated shaft that stuck out of the rear shoulder of Tetricus' cuirass.

'For the love of Venus, they did a number on you.'

Atenos, next to him, shook his head. 'Look again, sir.'

Fronto blinked and looked at Tetricus again, wondering what it was he was supposed to be seeing. The man was pale, having lost a great deal of blood, but he would live. The chances were good that both arm and leg would make it through, so long as the medicus did a good job. After all, the armour had prevented…

Fronto's brow furrowed as he leaned closer. What he had taken for a barbarian spear head beneath the thick coating of blood and mud was nothing of the sort. The bent and broken shaft that projected from Tetricus' shoulder was all that remained of a Roman pilum, the shaft broken off. Already knowing what he was going to see, his eyes dropped to the leg wound. Again, beneath the mud and blood, the shape of a Roman pugio dagger hilt was unmistakable when he looked closer.

'Who?'

Tetricus winced as he tried to put weight on his leg, but Atenos reached out and took a firm hold of the tribune.

'I don't know. Someone stabbed me in the thigh while I was still on the horse and pulled me off. We were in a thick mass of fighting, and I couldn't see who it was – there were legionaries and officers all round me. My horse ran forward and I staggered to my feet to go catch her when something hit me in the back and knocked me flat. I must have passed out for a moment, 'cause when I came to the fighting had moved on. I hauled myself under the nearest cart and waited.'

Fronto spun round, as though expecting to be able to find the would-be killer in plain sight, but only the occasional straggler from the Eleventh and Twelfth legions moved through the camp here, crouching to dispatch wounded barbarians and to deliver an occasional mercy strike to a fellow legionary who was beyond help.

'When I find the bastard responsible for this, I'm going to tear his face off with my teeth' Fronto snarled, as he reached out to take the other side of Tetricus. 'Come on. Let's get you to a capsarius.'

* * * * *

The three men, Fronto and Atenos all but carrying the wounded tribune between them, crossed the low embankment and moved slowly up the slope toward the Roman command section on the low rise. Caesar and his lieutenants sat on their horses in a small knot, gesturing at the camp below, deep in discussion. The artillery and the support wagons were still arriving slowly on the scene, and being corralled into groups. The medici and their staff were assembling three large tents to serve as temporary hospitals, while a number of orderlies stacked stretchers ready to run down to the camp and collect any wounded they could find.

By the time the three men were almost half way, the medical section had spotted them and two legionaries were running down with a stretcher. As they arrived and gently took control of Tetricus, lowering him to the ground ready to carry him back, Fronto caught one of them by the shoulder.

'Make sure he's tended first and best.'

The orderly looked for a moment as though he might counter with a sarcastic remark, but caught sight of Fronto's face and wisely bit it back, nodding instead. Fronto and Atenos waited for a moment, watching the two men rushing Tetricus toward the only finished tent, and then became aware of someone waving at them from the command section.

Changing direction, they jogged up the gentle slope to the officers, where Labienus walked his horse forward a few steps to meet them. Fronto saw the strain in the man's face and the risen colour that spoke eloquently of the arguments the man had been very recently involved in.

'Fronto? You've been in the midst of it. Tell me what's happening.'

The legate shrugged. 'As expected. We caught them completely unawares. They've fought a desperate defence across the camp, but it was hardly even an obstacle.'

'Do you think they'd surrender, given the opportunity?'

'I don't think they're organised and calm enough to surrender. I doubt they'd even listen to you. My guess is they'll flee the camp and try and get away. They certainly can't hold it.'

Labienus sagged, but Caesar, who had been close by and listening, stepped his own horse forward to join them.

'It looks like they're trying to float their rafts out into the river. If they can get across to the far bank, they'll be safe.'

Mules Marius' IV: Conspiracy of Eagles

Sabinus, nearby, nodded. 'There's a mass of them at the far side now too. You can just see them. They're running toward the Rhenus. We've broken them completely.'

Fronto glanced across at Caesar, whose expression suggested that the fight was far from over yet. He gestured to one of the mounted messengers who waited nearby. 'Get to the cavalry commanders. Tell them to leave the wagons and form up their men. Varus is still in recovery, so speak to his second. I want his wing to skirt the camp as fast as they can and cut off any survivors fleeing to the Rhenus. Galronus needs to take his men to the right of the field, along the river bank and deal with those men trying to get the rafts into the water. This fight ends here.'

Labienus turned to Caesar, a frown of concern creasing his face. 'And once they're surrounded and with no escape, general?'

Caesar turned a flat expression on his senior officer.

'They aren't just warriors, Caesar. This is three whole tribes who came across the Rhenus. There are women and children, old folk and babies. We need at least to try and behave like civilised soldiers.'

A flash of anger passed across Caesar's face at the scarcely concealed accusation of barbarism.

'Very well, Titus. If you want to save their old folk, go and try. Obtain their surrender.'

'But Caesar? You need to call off the pursuit first.'

The general's cold eyes regarded Labienus with steely dispassion.

'I will do no such thing. I have to consider the likelihood that you will not even get their attention. I will not give them time to regroup and face me properly.'

Labienus glared at Caesar for a moment and then turned and rode off down the hill, kicking his horse into speed as he raced toward what had now become a scene of slaughter and mayhem. Fronto turned to Atenos.

'We'd best get back to the Tenth and try and rein them in a bit' he said quietly, glancing at Caesar and hoping his words had been quiet enough to go unheard. But the general was paying him no attention, his gaze instead was locked on the two wings of cavalry that were now marshalling on the low rise and beginning to move down to their assigned tasks.

* * * * *

127

The camp resembled a mass grave as the two officers picked their way through it. All the wounded barbarians had been dispatched by the second and third waves of assaulting legionaries, and most of the Roman casualties had now been moved off by the capsarii and the medical orderlies, stretchered back up to the three great surgical tents being raised on the hill.

Fronto and Atenos picked their way through the field of bodies, wondering where the Tenth would be now. The sounds of distant fighting still echoed from the far end of the camp, and the two men made toward the sound as swiftly as they could.

The bodies that littered the ground were so numerous that it was impossible to not pay a certain amount of attention as they hurried through and Fronto noted with some distaste as he moved just how many of them appeared to be the women and children of whom Labienus had spoken. It seemed that not only had the attacking legionaries been less than selective with their targets, but also the Germanic tribesfolk had done nothing to try and shelter their civilian counterparts, the warriors having run alongside them and many women and children being left to die as the warriors ran.

A distant call from a buccina identified the location of the Tenth and the two men angled off to the south, toward the river Mosella. A sound like distant thunder told them that Galronus and his cavalry were converging on the very same spot.

The sounds of fighting became gradually louder and more distinct as they neared the river and finally, pushing their way past a large, partially collapsed tent, Fronto and Atenos laid eyes on the scene at the water's edge.

A detachment of legionaries – what looked like roughly half a legion in total – had pinned the barbarians against the waterside. The standards and flags identified the detachment as being composed of men from the Tenth and the Seventh, while Galronus' green cavalry wing, even as Fronto watched, crashed into the barbarians' flank along the river, jabbing down with their spears and scything out with swords, their organisation and fighting style still very much Gallic, as yet untempered by too much Roman influence.

With some dismay, Fronto noted that once again the barbarian force consisted of warriors, but also of women, children and old folk, and yet all of them seemed determined to fight back, women wielding weapons stolen from the dead, children swishing and stabbing with sticks, throwing stones, or hefting other makeshift weapons.

The reason for their combined and desperate defiance lay beyond, protected from the Roman attackers by a sea of flailing people: two dozen sizeable rafts, each large enough to carry twenty or more people, were being manhandled into the water, still tied to the bank with ropes to prevent them rushing away downstream. Even as Fronto watched, the first raft began to float out into the water. The occupants had no oars but, using heavy poles, they pushed the raft out into the deeper, fast flowing water before throwing the poles to the bank for the next group, then dropping their arms into the water and scooping their way out into mid-river.

The rafts were just as likely to return to this bank further down or hurtle downriver until they flowed out into the massive channel of the Rhenus as they were actually to cross here, but that seemed of little consequence to the fleeing folk before him.

Fronto paused.

'What are you thinking?' murmured Atenos next to him.

'I'm trying to decide whether Labienus is right. Perhaps we ought to just let them go. Look at them. They're in a panic and they're mostly civilians. This lot aren't going turn round and regroup. They won't stop running and swimming until they reach the east bank of the Rhenus again.'

Atenos nodded.

'It would be breaking the general's orders, though, sir. And these people *are* invaders. Don't forget that.'

Fronto turned to his centurion friend in surprise, but nodded.

'You're right. And, of course, slaves help pay for the campaign too. Come on.'

Breaking into a jog, Fronto and Atenos made their way to the scene of fighting, shouting at the rear ranks of legionaries to step aside, making for where they could see a group of standards wavering. Slowly, they managed to push through the crowd until they spotted Cicero's ornate helmet and white plume near the standards. Angling toward him, Fronto hauled men out of the way.

'Cicero!'

The man was busy bellowing orders to his men and threats to the barbarians only twenty feet away and roaring their defiance in guttural tongues.

'Cicero!' Fronto bellowed again as the two men reached the small command group. Two of Cicero's tribunes finally spotted the mud-spattered legate and his centurion and tugged at Cicero. The Seventh's commander turned and noticed Fronto.

'The bastards are getting away, Fronto. We can't kill them fast enough to get to the rafts.'

Fronto nodded.

'Galronus' cavalry are here now and they're pushing along the water's edge. They'll cut the enemy off completely in a few moments. Maybe three or four rafts will get away. That's all. Once their escape route's gone, they should surrender!'

Cicero smiled grimly and turned back to his men, shouting orders and encouragement.

'Had a bit of a fall, legate?'

Fronto turned to see Fabius standing nearby, a cold smile on his face. The centurion was liberally spattered with blood and wielded a gladius in one hand and his vine staff in the other.

'Horse threw me in the fight.' His eyes strayed down suspiciously to the man's waist, expecting an empty scabbard where the man's pugio should be, but he was a little disappointed to note that the hilt of the dagger rose proud from the sheath.

Fabius nodded a faint bow and then turned and pushed his way back into the fight. Fronto glared after him until he was lost from sight in the press. He would be willing to put money on the fact that, if he found Furius, the other veteran's dagger sheath would be empty.

A hand fell on his shoulder, causing him to jump slightly and he looked round to see Atenos smiling.

'The cavalry's behind them now. It's over, sir.'

Fronto tried to see across the crowd but, being more than a head shorter than the centurion, he could see little but a sea of milling legionaries.

'They're cutting the ropes' Atenos said with satisfaction. 'You can see the empty rafts drifting out into the water. Arms are getting raised too. Looks like they're surrendering.'

As Fronto listened, he could hear the distinctive sound of hundreds, even thousands, of weapons being cast to the ground in defeat.

It seemed that it really was over. The invaders had been smashed and beaten, their army destroyed, their camp ravaged. Survivors who made it to safety would be few and far between and there would be a lot of slaves taken. It was not even midsummer and the legions had already achieved their season's objectives.

Fronto smiled to himself, despite everything. The image of Lucilia and the memory of the warm waters of the bay below Puteoli sprang unbidden to his mind. Maybe, just maybe, he would be able to give her the marriage she sought this year after all.

* * * * *

Fronto took a deep breath and, rolling his aching shoulders and wincing at the pains he had suffered in the fall, glanced left and right at the crimson vexillum flags bearing Caesar's Taurus emblem in gold, and nodded at the two guards, who opened the flap.

'Legate Marcus Falerius Fronto' announced the cavalry bodyguard, ushering Fronto into the tent.

'Ah, Marcus. I'd been hoping you would deign this meeting worthy of your presence at some point.' Caesar's expression suggested that there was little intended humour within the sarcasm.

'Apologies Caesar' he replied with as little apology in the tone as he could manage. 'I have come straight from the medicus.'

'Your tribune?'

'Tetricus, yes. He'll live. He may suffer restricted movement in his arm and leg, but that's what we expect from Roman weapons: killing and wounding efficiency.' His sharp, almost accusatory words echoed throughout the quiet tent and he took a moment to cast his eye round the assembled officers, allowing it to linger on Cicero and his pet centurions. Neither Furius nor Fabius seemed fazed by the words.

'The matter *should* be investigated, Fronto' Caesar confirmed quietly, 'but you must be prepared to accept that it may have been an accident. In the press of war, accidents are inevitable, as you're well aware.'

Fronto harrumphed and fell into position in a sullen silence, glaring for long moments at the centurions before turning to Caesar.

'The figures appear to be more than acceptable so far' Caesar announced, running a finger down the tallies on the tablets before him. 'Currently they stand at forty seven men of the legions, including two centurions, an optio and a tribune, with a little over a hundred being tended by the medical section and nine unaccounted for. The cavalry lost twenty eight men and fifty one horses, due to the barbarians' unorthodox and effective anti-horse tactics. So, even assuming the worst, we lost less than a hundred men in total. I think we can all consider that a more than successful engagement.'

'And the enemy?' enquired Brutus.

'A little vague. Estimates range from thirty thousand to eighty thousand. Until the men have finished stripping the camp of anything valuable or useful and gathered the dead for disposal we won't have better figures. We'll never be able to be accurate, given that the number of tribesmen who were washed away in the currents of the Mosella and the Rhenus or sank without trace due to the weight of their armour will remain unknown. Suffice it to say there were a great deal more of them than us.'

'I see the men are already dipping into the funeral club coffers and building the pyres for the Roman dead' Fronto noted. 'Late this afternoon, I suggest you check the wind direction and make sure you stay upwind. It's likely to get a bit smoky. Didn't see pyres or pits for the enemy, though?' he added suspiciously.

'They will be left in piles for the scavengers in the wild' Caesar said flatly. Expressions of surprise and consternation rose on the faces of a number of officers, but Caesar blithely ignored them. 'Prefect Lentulus?'

A cavalry officer Fronto did not recognise stepped out of the circle of men.

'Tell us about the flight of the camp's inhabitants.'

Labienus stepped out and stood next to Lentulus.

'I can tell you about that, Caesar. I rode out to give them the opportunity to surrender, but this 'officer' here refused to rein in his men and stop chasing them, so I couldn't find a way to address them. In my opinion, this man was not ready for such a command and should be sent back to his ala.'

The prefect shot a sour glance at Labienus and took a step forward.

'As you are aware, general, the men under my command had their blood up. They were seeking revenge on the bastards who had ambushed them in the valley, and that was well known when we were assigned to the fight. Once they had the scent of the fleeing barbarians nothing short of chaining them to the floor was going to prevent the slaughter that occurred.'

Fronto frowned. A look had passed briefly between the prefect and the general; a look of recognition; understanding; possibly even approval.

'It was unnecessary and entirely avoidable!' snapped Labienus. Lentulus turned away from Caesar and fixed his glare on the seething senior commander. 'Once Commander Varus' cavalry had cut off their escape route, it was inevitable that my men would take the opportunity to exact revenge for their own defeat and losses. No man – not even you, commander – would have been able to stop them.'

He turned back to Caesar. 'And, I will state for the record that, had I been *able* to prevent it, I would not have done, regardless. The scum got what was coming to them. And with it we've ended the presence of the invaders here and achieved what we set out to do.'

Labienus continued to glare coldly at the man, but Caesar clapped his hands and drew everyone's attention.

'And that is the pertinent point. We have crushed the invasion. Now all that remains is to make sure that it never happens again. I will be organising further strategy meetings in good time but, for now, we should lick our wounds, such as they are, and tot up our successes.' He turned to Varus, who stood tall and steady, despite the sling that held his broken arm tight and the padding beneath his tunic where the hip wound was bound. 'I would like you to arrange mounted patrols and scouts to range up to twenty miles each way along the banks of the Rhenus and twenty miles back along the Mosella; long-range scouts out to the south, as well. I want continual and up to date information on the location and movements of the enemy cavalry that we know are still out there. We cannot afford to be taken off guard.'

Varus, standing painfully, his arm tightly slung and leaning on a stick with his good hand, started to rattle off figures and facts and Fronto's mind began to drift along to the drone of planning. As the conversation hummed slowly around him, his eyes fell on Lentulus, now stepping back into the line, a virtual crackle of angry electricity between him and Labienus. The more he ran his mind back over the statements and the shared looks between prefect and general, the more convinced he became that the man had been following Caesar's direct orders to wipe out as many of the barbarians as they possibly could and prevent the possibility of surrender. It would, after all, hardly be unlike the general to do such a thing.

Once more, his gaze passed to Cicero and the two centurions. Could Furius or Fabius have been responsible? They both bore their pugio at their belt, but a replacement would hardly be difficult to obtain had they lost one on the battlefield. A centurion did not carry a pilum into battle but, again, it would hardly be difficult to lay hands on one, even at a moment's notice, in the press of men.

He wondered where the two weapons used were now. Had the medicus kept them when the wounds were tended? Had Tetricus taken them? It was, of course, possible that one of them had some sort of distinguishing mark that could tie them to their owner.

The meeting rolled on with discussions of the logistics of moving the army closer to the Rhenus compared with making use of the enemy's partial fortifications and setting camp in their current location. Priscus stated his case with his usual brusqueness, Cita arguing his corner at every turn, other officers making their feelings known whenever the questions touched their commands.

Through the next quarter hour and more, Fronto stood silent, letting the murmur of complications and disagreements wash over him. His thoughts drifted over the river and past the plain where the enemy cavalry raided somewhere out of scouting distance, past the great oppidum of Vesontio, over the mountains of the Helvetii's land, past Caesar's province of Cisalpine Gaul, across mile after mile of tilled and mined land in Italia.

His mind's eye focused in like the view of a circling bird. A great mountain by the sea in a bay that looked from above as though a Titan had taken a bite out of the land. Cities in glorious marble and brick. Circling down away from the mountain, past the old Greek port, past the bubbling mud and steaming white crater of the Forum Vulcani, down toward the port where Fronto had spent the blistering summers of his youth.

The villa on the hillside with its familiar outbuildings. The patio where his father had first taught him how to hold a sword. And finally there she was: Lucilia, standing in a stola of midnight blue, with her back to the glittering waters of the bay far below, leaning on the balustrade and smiling at him.

'When are we going home?'

Only as a stunned silence settled around him did Fronto realise that he had voiced the thought out loud. His mind reeled back across the hundreds of miles, leaving that wondrous figure above the shining sea and refocusing on the tent full of sweating officers.

Everyone was staring at him. Priscus was still standing in the centre of the tent, his finger wagging at Cita redundantly.

'Fronto?' Caesar frowned.

The legate felt a surge of automatic panic flowing through him.

'That came out wrong. Sorry. What I mean is, though, that we're almost done here. You and Varus both said so. Once we can round up the stray cavalry they sent across the river, we've completely destroyed the invaders. Very few will have fled back across the river, and they'll have their own trouble dealing with the Suevi who pushed them here in the first place.'

Caesar simply raised his eyebrow questioningly. Fronto recognised the warning sign, but he had accidentally committed himself now.

'So I imagine that once we've smashed that cavalry force, we can report the invasion dealt with to the Gallic council, quarter the troops and then go home?'

He realised with some distress and annoyance that his voice had taken on an almost whinging tone toward the end, like a petulant child wanting to leave the table half way through a meal.

'You believe that the situation will be settled then, Marcus?'

'Well, I see no reason...'

'And what of those who return across the river, and the other tribes that live nearby? What if the advance of the Suevi is too much for them and they feel compelled once more to cross the river? What if the Suevi themselves decide to cross? How can we report this border of Gallic lands safe from invasion while we allow a threat to remain?'

Fronto frowned. 'You intend to crush the Germanic tribes, Caesar? Now that Gaul is peaceful, we move on east? A dangerous decision I'd say, general.'

Caesar's knuckles had whitened where his hands were entwined on the table.

'A demonstration to the tribes across the Rhenus, Marcus. A little warning of what we are capable of and willing to do. We will cross the Rhenus and punish them to discourage them from ever considering crossing the water again.'

A number of heads nodded in agreement. Fronto was hardly surprised to see Cicero, Labienus and a few of their cronies begin to argue in hushed tones, quietening only when Caesar threw a glance at them.

Fronto drew a deep breath. 'A punitive strike across the Rhenus, then. Fair enough, general. I can see the sense in the move.'

The discussions rose once more like a wave of noise and Fronto stood quietly and listened for a few moments more until Caesar drew the meeting to a close with an irritable sweep of his hand, his flinty gaze passing over Labienus and resting on Fronto. The legate pretended not to notice and waited as the officers began to file out, falling into the line and exiting the tent with some relief.

So it was not over yet. His mind reached back over the weeks and months to Balbus' villa above Massilia. 'He will push back the Germanic tribes across their river, settle the veterans there to make sure it doesn't happen again, and then he'll return to his gubernatorial duties, I presume', Balbus had said with a faintly challenging tone. Fronto had refused to listen; refused to acknowledge any possible truth in the accusation of Balbus' words. 'Watch what happens' he had added. 'If the general settles veterans and returns to political life after he's saved the Belgae, I'll eat my own cuirass.'

Fronto's gaze passed across the assembled legions and auxiliary cavalry. He had not questioned the general about the possibility of settling the veterans here, but it would be a solution; a good one. With a permanently resident force of veteran ex-soldiers, able to take up arms and defend their land, no Germanic tribe would find crossing into Belgic territory so easy in future. But this was clearly not the general's intention. He wanted a push into their own lands. The senate would have a fit when they heard. The people would celebrate and praise the general, but the tide in the senate would turn against him all the more.

'Cicero!'

Spotting the commander of the Seventh, for once lacking the company of Furius and Fabius, Fronto hurried to catch up.

'Fronto.'

'You heard about my tribune?'

Cicero nodded. 'Nasty business. You actually believe he was deliberately targeted by our own people?'

'It seems the only conclusion I can draw from finding a pilum and a pugio sticking out of him, yes.'

'Unfortunate. I don't really know the man, but I gather he's something of a hero. A clever engineer they say. Wasn't he involved in the fight at Geneva?'

'Yes. He's a good friend, Cicero. I will be... vexed... when I find out who's behind it.'

Cicero paused and turned to him, his face darkening.

'A threat, Fronto?'

'Not at all. Why would I threaten you, since you had nothing to do with it? No. But a couple of centurions with a grudge against him might want to keep one eye open for the rest of their lives.'

Cicero sighed and strolled on. 'You have to stop letting your personal prejudices against my men inform all your opinions and actions, Fronto. I may not agree with Caesar or even you at times, and Furius and Fabius may have been Pompeian veterans, but they fought like lions yesterday for our cause. Whatever else happens, Fronto, we're all Romans. Remember that.'

Fronto came to a halt and watched as Cicero strode off toward the camp of the Seventh.

Just how far could any man be trusted in the army of Caesar these days?

ROME

Balbus ducked behind a pillar of the temple of Saturn, his gaze playing across the small crowd outside the basilica Aemilia. Cicero had emerged less than a quarter of an hour ago from a public haranguing of Caesar and his 'needlessly self-glorifying personal crusade to conquer the world' and behind him had come half a dozen togate men, clearly of like mind. At least three of them were senators, known to Balbus from his regular visits to the forum to keep an eye on things.

Since Lucilia and Faleria's somewhat troublesome and dangerous visit to the lady Atia's villa and the revelation that Clodius was now running small gangs of thugs from the houses of Caesar's family – and therefore almost certainly at Caesar's command – he had been expecting to see trouble in the streets surrounding those who spoke out against Balbus' former general.

Cicero and two of the senators shared a private joke, laughing hard, and then clasped hands and separated. Balbus frowned as he watched them move out across the forum square. The pair of senators, still laughing and joking, strode along the Vicus Iugarius toward the meat and flower markets and the river, their togate forms blending into the general tide of humanity that flowed this way and that along the street.

Balbus' eyes pulled back from them, aware that, even with the unusual shock of red hair that marked one of the senators out in a crowd, he might well lose them in the press as soon as he shifted his gaze. Instead, he watched Cicero as the man stood for a long moment, tapping his lip as though struggling with a difficult decision. Finally, the great orator nodded in answer to some internal question, and strode across to the dilapidated arcades of the ancient Basilica Sempronia. Balbus frowned again as he watched the man enter the building.

Once the main venue for matters of law and public and political debate, the Sempronia had been damaged several decades ago by a tremor in the earth and cracks cobwebbed the walls and columns. It was far from unstable, but generally considered poor quality and unlucky so most business had now moved to the basilica Aemilia across the forum. Why Cicero should want to be in there, he could not imagine.

138

He felt torn. Watching Cicero could be very interesting, but the Sempronia was rarely frequented by more than half a dozen people these days, and the interior was bright and airy. He would find it difficult to observe the orator without being easily observed himself – at least close enough to overhear any conversation. Perhaps that interesting meeting was a task for another day. Conversely, with the press of people in the streets, it should be easy enough to catch up with the two senators and see what they were up to.

Plagued by indecision, Balbus finally settled on Cicero, hurrying across the forum to the stained and badly-maintained walls of the Basilica Sempronia. Clambering up the steps two at a time, he paused, heaving in heavy breaths. Despite his waistline, Balbus knew he was fitter than many men his age, and probably almost as fit as he had been most of his military life, but his illness last year had put a strain on his chest and he could feel the labouring of his heart when he did things like this.

Slowing, carefully, he ducked beneath the columns of the basilica's façade and scurried along in the shadows to a doorway – one of the numerous in the basilica's wall, but not the one through which Cicero had entered.

Pausing, he peered into the interior, his gaze scanning the open hallway until he spotted Cicero standing before a statue of the brothers Gracchus, the great statesmen of the previous century. The man was standing with his back to the entrance and therefore to Balbus, and waited patiently. Moments passed, Balbus struggling with the decision of whether to stay and wait too, or to run off after the other senators. Just as he straightened to leave, a second figure strolled out of the shadows and crossed to Cicero, the two men clasping hands in greeting before turning back to the statue and conversing in tones that Balbus would never hear unless he loitered nearby.

The second man turned for a moment, gesturing expansively at the interior of the basilica and Balbus pressed himself against the wall, his heart thumping with recognition. Titus Annius Milo, former tribune, commander of one of the largest private forces in Rome, and loyal client of Pompey. So... Cicero and Pompey. Not unexpected, and also not good for Caesar.

Nodding to himself and aware that he was unlikely to glean any further information here without his presence becoming known to the two men, Balbus left the doorway, skipping down the steps, and pushed his way into the crowd in the Vicus Iugarius. The chances of him finding the two senators so long behind them, were small, but he was not expected back at the house for almost two hours yet and, if all else failed, there was a nice little tavern on the edge of the Forum Holitorium that served a surprisingly good wine.

Balbus grinned to himself as he moved through the crowd, laughing at how much effect Fronto had had on his life and habits in the three years of their acquaintance.

Few along the street wore togas, this street leading into a lower-class, more mercantile area, with the markets, the sewer outflow and the dung piles mucked out from the Circus Maximus, and Balbus found himself peering intently every time he spotted someone wearing the bulky garment of the wealthy and noble citizenry. He himself wore a simple tunic and cloak that could have marked him out as anything from a trader to a dung-shoveller. Sometimes anonymity was preferable to status.

There were no togate figures moving in pairs and Balbus admitted with some disappointment that there was every chance that the two had now separated. If that were the case, he would only stand a chance of locating the red-haired one. The other would blend in too easily; he was too average for easy recognition.

With a sigh, as he stood at the crossroads at the entrance to the forum Holitorium, Balbus gave up. A nice wine, well watered, and a nibble at some of the sweet treats in that pleasant little tavern would help pass the time until he was expected back at the house.

Ducking off to the side, he moved into a less packed street and turned into a side alley that would provide a convenient, short cut-through to the street on which his tavern stood. A woman flapped a rug from a window in an upper floor scattering dust, detritus and dog hair down over him and the narrow empty alley. A few paces ahead, someone had emptied a number of piss-pots from a great height and left a wide, reeking puddle. Stepping gingerly round the edge of the ammonia lake, Balbus happened to glance down a narrow, shady side alley and paused, one foot raised above the golden liquid.

Squinting and frowning, he stepped back and peered down the shady lane. A pile of something white and red at the far end could have been almost anything from discarded laundry to the carcass of a sheep or goat... but for the shock of bright red hair that glinted in a ray of sunlight that happened to find a way down into the gloom, reflecting off a brass pot in a window. That mop of red curls caught

Balbus' breath and made his heart race. The healthy state of his footwear forgotten, Balbus jumped across the small puddle of stinking yellow, landing in a spatter, and ran down the shadowy alley until he reached the pile.

His initial fears confirmed, Balbus used his urine-soaked sandal to heave one body off the other, the corpse rolling onto its back, arm flapping limp against the filthy cobbles, denting an expensive gold signet ring. All their gold still intact about their person stated beyond doubt that this was no common robbery, had Balbus suspected for even one moment that that was the case.

No. Both men had been murdered with repeated blows to the chest and gut from a narrow bladed knife of some kind. Blue lips and bruising already flourishing around the mouth suggested that they died of their wounds with a hand clamped over their face to prevent the screaming attracting any unwanted attention.

More damning than anything, though, was the statement that had been made with their death. These murders were as much a message as they were deliberate assassinations, for both had been mutilated, their foreheads sliced and shredded, blood slicked down across their faces and necks and soaking into the white togas.

For both men had had the same symbol carved into their forehead, and Balbus was left with no uncertainty as to the reason for their death.

Turning his back, he walked away, his face sour and angry, leaving the two men bearing the carved 'Taurus' bull emblem on their face as a badge on their journey to the underworld.

Chapter 8

(Roman camp near the Rhine)

Galronus nodded. 'Lentulus is the obvious choice.'

'No, no, no, no, no' Fronto grumbled, the wine – less watered than anyone else's in the tent – sloshed over the side of his cup and added a fresh spatter on the legate's breeches. 'Lentulus let his men go berserk chasing down the fleeing tribesmen. Possibly on Caesar's orders, but a cavalry commander needs to have full control.'

Varus leaned back against a prop of cushions, his sling undone and resting the rigidly-splinted arm on a padded pillow. Despite the argument and concerns of the medicus, he had been in the saddle again the morning after the battle, unarmed of course, and wincing with every thud of the horse's hooves, but where he belonged. Between rides, however, he seemed to be mollycoddling the break. He shared a look with Galronus and pursed his lips.

'Marcus, Lentulus *was* in full control. It was a command decision, whether his or Caesar's, to sacrifice mercy and potential slaves in order to allow that cavalry wing their revenge. I honestly can't say whether I'd have tried to rein them in myself. You agreed with him in the debrief! What would you do if the Tenth were hacked to pieces and then given the opportunity to take it out on their attackers?'

'I'd restrain them.'

'No you damn well wouldn't, and you know it. What is all this about, Marcus. You're all over the place these days. One moment you're standing up for Caesar and supporting any amount of bloodshed he might suggest, and the next ranting about him over the deaths of enemy civilians. I realise that you've always had your differences with the general, but I can't figure out what's going on in your head. Sometimes you're starting to sound like Labienus.'

Fronto glared angrily down into his cup.

'I don't know, Varus. I've never really been able to figure Caesar out. Sometimes he's the very model of a generous, merciful commander and a good man; other times I see things in him that really worry me; twisted things.'

'Nobody is simply good or bad, Marcus' Galronus shrugged. 'That's a very simplified way of looking at the world.'

'If it hadn't been for what happened in Rome – the gladiators and Clodius and his men – I don't know whether I'd even be here this summer. Caesar saved my family, and that's hard to forget and let go. But something Balbus said to me a couple of months back has really stuck in my head. And then there's all these divisions in command, and new men drafted in that I wouldn't turn my back on, just in case.'

Varus shook his head. 'I have to admit that the army does seem to be drifting into factions. It's Caesar's army, and he pays the men and gives his patronage to the officers. But...' he lowered his voice, 'there are clear pockets of men who are plainly anti-Caesarian. It shouldn't be worrying, but, let's face it, Caesar wouldn't be the first praetor to have an army turn against him.'

'You think Labienus would wrest command from the general? You even think he *could*?'

Varus sighed. 'I've heard how the tide of opinion flows in Rome, Marcus. Caesar's got the mob in his pocket, but that's only so much use. Pompey wouldn't fart to help Caesar if he needed it and Crassus is busy flouncing about in the east trying to emulate Alexander the Great and building up to invade Parthia. The senate are well-stacked against Caesar and only favours and threats are keeping them from hauling on the leash and dragging him back to Rome.'

Fronto stared at him. 'I didn't realise you were so politically minded, Varus?'

'I just keep my eyes and ears open, Marcus. The thing is: Caesar is balanced on a knife edge these days. If things went wrong, we might find the senate rescinding Caesar's position and command. They could even prosecute him... hell, if Cicero has his way they'll declare him an enemy of the state. It sounds so ridiculous and unlikely, but it really isn't that fantastic.'

Galronus frowned as he thought it through. 'And if the senate ends Caesar's command, Labienus has the authority to turn around and take the army off him; maybe even assume the governorship. Is that really likely?'

'As I say, it all depends on the amount of support Caesar can maintain in Rome. As long as the senate either supports him or is frightened enough not to cross him, he'll be fine. He still has enough influence, money and men to assure both, I believe. The people love him for his victories, so he's never short of loyal muscle to hire, if you get my drift.'

Galronus scratched his chin. 'It's maybe worth noting that Caesar hasn't put Labienus in command of a single action so far this summer. I would guess the general has thought this through to the same end. How long do you think it'll be before Labienus ends up attached to Cicero's Seventh and all the other untrustworthy dissenters? I just don't understand why he hasn't sent Labienus and Cicero home just to be certain.'

'Because you can't waste talent on suspicions' Fronto said with a shrug. 'Labienus may be arguing a lot and disagreeing with Caesar, but the man has obeyed Caesar's every command regardless. Disagreement is a long, long way from mutiny, and Labienus is still one of the half dozen most talented military strategists on this side of the Mare Nostrum. Can't afford to let a top man go because he's argumentative.'

'And Cicero?'

'Would you want to send him back to Rome in disgrace where he can join his brother and stir up even more trouble? No. Cicero is safer under Caesar's nose.'

A knock at the wooden frame of the door interrupted the conversation and Fronto made shushing motions at the other two.

'Who is it?'

'How many people are you expecting?' barked the irritable voice of Priscus. Fronto relaxed back to the cushion and refilled his cup, adding the slightest dash of water for modesty. 'Come on in.'

The door flap swung out to reveal the figures of Priscus, Carbo and Atenos.

'You said there'd be dice' Priscus noted hopefully, 'and wine.'

'Help yourself to the wine. Now that you're here I'll dig out the dice. We were just discussing the divisions in command. Labienus, Cicero, Caesar, the senate and so on. Any opinions?'

'My opinion is that it'd be a better discussion without me' grumbled Priscus, slumping to a cushion and pouring himself a generous cup of wine, watering it healthily.

'I wonder who's going to be left in command of the winter quarters once we've rounded up the rest of the invaders' mused Carbo, reaching for a dark, earthenware cup.

'Not Labienus, for sure' replied Atenos with a grin.

'I think you're getting ahead of yourself' Fronto said quietly. 'This isn't the end of things. I argued with Balbus back at Massilia, but I'm more and more convinced he was right as the weeks roll on.'

He glanced up at the silence and realised the other five men were frowning at him in incomprehension.

'He feels that Caesar will continue to push even when there's no reason. For glory and the applause of the mob in Rome. The senate are never going to root for him, so he needs the support of the people, and that means he can't stop conquering and winning glory for Rome. He won't waste the campaigning season when he could be drumming up popular support.'

'So you mean the general is going to spend the rest of the season ploughing into the lands across the Rhenus? All to please the poor and the homeless back in Rome?'

'That would be my guess.'

'Any news about the tribune?' Carbo asked quietly, deftly changing the subject.

Fronto sat up a little straighter. 'He's recovering nicely apparently. Not as quick as the invincible horseman over there' he gestured at Varus, who grinned. 'Looks like Tetricus was very lucky; the wounds could have been that much worse if just a finger-width different. I think he's lucky he was moving and there was a big fight on. If the bastards had cornered him in an alley, it would have been a different matter.'

''Bastards'?' enquired Atenos with a frown, noting the plural.

Fronto shrugged. 'I'd wager a fortune on who the culprits were, and there's two of them.'

'Fabius and Furius of the Seventh' Galronus said quietly. 'How sure are you?'

'Pretty convinced. No evidence, though. I can accuse them all I like, but Cicero will back them to the hilt and it's no secret that those two and I have a mutual dislike. It'll just look like me being vindictive if I make any kind of accusation without evidence. I had a look at the weapons they used, but they're bulk legionary issue with no way to distinguish them.'

He narrowed his eyes. 'I'm beginning to wonder if the world might be a brighter place if those two wake up dead in their tent one morning.'

'You'd not sink to that level, Marcus. If you were the kind of man who did, the Tenth would have done away with you years ago.' Priscus shook his head. 'But it's a mess, Marcus.' he announced wearily. 'This whole thing is a mess. Labienus has been sounding people out, you know? He came to see me; ostensibly it was a perfectly acceptable enquiry for the camp prefect, but he asked me some pretty telling questions.'

Fronto narrowed his eyes at his old friend.

'And you said?'

'I said I was Caesar's camp prefect. That seemed to shut him up.'

Another knock at the tent door drew their gaze and attention.

'You invited anyone else?'

Fronto shook his head. 'Who's there?'

'Message for the legate of the Tenth, sir.'

Struggling to his feet, Fronto hobbled over to the door and pulled aside the flap. A legionary stood outside, looking nervous.

'Well?'

The soldier held out a cylindrical case; small and made of wood. 'This arrived by courier a few moments ago at the gate, sir, with instructions to be passed to yourself.'

Fronto nodded and waved the soldier away, taking the case and retreating into the tent. Unstoppering the end, he slid out a small roll of expensive parchment. The wax seal that held the scroll tight bore his family's signet, marking its source as either Faleria or his mother.

'Letter from the missus?' Priscus grinned.

'From home' Fronto said absently, snapping the seal and unrolling the short missive. His eyes strayed back and forth along the lines, his expression undergoing a number of changes as he read, and darkening as he neared the end.

'The bastard!'

The tent's occupants looked at one another and then at him.

'What?'

The legate thrust the parchment angrily at Priscus, who ran his eyes down the text until he reached the bottom.

'Maybe she's mistaken?'

'No. No mistake. I should have known when we confronted him in Rome that Caesar would get his talons into the man.'

'What?' Galronus was half-raised from the floor now.

'Caesar's got Clodius Pulcher working for him now, running gangs of thugs from his niece's house to frighten those daft old buggers in the senate who chunter about this campaign. After everything Clodius did to us last year! Caesar stood with me and fought the cheap little bastard and his men, and then he hires the prick? Clodius is as treacherous as a snake and as slippery as an eel.

146

The little bastard needs to be filleted and dumped in the Tiber, not employed!'

'Remember what I told you, though, Marcus' muttered Varus, wincing as he carefully tightened the sling around his arm once more. 'Caesar's only maintaining his command and his position because the senate are scared of him. That's what Clodius is: a cestus. An armoured glove of the general closing on the throat of the senate.'

'Still, if that little prick is swanning about in Rome when I get back, Caesar or no Caesar, I'll gut him myself.'

Galronus' brow furrowed. 'Why in Rome but not here?'

'What?'

'Why would Caesar have hired men frightening the senate into supporting him – which is extremely dangerous and could land him in court or prison – and yet leave those who disagree with him in important places in his army? I know you say Labienus is worth too much as a commander, but if the general would go so far as to threaten patrician class senators, would he really stop at his officers?'

'Caesar has always been a man of the army. His legions love him because he's one of them. He'd lose their love and respect pretty damn quick if he started doing away with officers he didn't like.'

And yet, even as he spoke, in his gut Fronto could not escape the feeling that perhaps there was some truth in Galronus' words. His mind conjured up pictures of Paetus – the former camp prefect whose family Caesar had allowed to die needlessly, turning him against the general. Of Salonius – a tribune who had stirred the legions against Caesar three years ago and who had disappeared without trace. Of the Fourteenth who had spent two years repeatedly being given the more ignominious duties in the army due to their Gallic nature. Of the Seventh, who now contained all the general's 'bad eggs'.

Caesar could be a hard man and an unforgiving one. Would he really allow potential enemies to stay in command in his own army?

Fronto reached for the wine again, ignoring the jug of water nearby.

* * * * *

Tetricus winced and lowered his head back to the cold, crisp bed. It never ceased to amaze him how the legion's medical staff could erect a fully working hospital in the middle of a muddy field. He smiled and allowed his eyes to close.

The wound in his back sent shock waves through him every time he lifted his head or turned over, meaning that he had moved remarkably little in the eternity he had spent lying here. Still, he had to consider himself lucky. Between that wound and the one in his leg that had been brutal, true, but had managed to narrowly avoid completely severing a muscle; he was in discomfort most of the time, even despite the medication the staff had him on that made him weak and filled his head with fluff. But he only had to concentrate to hear the moans and constant shrieks of those who fared worse in other parts of the hospital. Or to imagine that silent tent at the far end where those who were not expected to pull through lay in stupefied and putrefied agony.

No, he could have been in a far worse position.

And, of course, his rank had afforded him a private 'room' – a section of the large ward tent that was partitioned off with internal leather sections. Four such rooms existed and he knew from listening to the activity around him that two centurions and an optio occupied the others. The optio was recovering from a spear wound to the neck that had left him unable to speak, and the centurions had various lost a hand, suffered a head wound, and taken a blade in the gut, though who and in what combination, he had so far been unable to determine.

A sigh escaped his dry lips. Perhaps soon an orderly would come and he could request some water. Or maybe even something a little stronger.

The medicus and his assistants had been extremely noncommittal when he had asked how long he would be bed-ridden. Fronto had come to see him, of course, as had Priscus, Carbo, and the other tribunes of the Tenth as a mark of appropriate respect. And Mamurra, Caesar's senior staff engineer and a personal hero of Tetricus'.

Mamurra represented the major reason he was twitching to get up and about. The man had intimated that Caesar was considering something big – something that made Mamurra's eyes glint with that heart-deep excitement an engineer felt when presented with a challenge. The world-famous engineer was almost vibrating with eagerness, and had alluded to the possibility of Tetricus being in on the task if he was returned to duty in time.

And so he must be.

Somewhere beyond the leather walls of his small world there was a tearing sound, like a medical dressing being ripped open, though louder. Tetricus frowned in his strange and sterile compartment. Sounds had been his main companions these many past hours, and he had become used to every sound the hospital had to offer.

This was new.

Tetricus' world went white.

Panic gripped him as he jerked his head to one side, causing a fresh wave of pain to shoot through his back and shoulder. The curtain of white – linen apparently – slipped away from one eye and he had a momentary glimpse of a muscular arm coated in fine brown hairs, the wrist enclosed in a bronze vambrace embossed with a protective image of the medusa head. Even as the white veil slipped over his eyes again, he felt his arms thrust down against the bed by powerful hands while another pushed a vinegar-soaked rag, likely gathered from the hospital floor, into his mouth, stifling his cry before he could even issue it.

At least two people; his arms held down and his mouth gagged and eyes covered. Panic rose to a crescendo. He tried to kick out, but the agony in his wounded leg caused him to slump back, his breathing horribly restricted by the linen and the rag that covered his face.

Surely such a thing could not happen in a hospital? Where were the orderlies? Where was the medicus? Was he not due another dose of the drug?

No amount of struggling would free his arms; he was simply too weak. His chest heaved with the difficulty of breathing through the white cloth. Was this what they were trying to do? Smother him? Why?

Officers of Caesar's army killing other officers? What was happening to the world?

Despite the gag, he did manage a sharp squeak and a whimper as a long, tapering blade crunched down through his breastbone and slid deep into his chest, severing blood vessels and piercing organs before grating between ribs at the back and punching into the bed itself.

Tetricus gasped at the killing blow. Despite the wounds he had taken from the dagger and the pilum and the half dozen other injuries he had suffered these past three years since Geneva, nothing could have prepared him for this white hot agony.

He could feel the grey closing in around him almost instantly. His voice would not respond. He could do little but shudder and shed a silent tear. His last breath issued as a simple wheeze with a crackle and a rattle. He barely recognised the feeling as the blade ripped back out of his chest, grating on the bone and releasing the flow of blood. His heart had already stopped, a hand-breadth of steel driven through the centre with professional accuracy.

Tetricus passed from the world of men bare moments before the orderly arrived with a small vial of henbane and mandragora solution, finding only the body of a tribune in a lake of blood and a large slit in the tent wall.

* * * * *

Fronto stomped across the grass, his eyes burning with a fire so hot that legionaries and officers alike scrambled to get out of his way. There was that something about his appearance which challenged anyone to stand in his way.

The hospital tent stood gaunt and bleak at the bottom of the slope by the river and at the downstream end of the camp for the sake of hygiene. Two contubernia of legionaries stood guard around its perimeter, as they did at the other two hospital tents and, as the legate approached, the optio by the tent's doorway stepped aside and saluted.

'Legate Fronto. The medicus is waiting for you.'

Fronto, acknowledging the man's very existence with only the merest of nods, strode into the tent and fixed his eyes on the man in the white robe, standing deep in conversation with one of his orderlies.

'Ah, legate. Come.'

The man handed his wax tablet to the orderly and stepped through a divide into one of the partition rooms. Fronto, his heart a lead weight in the base of his stomach, followed, steeling himself.

Tetricus had been left as found and, despite his preparations, Fronto found a small volume of bile rising into his mouth, his flesh falling into a cold sweat.

The tribune, dressed only in tunic and undergarments, lay on the waist height bed, the sheet that had covered him rucked up, presumably during his death throes. A white linen wrap lay draped across his face and a bloody, brown rag protruded from his mouth. The chest of his russet-coloured tunic glistened black, soaked with the blood that had run in torrents down both sides of the man's torso, pooling on the bed around him before dripping onto the floor and creating a dark red lake.

Fronto was momentarily taken aback by the wrap covering his friend's face until the medicus reached out and removed it, revealing the expression of shock and excruciating pain that had locked on the tribune's face in the moment of death.

Fronto felt the bile rise again and fought the urge to replace the covering and hide his friend's face.

'The wrap was used to cover his eyes – presumably to obfuscate the killers so that if something went wrong they could not be recognised.'

'They?' said Fronto sharply.

'There must have been at least two. These marks show that the tribune's arms were forced against the table while the blade was driven through him. Possibly a third man kept the face covered, although that could have been managed by the man with the sword. After all, the tribune was weakened both by his wounds and by the medication we administered. He could not have fought back very hard. It does appear that the entire attack was over in moments.'

Fronto told himself that at least that was a relief. Tetricus had died very quickly. Somehow it did not diminish the pain and anger he felt.

'Anything you can tell me that might give us an idea of the killers' identities?'

The medicus shook his head.

'All I can confirm for definite is that they were Roman. I've treated enough gladius wounds in my life to recognise such a thing. They entered the tent by slitting the leather in the outer wall of this room, and they must have chosen an opportune moment to effect entry and escape, given the number of soldiers who are always milling about around the tents. I've already got an optio interrogating everyone to check whether anything was seen, but I hold very little hope. The attack seems very professional to me, and I cannot imagine the assassins making such an obvious error.'

Fronto nodded, a hollow emptiness starting to settle within him.

First Longinus had gone in a cavalry action. Then Velius in the madness of the Belgic campaign. Then Balbus had retired to civilian life. Now Tetricus had been torn from him. The number of people he felt he could trust or rely upon within the army was dropping every year. But somehow this was worse than any other friend he had lost in this bloody war. Because Tetricus had been dispatched by his own compatriots in cold blood.

Something cold and hard formed in the pit of his stomach.

Revenge for this would come, and it would come with the full force of Nemesis behind it.

Nodding along to the rest of the medicus' report, he hardly heard a word, his eyes taking in every detail of the body before him, memorising every line and shape such that he would be able to recall his friend in minute detail the day he stood with a sword at the killer's throat.

Finally, the man finished chatting and Fronto nodded, thanked him, and turned, leaving the hospital tent and striding out into the warm, fresh air. Pausing outside, he took a deep breath and paced away across the grass. Briefly he had considered visiting Cicero and facing down Fabius and Furius, but he was currently in no state to do so. Right now he would very likely run them through before they could get out a word, and that sort of act would hardly help matters.

Striding from the tent, he made for the encampment of the Tenth and the jug of wine that his remaining friends would have waiting for him.

With irritation, he realised that something was flapping on his foot and he bent forward to examine the length of bloody wadding that had stuck to his boot – a chance manoeuvre that saved his life.

He only realised what had happened as he tumbled forward. The whirring noise that accompanied the missile clearly defined it as a lead sling bullet. Certainly it *felt* like lead as it caught him a glancing blow on the crown of his head, ripping away a tuft of hair and tearing the flesh. He allowed himself to fall forward into the grass, hopefully out of shot of the would-be killer.

For that was clearly the case.

Had he not chanced to duck his head forward, the bullet that had skimmed his crown would now be embedded in his temple, and he would be shuddering out his last breaths as the lead lump lodged in his brain killed him in convulsive moments.

He lay for a long moment in the warm, springy grass and listened. The optio back by the medical tent had shouted in alarm. Not a warning or command, though. All he had seen was Fronto pitch forward to the ground, no sign of an attack.

But despite the background sounds of men running to help him, the noise he was half-expecting to hear remained absent. No 'whoop, whoop, whoop' of a sling being spun. No further missile would come. The attacker had lost his opportunity with his first miraculous failure and had almost certainly cut his losses and run.

Fronto's hand closed on the small figure of Fortuna that hung round his neck on a thong. The Goddess was certainly putting in the hours looking after him today. Shame she had not dropped in on Tetricus.

Slowly, carefully, Fronto rose to his feet, his head throbbing and a pain wracking his scalp. Suddenly half a dozen men were around him, hands reaching out to help steady him. He did nothing to stop them.

'Sir?' queried the optio. 'Are you alright?'

'Sling bullet' Fronto said quietly, touching his scalp gingerly and pulling away a hand spotted with blood. The optio blinked in surprise.

'A bullet? But from where?'

Fronto glanced around, his eyes coming to rest on a small copse that had remained within the bounds of the camp, gradually reducing in size as the timber was cut from it.

'There. Only place with a clear view where a man could hide. I suggest you detail men to surround it and search it, but I'm sure beyond doubt that you'll find no one.'

The optio sent men to the small knot of trees and undergrowth, while he and two men remained by the legate.

'Come on, sir. We'll escort you back to the hospital, just in case.'

'Bugger the hospital. I'm going back to my tent.'

'But sir? Your head?'

'Will feel much better with half a jar of wine in it. Thanks, optio. Let me know if you find anything.'

As he trudged on up the hill, Fronto could not stop his eyes searching every face in the camp, peering in through tent flaps and checking every shadow. Suddenly it was beginning to feel quite dangerous being an officer in Caesar's camp.

* * * * *

Fronto was quite clearly very late and, as usual, could not care less. Aulus Ingenuus stood with his men on guard by the entrance to Caesar's headquarters tent, his horse guard positioned all around, the prefect rubbing the stumps of his missing fingers, as was his habit. The young commander of Caesar's bodyguard raised an eyebrow questioningly at the dishevelled figure approaching the tent.

Fronto knew what he must look like and pondered for only a moment what it said about his reputation that turning up to Caesar's briefing in a wine-stained, rumpled tunic and muddy boots and with spatters of blood across his temple and forehead warranted only a raised eyebrow. Once upon a time, not so long ago, he had taken pains to look his best for command briefings.

But then, with this as with everything else, today he would likely be given more leeway than most.

Ingenuus gave him a nod and the two guards stepped aside, allowing him entry to the command tent. The briefing and conversation was already in full swing as he slipped in through the tent flap. The speech halted instantly, all eyes turning to the new arrival. All around the edge of the tent burnished, shining armour and neat crimson cloaks did their best to amplify the effect of his dishevelled appearance.

'Fronto?' Caesar did not look angry quite so much as confused and concerned.

With a visible lack of effort, Fronto threw out a half salute and slumped into a chair near the door.

'Fronto?' the general repeated, slightly quieter and with... trepidation? 'Is something amiss?'

Varus, his arm bound once more in the tight sling, stepped out from the tent's edge, the wound at his hip making the move jerky and uncomfortable.

'Symptoms of mourning, Caesar.'

Caesar's brow furrowed.

'Mourning, Marcus?'

Fronto slumped deeper in the chair, but something in the general's voice drew him out of his shell a little.

'For Tetricus, Caesar.'

'Ah yes. I noticed his name in the medical reports. I have to admit to some surprise, since I was led to believe that his wounds were far from life-threatening.'

It was now Fronto's turn to frown. 'His wounds, Caesar?'

Varus was stepping forward again. 'Caesar, the tribune did not pass from his wounds, but from the attack.'

Fronto's eyes zipped back and forth between Caesar and Varus. Had the medicus assumed that speaking to him, as a senior legate, would suffice for reporting the incident, and not mentioned it to the general?

'An attack?'

Fronto, despite the bleariness of having spent the previous afternoon and the whole night drinking away unhappy hours with a succession of friends and companions as their sleep-patterns and shifts allowed, suddenly perked up.

'Tetricus was murdered, general. Yesterday morning, in the hospital.'

A stony hardness fell across Caesar's face, but Fronto swore that for just a tiny moment a flash of panic flitted through the general's eyes as his gaze flicked to one side. Fronto peered over to the left, in the hope of identifying to what or whom Caesar had turned in that strange, unguarded moment but saw nothing out of place.

'That is entirely *unacceptable*' Caesar said quietly and angrily. 'I will not have valuable officers dispatched in such a manner in my camp.'

Fronto leaned forward, a dozen warning triggers firing in his head at the strange reaction. What was more worrying? That it seemingly applied only to 'valuable officers'? That just for the briefest of moments, Caesar seemed to have lost his iron control and given way to an element of fear? That he had cast an intense momentary glance at someone or something that Fronto could not identify? That only the manner of dispatch apparently mattered?

No. What worried – or, more correctly, *irked* and worried – Fronto the most was this virulent reaction to the death of an officer with whom Caesar had been passingly acquainted at best, while a couple of months ago the information that his own nephew had been brutally murdered in an inn in Vienna had warranted merely the word 'inconvenient'.

Fronto glared at the general with genuine disgust for a moment before forcing a nondescript expression across his face and nodding.

155

'I presume, then, that no one has informed you of the attempt on my own life. An added 'inconvenience', at the very least, I'm sure you'll agree.'

He narrowed his eyes, watching for Caesar's reaction, but the general seemed genuinely shocked.

'This is harrowing news indeed. Ingenuus!' he bellowed.

The commander of his bodyguard pushed open the tent flap.

'Caesar?'

'After this briefing, put yourself and your best men at Fronto's disposal. It appears we have a traitor in the ranks who is intent on picking off my best officers. I want the matter resolved before we move out to the Rhenus.'

Fronto scratched his head, wincing as he accidentally rubbed off a newly-formed scab.

'We're moving out already? What of the cavalry across the Mosella?'

Caesar nodded calmly. 'I understand why you missed the first part of the meeting, Marcus, and how you may have been out of the loop a little over the past day. Let me give you a quick rundown of what has occurred.'

He stepped out from behind the desk and began to pace back and forth across the tent, one hand behind his back and the other gesturing in the air with his words.

'I have had a report from the scouts that the remaining enemy cavalry were somehow informed of our victory over their tribe. Rather than come and face us in honourable battle or offer a sensible surrender, they fled across the Rhenus somewhere to the south and have allied with a Germanic tribe called the Sigambri, to whom they are in some way related. I am still hoping to find out how they crossed the river' he added with a hint of irritation. 'There must have been a fleet of boats miraculously waiting for them, or someone on this side of the Rhenus gave them aid.'

He turned and paced back, waving his finger.

'Thus our enemies have fled our clutches and believe themselves safe across the river. They make the fig sign at us from their theoretical safety. At the same time, the Ubii, who control lands on both sides of the Rhenus, have sought an alliance with us and, while I had been set on refusing such alliances with these tribes, the line blurs a little with the Ubii, since they traditionally occupy both banks. They have offered us boats, manpower and gold if we will aid them in protecting their tribe's territory across the river from these vicious Suevi that have been pushing the tribes west.'

Fronto rubbed his temple. It was everything the general had intended anyway, but the flight of the cavalry and the request of the Ubii had provided him with the excuses he had needed to make the whole thing legitimate.

'So crossing the Rhenus is no longer a matter of discouraging those tribes on the other side from ever coming here again, but is now actively a campaign against the enemy cavalry and the Suevi? I hope you realise, Caesar, that this could be every bit as long, protracted and costly as Gaul has been?'

Caesar's eyes flashed angrily for a moment before control was reasserted.

'I do not intend to launch an invasion, Fronto. We will chastise the cavalry and the Sigambri for sheltering them, and we shall consolidate the frontier of Ubii lands, but go no further. We need to impose our strength on them just enough to make them aware that we are both capable of this and willing to do so at any future time we deem necessary.'

Fronto's eyes slipped to Labienus and Cicero and their small group, including the two centurions who made his blood boil at their very presence. Labienus had the defeated look of a man who had argued until he was blue in the face and knew he had lost. Suddenly Fronto was rather grateful that he had not been here for the start of the meeting.

Caesar leaned back against his table, palms flat down on it.

'That's all for most of you for now, I think. It might be prudent in the circumstances to draw this meeting to a close. I will require a few of you to stay behind and consult with me on the logistics of our move to the Rhenus – Labienus, Mamurra, Priscus, Sabinus and Cita, if you five would remain. The rest of you feel free to go about your business. Fronto? I would suggest you wash, get some sleep and then find Ingenuus and get to work on finding your tribune's killer.'

Fronto watched the general as the men began to salute and file out. Once again, Caesar's gaze flicked to the side for a brief moment and Fronto tried to follow it. Somehow he had half expected it to rest on Labienus or Cicero, or Fabius and Furius. But no. Whatever or whoever he had looked at Fronto could not tell, but it was not who he'd thought.

Something was definitely going on with the general, though: something strange and unsettling.

Chapter 9

(On the west bank of the Rhine)

Caesar scratched his chin.

'It truly is one of the greatest rivers in the world, as they say. I have rarely seen its like in width, depth or current. It is a matter of supreme amazement to me that a tribe of backward lunatics managed to cross and even to bring their worldly goods and their cavalry with them.'

Labienus pursed his lips. 'I suspect it is that very lunacy of which you speak, Caesar, which is the only thing that would lead a man to try to cross it. It will take days to construct the boats and even then I'll be making a very hefty offering to every god who listens this far north before I go out on those waters.'

'It may be an impressive one, but it's still a river' muttered Fronto sullenly.

'You're in good humour, Marcus.' The general turned back to the group of a dozen or more officers. 'The Ubii have offered us a score of boats that they use to cross the Rhenus on a regular basis. It is small help, admittedly, but a useful gesture regardless. Fortunately, I do not believe that such use will be necessary.'

Mamurra, the renowned engineer, stepped a little closer to the bank and frowned. 'The feasibility is still a matter for debate, general.'

'The chief engineer and surveyor in the Eighth are both experienced in such matters and they inform me that it cannot be done. A 'matter for debate' is an advance on impossible. Talk to me.'

The engineer tapped his lips thoughtfully as his eyes roved across the surface, taking in the banks and the whole length of the river visible from this point.

'No bridge like it has ever been attempted.'

Fronto, his surly mood punctured by a dart of surprise, wheeled on Mamurra.

'A *bridge*? Are you *mad*?'

'May I point out, Marcus' the general said quietly 'that the *idea* is mine.'

'I've seen near a hundred bridges thrown over a hundred rivers in the past two decades. Some have been simple and small and taken a few hours. Some have been grand affairs across wide flows that have taken days. No idiot in the history of bridge building has ever crossed something like that. It's the reason boats exist.'

Mamurra gave a noncommittal shrug. 'It will be difficult. There's no denying that. But I don't believe it to be impossible. I wish your engineer was here though. He was very good with bridges.'

The older engineer became aware too late of Caesar making shushing motions. Fronto's expression darkened once again as the image of Tetricus splayed out bloody on a table smashed aside his thoughts. Despite Caesar's vehemence that the matter be investigated and resolved immediately, Fronto and his associates had, unsurprisingly, been unable to glean anything beyond the obvious. Another brief conversation with Furius and Fabius had once again turned into a sour slanging match that had left no proof, only a bitter and angry legate. Fronto grunted.

Mamurra turned back to the river and immediately switched to a professional tone.

'The first thing to do is to tether a couple of boats and get out there with some long poles and a weighted line of knotted cord – and me with my stylus and tablet. We need to know how deep the water is across the whole section, and how malleable or supportive the river bed is. Given the length of the river and the dirt it carries out to the sea, I have the feeling that the bed will be unpleasantly soft and with a very thick layer of mud.'

'And that would make it impossible?' Labienus said hopefully.

'That would make it more difficult. With a good grounding in the sciences and the legions at our sides, impossible is not a word I like to use. Impossibility is a myth; only *feasibility* matters. The flow is fast on the surface. Given the size of the river, I fear that below the surface, the current will be a great deal stronger.'

His gaze wandered around the bank. 'These trees will be of little use to us other than for lesser struts and decoration. For all supporting and structural beams we want tougher, taller, thicker and more seasoned wood: oak for preference. There was a forest some eight miles back that had the sort of trees that I would expect to use. We will have to set up a constant transport system from the work gangs there to deliver the cut boles here, where they can be shaped and treated.'

Fronto was shaking his head as he looked out across the flow. 'I've seen bridges built across currents like that. Even across a narrow river, the pressure on the piles will be immense. Given the length of a bridge across this, the whole thing will just disappear like a pile of kindling before you can even get near the far bank.'

'I had no idea you had such a grasp of engineering, Fronto' Mamurra smiled.

'I don't. I have a fear of bridges folding up underneath me and plunging me into deadly rivers. You surely can't be considering this? I get seasick, you know.'

Mamurra had already turned his attention back to the water.

'It will require the piles to be driven in deeper than anything I've ever attempted, and they will have to be driven in at an angle to counteract the current. The structure will have to be built in sections, one trunk-length at a time, each section consolidated and completed before moving on to the next. We will slowly edge our way across the river.'

'Not slowly' Caesar said quietly.

'Turn of phrase, Caesar. Two weeks should be sufficient.'

'A week.'

'With respect, Caesar, remember my stand on feasibility? One week: unfeasible. Two weeks: feasible.'

'In a week I want to be on that far bank ravaging the enemy and earning the thanks of the Ubii. Bend your will to it and drive the legions as hard as you must.'

'The first time a drifting tree trunk comes down that flow from upriver and hits one of your piles, the whole damn thing is going to collapse' Fronto grumbled. 'I don't care how much you angle them, it won't help.'

'A fair point, Fronto. So we need a separate set of piles a few paces upstream, driven in just as heavily, but only just protruding from the surface. They will be more secure and solid and should stop any drifting debris from striking the piles of the bridge.'

The engineer's face took on a happy glow.

'Such a structure will be the envy of the civilised world. I wish we had the time and facilities to add concrete supports. But even in timber, if well-tended, it could stand for several lifetimes.'

'It will be torn down before winter' Caesar said quietly. Mamurra stared at him.

'Caesar?'

'We are on a punitive mission. I want a safe, secure, and speedy way of transporting the army across the Rhenus and back, and a simple route for resupply while we campaign on the far bank. But this is a temporary advance and I have no intention of leaving behind us a simple method for the enemy to cross the river and repeat their occupation. Once we have given them something to think about we will be tearing down the bridge.'

In other circumstances, Fronto would have laughed at the struggle and conflict in Mamurra's expression; faced with the opportunity to build something unique and astounding, and the knowledge that it would later be torn down and vanish from history. Tetricus' face would have been just the same.

'All things being equal, I think I'll let a few dozen wagons and an ala of cavalry cross the finished work before I test it with my own weight' Fronto grunted, seeing the emphatic nods from Labienus.

'The far bank' Caesar noted, gesturing with an extended finger, 'is Ubii land. Theoretically their alliance with us should protect us from aggression by other more dangerous tribes until the army is fully marshalled on the eastern side. Theoretically.'

He turned to Labienus.

'Titus, I want you to take command of the Seventh and Fourteenth once the final section of the bridge is underway. Despite the Ubii's alliance, we will take no chances. As soon as the last section is crossable, even before all the boards are in place, you will lead your two legions across, along with two alae of cavalry and two of the auxiliary missile units. You will set up a bridgehead and send out patrols while the rest of the army is marshalled.'

Labienus' face fell and Fronto could not help but notice how Caesar had saddled him with the 'bad egg' Seventh and the disfavoured Fourteenth.

'We will, of course, have to set up a general guard over the bridge to maintain security for our supply lines while we work on the far side. I think…'

He stopped mid-sentence and the rest of the officers turned to follow his gaze. A rider was cantering down the slope toward them, dust kicking up in clouds behind him.

Fronto watched as the man approached and slowed before reining in his horse. Despite the state of the rider, he looked oddly familiar. The man wore the broad striped tunic of a senior tribune and the leather smock with the pteruges normally seen beneath a cuirass. A career soldier, then, and a senior officer.

162

'Pleuratus?' Caesar said in surprise as the man swung himself down from the beast's back and stamped his feet for a moment, allowing his circulation to return. Fronto shuffled a few steps to his left to where Priscus was standing gazing out over the water with a thoughtful look.

'Pleuratus?' he whispered, leaning close.

Priscus looked round in surprise. 'Senior tribune of the Ninth last year. Reassigned over the winter outside my jurisdiction.'

Fronto frowned for a moment, his mind furnishing him with a different picture of the dusty, tired looking tribune. Neat and clean, well-shaven and clad in a toga. He was entirely unsurprised when the man spoke and his words carried the twang of a Greek-speaker.

'Apologies for my appearance, Caesar. I bear a missive from Rome for you.'

Caesar narrowed his eyes as Pleuratus proffered a sealed tablet. Taking it, he snapped the seal and opened the letter, his eyes running down the text as the tribune stood, breathing heavily and shaking slightly from what appeared to have been a long and fast ride.

An expert at reading Caesar's moods, Fronto saw the tiny flicker of annoyance pass across the general's eyes, while his countenance remained stony. Without a word, Fronto stepped behind Mamurra and Priscus, out of Caesar's direct view.

'A *Taurus emblem*?' Caesar said, quietly and with cold anger. 'A damn bull? Is the man an idiot? I should employ donkeys instead of men.'

Suddenly aware that his officers were standing in a half circle, silently waiting, Caesar took a deep breath. 'Thank you, Pleuratus. Make your way back into camp and get yourself cleaned up and fed. I will have to ponder on my reply for some time before sending it.'

Pleuratus nodded, saluted, and reached up to the reins of his tired, placid steed that had been calmly munching on the rich grass. Turning the beast, he walked slowly and gratefully away toward the camp. Caesar frowned for a moment and then lowered his gaze and pinched the bridge of his nose. 'I fear I have a headache coming on. Gentlemen, we will reconvene when Mamurra has all his measurements and plans. For now: dismissed.'

The officers began to scatter, going about their business, and Fronto watched for a moment before striding up the slope, passing the others and catching up with the tribune and his weary steed.

As he approached, the man looked round at the noise and, spotting Fronto, nodded a greeting. The legate fell in beside him and matched his tired pace.

'Pleuratus. I remember you. You came to my house last year from Illyricum with Caesar.'

'Yes. It was not the most friendly of meetings, if memory serves. I fear that we were over-haughty and unused to your ways, while you were not prepared for our uninvited intrusion.'

Fronto shrugged.

'I was probably having a bad day.'

'You were hung over. But then, after a year in Gaul, I have to admit to waking with a thumping head more often than used to be the case.'

Fronto paused for a moment, trying to work out whether he should be taking offence at the words. Deciding it was probably a gesture of equality rather than an insult, he smiled.

'You were assigned to the Ninth last year' Fronto said. 'But not this year? Strikes me as a bit demeaning? A tribune on courier duty, I mean.'

Pleuratus nodded, his face slightly sour.

'It does not sit well with me, I must admit. I agreed to act as a courier for personal missives with the general's family, not to carry messages for thugs and lowlifes.'

The tribune glanced up at Fronto as if suddenly realising that he had said something he should not. 'Still, at least I won't have to traipse into the forests of Germania and share a sponge stick with anyone, and that has to be a bonus.'

Fronto nodded and plastered a smile across his face as, behind it, his mind raced back and forth between the general and his 'special' courier, Clodius in Rome following senators around, and his sister, his sort-of-betrothed, and his old friend in the depths of the city's intrigues. His spine began to itch at the thought.

'Can you do me a favour, Pleuratus?'

'What would that be?'

'When you get back to Rome, find the house of Quintus Lucilius Balbus on the Cispian hill and deliver a message for me?'

'Of course, Fronto. I'll come and see you to collect it before I leave. It may be a few days yet, hopefully.'

Fronto nodded absently. Something about the way Caesar had reacted to the letter suggested strongly that Clodius had once again overstepped the mark. The very thought that Faleria, Lucilia and Balbus were caught up in the affair make the hair stand proud on his arms.

* * * * *

Fronto stood on the ramp and took a deep breath.

The earth embankment rose from the downward-sloping turf near the bank to a full height of some ten feet, where it gave onto the first sections of the bridge.

Four days of construction and the beast of a structure now spanned some thirty or forty feet of the water. For four days Fronto had managed to avoid having to set a single foot on the thing. In the selfish corners of his soul he was grateful that Caesar had given the bulk of the construction work to the Seventh and not the trusted Tenth.

No matter the numerous and high quality libations and offerings the officers and men of the legions made to every Roman and native god they could name, progress was slow and dreadfully dangerous.

Each of the last three evenings, the reports had come in with fresh and wearying results: legionaries crushed by falling timbers, tipped into the swift flow and carried away screaming toward the sea, succumbing to a myriad of insane accidents. It was almost as though the construction was cursed.

Fronto eyed the timber with suspicion and nervousness.

What was already built certainly looked solid enough, but the thing still put the shits up him beyond all thought and reason. He had the horrible feeling that something nasty was lined up by the Fates to happen to him today.

The legates were taking turns on duty at the bridge construction site and, fight it all he could, today was Fronto's turn. He'd woken with a feeling of dread and disgust, only to discover that the thong on which his Fortuna pendant hung had broken and the lucky charm itself had vanished somehow, despite never having left his person outside his tent.

It was a bad omen.

As was being summoned by the centurion of the works, via a tired looking legionary with a bruise on his face the size of his hand – the result of yet another accident.

With pulse racing, Fronto stepped the last few paces of the great turf and rubble embankment and placed a foot warily on the timber walkway of the bridge.

Eleven deaths and twenty eight wounds – seven of them crippling – in just four days of work. Fronto had been determined not to add his own name to that grisly list, and had had a small tent erected near the bridge from which he could watch the work in the safety and comfort of the shelter.

And now, despite all his precautions, ill luck and the actions of others had conspired to bring him to this point: standing on the recently cut and shaped timbers, watching the grey-brown torrent rushing past below, visible through the side rail. The bridge wanted him, of that he was beginning to become convinced.

With a deep breath and a nervous swallow, he took a step forward, alarmed at how the beam bowed very slightly beneath his foot. Lifting it urgently, he retreated a pace. The legionary beside him, sweating from his exertions and wiping away blood from a narrow cut on his forehead, frowned.

'It's alright, sir. It's just settling very slightly. There's going to be a small amount of give until it's properly bedded-in. Once a few carts have been across it it'll be solid as a rock.'

'And in the meantime, I'm supposed to trust my weight to wood that bends?'

'Look, sir.' The legionary grinned as he jumped up and down heavily on the plank, his hobnailed boots leaving small indentations, clouds of sawdust billowing out from beneath the walkway. Fronto grasped the rail in horror, holding on for dear life.

'Stopthatstopthatstopthatdstopthat!' he rattled out nervously.

'Safe as houses, sir.'

'I've been in houses that have fallen down. Come on.'

Swallowing his nerves, he took three quick steps before allowing himself a breath. The bridge seemed unnaturally high, and the far bank distant enough that the woodlands covering much of it blurred into a single mass of green.

Tearing his gaze away from the far side and the river rushing beneath him, Fronto fixed his eyes on the centurion standing close to the current work site at the far end of the walkway, a small group of workmen and engineers gathered around him. Avoiding thinking further on the planks beneath him, he concentrated instead on the men.

They stood in a knot around a small mound that was barely recognisable in shape – just a grey-brown lump on the timber surface.

'Legate?' the centurion saluted as he approached. Most of the workers turned and followed suit, others unable to do so due to the burdens they bore.

'Your man tells me we have another fatality to add to the list.'

The centurion gestured to the men around him and, saluting, they scurried off past Fronto toward the landward end of the bridge, their passage shaking the timbers worryingly. Fronto gripped the rail until his knuckles whitened and frowned as he looked down at the dirty lump that lay between the two of them. The last workmen lowered their burdens and moved off out of earshot at the centurion's gesture. Once they were alone, the centurion crouched by the body.

Fronto could not help but notice with a heart-stopping realisation just how close to the open end of the bridge the man crouched. A strong gust of wind might just blow him back into the water. He resisted the urge to tell the centurion to come away from the edge. Gingerly, he crouched to join the strange conspiratorial tableau.

'Well?'

'I tried not to let too much on to the men, sir, but we fished him out from the debris where the next pile was being settled half an hour ago. He's been in the water a day or two now at least.'

The centurion reached out and rolled the bloated, discoloured thing onto its back so that Fronto could see what he was explaining. The legate felt the bile rise in his throat and had to swallow it and steady himself with his fingertips on the timber floor. The body was barely recognisable as a human, the skin blue-grey and bloated, with a waxy sheen. A green tint of algae had mixed in with the black, curly hair, along with scum and weed. The man's white tunic had been stained an unpleasant grey-green.

'Not pretty, is it, sir.'

Fronto shook his head, trying not to breathe too deeply.

'We'll have to try and check into missing soldiers – see if we can identify him.'

'That shouldn't be hard, sir.'

Fronto frowned in incomprehension. 'Meaning?'

The centurion reached out with a pointing finger and jabbed the stained tunic. 'A white tunic, sir. Not a red one. He's an officer, not a legionary.'

Fronto blinked. How had he missed something so obvious? A white tunic. His eyes ran down from the face, past the shoulder and to the upper arm. Yes. There it was: a broad stripe. A senior tribune.

He rocked back on his heels and nearly fell as he realised he was looking at the days-old, bloated corpse of tribune Pleuratus, Caesar's personal courier. He'd assumed the man was still mooching around the camp waiting for the general's summons to ride back to Rome.

'How the hell did he end up in the river?' Fronto asked quietly, already acknowledging the cold certainty in his belly that it had been no accident.

'That's one of the reasons I sent everyone away as soon as I'd had a good look at the body, sir. Rumour will get out, of course, but not for a day or two.'

His pointing finger moved on from the white tunic to the bloated grey-blue flesh of the man's hands and lower arms. A dark, black ring ran around the wrist. A glance across at the far side confirmed that the mark existed on both wrists.

'His arms were bound?'

'Behind his back, I believe. There's similar marks on his ankles. The rope's gone somehow. Don't know whether the knot had come undone, or maybe a fish ate it or something, but whatever the case, the rope's gone. That means I can't confirm it, but I'm pretty sure whoever did it tied a big rock behind his back and dropped him in the water. I'd guess they expected it to sink into the mud and disappear, but the rope's come away and the rock's sunk, so the body's floated up to the surface.'

Fronto stared at the tribune's body. A horrible suspicion was beginning to form in his gut.

'Do me a favour, centurion, Keep a lid on this as long as you have to. Threaten all the men who were here or bribe them; whatever you have to do to stop this becoming common knowledge. Help me wrap him up in that sacking over there and we'll take him to the medical section for now.'

* * * * *

'I thought there'd be wine and dice. The 'loose women' thing was too much to hope for, but one expects at least wine and dice in the tent of the great Fronto.'

The legate of the Tenth allowed his customary scowl to do its work in quietening Priscus and then sat back on his bunk.

'I thought, given the nature of this conversation it would be worthwhile being as sober as possible, though I have to admit to the temptation to be otherwise.'

He turned to Carbo. 'Did you station men like I asked?'

'Not a man within earshot and no one will get near without trouble. They're all good, honest men – as far as such a man can be found in Rome these days. The three nearest tents have been uprooted and moved just in case. Now, break the spell and tell us all what's so damn suspicious that we need such privacy?'

Fronto allowed his gaze to wander past Carbo and then Priscus, over the rest of the men he'd called to the tent. They represented every man whom he trusted with his life. Each man in this tent he would willingly leap in front of a pilum for and he was almost certain the same could be said in return. In a way it was an impressive thing to ponder on, but pondering on it too much led to a certain dismay at the diminished number of them, and at the missing faces he would have on that list: Velius and Balbus particularly.

Representing the Tenth: Carbo, Atenos and Petrosidius, the chief signifer and a longstanding colleague. Priscus: the camp prefect. Varus and Galronus of the cavalry. Balventius, the primus pilus of the Eighth. Crispus, the legate of the Eleventh and Galba, that of the Twelfth.

Nine men.

Nine men he felt he could trust beyond reason and word.

Nine men that he would accept the opinions of and who felt at ease speaking to him as though to a friend rather than a superior or colleague.

'It's about these deaths' he said flatly.

'Deaths?' Crispus sat upright. 'You mean Tetricus? I was hoping to share a libation with you to his memory after the funeral, but duty seems to have kept us apart. There are more deaths than Tetricus?'

Galba shuffled in the seat next to him. 'Others caused by… by Romans?'

Fronto sighed. Time to fill in all the missing details.

'I realise that we've been almost constantly active since we met up in Mediomatrici lands. We haven't had the customary weeks of reacquainting ourselves and we haven't had our usual social meet-ups. Let me give you a bit of a rundown.'

Holding up a hand, he extended his forefinger.

'Publius Pinarius Posca. I expect some of you know the name. I didn't. Nephew of Caesar; son-in-law of his eldest sister. He set off from Ostia on the same trireme as myself, as well as Galronus' he nodded at the Remi chieftain who was nodding grimly, 'and also the Pompeian centurions Fabius and Furius from the Seventh, and Menenius and Hortius – those peacocks in the Fourteenth. It would appear that we all separated as groups for our journey north. Whether Pinarius took on local guides and guards I don't know. I assume so, as he hardly seemed rugged and capable – I suspect he was still breast fed into his twenties. Either way, he only made it as far as Vienna, north of Massilia, where he was dispatched with a single pugio thrust to the heart. Stabbed in the back and buried under firewood.'

The number of surprised looks shared by the occupants of the tent clarified just how little had been said about this.

'*Caesar's* nephew?' Balventius sat forward. 'Murdered en route to the army? What has the general done about it?'

'Precisely nothing. He seemed to be less than impressed with the poor young moron. In fact, he seemed to think it would make his life easier; it was certainly hardly advertised. I was intending to investigate as much as I could and I made a few enquiries, but the business of war has somewhat impeded any investigation.'

Crispus frowned. 'You should have enlisted us all.'

'At the time, I thought it better to keep it as low-key as possible. Things have now changed.'

'So,' Varus said, hissing through his teeth as he moved his slung arm without thinking. 'So, you're convinced that the person who put a Roman knife in Caesar's nephew stuck the same knife in Tetricus? It does seem rather too much for coincidence.'

Fronto and Galronus were both nodding.

'It gets better, Varus. The head wound I saw the medicus about a few days ago was not, as is generally believed, a drunken fall. I know the rumours my reputation sows, and in this case I've fostered the rumour. But in fact, the thing that nearly took the top of my head off was a sling bullet. Someone hidden in the trees tried to send me to Elysium hot on the heels of Tetricus. Less than an hour later, in fact.'

Carbo and Atenos exchanged glances. 'Then we need to tighten security in the Tenth. It's time you formed yourself a bodyguard like legates are supposed to.'

Fronto shook his head in irritation. 'Firstly, I can quite do without having half a dozen men accompany me every time I go to the shitter. Secondly, I want to catch these bastard murderers in the act, not make it impossible for them to strike. If they've failed to get me once, they're likely to try again, so I need people to keep their eyes open around me rather than stand with their shields raised.'

The nods around the room were accompanied by the soft burble of low conversation. Fronto waited for a moment and then cracked his knuckles as he took a deep breath.

'There's more to it yet, though.'

Silence fell, leaving an expectant vacuum.

'A couple of hours ago, while on duty at the bridge, the centurion in charge hauled a body out of the Rhenus. He'd been there for around three days by the medicus' estimate. We've kept the lid on this so far, but it'll get out into the rumour mill soon enough. The man was Caesar's personal courier, a former senior tribune in the Ninth.'

Priscus unfolded his arms, leaning forward. 'Pleuratus?'

'The very same. Tied to a rock and dropped in the river so that we'd never know had the ropes not come away.' He took a deep breath and leaned back, steepling his fingers for a moment until he realised just how much he must look like Caesar in such a pose and quickly unknotted them.

'So that's the situation. Three men dead: Caesar's nephew, his private courier, and my senior tribune, along with one attempt on my own life. And things seem to be speeding up. Before anything else happens, I think we need to try and shine a light on the culprits. So what links us all and who might want us all dead?'

Galronus scratched his chin and looked around the group of friends. 'Am I stating the obvious when I mention Fabius and Furius? Where have they been on each occasion?'

'They claim, as you know, to have been travelling separately to Pinarius. They were certainly in the thick of it in the Germanic camp when Tetricus was first attacked. Other than that, Tetricus' murder, the attack on me and the drowning of Pleuratus have all happened in camp. We can enquire about the pair, but the chances of being able to narrow down their exact location are tiny, especially with Cicero hovering protectively round them like a mother hen.'

'But you suspect them' Priscus said quietly – a statement rather than a question.

'I would like to. People keep telling me that it's my prejudices against Pompeian veterans serving with us, but I hope not.'

'As an outsider – of sorts' Atenos added, alluding to his Gallic origins and his centurion status, 'I would have to point out that if the attackers *were* anti-Caesarean, then the link is fairly self-evident.'

'Go on.'

'Well. Caesar's own kin. The man to whom he entrusts his personal letters. Yourself?'

'Me? I argue with the hard-faced old bastard more than anyone in the command.'

'Yes,' Priscus said quietly, 'but usually to save him from himself. You've been supporting the man all the way through Gaul. You defend him when he's attacked. Whatever you consider yourself, to an outsider you're Caesar's man through and through.'

'And what of Tetricus?' Fronto said calmly. 'He's no Caesarean man.'

'But he's yours. Perhaps that's enough.'

'Or' Varus added quietly, 'that's something different entirely.'

All eyes turned to him.

'Well I'm sure I'm not the only person who saw those two centurions cast the evil eye over Tetricus in a briefing a while back. There's no love lost between the three, I'd say.'

'So is that what we think?' Fronto said quietly. 'That two men, possibly even still in the pay of Pompey Magnus are taking opportunities to do away with Caesar's closest or most important men?'

'It seems feasible at least.'

Fronto nodded as his mind furnished him with a damning image of Furius and Fabius gripping a broken pilum and a bloodied knife. How to get them to reveal themselves without Cicero interfering? Now that was the next problem.

* * * * *

Something was clearly screwed up with the planning, that much was certain. Fronto stood looking at the ramp from his little duty officer's tent and thought dark thoughts about Priscus, the man who was almost certainly responsible.

He had never been that good a student and mathematics was far from his strong point but, to his mind, they were on the eighth day of bridge construction and there were eight legionary legates present. How he had drawn the duty twice was not a question of mathematics, but one of wicked intent.

Priscus.

He could almost see the camp prefect grinning as he made the marks on the duty roster by the flickering light of the oil lamp in his tent.

An unseasonal shower had woken the legate before dawn, pattering on the leather of the tent roof, and had not let up all morning, finally beginning to penetrate into the parched, cracked, dry ground, softening the turf and dampening the moods of the men in general. The drizzle seemed set in for the day, pattering down from a pale grey, gloomy sky and slowing work on the bridge, making conditions on the slippery timber piles even more dangerous.

Still, it would soon be over.

The great span of Caesar's – Mamurra's – masterpiece stretched out across the wide Rhenus toward the far bank, with only three sections remaining to be put in place. The engineer had confirmed that the bridge would be complete by nightfall the next day – a spectacular nine days and almost to the unrealistic schedule that Caesar had set. Of course, the engineer had set his estimate back by a day this morning, given the turn in the weather, but even *ten* days was still an astounding feat.

And Fronto had to admit that when he'd taken the morning stroll across the completed sections, they now felt as secure as any bridge he'd ever crossed.

He paused in the act of giving himself a shave with his dagger and listened intently, frowning. There had been a change in the general distant murmur of noise. Only a tiny change and only for a moment, but a change that any experienced officer would spot instantly.

He was already running, pugio sliding back into the scabbard at his belt, when the cornu rang out with the warning call. As Fronto pounded up the ramp and onto the slippery timbers, he could already see men running back across the bridge. Behind him almost a century of armed and armoured legionaries answered the call, running onto the ramp, shields held ready and blades out, preparing to leap into action.

The unarmoured work gang legionaries had dropped their tools and loads, while the eight man contubernium that was the entire fighting-ready force on the bridge itself could be seen at the far end with the centurion's crest bobbing around among them.

Slipping a couple of times on the slimy wood, Fronto managed to keep his feet along the length of the structure, the near-eighty men on military duty hammering along behind and gradually catching up.

Fronto, wondering what had caused the warning, found his answer as a legionary ran past him, panting, without even raising a salute or looking at him, clutching his left arm from which the shaft of an arrow protruded, the scraggy grey feathers dirty and unpleasant. Rivulets of dark blood ran down his sweating, dirty arm, joining the grime and diffusing in the rain.

The legate turned his attention back to the group ahead and could now see that the centurion had formed his eight men into a small 'testudo' tortoise formation to shelter them from the dozens of falling arrows and to provide a shield to protect those men who were still fleeing the construction area.

Fronto's practiced and professional eye told him that they were at the very furthest range of the unseen archers. Most of the arrows were plummeting into the grey-brown torrents of the Rhenus, stippled by raindrops. A few had struck the timbers and lodged there, and perhaps one arrow in a dozen was actually making it to the bridge works.

The section that had just been lowered into place was still loose; the ropes, pegs and nails that would secure it lying untended on the deck.

'Get back!' Fronto bellowed at the centurion and his small party. The legionaries behind him finally came alongside as the centurion turned to see the legate pelting toward him.

'Not yet, sir!' His eyes flitting to either side of the legate, he addressed the arriving soldiers. 'First four contubernia join your mates and form a barrier. The rest of you lash and nail this bastard in place as quick as you can and then we'll pull back. I'm not having this section wash away on *my* watch!'

Falling in behind the small testudo of shields, Fronto crouched a little next to the centurion who stood proud as though nothing in the world could harm him. Men fell into place around them, creating a solid shield barrier against the arrows falling all across the bridge's lip.

Behind, the other men had dropped their shields and swords and were hurriedly securing the latest section of bridge. Despite the shield wall and all the protection it gave, even as they all fell into place and went about their tasks, two men dropped among the ropes and beams with black shafts protruding from head or chest. Another fell from the shieldwall, a man who had kept his shield too high, screeching as an arrow slammed into his shin just above the ankle, almost pinning him to the bridge. As he fell backward, other shields resettled to fill the gap.

'We have to pull back. There are hundreds of them.'

'As soon as we have the bridge secured, sir.'

Fronto watched with desperate impatience as the men hurried about the business of nailing and roping the section down.

'They'd better be bloody quick. We're going to lose a lot of men if we stay here.'

Even as he spoke another worker shrieked and vanished over the side into the roiling water, an arrow protruding from his neck. A grunt from the shieldwall announced a glancing blow.

'This is nothing, sir. You wait 'til we start the next section and we come into proper range.'

Fronto shook his head in anger. 'We can't have the men work under these conditions. It's not viable. Can we maybe have a missile troop drawn up here to clear out the far bank?'

Two more screams sounded as men collapsed to the ground, writhing and groaning.

'No good, sir. We can't fit an archery unit on here while the men work around them, and if you just put the archers up here and try and clear them out, they'll just disappear into the woods and wait until an easy target turns up. They're barbarians, but they're not daft.'

Fronto reached out and pushed a man's shield back into place.

'Stop paying attention to us talking and keep that bloody shield in place!' he snapped and, turning back to the centurion. 'Well, we'll have to do *something*. We've got to clear those archers out if we want to finish the bridge.'

One of the legionaries bellowed from the side that the section was secure and the centurion smiled grimly.

'Sound the defended retreat. Shields up until we're at least twenty paves along the bridge. *Then* you can run!'

Fronto turned, feeling the slight give in the boards underfoot, and fell in with the legionaries as they beat an ordered retreat along the bridge, workers picking up their shields and blades as they moved, joining the defensive lines.

A dozen paces further and the last arrow fell a long way short of the men, the enemy shots ceasing and leaving just the eerie patter of rain on the timber. Fronto looked around the sullen century of men who stomped alongside him, five casualties being helped along and two dead carried by their companions. At least two more had disappeared beneath the surface of the Rhenus.

As the rain spattered his face, Fronto nodded in answer to his own silent question. There was only really one solution to the problem.

Chapter 10
(The Rhine)

Fronto held on for dear life as the wood clenched in his whitening fingers bucked and spun.

'Whose stupid shitty idea was this?'

'You really need an answer to that, sir?' Atenos grinned from the front of the low, flat boat where he stood boldly in a pose reminiscent of the great Colossus, seemingly uncaring of the lurching of the vessel with every churning trough or peak of the roiling surface. The rain, now a constant sheet of water, battered their forms, pinging off the metal of their armour and soaking into every inch of clothing.

'*I* shouldn't have come, though. You could quite easily have done it without me.'

'I think it's better that you did, sir, in the end.'

Fronto looked up from the rail and noticed the huge Gaulish centurion's eyes flicking meaningfully past him to the rear of the boat. Trusting in Fortuna and releasing one claw-like hand from the boat's hull, Fronto turned, his gaze taking in the dozen other boats in the small, scattered flotilla before coming to rest on the figure at the rear: the object of Atenos' scornful look.

Tribune Menenius of the Fourteenth sat alone on the bench, the rest of the men keeping away from him – possibly out of respect for his rank, though Fronto somehow doubted it. The youthful, foppish tribune looked utterly dejected and a little frightened.

Once again, Fronto cursed his luck for ending up with the ineffectual little turd as a second in command. It would be easy to blame Plancus, the legate of the Fourteenth, but Fronto knew deep down it was a symptom of having lost his Fortuna pendant.

The plan had been simple enough: to take the boats the Ubii had donated and use them to ferry a small force across, downriver and out of sight, then to move stealthily up the east bank and fall on the archers that plagued the building work.

Simple.

So simple that anyone could have commanded it.

A dozen Ubii scouts had been brought into the force, but the bulk of the expedition would be made up of the men of the

Fourteenth: Gauls themselves, who may be able to pass as locals along with the scouts during the stealthy approach. So simple.

Until Plancus had volunteered to lead the mission, given that it was his men who had been selected. Fronto had suffered a momentary premonition of how the attack might proceed under the cretinous direction of the unimaginative legate of the Fourteenth. So harrowing was his mental image that he had found himself standing forward and demanding that he lead the attack, it being his idea. Plancus had been so outraged he had almost spat teeth, but Fronto was adamant; his plan, his responsibility.

And so, having tricked himself into coming along, he had added a century of his own men from the Tenth into the force, troops upon whom he knew he could rely. Specifically the men of Atenos, the first century of the second cohort, a number of whom shared the Gallic origin of their officer. It seemed the only sensible course of action.

Yet Plancus had still refused to relinquish control of his men to his brother legate and the resulting appointment had left a sour taste in Fronto's mouth. Menenius, a junior tribune with, apparently, no combat experience, would accompany him as a second.

The tribune looked up from beneath his sodden brown cloak, feeling the eyes of the other two officers on him. He cast an unhappy glance back at them and then lowered his eyes to his feet once more, lifting his sopping boots from the quarter of a foot of water that filled the bottom of the boat – yet another thing that sent cold shudders down Fronto's spine.

Like it or not, he was clearly saddled with this man. Gritting his teeth and holding his breath, the legate of the Tenth nodded to Atenos and stood, rocking unsteadily as he gingerly made his way along the wide, flat craft between the legionaries pressed together against the rain, rowing for all they were worth to try and stay with the other boats despite the unbelievably strong current.

With a great sense of relief, Fronto arrived at the space around the tribune and sank to the bench opposite. Menenius looked up and tried to smile. The man looked like a fish – a fish out of water, Fronto thought sourly. The legate smiled with forced sympathy at his second in command.

'You don't like boats either?' he hazarded, well aware in truth of the cause of the man's nerves, but offering him an out.

Menenius sniffed, a droplet of mucus forming on the end of his nose like a six year old, which made Fronto simultaneously want to wipe it away and cuff him around the ear.

'Once we land, stick close to me. Your best centurion in the unit is Cantorix. I've met him before and seen him in action. When I give orders, Atenos will deal with his century. You relay them to Cantorix and he'll diffuse them as necessary among the other three centurions from the Fourteenth. If we get separated, remember the goal. Go as stealthily as you can to the bank opposite the bridge and separate out into a wide arc before you pounce, so they have less chance of getting away. Then keep moving the arc around so you can close them in against the bank.'

The look of panic that flashed across Menenius' face only served to increase the ire in Fronto, but he held his breath and forced the patience back into his voice.

'Have you had no experience of a fight at all? You've been a junior tribune for more than a year now in different legions. You must have been in the battles we've fought?'

'I've stood at the back, Fronto. I've occasionally had a musician send messages when required. I'm not at all cut out for this kind of thing, though. This is what centurions are for, isn't it?'

Fronto smiled, though without genuine humour.

'The centurions will do nearly everything. Just stick with me.' He reached out and tapped the ornate scabbard of the tribune's gladius. 'With any luck you won't need to use that.'

Menenius looked at the sword and sighed. Reaching down, he drew it slowly with a well-oiled hiss.

Fronto eyed the blade as it came free. Despite the showy scabbard and the eagle-embossed pommel, the blade itself was rust-free and unpitted, perfectly oiled and maintained and clearly sharp. Near the point where the tip began to taper, a pair of small nicks was visible.

'You keep your gladius in good condition, but it seems to be marked?'

Menenius looked at the blade in surprise, then spotted the nicks and nodded unhappily.

'My father. It was his sword. He served under Sertorius in Hispania – with distinction apparently, a fact that he never let me forget until his dying day. I sometimes suspect that if I let the blade rust, he'll find a way to come back from the dead just to punish me.'

Fronto sagged. The tribune was clearly more suited to some administrative role somewhere.

'Just stay close and try to stay alive.'

Menenius nodded unhappily. 'I wish Hortius was here. He'd know what to say.'

Fronto cast thanks up to the heavens to any god that was listening that this was not the case, but fixed the fake smile of sympathy to his face again and turned at a shout from Atenos.

'We're closing on the bank, sir.'

Sinking to the bench, the legate grasped the side of the boat again and clung on, watching the grassy slope approach at a worrying speed. Despite the swiftness of the river, the boats had managed to stay in reasonable formation, drifting downriver only a little more than planned.

The surface of the Rhenus hissed and spat as the rain hammered down into it, the boat's bottom wallowing in half a foot of freezing water. Fronto felt the numbing cold seeping in through the soft leather of his girlish boots and saturating the socks beneath and once again cursed Lucilia for offloading them on him and disposing of his good old hard boots. He really must get around to getting a new pair from Cita. Lucilia need never know.

The boat hit the bank with a crunch, jerking forward for a moment, the occupants lurching around briefly before leaping into action. At Atenos' command, two men leapt over the bow with a mooring rope. One produced his mallet and a heavy wooden stake and proceeded to smash the peg into the ground to make a mooring post, while the other looped the rope ready and then tied it off on the heavy stake.

As soon as the boat was secured, the rest of the legionaries and the optio disembarked and began to disperse. Within moments of the boat touching earth, the men were formed up on the grassy rise, while the two Ubii scouts drifted toward the edge of the woods that surrounded them.

Fronto clambered from the boat with a great sigh of relief, feeling his gut begin to steady itself again and his bowels unclench for the first time in more than a quarter of an hour. Scanning the ground, he nodded to himself. The landing site had been well chosen. Three miles downriver, the boats would have been invisible from the building site as they crossed even in clear weather. In this torrential downpour, they would be obscured from even close range. The landing was a gentle, grassy slope where the legionaries could assemble.

Around the river-side clearing, the woodland stretched out who knew how far. This territory was beyond the ken of any of them and the forest could cover every pace from here to the end of the world for all they knew. But as long as they kept the river in view to their right, they would locate the construction site and the enemy enclave opposite soon enough.

It seemed odd to look at the men formed up as they were: in the efficient lines of parading legionaries, yet dressed so nondescript.

The reasoning had been simple: They would in theory need only a small force to deal with the lightly armoured archers they were to face and, between the element of surprise, their superior tactics and discipline and the quality of their weapons, they should not need their pila, helmets, shields or any such kit that would clearly mark them as Roman to even the least observant passer-by.

And so the men of the Tenth and Fourteenth stood with the disciplined straight backs and raised chins of the legions, wrapped in plain wool cloaks, their only concession to equipment shirts of mail and a gladius on their belts hidden beneath the folds of wool.

In a way it irritated Fronto that while, for the first time this year, he had the opportunity to control and command a military mission with a simple battle objective and no argument, discussion, or treachery, it still required subterfuge and sneaking. It would have been nice to arm up like a legion at war and tramp the grass toward a prepared and worthy enemy, rather than to run through the woods in disguise and fall upon a poorly-armed and soggy missile unit.

Somewhere deep inside, Fronto chided himself for hoping that the enemy were better armed and prepared than expected and the possibility of a proper fight, but looking across at Atenos, he realised that the big man was clearly thinking along similar lines.

Still, a fight was a fight, and anything was better than endless arguing while good men were knifed in the back by their own side.

Menenius fell in beside him, one hand wrapped around the hilt of the gladius beneath his cloak, the fingers white with pressure.

'The last of the boats is landing, legate' he reported, his voice cracking slightly with nerves.

The men poured out of the boats and fell in alongside those already gathered in the clearing. Fronto looked across the force: five centuries of troops. Three hundred and eighty two men, given the fallen and casualties back across the river; plus the two senior officers and twenty native scouts.

Four hundred and four men. And of them, perhaps only fifty who had no command of the Gallic language. Hopefully, if anything went horribly wrong, the Ubii scouts would be able to handle it, claiming to be the warriors of a large Ubii village from downriver, forced south by Suevi advances. The women and children and wagons would be following on.

'You all know why we're here' he shouted through the siling rain. 'To finish the bridge, the enemy archers on this bank must be dealt with. We have no idea about the disposition of enemy forces on this side of the river, so go carefully and quietly. If I hear a single Latin word spoken aloud once we leave this clearing, I'll tear that man's balls off and nail them to a tree as a warning to the rest.'

The officers, of course, were discounted from such strictures, given Fronto and Menenius' almost total lack of comprehension of the local language. But then the tribune hardly seemed his usual loquacious self and, given the way he was still shaking gently, he was unlikely to draw any attention to them in enemy territory. And Fronto knew he could restrain himself.

'Leave any encounter to the Ubii if you can. If not, let those with the best Belgic dialects handle it. There should be very few native settlements or groups around here. The Ubii are all on the move due to the advances of enemy tribes, so it's likely that anyone we meet will be hostile. I'm afraid we'll just have to play it by ear. Listen to your officers and do your duty and in a few hours we'll have cleared out the east bank and Caesar's bridge will be marching toward us again. Right,' he pointed to the woodland at the northern side of the clearing where two Ubii scouts were waiting patiently 'move out!'

* * * * *

'It's a local farm' Cantorix said, so quietly he was barely audible over the rain. 'Still occupied apparently. Though I see no animals, there's smoke pouring out of the roof hole.'

Fronto leaned against the tree. For two miles as they had crept through the woodlands they had seen no sign of life, the only mark of habitation was one farmstead that had been burned out, leaving only shattered fences and the blackened stumps of a timber building. In a way, Fronto was pleased to discover life, as the journey had

182

been too tense and silently uneventful for his liking; as if they were tip-toeing across a field where he knew there was a bull hidden in the mist.

'Anything else?'

Cantorix shook his head. 'Just the smoke from the hearth. I've sent the scouts out to circle through the surrounding woods, just in case.'

The legate nodded. Two of the Ubii remained with them at the heart of the expeditionary force to act as advisors and, if necessary, interpreters. Turning, one hand on the hilt of his gladius, Fronto shook his head, creating a cascade of water from his sodden hair, and gestured to one of the guides, pointing at the farmstead, barely visible through the boles of the trees.

'What's your opinion?'

'Commander?'

'Is it likely we would encounter an isolated farm still occupied by your people, but without animals?'

The scout shrugged.

'Many still trap this side of river. They leave village; go hide when enemy near; then come back when they gone. Could be.'

The legate sighed. Hardly conclusive, as answers went.

'We'll wait for the scouts to check out the woods before we move through.'

Menenius, standing nearby with wild, nervous eyes, nodded emphatically.

The men stood among the trees, so many drab shapes blending in with the endless trunks of the woods, the rain here channelled from a constant battering force to form heavy, huge droplets that fell, swollen, from leaves and branch-tips, drenching the men beneath.

'That's the signal' murmured Cantorix.

Fronto, Menenius and Atenos stepped forward to peer between the grey boles to the misty, rain-occluded farmstead. It took them a moment to see the scouts and the legate could only commend the centurion on his eyesight. Barely visible across the farm clearing, two of the Ubii had reappeared and stood, tiny figures in a grey, wet world, waving their arm in the signal that all was clear.

The officers deflated slightly.

'Menenius? You and Cantorix take these two scouts and go speak to the farmers. We should be able to get a good deal of information about the current situation in the area. Cantorix: take a few of your men in with you but not enough to frighten the civilians. The others can form a perimeter around the building. The rest of you, with Atenos and myself, will scatter in groups around the farmstead and search, consolidate and hold until we're ready to move off again. We should be on the enemy archers sometime in the next half hour or so.'

The officers all nodded and moved off; Menenius hovering all too close to Cantorix for a Roman tribune. Fronto caught the Gallic centurion's expression at being saddled with the fop and tried not to grin.

With long-practiced hand signals, Fronto directed the centurions who stayed with him, splitting them into four groups, two of which would move around the edge of the clearing, one in each direction, keeping the woodland under surveillance alongside the scouts, while the other two would spread out across the farmstead and its buildings.

The legate grinned happily as he moved along the eastern edge of the clearing, imagining the fun Cantorix was going to have with Menenius and the scouts in the farmer's hut.

The centurion of the unit with whom Fronto moved pointed to the two scouts standing by the wood's edge, others having now returned from the shadowed forest. The two men were waving their arms again and gesturing. The centurion, his voice low and in Latin but with a noticeable Gallic accent, leaned close. 'What do they want now?'

Fronto shrugged. 'Best check.'

The centurion nodded, made a couple of arcane signals to his optio and then jogged off forward to the two scouts, who were gesticulating expansively. As the centurion closed on them, the optio strolled up alongside Fronto.

'The men are separating out into contubernia to patrol the edge, sir.'

The legate nodded his understanding and squinted through the rain at the scene ahead.

'Why are they waving like that when we have so many arranged hand signals?'

He felt the optio stiffen beside him and the man's hand grabbed his upper arm.

'Because they aren't Ubii, sir!'

Fronto frowned as the centurion ahead reached the two scouts, demanding quietly of them what all the fuss was. The legate jerked back as he saw the tip of the Germanic long sword suddenly burst from the centurion's back in a shower of blood. Even as the forest's edge erupted with warriors, Fronto turned to order the musician and signifer to raise the alarm, but too late. A bellow of shocked pain rang out from the farmer's hut and was immediately joined by others from the various buildings as the trap snapped shut.

The discordant, horrible Celtic horns rang out and Fronto was drawing his sword and letting his cloak fall to the floor even as he saw Cantorix stagger out of the central hut clutching his side and swinging his sword, bellowing at his men. No sign of Menenius yet. Suddenly, what looked like half the world's barbarians were pouring from the treeline into the clearing.

The cornicen a few paces from Fronto was busy bleating out the alarm when the notes became a gurgle, a tribesman's sword slamming into his neck in a backslash hard enough to snap the spine. In a sudden explosion of activity they were in the midst of battle. The century around Fronto had not had the time and warning to form a defensive line and lacked shields and helmets, the fighting already devolving into a melee of individual duels.

There was no opportunity to call out a strategy or gather the men to him.

Turning again, his sword out, Fronto barely had time to raise it and knock aside the blow that was coming for him, the sheer strength of the strike when the blades met numbing his arm and sending shock waves through the joints up to his shoulder. He looked into the eyes of his opponent, a Germanic brute a good foot taller than he, with a dense, unkempt beard and his hair only kept from his eyes by a topknot. The man wore nothing but bronze arm rings and a torc at his neck, his nakedness no shame or hardship in combat, with designs drawn on his chest in black mud. His eyes bore that crazed, unstoppable look that Fronto had seen before. A man who could only be stopped with a hard death.

The barbarian drew back his sword and swung again. Aware that his gladius was barely able to deflect the strength of a powerful blow from such a long weapon, Fronto slackened his knees and dropped into a crouch as the sword swung past above him at his former neck height.

Ridiculously, even as he stabbed up with the gladius into the big man's vitals, the thoughts that suddenly crowded his mind were of how much his knees ached when he dropped and how much effect his age was having on his combat abilities. Would he really, realistically, be able to lead an assault like this for much longer?

The roar of the stricken barbarian stirred him from such disturbing and poorly-timed thoughts and he sank back into the crouch, ripping his blade from the man's bladder, twisting it as it came out. Roaring and spraying blood down onto the legate, the tribesman seemed oblivious to the mortal wound he'd been dealt, apparently entirely impervious to the pain as he rocked back and clasped the hilt of his huge sword in both hands, preparing to bring it down on Fronto in a chop.

The legate stabbed up again with his blade, severing the man's thigh artery and slicing through muscle in an attempt to unbalance him. Still standing solid despite the wounds, the barbarian's sword came down like the falling sky, preparing to end the life of the last scion of the Falerii. Fronto left his sword jutting from the huge, bulbous thigh and dropped, trying to fall out of the way of the blow, horribly aware of the fact that the falling sword was moving too fast to dodge.

His last moments of thought were of the missing Fortuna amulet, then of the men he had led to their doom and finally, painfully, of Lucilia standing by the threshold of the newly-renovated Falerius townhouse, the sacrificial bull lowing nearby as she waited for the iron ring he would never be able to give her.

The glinting blade swept down to split his skull and was met by the upward swing of a gladius and a pugio that crossed to block it. Fronto stared up at the meeting of three blades, a shower of sparks raining down on him, and felt his bowels give just a little at how close he'd just come to being an ex-legate.

As another sword took the barbarian in the chest and drove him away from sight, the sword and dagger uncrossed and the face of the optio appeared, all concern.

'You alright, sir? Thought you were a gonner for a moment.'

'Juno's arse, so did I' Fronto grinned up at him as he clambered to his feet, knees creaking as he went. He almost fell again as his left knee gave way, painfully twisted.

'Looks like we're starting to get it together sir.'

'We are?' Fronto looked around in astonishment and saw that it was true. In less than two dozen heartbeats, the men around the clearing had gone from being beleaguered groups into defensive squares, holding their own against the enemy. It was astounding, given the speed of the sudden turnaround and the fact that Fronto had been unable even to think about giving the right signals.

Signals.

That was it. He was suddenly aware of the cornu calls ringing out across the farmstead and the circling standards organising the centuries into fighting forces.

That was a command call.

His eyes drifted toward the farmer's hut, where a dozen men stood in a defensive knot around Cantorix and Menenius. The Gallic centurion was leaning heavily on a stick and clutching his side, but Menenius was gesticulating with the centurion's vine staff while standard bearers and musicians relayed the tribune's orders across the open ground.

Fronto stared in disbelief and yet, even as he watched, the century around him reformed in the face of brutal attack, creating an organised defensive line. Their lack of shields was resulting in a much higher casualty rate than one would normally expect but at least now they were holding, rather than being slaughtered in a disorganised chaos.

He turned to the optio.

'You got everything under control here?'

'We'll manage, sir.'

With the briefest of nods, Fronto turned and limped at speed for the central buildings of the farm. His mind formed a picture of the optio who had just saved his life and he committed that image to memory so that he could find him later and buy him enough wine to float a quinquereme. In fact, given the fate of his commander, the man would probably be a centurion by the time Fronto got to thank him properly.

The centre of the farm showed signs of hard fighting. Eight or nine barbarian bodies lay around in the dirt, the rain diffusing the blood from their wounds into the muddy puddles. Three legionaries lay among them, and Cantorix was clutching a torso wound from which blood was blossoming, leaking through the links in his mail. Apart from the inconvenience, he seemed to be ignoring the wound, which was entirely in keeping with the centurion Fronto remembered from the thickest fighting last year.

The big surprise was tribune Menenius. Standing as straight and tall as one of the statues of the great generals that stood in the forum, the tribune's sword hung by his side in his right hand, watery blood coating the blade, while he continued to issue commands, pointing with the stick in his free hand.

Fronto stared as he staggered forward wearily, his knee clicking painfully.

'Menenius?'

The tribune spotted Fronto and his face broke out into a wide, relieved smile.

'Legate Fronto? Thank the gods. I think we're going to survive, sir.'

'How the hell?' Fronto stared at him, using his free arm to take in the whole battle with the sweep of an arm. 'What did...?'

Cantorix straightened, holding his wound. 'The tribune shows a remarkable grasp of military strategy, legate.'

'And he's bloodied his sword too.'

The centurion nodded. 'Saved my damn life, sir. Fast as a bloody snake, sir.'

Fronto's stare turned into a frown. 'Menenius?'

'Sort of lucky with the sword, legate.'

'Lucky, my arse' Cantorix grinned.

'My father paid for some very expensive weapon training in my youth' the tribune said humbly. 'Not had much chance to put it into action before, but it seems I can remember enough.'

Cantorix's eyes told Fronto that it had been a little more than that, but he let it go for a moment. 'And you put out the signals?'

'With the centurion's advice here.'

'My arse' repeated Cantorix.

'I've studied the historians, sir. History is replete with examples of how to turn an ambush against the ambushers. It's all a matter of maintaining control. They expected easy pickings and panic. As soon as we take control the panic passes to them.'

Fronto glanced around the clearing. The barbarians were melting away into the woodland, their easy victory snatched from them in moments.

They had *won*!

'We were hit hard' he noted, assessing the situation with the practiced eye of a man who had surveyed many a battlefield. 'I reckon we lost over a third of the men; maybe even half.' He turned back to Menenius. 'But without your help, we'd have been lost altogether. Caesar'll hear about this, tribune. I may have underestimated you, and I think the general needs to hand out a few phalera for this.'

Menenius looked down with a strangely shy, boyish smile.

'I'd rather go unsung, if you don't mind, sir. Cantorix here deserves the real credit.'

Fronto, surprised at meeting a self-effacing junior tribune, looked at Cantorix and the man's expression left him in no doubt as to just how much of this was the tribune's doing.

'Perhaps, Menenius, but I'd love to transfer you to the Tenth.'

* * * * *

The men of the Tenth and Fourteenth legions jogged through the woods as fast as the terrain and unit cohesion would allow, their cloaks discarded to prevent snagging on branches or entangling in armour and scabbards. All pretence had now been thrown to the wind in favour of speed. Fronto had bound his weak knee with a thick strip of torn cloak, and tried to limp as little as possible, biting his lip against the pain and discomfort. A number of the men, in fact, had used the discarded cloaks to bind or pack wounds that they could run with, including Cantorix who had pushed half a garment beneath his mail shirt and proceeded to completely ignore the wound at his ribs.

In the light of the enemy's recent attack and the lack of information about the barbarians' disposition it had been a difficult decision to make. On the one hand, perhaps this had been an entirely coincidental encounter and this band of warriors was unconnected to the archers at the riverbank, in which case by discarding their disguise they further endangered themselves on the journey. More likely, though, this attack had been carried out in concert with a grand plan and therefore the barbarian archers must know they were coming. In that case speed was now of the essence. To move slowly or indecisively was to allow the possibility that the ambushers would regroup and link up with the archers.

Fronto swallowed as he ran, tense at that very thought. They would have roughly equal numbers to the archers now that they had lost so many men, but enough ambushers had escaped to make the odds almost three to one if the two barbarian forces joined up. Not good odds when lacking shields, pila and helmets.

'Sir' barked Atenos, away to his right, ducking through the trees as though born to the forest, his great size apparently causing him no difficulty.

Fronto angled his run and jumped a fallen branch, almost falling as he landed favouring his bad knee, and falling in alongside the huge Gaul with a slightly more pronounced limp.

'What?'

'The bridge' Atenos pointed off to the side. Fronto squinted and could just make out between the blur of passing tree trunks, through the mist of torrential rain, the dark grey mass of Caesar's bridge arcing out of the distant mist, rising as it strode toward them. For the first time, seeing it from this side and angle, he realised just what an impressive piece of engineering it was.

Fronto nodded. 'Pass the word.'

As Atenos turned and yelled for his men to pull closer together and watch for pickets, Fronto moved left and bellowed the order to Cantorix and the others. Menenius, pale and apparently as shaken by what he himself had done as by what had been done to them, moved along behind, his hand gripping the hilt of his gladius as though it might leap from the scabbard and start slicing people.

Fronto faced forward again, just in time to see movement ahead. A grey shape like the ghost of a warrior disappeared behind a tree, just as another humanoid bulk loomed in the mist and then faded again. Ahead, a cry went up in a deep, guttural tongue, quickly taken up by other voices.

'Take 'em fast, lads. Fast as you can, then rally at the riverbank!'

Ignoring the bulbous raindrops bursting against his face, Fronto hefted his gladius and ran, leaping over fallen wood and ducking the worst of the branches, ignoring the fire burning in his knee and the constant danger of folding up into the undergrowth. His heart pounded as something passed close to his ear with a 'zzzzzip' noise and thudded into a tree.

The air was suddenly alive with arrows, whipping through the woodland, many thudding into trees or being pushed off course by fronds and leaves, but too many for comfort sheathing themselves in the men of the legions.

A soldier was suddenly at Fronto's left, sword in hand, teeth bared as the rain battered him. Fronto turned to give him an encouraging grin but was too late as an arrow took the man, dead centre in the neck, punching through his throat apple and hurling him backward to fall gurgling among the undergrowth. A moment later another man joined the legate, and he spotted Cantorix just beyond the new arrival, ahead of his men and bellowing a battle cry in a Gallic tongue that Fronto was surprised he was starting to understand a little.

The depths of the forest became slowly, imperceptibly lighter, though the running legionaries were too busy to notice. Fronto's battle-honed wits began to tell him that something was wrong as the mist brightened and it took him only a moment to realise that the arrows had ceased. Not a single missile whipped through the shade.

'Halt!' he bellowed urgently, too late for some.

The front runners, those eager for the kill and for revenge on these damned Germanic warriors who had ambushed them and killed good friends, suddenly found they had run or leapt clear of the edge of the forest in their enthusiasm.

A few paces behind, Fronto and Cantorix came to a halt, most of the legionaries joining them, watching with held breath as the scene unfolded.

Almost a score of men had burst from the forest's edge, yelling their blood lust to the sky, to the waiting ears of Mars, Minerva, Jupiter and Fortuna, and suddenly found themselves on springy turf, enveloped in a mist formed by wind-swirled rain. Slowing to a confused halt, they exchanged worried glances, the impetus of their attack suddenly swept away, swords ready for an enemy that was not there.

Somewhere behind them they became aware of their centurions and officers calling them back, but even as they recognised the orders, the mist parted like billowing curtains in front of them to reveal a wall of humanity, three men deep and stretching from side to side, the ends lost in the grey.

And they all had bows, the strings drawn back to their ears the arrows nocked and ready.

'Shit!' yelled Artorius, excused duty legionary of the third cohort, second century of the Fourteenth legion, and closed his eyes.

Fronto watched with leaden expectation as the arrows of three dozen archers punched into the chests of the exposed legionaries, every man felled like a tree, falling to their knees and then faces, or thrown back onto the grass, staring up into the grey, searching for the gods that had deserted them.

The men of the legions remaining in the forest instinctively began to move back between the trees, further away from the threat.

'How far do you reckon that open ground is?' Fronto called across to Cantorix.

'About thirty paces, I reckon, sir.'

'So it'd take an exceptional archer to get off more than one shot while we crossed it?'

Cantorix grinned. '*Exceptional*, sir. And they'll be using sinew bowstrings. The rain'll be playing havoc with 'em, sir. Half of 'em will be useless already and the rest'll only manage a couple more arrows before they're ruined.'

'On me!' Fronto bellowed, stepping deeper into the forest and hoping that the cover of the woodland would protect them; also that the enemy's grasp of Latin was small or non-existent. He watched the two hundred or so men of his force converging on his position and held his breath, hoping that the enemy were nocked and waiting for another charge. If they started firing randomly into the woods again they would likely reduce the force considerably and very quickly. Fortunately no arrows came as Fronto looked around at his men.

'We can't spread out to take them. The river hems us in to the right and who knows what's left, but we *do* know there's a force of warriors from the ambush out there somewhere and we don't want to blunder into them. So we're stuck. We have to take them head on and they're prepared. So here's what we're going to do: we're going in as a wedge.'

Menenius, standing next to Fronto, turned his head and flashed an incredulous look at him.

'We go in as fast as we've ever run in our lives' Fronto went on. 'Every archer out there will get one shot. After that, they're screwed, because we'll be among them, and we all know that a gladius beats a bow in close combat. Once we've punched into the line, we peel off. Cantorix and Atenos and their centuries will head right toward the river and carve up every archer they find. The rest of you, with me, will turn left and make sure we get every last mother's son among them. Only when every archer is eating turf do we stop and re-form. Got it?'

The tribune reached out gingerly and tapped Fronto on the shoulder, drawing close.

'Are you *mad*, sir?'

'Quite possibly. It has been suggested before. But if you can think of a better way, enlighten me.'

'We go back to the boats, cross to the west bank and come back in force, armed properly.'

Fronto shook his head wearily. 'The chances of us getting back without another ambush are tiny. They know we're here now, and we're at our objective. We set up a bridgehead and hold it for a few hours – a day at most – and the bridge will come to us.'

'Fronto? That's madness!'

'So...' the legate turned back to the men, 'quite a few of us will die in the next few moments, but... well, that's what we signed on for, wasn't it? Those of you who will be in the rear centre of the wedge, I want you to remove your mail shirt and pass it to a friend. By the time I count a hundred I want half of you unarmoured in the centre and the rest of you wearing two mail shirts – preferably the really muscly buggers, as you'll have to run fast wearing two lots of armour. It'll be like wearing a cart.'

He grinned. 'You,' he pointed at a man 'give me your shirt.'

'What?' barked Cantorix. 'Can't do that, sir.'

'You damn well can. It's an order. I'm the front of the wedge.'

Atenos was suddenly next to his fellow centurion. 'He's right, sir. The head of the wedge is a prestigious position, sir. A guaranteed commendation and worth a phalera and a fortnight's leave at least. We can't let you deprive a man of that, sir!'

Cantorix grinned. 'A centurion doesn't get enough leave, does he? Shall we toss a coin?'

Fronto shook his head and tried to reach past them for the mail shirt now being proffered by the legionary. The two centurions leaned toward each other, blocking him off.

'My duty, I think' Cantorix grinned. 'The Tenth have reputation to spare, but the Fourteenth never seem to get the glory.' Atenos looked hard at him for a moment and then nodded.

As the centurion from the Fourteenth grabbed the shirt and pulled it over his large, muscular frame, covering his own mail that glistened red with the blood from his earlier wound, Fronto looked helplessly at Atenos.

'This was *my* plan. I'm not going to let anyone else grab the shitty end of the stick.'

'Tough, sir.' Atenos smiled. 'Get that shirt off, sir, and get in the centre. If this works, you'll need to be around to organise the defence until the bridge is finished.'

Fronto opened his mouth to argue, but the look on the centurion's face was adamant and he simply nodded and began to peel off the heavy, wet armour. Next to him, Menenius had already divested and passed his mail shirt to an enormous Gaul, who was having trouble struggling into it.

A long moment passed in tense expectation as the last of the armour was transferred and men fell into their assigned places, allowing for the fact that they would not be able to consolidate into the wedge properly until they left the woodland. Finally, the archers in the clearing seemed to have come to the end of their patience and occasional arrows whizzed into the woods, burying themselves in timber here and there. Fronto smiled grimly to himself. Every shot they took lessened the chances of that man being able to shoot during the charge.

'Are we all ready?' Cantorix waved and gestured for everyone to settle into their final positions. 'As soon as you pass the last tree, get as tight into formation as you've ever been. I want you all to be able to feel the breath of the man behind on your neck. Tight and fast, then break as soon as we're there.'

The men murmured their agreement. Fronto looked around from his position in the midst of the unarmoured centre, grumbling at his secure and unadventurous place. He could not see Atenos or Menenius in the press, nor Cantorix, though he could hear the centurion at the head of the wedge.

'Go!'

And suddenly he was running, along with everyone else, his concentration now fully on the men around him and the forest floor, watching for treacherous branches or bumps that could foul him and ruin the formation, aware of the weakness of his knee with every painful click.

A sudden image flashed into his mind of a legionary being beaten within a shadow's breadth of death on the orders of centurion Fabius for tripping in manoeuvres and fouling his unit. He'd been so outraged by the man and now, as he ran, barely missing a tangled root with his left foot, he felt that perhaps…

Angry, he pushed the thoughts away and concentrated on the run.

Arrows were now coming thicker and faster. The sounds of them thudding into trees were fewer and farther between, while the sounds of them crunching into mail or the screams as they punched into flesh were all more common. Here and there an archer was casting aside his bow, the string now ruined, and drawing a sword.

The stygian gloom of the woodland gave way to the pale, misty grey of the clearing and the men closed formation as only legionaries could, Fronto finding himself so tightly packed in the press that he could hardly move.

A tense heartbeat, and there finally came the expected sound: the collective twang and rush, whirr and zip of countless arrows being released simultaneously. Another single heartbeat and the result manifested in the screams of dozens of men and the inevitable slowing of the wedge. Three more heartbeats and the front of the Roman unit seemed to meet the archers, the sounds ringing out eerily through the swirling mist.

Fronto lurched, tripping on a body that had fallen in front of him and his eyes momentarily ran across it, almost certain it would be Cantorix, only to see a legionary he knew not, three arrows jutting from his face, chest and belly. He must have been one of the front men, though, to take three shots. Fronto found that he was praying subconsciously to Mars that Cantorix made it, despite the fact that such a notion was ridiculous.

Two more heartbeats and the press opened up in front of him, men veering off as assigned, moving left and right along the line of archers. Somehow, strangely, Fronto found himself staggering to a halt with no enemy to fight.

Turning this way and that, he peered into the barely-penetrable gloom, the rain hammering at him and plastering the tunic to his torso. It seemed that the archers had broken and routed as soon as they realised they could not stop the Roman force. In the subdued fog of rain, he could hear the sounds of fighting off to the left and right, but here there was no one, apart from a few legionaries looking as lost as he; a few wounded, staggering with an arrow in the thigh or clutching one jutting from an arm.

Turning, he looked back toward the barely visible treeline. Bodies littered the ground between here and there, the grisly graveyard disappearing into the mist. A lot of men had died there, but it appeared that they had completed the mission. The bridge site was safe for now.

Rubbing the excess water from his hair, Fronto looked around for a centurion, optio or tribune, but saw none. He would have to pull them together and get down to the river. This was unlikely to be the last they would see of the barbarians before the engineers reached this bank.

'On me!' he yelled. 'Re-form!'

Time to establish a bridgehead, somehow.

Chapter 11
(East bank of the Rhine)

Fronto walked across the grass toward the approaching men, legionaries looming out of the mist like some sort of demon horde, grinning maniacally at having survived such an insane charge. Many of them, he noted, carried some trophy of their kills, the Gallic legionaries of the Fourteenth tending toward the more grisly. It was not something that Fronto particularly approved of in the aftermath of battle but it was hardly unknown, particularly among the Celtic peoples, and he could hardly chide them for such a petty thing after their brave sacrifices.

'Any officers among you?'

Two figures stepped out ahead of the men returning from the east, a centurion and, Fronto was pleased to note, the optio who had saved his life at the farmstead. Behind them, a cornicen and a signifer came striding forth, the standard bearer dragging a wounded leg.

'Over here' called a voice from behind, and Fronto turned gratefully, to see the figure of Atenos appearing from the mist in the direction of the river.

'Anyone seen Cantorix or Menenius?'

No one spoke, and Fronto felt the leaden certainty in his gut that the centurion had not made it. The front man of a wedge never did. Rarely did the front third, in fact. Menenius, on the other hand, was in the press of safer men at the back. They would turn up soon enough, whatever had happened to them.

'Right. I want pickets stationed all around the edge of the forest. The men with the best eyesight and hearing, and those who can whistle loud enough to be heard half a mile away. Atenos? I want you and this musician and standard bearer down by the water. Get the duty centurion's attention on the far bank. When you can get him onto the bridge to speak, let me know and I'll come talk to him.'

Atenos nodded and, the two signallers falling in at his shoulders, jogged off to the river.

'You' Fronto pointed to the centurion he did not know. 'Set up the pickets.' The man saluted and began scouring the surviving legionaries for the best men, hooking them out with a beckoning finger.

'And you' he gestured to the optio. 'I want a work party to gather every last Roman body they can find, as well as the casualties, and bring them down to the river bank, and then I want a full headcount of who we have left. How many men, officers, signallers and so on.'

The optio saluted and Fronto gave him a weary smile. 'What's your name, soldier?'

'Vitiris, sir. Chosen man of the...'

'Centurion, I think' Fronto interrupted. 'Just make sure you live long enough to requisition the crest from the quartermaster.'

As the men moved off, assigned to either work parties or picket duty appropriately, Fronto limped wearily down toward the river bank, making for the call of the Roman cornu he could hear. Now that the rush of battle-induced adrenaline had worn off, the ache in his knee was becoming unbearable. Pausing and reaching down, he ran his hands over the joint and was momentarily taken aback by just how swollen it was compared with the right knee.

Grumbling and muttering about the effects of age, he limped across the grass, wincing occasionally.

Here, the river bank rose above the flow with a drop of some four or five feet into the roiling, seething waters; a good height for the bridge to make landfall. As he approached the bank, he could see the figures of Atenos and the signallers on the turf.

Once more brushing the excess water from his hair and shaking his head to clear as much as possible, Fronto limped over to them.

'Any luck?'

The big Gaul turned and smiled, pointing across the water. Fronto followed his gesturing finger and squinted into the sheeting rain, picking out the image of human shapes approaching on the bridge. The small party of half a dozen men reached the truncated bridge end and gathered there. Fronto half expected to see Caesar, but the general had not come yet. These were the officers currently on duty at the bridge site. The legate stepped as close as he dared to the drop into the water and cleared his throat.

'Centurion? Can you hear me?'

The distance-and-rain-muffled voice of the officer called back 'Just about. That legate Fronto?'

'Yes.'

'Thank Juno. We were starting to worry.'

Fronto, his voice hoarse from shouting into the rain, took a deep breath. 'We've destroyed the archers and routed another force, but we're still in danger and poorly equipped. Can you send over some equipment for us?'

'Of course, sir. We'll launch a rope over by arrow and set up a ferry from the bridge. What do you need?'

'Everything. Have someone fetch our helmets, shields, pila and everything else. It's all stockpiled ready. We could also do with a few archers if they feel up to hand-over-hand-ing it across a rope?'

The centurion let out a laugh. 'I'll see what I can do sir. You sit tight while we get the ball rolling.'

Fronto turned and breathed deeply.

'Soon as it all arrives, can you get it distributed appropriately?'

Atenos nodded. 'Of course, sir.'

'I'll be sat on a rock somewhere hoping the bottom half of my leg's not about to fall off.'

Atenos grinned. 'If he's still alive, there was a capsarius in my century. I'll look into it and if he's here, I'll send him to find you.'

Fronto nodded and wobbled off across the grass in search of somewhere solid to sit down that would not churn with mud. Men were beginning to make their way into the clearing, carrying the bodies of the fallen and supporting those too wounded to walk on their own. It was somewhat disheartening to ponder on the numbers, but then the assault had apparently been anticipated, which had rendered their mission considerably more dangerous and costly than expected. Exactly how the enemy had known they were coming was still a mystery, but the more he thought on the ambush at the farmstead, the more he was convinced that someone had tipped them off. Presumably the Ubii.

Fronto's eyes widened as a familiar shape loomed out of the seething white rain-mist.

Cantorix could hardly stand, and was being gently carried along by two legionaries. Fronto noted without surprise the stumps of arrow shafts jutting from his right shoulder, left hip, right arm, and both legs, apparently all broken off when he fell to the ground, driving them deeper in. He was deathly pale but grinning through a mouthful of blood.

'Looks… looks like we got 'em, legate Fronto.'

Fronto tried to stand, but the strength had left his knee.

'You look in a sorry state, Cantorix.'

'Didn't have time to shave, sir' the centurion grinned, spitting a wad of clotted blood to the turf.

'Don't you dare die on me now, centurion.' He said, smiling back, but only half-jokingly.

'I have no intention of dying, sir. I'm owed a couple of weeks' leave.'

* * * * *

Fronto sighed and stood slowly and awkwardly, favouring his right leg, as the legionary ran across the sodden grass toward him, splashing up crowns of water with each heavy step.

'What's happening?'

The legionary came to a stop and saluted. 'The outer pickets to the east have spotted movement in the woods and confirmed a sizeable force, sir.'

Fronto nodded and stretched wearily. 'Tell them to fall back to the inner line at the woods' edge. The inner pickets can come in now. As soon as they're visible from the inner line, they're to pull back too.'

As the legionary ran off again, Fronto turned and peered into the incessant downpour, trying to spot Atenos. The towering Gaul was organising things near the water's edge, gesturing to groups of men who were dashing around with piles of equipment or digging the trench.

Hobbling over toward them, Fronto was impressed at how quickly things had progressed. The pickets had been in position for only two hours, but already two rope lines had been slung from the construction to ferry goods and support to the bridgehead. While the engineers and their work parties carried on the work at an impressive forced pace, Atenos had groups of legionaries preparing what resembled a tiny marching camp on this bank.

The headcount had come in and, of the four hundred or so men who had crossed the Rhenus, Fronto's command now numbered ninety seven, including himself and the two remaining Ubii scouts, who remained under close scrutiny on the suspicion that it was they who had warned the enemy about the mission. One mystery that niggled was the continuing absence of tribune Menenius, last seen when forming up for the wedge assault.

Of those ninety four officers and men, thirty two were posted to picket duties in four-man groups, the rest rushing around and carrying out Atenos' commands. A ditch, currently three feet deep and three wide surrounded the site in a 'U' shape, seventy paces in length and almost completed was being excavated, while four men sharpened cut branches and planted them in the hollow, angled toward the enemy approach. The upcast, forming a three foot mound within the perimeter formed by the ditch, protected a scene of organised chaos within.

The capsarius who, wounded himself, had set up a small field hospital and was working manically to treat those who stood a chance of survival, had been joined by a fellow medic from the camp who had shown the gumption to hand-over-hand it along one of the ropes, and the two men dealt with a constant supply of wounds. A peremptory and none-too-gentle prod of Fronto's knee had elicited little sympathy from either medic. Cantorix lay wrapped in a blanket, pale grey and sweating, delirious with the compounds the capsarii had forced into him. When pressed on whether the centurion would make it, both men had looked doubtful and shrugged.

Two men worked a pulley and bag on one rope, retrieving rations, weapons, entrenching equipment and, on the legate's orders, a few jars of watered wine, and distributing them among the men as required. The other rope delivered a slow but growing supply of Cretan auxiliary archers, none of whom looked particularly enchanted with their method of arrival, but who were starting to take positions behind the low rampart, jamming their arrows point first into the ground for quick retrieval.

Even as Fronto made for the newly-promoted centurion, he spotted a familiar, if bedraggled face, clambering down from the rope: Titus Decius Quadratus, the prefect of the auxiliary unit and a man who, despite the gulf between their commands, Fronto had held in high esteem ever since the defence of the Bibrax oppidum two years previously. Decius spotted Fronto lurching toward him as he nodded a greeting to Atenos and his face broke into a wide grin.

'When I heard that the legate of the Tenth had holed up in enemy land and needed archers, I said to myself 'just how long is Fronto going to hold out without me?' When I answered the question, I came running.'

'Decius, it's damn good to see you. I hope your men are ready quickly. The enemy are on the move.'

The auxiliary prefect scratched his stubbly chin and gestured back at the rope, where two figures were crossing at once, very slowly and carefully.

'It's a slow job. I've got maybe twenty or so men here now and more coming across but the rain's making that rope treacherous. I've lost two men into the river already and only one made it to the bank. Hell, I nearly went in myself. The big thing is: my lads are really unhappy about taking their bows out in this weather. They've each got a spare string, but just the one.'

Fronto sighed and sank to the rampart, rubbing his swollen knee.

'They'll just have to deal with it. If I could turn this rain off, believe me I would! And I'd have liked to get a palisade up but we just don't have time. To be honest I'm surprised we've had this long without being assaulted. The staked ditch and mound will just have to do the job. At least we've got shields, pila and archers now. We'd have lasted about ten heartbeats without all this.'

'What have you done to your knee?'

'Just a bad twist. The capsarius says to stay off it, as if that were a remote possibility. Here.' Unceremoniously, he thrust one of the wine jars he'd commandeered at the prefect. Decius took it without comment and swigged gratefully, brushing the rain from his forehead.

'It's been a noble effort, Decius, despite our horrible losses, and they're working like madmen on the bridge, but I can't see much hope of us holding off the entire Germanic people until they get to this bank. It's going to be a day yet, even if they work through dark.'

'I swear, Fronto, that if you get any more negative, you'll change colour. It's not about holding off an entire nation.'

'No?'

'No. It's about dealing with the first attack so brutally that they daren't try again.'

Fronto perked up, his eyes narrowing. 'You think we can hit them hard enough to make them withdraw?'

'You and me? The defenders of Bibrax? Ha!'

The legate stood, slowly and painfully, and grinned. 'What have you in mind?'

* * * * *

The first assault came less than an hour later. The pickets had withdrawn to the fortified boundary and the defenders had watched the barbarians moving around just inside the shadow of the woods, their numbers uncertain.

It began as a roar somewhere inside the treeline, followed by a crash as the Germanic warriors slammed their weapons against shields, other weapons, or just tree trunks, raising a noise that shook the world. Then, half a dozen heartbeats later, the enemy poured out of the forest, yelling their guttural battle cries, mostly unarmoured, often unclothed, but with every weapon honed to a killing edge.

Fronto, standing on the low embankment, was pleased to note the lack of enemy archers. Not a surprise, really, given the utter devastation their wedge-formation charge had wrought on the lightly armed missile troops. Very few bowmen had escaped alive into the woods, and those that did would be in no hurry to return. These men were very likely the remaining warriors of that first ambush at the farm. If that were the case, then it suggested to Fronto that perhaps the rest of the tribes were staying safely back in their own territory, watching the Roman advance carefully. If that *was* the case then Decius could be right. If they broke this attack, they might survive until the bridge was complete.

'It all sounds a bit unlikely to me' he muttered to Decius. 'Are you really sure they're that good? They look a bit shaky to me.'

The prefect grinned. 'They're just still recovering from that rope trip. But remember Bibrax? And we've been training on small target shooting since then, so watch and learn.'

Fronto cast a distinctly uncertain look at the archers, but nodded. They all looked worried and shaky. Not that he blamed them. If he'd had to cross that wet rope above the churning currents of the Rhenus, he would probably have lost control of his bowels by now.

'Legionaries prepare! Front rank ready! Rear rank ready!'

As he glanced along the rampart, the sixty five men forming the front rank stood with their shields forming a defensive 'U' within the defences of the tiny fort. Swords were held poised, ready to flash out each time the shields parted a couple of finger-widths. The rear rank of twenty five men stood five paces back, each holding a pilum ready, five more jammed into the ground, ready to throw.

Decius waited until Fronto's voice had echoed away and straightened. The forty archers who had crossed knelt on the embankment, arrows jammed into the earth.

'Remember the range. Only loose when you're certain of a hit. Mark your targets carefully. Section one: you're looking for the largest, least armoured men. Section two: release at will, but be selective and mean!'

Fronto looked along the line of archers and then glanced back and watched with regret as the two ropes splashed down into the water and were withdrawn to the bridge, a precaution against giving the enemy any advantage should the bridgehead fall.

It quickly became clear as the barbarians swarmed across the open grass that their numbers had been somewhat bolstered since the ambush at the farm. Even as the lead warriors – bloodlust filling their eyes and minds, swords raised for a first blow – closed on the small, hopelessly inadequate fortlet, more were still pouring from the woods in a seemingly endless supply.

'Steady' called Decius in a calm voice. Fronto glanced nervously across. Surely they were close enough now. He could almost smell them. In return, the tanned prefect grinned at him and, producing one of the wineskins, took a quick pull from it and winked.

'Loose!' he bellowed.

Fronto felt his eyes drawn back to the enemy by the arcing of the missiles. The initial volley seemed to have failed in its intended effect for a moment and Fronto was about to order the archers back, when he watched the results unfold with interest.

The nine archers of 'section one' were Decius' best shots. The most accurate and consistent archers to be found in the whole unit of Cretans, most of whom were still trapped on the far side of the Rhenus.

Now Fronto could see how they had earned the blue scarf that marked them out as double-pay men. Each of the nine arrows sailed straight and true and only one missed the intended mark, by a tiny enough margin that the effect was the same.

The result was impressive. Each missile had been aimed for the knee of one of the largest and most powerful barbarians and had struck home with impressive accuracy. The bulky warriors had floundered with the crippling blows and fallen sideways in the direction of the damaged joint, bringing down several of the other charging barbarians in the mess.

The rest of the archers were firing and nocking, firing and nocking, firing and nocking at a rate that Fronto simply could not believe, their victims collapsing to the wet ground with cries of agony. Precious few arrows went astray, and even those that did caused some damage due to the press of the enemy.

The effect of the targeted knee shots was remarkable. Where a moment earlier a solid row of howling barbarians had been running, trying to out-sprint one another, now few pockets of men were still running, while most of the front five or six ranks' worth of warriors were down, floundering in the churning mud while the mass behind them tried to leap over or clamber across them in their lust to get to the enemy.

Fronto had a momentary image of that hillside at Bibrax two years ago, the slope wet and muddy, churning and becoming more slippery and treacherous with every fallen struggling man. The same was now happening on the field before him. The floundering ranks of attackers were churning the mud and creating a mire that made it increasingly difficult to gain a footing and stand again.

As the entire attack ground to a comical, messy halt, the chosen men of the unit joined their compatriots in the simple nock-release-nock-release that was having a devastating effect on them.

Finally the warriors from the bulk of the enemy force managed to make headway, clambering across their fallen countrymen, using the wounded or dead as a walkway to cross the roiling mud.

'Your turn!' Decius shouted with a grin, even as his men continued their impressive rate of shooting.

Fronto nodded and raised his voice. 'Second rank, throw at will!'

As the barbarians continued to fall to the fletched hell that Decius had unleashed, the men of Fronto's legionary force began to cast their pila. They could not see their targets with the men of the first rank, the mound and the archers in front, but they cast their missiles high and hard, the pila falling somewhere deep in the mass of barbarians where they were almost guaranteed a kill.

And for long moments the battle seemed frozen in time; a constant repeat of actions. Arrows flew from the rampart, plunging with astounding precision into the nearest barbarians, holding back the surge, while pilum after pilum arced up and over, falling into the press of flesh.

Fronto stood on the mound watching the tableau with a professional eye, noting the slowing of the enemy force – not due purely to the damage being done them by the constant barrage of missiles, but also showing a growing uncertainty about their attack.

Their enthusiasm was waning, their sureness of victory drained with every death and wound.

It would be a close thing.

There were still enough warriors in that field to completely swamp the hundred and thirty or so men defending the bank. If they could be pushed a little harder, the resolve that weakened with every moment might break completely and, if that happened, his small force had won. The barbarians would rout and leave the field and the bridgehead would hold, while fresh supplies and more men could be brought across.

But even as Fronto felt his breath come and his tension ease, his gaze took in the arrows jammed into the turf along the defensive line. Few archers had more than two or three shots remaining. In the moment he registered the change in the situation, the last few pila arced up and over, signalling the end of that particular advantage.

Decius was grinning as he turned to Fronto.

'That's us. Your turn now!'

The last few arrows whirred into the enemy, picking off the closest and biggest of them. As the final missile flew, Fronto took a deep breath. 'Ranks part!' he bellowed.

All along the defence, the line of legionaries shuffled to create gaps through which the archers could move to the relative safety of the camp. Decius ran along the mound to Fronto and gestured. 'We'll do what we can from behind. Good luck!'

Fronto nodded, casting a last glance at the enemy. Perhaps two or three hundred men had fallen in that brutal assault – more than a third of the enemy force. The rest came on slower, a little more carefully, watching the defenders suspiciously, with the blood lust gone from their eyes. With a deep breath and a murmured prayer to Fortuna, he dropped down the slope and moved between the parted ranks where he collected a shield and fell in with the second rank.

'Front line, close ranks to shieldwall!'

As the shields slammed together, the legate closed his eyes for a moment, willing the enemy to break fast. The second rank, himself included, would be ready to plug any holes in the shieldwall, but until a gap opened, all he could see of the enemy was a general mass of howling flesh in the tiny openings between legionaries.

'Ready?' came a voice from behind and Fronto turned to see Decius and his archers gathered in small groups, hefting hammers, mattocks and stakes that had been brought over to help with the work

– even a few empty and discarded wine jars. Even as he frowned at the prefect, the first man swung hard and released a heavy-headed mallet, which arced up over the defenders, falling somewhere among the enemy.

Decius caught his glance and grinned.

'Anything that might help, eh?'

A mattock, heavy and sharp, thrummed overhead, plunging into the mass of the enemy, barely making it over the heads of the legionaries and causing a brief bladder release in the soldier who had almost lost his head to a flying spade.

'Careful!' Decius snapped. 'High and far... high and far.'

He turned his grin back on Fronto, who shook his head but could not help but join in with a disbelieving smile.

The crash of close combat drew his attention back. The enemy had finally reached the shieldwall, though from the screaming and gurgling more were still falling foul of the sharpened branches jutting up from the ditch.

From his position in the rear rank, Fronto watched the men of the Tenth and Fourteenth going to work, their shields changing angle every few moments in a single movement that opened up a foot wide gap through which every gladius in the line lanced out, biting into flesh before twisting and withdrawing behind shields that closed once again.

It was an almost mechanical process and the enemy began to pile up on the far side of the rampart, several of them falling foul once again of the slippery conditions underfoot, the combat ripping the turf and earth beneath and churning it into a soup of treacherous mud. Here and there a legionary slipped, but managed to maintain his footing due to the heavy hobnailed sandals they wore. The barbarians, largely unshod or clad in flat-soled boots, were less lucky, every slip bringing them down into the sucking mire, where they floundered as their own tribesmen clambered across them desperately.

Fronto counted almost a hundred before the first legionary went down, an overhead blow cutting him almost in two. The gruesome corpse slopped backward and splattered into the pool of watery grass behind, staining it with a spreading pink tint. The legate opened his mouth to give the order, but a man was already moving forward to fill the gap.

That was the moment in every battle, though.

The legions fought their mechanical fight with a feeling of invincibility until that breaking point. The first death seemed to trigger it, and Fronto prepared himself as first one and then two, then three men fell, some slumping forward onto the earth bank, their heads smashed and slashed, their bodies opened and spilling their vitals to the wet ground, others tumbling backward.

Each time, one of the second rank ran forward, stepping into the gap and slamming his shield into place, continuing the butchery.

The legate watched with held breath as his small force of reserves dwindled more and more, twenty five men now down to fourteen. Now thirteen. Now twelve.

Even as he realised he was about to run out of reserves, Fronto blinked in surprise. Three of the auxiliary archers had joined the line of men, armoured in their light mail shirts, less than half as protective as a legionary version, but gripping spare legionary shields and hefting their backup blades ready to join the fight. Decius fell in beside him, grinning, as more Cretan archers armed up and joined in.

'Ran out of things to throw' he shrugged, hefting his sword.

Only seven legionaries were left and now eight auxiliary reserves. Fronto took another deep breath. 'Think we might be in the shit, Decius.'

'Seems that's the only place I ever meet you!'

Fronto laughed a hollow laugh and turned back as a man howled in front of him, falling back with a spear impaling his chest, snapped off near the solar plexus. 'My turn!' he shouted and shuffled forward, limping over the fallen, groaning man with difficulty. He barely got his shield into position before the next blow carved a small sliver off the curved corner of it.

'Bollocks, that was close!'

The legionary next to him grinned and thrust his sword into a man whose hands had risen for an overhead chop with a heavy axe. Even as the man fell away and Fronto stabbed at the nearest open flesh, his eyes strayed up and over the press of men.

'Mars be praised.' The field was largely empty of enemy warriors, more than two thirds of the Germanic attack now lying in heaps around the field or piled up like cordwood before the shieldwall.

'Nearly done 'em, sir!' the legionary grinned.

'Why haven't they broken? We must not have frightened them enough.'

'They know we can't hold forever, sir. They'll still win in the end.'

The legate turned a vicious smile on his men. 'Not today.'

Withdrawing his sword and closing the shield gap again, he rolled his shoulders and took a deep breath.

'Soldiers of Rome: advance!'

Despite the gasps of surprise around him, Fronto smashed forward with his shield and then turned it slightly, lancing a speedy blow that cut through a man's neck cord. The warrior fell away, shrieking in pain, his head lolling obscenely to one side, and Fronto took a step forward and then another, almost collapsing as his bad knee negotiated the slope.

Next to him, the other legionaries had reacted with professional discipline, despite the unexpectedness of the command, smashing the nearest enemies out of the way with their shields and stepping forward, reforming the line. Suddenly, Decius was there, pushing his way into the line, half a dozen men along.

'You're not winning this one without me, Fronto!'

And the auxiliaries were there too, no longer plugging gaps, but forcing their way into the line, expanding it and extending it, following the lead of the legionaries on either side of them, learning the new tactics of legion fighting in the melting pot of battle itself. The men of the Tenth and Fourteenth reacted momentarily with the traditional distaste of legion men regarding the 'inferior' auxilia, but these men had proved themselves once and were doing it again, and within moments, the legionaries were giving their new compatriots enough space to work and yelling encouragement.

The barbarians, until a moment ago throwing themselves against an ever-diminishing line of defenders, suddenly quailed in the face of the unexpectedly violent and enthusiastic advance. Across the field, shouts of consternation were raised in the guttural Germanic tongue and, through the periodic flashes of vision Fronto caught every time the shields parted for a sword blow, it was clear that the rear ranks of the remaining barbarians were now turning on their heels and plummeting into the forest in an effort to escape the scene.

The sudden change in the fortunes of the enemy caused a moan of dismay to ripple across their massed ranks and, as they began to pull back en masse, a cheer went up among the men of the Tenth, the

Fourteenth and the Cretan auxiliaries, accompanied by a fresh push of energy.

The Roman line surged forward, each step accompanied by the smash of the shield boss, no longer a teeth-gritting, muscle-rippling heave against a wall of sweating flesh, the pressure easing as the enemy ranks thinned.

A legionary a few men down from Fronto roared and stepped out of the line, desperate to deliver a killing blow to the man with whom he'd been struggling and who had now pulled away and opened a gap between them.

Before Fronto could shout a warning or an order to return to the line, the man fell foul of three of the enemy who paused in their flight to dispatch the careless Roman. The legionary went down under the blows of two axes and a sword, hacking chunks from his upper body. The line surged a little faster again as the legionary's compatriots made an attempt to reach his killers without making the same suicidal mistake themselves. The barbarians, though, were now intent on self-preservation, the attack having fallen apart around them, and were already out of reach and accelerating.

'What are your orders, legate?' Decius bellowed along the line as the Roman force moved across the soaking, body-strewn grass at a steady pace, the barbarians fleeing ahead of them.

Fronto peered off through the rain, which looked as though it might be finally lightening. 'Hold ranks until we reach the woods. Then we're going to split: I'm going to take half the men a few hundred paces inside the treeline just to be sure they're not thinking of forming up for another performance. You'll take the rest and return to the camp. Get the ropes going again and get the men resupplied and some more support brought across.'

Decius grinned as he stepped over the twisted body of a wiry barbarian, pinned to the wet, sludgy grass with the sharp blade of an entrenching tool where his head should have been.

Fronto took a deep breath and very carefully negotiated every grotesque obstacle with his swollen knee screaming at him. It was almost over. He could not believe they had done it with the few men and supplies they had, but Decius was almost certainly right: the barbarians would not be back. Everything that had happened on this side of the river had been the work of one tribe, while the rest seemed happy to sit back in their own lands and watch. The horrible defeat that had just been inflicted upon them by a tremendously inferior force would ensure that no further danger came Caesar's way.

The shields had stopped opening and closing to allow strikes now. Not a single living barbarian faced the wall of steel, iron, bronze and flesh moving inexorably across the turf. Indeed, the last few of the enemy were even now being lost to sight among the boles of the trees, going to ground in an attempt to evade death or capture.

Decius' voice rang out along the line. 'Every second man withdraw to the defences!' Stepping back himself, he saluted Fronto as he took twenty three men back to the fortlet, leaving the remaining twenty four with the legate.

Without needing a command, those men closed ranks as they moved and, within moments they had reached the edge of the forest. There was no longer any sign of the stragglers, but Fronto knew from horrible experience how dangerous it was to assume all was clear. There would likely be a few barbarians, willing to sacrifice themselves in the name of revenge, who would be hidden in the undergrowth in the hope of taking a number of heads with them when they went to meet their dung-ridden gods.

'Be wary now, lads. Stay within sight of one another and move carefully. Watch every bush and every tree for movement. Be aware of your surroundings and every noise. We move in for a count of three hundred only and then turn and withdraw. No chasing any juicy Germanic women, no matter how naked they might be!'

A few laughs rippled out down the line as the soldiers moved into the woods, spreading out and forming a wide cordon to clear any hidden ambushes. Fronto realised very quickly that he was lagging, his knee was a serious impediment in the troublesome terrain of the forest, and he was grateful when Atenos and one of the other legionaries noticed. The centurion nodded at him and closed the gap, allowing the legate to fall back and leave the line.

Fronto watched as his men very ably and professionally stalked deeper into the woods, and stumbled over to a fallen tree trunk, onto which he sagged with great relief, examining his swollen knee and worrying about whether it should be turning the shade of mauve that it appeared to be.

He sighed with happiness and never noticed the heavy, shiny object descending before it smashed him over the head, obliterating all consciousness and driving him into darkness.

* * * * *

White light brought with it the sort of pain that Fronto usually only associated with heavy drinking bouts, though this was clearly not the result of any such activity. With a groan, he sat up, his hand going to his head to feel where the throbbing was coming from.

When he regained consciousness the second time, he was lying awkwardly and the smell of relatively fresh vomit assailed his nostrils. He opened an eye a fraction and then squeezed it tight shut against the terribly painful light. The vomit was apparently his and had seeped into his clothing, despite having been peremptorily wiped away with a cloth.

'He's awake.'

'If you can call it that.'

'Did you bring the wine? Wine always heals Fronto' Even with his eyes closed and the fog of agonising unconsciousness still clinging to his senses, Fronto could almost hear the malicious grin on the face of Priscus, to whom he knew the voice belonged.

'Piss off.'

'It speaks!'

Fronto cracked an eye open again, but held it so narrow that his lashes formed a veil against the light. Above was a white leather roof. Too high to be his own tent, so it was clearly a hospital one. His wandering gaze took in the beaming faces of Priscus and Carbo, with Decius sat next to them, the only one wearing any sort of expression of concern. Fronto noted with interest, his professional eye taking over despite the circumstances, that Carbo sported a recent cut to his cheek that had not been there last time they had met, just before the river crossing. A suspicion began to form.

'How long have I been out?'

Priscus and Carbo exchanged glances and then looked across at Decius. 'Not sure. Who are the consuls this year, prefect?'

Decius gave them a weary smile and focused on Fronto. 'A little over a week.'

'A *week*?'

'You took a bad blow to the head.'

Priscus laughed out loud. 'It was a truly magnificent wound. One of your best yet. The medicus said he thought he could see your brain, but I assured him that was unlikely.'

212

The camp prefect burst out laughing and Carbo grinned evilly. 'Actually, in all truthfulness, the medicus did say that you've got one of the thickest skulls he's ever seen and that was probably what saved your life.'

Fronto frowned and the pain the muscle movement caused almost made him vomit again.

'What happened? I remember stopping because of my knee and then nothing.'

Decius shrugged. 'We're still not sure. It appears that Menenius saved you.'

'*What?*'

The auxiliary prefect gestured to the bed on the other side of the spacious partitioned room. 'When we found you, you were together. You'd been brained and Menenius had two stab wounds and an arrow jutting from his chest. But there were three dead barbarians around you too, and the tribune's sword was good and bloody.'

Fronto stared across at the still form of Menenius, whose chest rose and fell in shallow breaths. 'Is he…'

'He's suffering a fever. Not been lucid yet and keeps dropping off for half a day at a time. The medicus said his arrow wound was infected. He should pull through, but nothing's certain yet.'

The legate shook his head in disbelief. 'I'm going to owe him a few drinks apparently, if he recovers well enough. Any news of Cantorix?'

'After a fashion. He's lost his right arm at the shoulder, can't feel a thing in his left leg, and swears every time anyone touches the right. But, somehow, the big Gaulish bastard seems to be getting stronger. It's the end of his soldiering career, of course, but it's impressive nonetheless.'

A resounding crash made Fronto start and he almost sat bolt upright. 'What in Hades was that?'

'That was the bridge coming down' Priscus shrugged. 'It's nearly done now.'

'Down? It's only been a week!'

'A week's been enough' the camp prefect shrugged. 'Looks like the bridge and your little party on the bank have put the shits up even the hardest bastards out there. We hardly had the legions across the bridge before we started getting ambassadors and tribute, hostages, promises and so on. Most of the tribes have capitulated and agreed terms with the general.'

'And the rest?'

'That's what took the week.' Carbo leaned forward. 'The dangerous tribes – even the Suevi – all abandoned their conquests and territories and melted away into the forests to the east. Doesn't look like they'll be coming back in the near future... especially given that we burned all their settlements, harvested their crops, slaughtered their livestock and poisoned the wells. Caesar's declared the Germanic threat nullified and now we're consolidating while the bridge comes down.'

Fronto sank back to the comfortable surface.

'Then it's over. Any word on when we move out? Are the legions wintering here or do they get to come south this year?'

The three officers looked at one another uncomfortably.

'Not south, Marcus' Priscus said with a sigh. 'West. To the coast.'

When the legate frowned in confusion, the camp prefect sat back and squared his shoulders. 'Caesar has it in mind to do to the tribes of Britain what we've done to Germania.' He lowered his voice to a conspiratorial whisper. 'He claims to still be smarting over their support for the Veneti last year, but the general consensus is that he wants to double the glory and tribute we've taken so far before returning to Rome. I'm not sure I disagree, mind. Cartloads of gold and a long chain of slaves. Every man in the army's going to be quite well off this winter.'

Fronto allowed his eyes to close as his mind formed a fantastic and somewhat worrying image of the strange and unknown island full of monsters and evils that lay across the ocean to the north.

Fabulous.

Just wonderful.

An image of a smiling Lucilia that he had not even been aware was in his head until now started to fade, replaced by a screaming horde of yet more Celts.

'Think I'd better rest again.'

ROME

Lucilia smiled. 'Father has such old-fashioned tastes. I tried to get him to buy a statue of Priapus or 'Pan and a goat' for the atrium, but he refused. So we're stuck with a bust of my great grandfather who, to be quite honest, does not appear to have been a particularly handsome man. Who wants a party in such surroundings, I ask you?'

Faleria laughed lightly.

'Such statues as you favour might well lead to the kind of party that you'd be well advised to avoid, while your husband-to-be is still absent fighting the enemies of the republic. Let us concentrate on the important things. The wine is already taken care of, but we need to order the meats, cheeses and fruit at least this afternoon. And before we head back, we should see what musicians are for hire. No offence to your father's household, but if I have to listen to that wailing cat of a piper again I shall stuff his pipes with his own innards.'

Lucilia grinned. 'Perhaps we should head onto the Aventine and see how your house is coming on? Most of the roof should have been replaced this week.'

The older of the two shrugged. 'If there's time. The work will go on whether observed or not.'

The pair turned into the side street, the noise of the forum fading a little behind them as the buildings muffled the din. Faleria frowned as she glanced back over her shoulder.

'Where's that useless Thracian? If he's gone off on his own your father will have him flogged!'

Lucilia turned to look and her shriek was cut off sharply as a sack fell over her head and tightened around her neck, a pair of strong hands grasping her wrists and yanking them up painfully behind her. She tried desperately to call out to Faleria from the suffocating, blinding confines of the sack, but was instantly aware of the cries of anger and pain from her friend, apparently being similarly manhandled.

More hands grasped her shoulders and elbows and pushed her, almost knocking her from her feet. She was vaguely aware of the distinctive sounds of Faleria struggling and cursing their attackers and bit down on the fear and panic that threatened to overwhelm her, concentrating instead on yanking an elbow free from someone's grip and then landing it in someone's stomach. She was rewarded with a rush of air and a groan, but then the hands tightened around her and she found herself totally restricted and all but carried, her toes brushing the ground as she moved.

The only indications that the pair had been dragged and carried inside a building were the oppressive heat of an unventilated room and the further muffling of the background city noises. The sudden change in environment also allowed Lucilia to pay better attention to the more intimate sounds as they were shuffled along corridors, through rooms and, toward the end, down a short flight of stairs.

She could identify at least five sets of footsteps and there were three voices, not speaking, but grunting or swearing, all in accents local to Latium or at least the central regions of Italia. Not pirates, then, and unlikely to be slavers. Thugs. And thugs always answered to a boss.

'If you had any idea who it is you've just accosted, you'd release us straight away and pray to whatever lowlife deities would have you that we say nothing more about this.'

Two deep, guttural laughs greeted her statement and she found her arms released as she was pushed from her feet and fell in a heap painfully on a cobbled floor. Stretching her shoulders and making sure there was no serious damage, she reached up and pulled the bag from her head just as Faleria landed by her side. Reaching over gingerly, she helped Faleria remove the sack from her head and they both looked around at their location and captors.

They were clearly in a cellar, from the construction and the lack of windows. There was the sound of water rushing somewhere beneath them and just beyond one of the walls. The room was dim, lit only by two small oil lamps, though an orange flare added more detail as one of the thugs lit a torch.

The room was less than five paces across each direction. Square and featureless apart from...

Lucilia's heart lurched and she swallowed nervously as her eyes took in the meat hooks on the ceiling and the iron rings in two walls. A meat storage cellar. In fact, now that she knew, she could definitely smell the long-faded iron tang of blood. She was grateful at least that the cellar appeared to have been cleaned at some point since its original use.

Six men stood between the women and the doorway, beyond which they could see a second room and a flight of stairs rising to the ground floor. The men were all bulky and ugly, with an assortment of misshapen noses and bulbous ears; fighters all. Two men, standing at the edges and with less leery passion in their gazes, had the distinctive look of professional soldiers, something both Lucilia and Faleria could spot a mile away, after years with Fronto and Balbus.

'I am Faleria, daughter of the senator Lucius Falerius Fronto, a citizen of Rome, and this is Lucilia, daughter of Quintus Lucilius Balbus, former commander of the Eighth Legion. If any harm should come to us, I'm sure you can picture the trouble that will befall you?'

The men remained silent and Lucilia was suddenly aware of the tip-tap of light leather shoes on the flagstones beyond the door. It came as no surprise to either woman when the slender, graceful figure of Publius Clodius Pulcher stepped through the archway, his glossy black hair shining in the torchlight, his pronounced cheekbones and handsome face split in a less than handsome smile.

'Dear ladies, how remiss of me. I have offered neither of you refreshment.'

'Clodius, you hog-breath'd son of a Thracian whore!' Faleria spat with such venom that even Lucilia looked around in surprise. The thugs took an involuntary step back from this bile-ridden woman, but Clodius simply smiled and stepped forward, in front of his men.

'Dearest Faleria, but we are old friends, are we not? Let us not stand on ceremony.'

Without warning and like a coiled snake striking, Faleria was suddenly up and lunging for their captor. With neat economy of movement, one of the two professional ex-legionaries swept a cavalry long sword out and rested it on her throat, bringing her to an abrupt halt four feet from Clodius.

'Tut tut, Faleria. An unwise move in this company, and one that could result in something very unfortunate happening.'

'What do you intend to do with us?' Lucilia snapped, glaring at the legionary who held Faleria still with his sword.

'We know you serve Caesar now' Faleria snarled. 'He is a friend of my brother and our family and will gut you and string you up for the crows when he finds out about this.'

Something about Clodius' smile suddenly unnerved Lucilia and she realised she was less than convinced of that fact.

'Faleria...'

But Clodius simply reached out and took the long sword from the soldier and slid it back into its sheath. Faleria made no move further forward despite the impediment having gone.

217

'I have Caesar's utmost confidence, my dear ladies, and an open remit to do what I must to prevent anything getting in the way. You see I have very specific goals and a limited timescale and opportunity to carry them out.'

'Caesar will take exception to…'

'I suspect not. Things move apace for the general and he has more on his mind than continually bothering himself with the minutiae. However, I will grant you your wish.'

'You'll release us?' Lucilia asked in suspicious surprise.

'Gods, no. Apologies, you charming young lady, but that is quite impossible at this time. I will, however, send word to Caesar and request his instructions on how to proceed with you.'

Lucilia blanched. 'But that will take months!'

'Yes. Even with fast couriers, it will not be quick. But you see, I am bound to obey the commands of my patron, and to release you without permission would be to countermand Caesar's own orders.'

Lucilia narrowed her eyes. 'And, of course, word will no doubt reach my father that something unpleasant might happen to us unless he loses all interest in your activities?'

'I think not, I'm afraid. Your father shares certain traits with your betrothed, and I suspect that, should he have any confirmation of our involvement, an entire mercenary army would be knocking on my door in a matter of hours. Sit tight ladies. I will have the room made more comfortable for you and make sure you are well looked after until I have word from Caesar.'

Lucilia and Faleria watched with acerbic glares as Clodius and his thugs left the room, the last man placing one of the two lamps on a niche near the door to keep the room lit before closing the door and locking it from without.

The older of the two women waited until all was quiet and then turned to her friend.

'It's all down to us, Lucilia. Tell me everything you noticed on the way here.'

Lucilia frowned. 'Let's not do anything potentially dangerous, Faleria. Father will look for us anyway and he'll know who's to blame. And even if the worst comes to the worst, Caesar will order him to release us.'

'I doubt that word will ever reach Caesar. There is no courier and no message. Clodius gives us that hope to help keep us quiet and malleable. We cannot look to Caesar for help, and your father may well find us, but Clodius would as quickly slit our throats as let him find us alive and able to testify against him.'

She sighed. 'No. It is up to us to find our way out of this. I memorised the journey through the building, I think. Find me a loose stone and we'll scratch a map on the wall before the memories fade.'

Lucilia stared at her friend. Courage, ingenuity and indomitability apparently ran strong in the line of the Falerii. She just hoped it would be enough to save them.

Never had Fronto's arms felt so far away from her as now.

PART TWO:

BRITANNIA

Chapter 12

(Nemetocenna in the lands of the Belgae)

The legions heaved a collective sigh of relief as they settled in for the night. The journey from the Rhenus had consisted of almost two weeks of interminable marching, scouting, constructing and deconstructing innumerable camps for each night. And so, when the walls of Belgic Nemetocenna – well known to many of the men – hove into view as the sun began its descent, each soldier in the army sagged with gratitude that semi-permanent military ramparts remained here from the past few years of wintering troops, saving them the effort of digging ditches and raising walls.

The huge, sprawling fort, with four separate and individually-ramparted sub-camps, had been fully constructed and thriving within half an hour of arrival. Sentries had been posted, pickets out, officers already in the settlement in deep discussion with the local leaders, negotiating the price for extra supplies to supplement those brought on the huge wagon train that was still arriving as an owl began to hoot. The Fourteenth legion, as usual drawing the short straw, began to file slowly into the camp, escorting the last of the carts and the siege engines.

Fronto stepped gingerly across the open ground, trying to avoid the areas that had been churned into glutinous mud by the endless pairs of nail-shod feet working to put up tents, stack pila and so on. He caught sight of the glittering armour of Plancus, the Fourteenth's legate, glinting in the orange light of the torches and fires that dotted the enormous camp.

Plancus sat his horse like a statue, his face the image of the traditional Roman officer: proud – if somewhat vacant about the eyes – haughty and confident. The tribunes of his command followed on astride their own steeds, followed by the standards bearers, musicians and the rest. Fronto ignored the rest of the arriving column.

'Legate Fronto?' Plancus narrowed his eyes as though he might be mistaken. 'Can we help you?'

'Could you spare me one of your tribunes for a while?'

221

Plancus shrugged carelessly. 'They all have assigned duties. I will send a man over as soon as he has completed his tasks, if you like. Who is it you wish to see?'

Fronto fought the urge to grind his teeth. It was a habit he'd noticed on the increase when dealing with that particular breed of officer that took to military life like a fish to gravel.

'I doubt that'll be necessary. I would like to see tribune Menenius. He's not with the medical column that arrived, so I assume he's back with his legion.'

A trace of irritation passed across Plancus' eyes and he cleared his throat meaningfully.

'Menenius is travelling with my baggage train, in relative luxury. Despite my insistence, he continues to maintain that he cannot ride a horse.'

Fronto found that, despite his decision, his teeth were grating off one another already. Of course the damn man couldn't ride a horse. Fronto had visited him in the hospital tent back at the Rhenus as soon as his head had cleared enough and stopped thumping. The Fourteenth's tribune had taken an arrow wound to the shoulder that had become infected, as well as two sword wounds to the arm and the thigh. Fortunately, both had been light blows, drawing blood and a little muscular nicking, but with no real damage. The fever that came with the infected wound had kept the man on the bank of the Styx for six days and he'd still been in the care of the medical staff until yesterday. He certainly should *not* be riding a horse.

You prat.

'So if you can spare him?'

'He claims to be unfit for general duties and for some reason the medicus supports the malingering wastrel, so do as you see fit.'

Grind, grind, grind.

'Thank you for your consideration, Legate Plancus. I'll just speak to him in the column, then.'

Without waiting for any sort of gesture of acknowledgement – which he felt he was unlikely to receive anyway – Fronto turned and strode slowly along the line toward the small group of wagons that carried Plancus' mobile palace, with every comfort he could muster.

A jutting tuft of grass turned his step uncomfortably, and a lance of pain shot up from his knee, making him stumble. Though he'd already regained most of his leg strength, it was clear that a certain amount of knee weakness was here to stay. It had taken Carbo very little effort to persuade him to ride these past ten days rather than the march he generally preferred.

'Bollocks!' he snapped at the mauve evening sky, grasping his knee and rubbing it before he straightened.

Hobbling across to the rolling wagons, he hopped a few steps and then fell into a steady pace, grimacing with every other footfall.

Menenius sat in one of the carts, wedged into place with bundles and sacks. His armour had been stowed, and he travelled in his uniform only, with his cloak spread out beneath and around him, providing a clean surface upon which to recline.

Fronto was surprised at how pale the man still was, but had to remind himself that Menenius had always been fairly white, displaying that particular skin tone found on men who spent almost all of their time surrounded by scrolls and books and oil lamps, who only saw the bounty of nature through windows.

Twelve days had passed since he'd dropped in on the tribune, at which time the man had been in the throes of fever, lashing out and thrashing around, totally oblivious to any visitor. Since that time something had settled into Fronto – something that had killed off any further urge to visit. He'd not known exactly what it was, but something in his gut had continually turned him from visiting, even when Priscus had urged him to do so.

The man had clearly saved his life, but his stomach turned over at the thought of admitting that the fop, who had stated his own dislike of all things martial, had had the courage and wherewithal to step in and fight off three howling barbarians while the strong legate, veteran of a dozen wars, had dozed unconscious with a cracked skull and a trick knee.

It rankled badly.

And yet, on this last day of journeying, he had found his mind wandering and focusing on the events of that impressive and insane foray to the east bank of the Rhenus, and he had gradually come to the conclusion that he was being childish – a fact that needled him even more, given how often Lucilia and Faleria accused him of the same. The tribune may be a fop with a flowery personality and a weak chin, and he may have no desire to serve in an actual military environment, but the man had shown natural, innate talent, both with command and with direct swordplay.

It had soured Fronto all the more to discover that the root cause of his reticence to visit and acknowledge Menenius was plain jealousy. Here was a young man who was destined for high position in Rome, thrust into an environment for which he was hopelessly unprepared, and yet he'd excelled in the position. Meanwhile, Fronto, who had long been the most soldierly and martial of Caesar's officers, was rapidly being forced to come to terms with the aches, pains and limitations that came with being the oldest of the serving commanders.

'Menenius?'

The tribune sat a little straighter and, Fronto noted, took a sharp intake of pained breath as he focused on the source of the call.

'Legate Fronto? Mayhap you are lost?'

Fronto fought the surge of irritation and jealousy that urged him to turn and leave, and shook his head as he approached the cart.

'No, it's definitely you I'm here to see.'

'I feared...' Fronto was further irritated to realise that Menenius was blushing, 'I thought that perhaps I had angered you or that you were disappointed with me. I would have come to see you, had not the medicus and my own legate been very restrictive with my movements.'

Fronto fell in alongside the wagon, his head level with the tribune's elbow.

'Of course not!' he snapped, instantly regretting his tone. 'Sorry. I should have come to see you sooner. How are you feeling?'

Menenius winced as he moved. 'Somewhat pained. The medicus tells me that the wounds are not bad, but I have to admit to suffering with them. I have never been wounded before, barring a broken arm as a child. It hurts surprisingly more than I expected.'

Fronto nodded. 'As the recipient of a hundred wounds in my time, I can tell you that they all hurt, and you never get used to it. Well, some do. Balventius in the Eighth seems to actually enjoy it.' He scratched his head. 'I wanted to ask you what happened. How did you come to be there when... when whatever it was happened? It's all so vague.'

The tribune's face took on a surprisingly sheepish look that made Fronto frown.

'What's up?'

'I... it's not a tale of bravery, I'm afraid.'

'Results suggest otherwise.'

Menenius gave an embarrassed smile. 'Sadly not. When you formed the wedge to attack the archers, my bowels almost gave way.

I have never felt so terrified in my life. It is distinctly possible that I actually urinated in my breeches.'

'But you killed three barbarians. How? I mean, we thought you must have died in the assault.'

'I never *took part* in the attack, sir. To my eternal shame, I let our entire force charge the enemy, while I dropped to the ground behind and hid in the undergrowth by a tree.'

Fronto stared at the man. This was starting to sound more like the Menenius he had expected. Instead of the loathing he expected to feel for such cowardly activity, though, what he was surprised to experience was a surge of relief. The tribune was not so damned perfect after all. Fronto still had the edge.

'But why didn't you follow on when we'd taken the place? We searched for the fallen and couldn't find you. I wondered whether the bastards had carried you off – there were a few missing men.'

Again, the tribune turned his embarrassed face away. 'I'm afraid that I fled. As soon as you'd all gone and the screaming started, I ran deeper into the woods. I was in a blind panic. I don't even know how long I ran or where to. I only stopped when I almost ran straight into the rest of the barbarians coming the other way.'

Fronto nodded to himself. 'You ran into the enemy from the farm ambush?'

'Almost. I stopped short and began to make my way back toward you all as best I could. But I had to move slowly and quietly, and I was not entirely sure of the direction. Eventually, they were almost upon me, and I had to hide. I stayed in that hiding place for a while, shaking and terrified. I didn't know what to do or where to go. I think I slept for a while, but I woke when the barbarians came crashing back past me, running for their lives. I could hardly credit it. It seemed that Fortuna was sheltering me that day.'

Fronto smiled 'And me, I suspect.'

'Well I waited until the Germanic thugs had fled, and I saw a few legionaries pass, and I was about to stand when I saw you approach and sit, rubbing your knee.'

The legate reflexively repeated the motion now, noting the gentle throb within.

'I stayed crouched for a moment. To be honest, I was less than sure whether I dared make myself known, after my cowardice. But while I tried to pluck up the courage to stand, I saw a few more of the barbarians rise up out of the undergrowth behind you. They must have been hidden just like me, and less than ten paces distant. Remarkable, really.'

'Very' Fronto nodded. 'And one of them smashed me over the head from behind.'

Menenius blanched again. 'I could have stopped that. I just do not know how I can apologise enough. Had I stood when I saw them or shouted a warning, you could have moved. But I stayed frozen. You fell heavily and I realised then that they would kill you.'

He lowered his eyes to the rattling boards of the cart beneath him. 'Something happened. I'm not sure what. It's all a bit of a blur, then. I think they spotted me before I stood, but possibly not. I drew my sword and... and... well it's all a bit confused. Next thing I knew I was being lifted up by legionaries, and my eyes wouldn't focus.'

Fronto nodded again. 'It would appear that your courage comes in fits and starts, tribune. The man who turned the tide back at that farmstead is the same one as the man who saved my life. But that man seems to be locked away inside a gentler, more peaceable man. I can't say I'm not grateful, mind.' He took a deep breath. 'But that dichotomy is no use in command of a legion. I would heartily recommend that when the campaigning season ends, you do not push to retain your commission.'

Menenius smiled weakly. 'I never had that intention, legate. I have already spent this summer planning my next step up the cursus honorum. My family wanted me to excel in the military. They pushed for me to repeat my year and try to shine, but it is time to resign. I know that now.'

'And don't let that knob Plancus assign you to anything like that again. Stick to shouting at people and making lists. In the meantime' he glanced at the wagon's driving seat, where the Gallic-born legionary was studiously examining the rump of the ox before him, 'don't repeat this story to anyone. Just tell them that you don't recall what happened. It'll do you no good in Rome if that story gets out.'

The tribune nodded gratefully. 'Thank you, legate.'

'And thank you. It seems that I owe you a life somewhere down the line. Let's pray to Mars that it's not necessary to collect on it.'

Leaving a slightly relieved looking tribune, Fronto strode forward again at a faster pace. Slowing briefly, he caught the eye of the legionary driving the cart.

'What's your name, soldier?'

'Catumandos, sir. Third century, Seventh cohort.'

'Well, legionary Catumandos, if any hint of that conversation I just had with the tribune ever surfaces again, I will know exactly where to look. It's not unknown for an unwary legionary to drown in a latrine trench. You get my drift?'

The soldier nodded, stony-faced. Fronto gave him a long moment of glare, just to push home the point, before strolling off back toward the tents of the settled legions.

Good. Cathartic. That was exactly what he'd needed to hear. So long as he never found himself sharing a command with the man again, everything would go swimmingly.

And now to address the other thing that had been filling his thoughts on the journey before dropping in on Cantorix at the medical section.

* * * * *

'Nice dagger.'

Centurion Furius turned to face Fronto, his face betraying no surprise, his eyes flinty and hard. The legate of the Tenth could hardly fail to notice the way Furius' hand dropped to rest on the pommel of his gladius in an automatic reaction.

'Legate?'

'I said 'nice dagger'. Shiny. New, is it?'

The centurion's jaw firmed. 'As it happens, yes. Can I help you in some way?'

'Costs a couple of coins, doesn't it. And Cita can be a bit stingy with replacements. Bet you had to shell out over the odds for that. Must irritate you.'

Furius squared his shoulders and looked the legate in the eye. 'Is there a reason you're keeping me from my duties, *sir*?'

'Just admiring the dagger. Lost your old pugio, did you?'

'If it's of any great interest to you, it broke during the battle at the Germanic camp. I requisitioned a new one the same day. I don't let any man attend duty with missing kit, let alone doing so myself. Are you quite happy now?'

'Tough luck, that' Fronto replied with a grin. He was starting to enjoy himself, and the more irritated Furius became, the more his own mood improved. 'I mean, the pugio's a strong weapon. Damn hard to break that blade. Tried to prise off a pilum head with it, did you?'

227

Furius simply glared at him and Fronto ploughed on, smiling.

'I mean, I've had my pugio since Caesar was a simple quaestor in Hispania and I was on his staff as a junior officer. Used it for the first time in a riot in Numantia, long before Caesar's proprietorship and my command in the Ninth. I'd say I've used it more than a thousand times since then, and it's still as strong as a vestal's underwear and has a wicked edge.'

'If you really must know, legate, my pugio snapped because I punched the bloody thing through a chieftain's bronze chest plate. I got it stuck in his breastbone and the tip snapped off while I was trying to remove it. I might have been able to free it, given time, but I was sort of busy fighting off two more of the bastards with just a gladius. Some of us fought like soldiers there, rather than poncing about on a horse.'

All the humour drained from Fronto in a breath. His eyes narrowed.

'I know your sort, Furius. You and that friend of yours. When I have proof of what you're up to, you'll wish you'd been cut down in battle.'

The centurion simply smiled coldly. 'Permission to speak out of turn, man-to-man, sir?'

'Granted by all means.'

'Why don't you just fuck off, Fronto? You spend all your time swanning around with a vine staff jammed up your arse, half-drunk and half-dazed. You're just an impediment to proper military organisation. You're too hard-arsed to support those liberal, girl-like officers who want Caesar to rein his army in and 'talk it out', but you're too weak and disobedient to serve properly and carry out the orders given to you by your superior without questioning every angle and complaining at it all.'

Fronto opened his mouth angrily, but Furius jammed a finger into his chest, almost driving him back a step.

'No. You gave me the right to speak. Your sort makes me sick. You have the skills and the courage to be a bloody good officer and leader of men. You could be a Pompey. Or a Lucullus. Or even a Caesar. But you're just too indecisive and wishy-washy. You have flashes of brilliance, I'll admit. Your little stunt across the river was good and I'd have liked to have been there. But in between, you continually sod it all up and drink away your effectiveness.'

There was a pause – a moment's silence – and yet Fronto, standing there with furrowed, angry brow and mouth open ready to retort, found himself somehow unable to speak, disarmed by words.

'See? You can't even put me in my place.' Furius took a deep breath. 'Now I have duties, like most centurions. I have things that need doing. You don't like me. I don't trust you. But we serve in different legions and we'd never even have to cross paths if you didn't make it your life's work to pester and accuse me. So why don't we agree never to speak again, and I'll just wait patiently until the end of the year when, if rumour in the Seventh is to be believed, you will lose your commission through your constant disobedience, and piss off back to Rome to swagger around the gutters there.'

Without waiting for a reply, which Fronto, almost shocked with anger, appeared totally unable to supply, Furius turned and strode away, vine staff jammed beneath his arm.

The legate stood and watched him go, turning over everything that had been said in his mind.

Rumour was that he was going to be decommissioned? Why?

Somehow, that small unpleasant revelation almost obliterated everything else the man had said. Should he speak to Caesar?

He stood still in the warm night air for a moment, listening to the general murmur of a camp at rest and the distant sounds of the civilian settlement going about its life.

A deep breath totally failed to calm him or settle the twitch he seemed to have suddenly acquired beneath his right eye. Grumbling quietly, he strode off back toward the praetorium.

The cavalry officers of Aulus Ingenuus, Caesar's bodyguard, were positioned around the command section of the main camp, by the important tents as well as in a general perimeter, their backs ramrod straight, eyes alert. Two of them twitched for a moment as Fronto approached, preparing to block his path but, recognising him as one of the staff officers at the last moment, they saluted.

'Password, legate?'

Fronto had to pause for a moment and dredge his memory. 'Artaxata. Why Priscus needs to keep dredging up the names of eastern shitholes for passwords is beyond me. I think he just does it to annoy me because he knows I'm bad with geography.'

The two cavalrymen smiled and thumbed over their shoulder.

'In you go, sir.'

'Is the camp prefect in?'

'He's in his tent, sir.'

Nodding his thanks, Fronto strode off toward Priscus' tent, gesturing at the guard standing beside that doorway. The legate himself had never bothered with a personal guard around his command as most senior officers did, but the praetorian cavalrymen had extended their remit from the general himself to the entire command section. Against all expectations, Priscus seemed to like it.

'Fronto, from the Tenth' he said to the cavalry trooper.

The man saluted, rapped on the tent's doorframe and ducked inside. Fronto heard his name being announced in a muffled voice within, and the barked command to let him in. Priscus sounded in a worse mood than usual.

Thanking the soldier, Fronto ducked inside. Priscus stood behind his large desk, leaning on it with his left hand, his right curled around a solid wooden wine cup. He looked up at the new arrival and Fronto caught the look of desperate aggravation within his friend's eyes.

'Bad day?'

Priscus nodded and slumped back down to his seat, the wine slopping in the cup. 'You have no idea. And you?'

'Bet mine beats yours.'

Priscus' brow rose and Fronto strode across and dropped into one of the two rickety wooden chairs opposite the prefect. 'I've discovered that I was saved from gruesome death by a wet little coward with no experience who *still* somehow fights better than me. I've been told I'm useless, drunken and old – more or less – by a centurion who, while he may be a prick, could just be right. And now I hear there's a rumour that I'm to be sent back to Rome at the end of the year. Top that.'

Priscus grinned.

'Good. Well, the tribune saved you and, whatever you think of him, you have to be grateful for that. You *are* old. You're older than me and I feel damned ancient these days. And you do drink considerably more than the others – myself excluded of course. Did you know that Cita keeps an emergency stock of amphorae that he calls his 'Fronto'? 'Useless' I'd be tempted to argue with, though I've seen you trying to ride a horse, so I might not. And I can squash that rumour for you. I have the list of officers whose tour is up by winter, and your name's not on it.'

'Good. But it's still been a bad day. What's got you so bothered, then?'

'Other than the standard camp crap, added to all the extra work provided by the presence of a civilian population? Caesar's got me handling all the bloody merchants that he's called in, and setting everything up for Volusenus.'

'What merchants? Who's Volusenus?'

Priscus slid the jug of wine across the table, indicating the three spare cups at the side. Fronto eyed it suspiciously for a moment, wondering how much of Furius' invective stream he would be proving right if he poured that drink and in the end giving up and doing so anyway. As if to cheat the centurion, he gave it an unusually healthy dose of water.

'Go on.'

'It's not general knowledge, but Caesar's had the call out for merchants who have knowledge of Britannia. He had local scouts sent out before we even left the Rhenus to gather information. Most of them, and the scouts, will be waiting for us at Gesoriacum, but a couple of the more enterprising ones have come here and met the column, hoping to get the choicest reward for their help.'

'So you've been collating all their information?'

Priscus' look was rather sour. 'It didn't take much collating. They've given us some scant knowledge of the tribes and the geography, but they all seem to disagree on everything but the most basic points. And on the one thing they've all emphatically stated.'

'What?'

'That it's too late in the season for safe sailing to Britannia. That if we attempt to cross after this month we risk the fleet being torn apart and sent all over the ocean with the army drowned. Apparently the autumn currents here are bloody awful. They all think we should wait for spring.'

'But Caesar doesn't?'

'Correct. Unless we get a lot more useful information at Gesoriacum – and that looks exceedingly unlikely if this lot are any indication – the general's going to send a scout across to check it out. Hence: Volusenus.'

'Still don't know him.'

'He's senior tribune of the Twelfth. Distinguished himself at Octodurus apparently. Anyway, he's apparently got history with ships, so Caesar's planning to send him across to Britannia in a bireme to fill in the gaps in the knowledge and clear up any points that we're not certain of. Can't say I envy the poor sod. But I've had

231

to have everything ready for him on the assumption that, as soon as we reach Gesoriacum, he'll be off to explore.'

Fronto glanced down at the desk and noticed for the first time the hastily drawn map of the Gaulish coastline, marked out in charcoal on a piece of expensive vellum. A short distance from the town marked 'GESORIACVM' a wavering line of grey denoted the coast of the land of the druids: Britannia. A shudder ran through Fronto which chilled him to the bone.

'No. Can't say I envy him either. But then we'll all get the chance soon enough. In three days we'll be at the coast. Then we'll just have time to recover and shave before Neptune gets to drag everything I've eaten for the last two weeks out of my face and make my life a living Hades.'

As Priscus took another pull on his drink, Fronto gazed across the map, trying to decide what would be worse: the journey or the destination.

* * * * *

Gesoriacum was everything that Fronto feared it would be: maritime-obsessive. Absolutely everything about the place was centred about its mercantile shipping, its port and its fishing industry. The whole place smelled of dead, landed fish and brine – a fact that had caused Fronto's first vomiting session before they had even clapped eyes on the rolling waves. He could remember a time when he'd enjoyed fish as a meal and slathered the 'garum' fish sauce from Hispania over everything he ate – not so now.

The population seemed to consist almost entirely of fishermen, fish-sellers, fisher-wives, retired fishermen relying on their fisherman families, and inns with names like 'Drunken Codfish', 'Thundering Barnacle' or 'Jolly Fisherman'. It was almost as though the gods had set out to create a native settlement perfectly designed to keep Fronto at maximum smelling distance.

The army had camped on the high point at the landward side of the town, forming a solid fortification that loomed over the native settlement, with a commanding view. The increased altitude and distance from the docks were the only reason that Fronto had remained a pale grey-pink colour for the last week, rather than tipping into the grey-green tone he'd gone whenever he'd had cause to visit the waterfront. At least on one such visit he'd managed to

232

secure a new 'Fortuna' pendant from a merchant. It looked decidedly like a bandy-legged Gallic fishwife to Fronto, but the merchant had been insistent that it was the Goddess of luck. Somehow he'd rested a little easier wearing it, for all its misshapen ugliness.

Barely had the legions begun the ditches and ramparts before the veritable army of native fishermen, traders and opportunists had descended on the camp, drawn by promises of a healthy reward for any pertinent information they could supply concerning the land of the druids across the ocean. Their idea of pertinent had apparently differed greatly from Caesar's, and many had left the camp with a scowl of discontent and empty pockets, glowering at the newly arrived and heavily armoured soldiers that reminded them so heavily of the armies that had passed by this way a year before, 'pacifying' the north coast.

A few interesting titbits had floated to the surface though, two of which had helped mollify the dreadfully unhappy Fronto: Firstly, three different men, all of whom had good credentials, had confirmed that the centre of druidic power in that horrible island was more than a fortnight's travel to the northwest. This was welcome news to every man in the army. The druids had caused enough trouble in Gaul; their religion, power and practices were still largely unknown and frightening, and Britannia was the home of that power. To know that the chances of an encounter were so distance-dimmed was a great consolation.

Secondly, the most warlike of the native tribes all lived in the north of the land. While those tribes to the south could be expected to be every bit as dangerous and duplicitous as the Gallic, Belgic or Aquitanian tribes; the talk had always been that the worst tribes of Celts had lived in Britannia. Nine-foot-tall cannibals with painted bodies, supposedly – reports delivered by enough trustworthy scholars that it was hard to refute. But to know that these tribes of monsters lived far in the north made a southern coast landing a little less worrying. Even Caesar, who had denounced such descriptions as preposterous, had donated generously to those visitors who had confirmed the vast distances between the south coast and these awful dangers.

Other details had come out too: the nature of the coast, with its intermittent areas of unassailable cliff and the location of several strong rivers; the swampy areas that lay along the coast to the north, and the names of a number of local tribes.

All in all, the information had been interesting and some of it of use, but little was detailed enough to warrant adding to the map of which Caesar and Priscus kept tight control.

And so, within half a day of their arrival and at the most favourable tide, tribune Volusenus, whom Fronto had finally exchanged a few words with – largely ones of sympathy – had boarded a small, fast bireme that had come up the coast from the anchor point of the Gallic fleet, and had sailed off into the endless waters and the unknown.

Two days later the rest of the Roman fleet that had been raised the previous year on the orders of Brutus hove into view and anchored at the southern end of the town.

Since then the army had settled in to wait. Fronto had deliberately moderated his drinking – a move made all the easier by the fact that not a day passed without his having to find a quiet corner in which to be sick – and had very carefully avoided any possibility of bumping into either centurion Furius or tribune Menenius, though each for entirely different reasons.

And now, with a week of misery under his belt, Fronto stood leaning on the fence of a horse corral, breathing deeply; the cavalry pens and the latrines were the only places outside mealtimes where the stink of fish disappeared beneath something else.

'Fronto!'

Taking a deep breath of horse sweat and dung to keep him going, Fronto turned at the familiar voice. Priscus stood in the main road between pens, his hands on his hips.

'Whassup?'

'Time to come and get involved.'

Fronto shook his head. He'd been ordered to attend the first two of the general's interminable meetings but after putting out a flaming brazier with a stomach full of bile last time, he'd been excused further attendance. He simply could not understand how the rest of the army endured the constant stench of brine and dead fish.

'I'm not required' he replied.

'You'll want to be there. Volusenus is back.'

'What?'

'Landed quarter of an hour ago. He just came into camp to give his report. I'm gathering all officers.'

Fronto nodded and heaved himself away from the railing and the smell of horses, bracing himself for the fresh waves of fish he caught as soon as the wind brought it wafting up. While he could still get away with not attending, to hear a first-hand account of their destination was an invaluable opportunity.

'Lead on.'

* * * * *

Caesar's headquarters tent was already thronging with officers when Priscus and Fronto fell in at the back. The Tenth's commander took a deep breath of sweat and body odour combined with the fumes from the four braziers and coughed.

Tribune Volusenus had already arrived and was busy adding marks and lines to the map on the table as the assembled officers stood around the periphery impatiently, tapping their fingers or stretching unobtrusively in the press. Gradually, over the next few moments, other members of the staff and senior field commanders filed in to take their positions, leaving Fronto smiling at the fact that he was, for once, not the last man to arrive. After a tense wait, Volusenus stepped back and admired his handiwork, frowned, added a couple more lines and adjusted the position of some splodge or other, and then stepped back again with a nod, dropping the charcoal stick to the table and folding his arms.

'That's all of it?' Caesar asked quietly.

'That's it sir.'

'Well it seems as though everyone's here. Why don't you fill us in, tribune? I am sure that every man in this tent is just as tense and expectant as I.'

Volusenus nodded again and cleared his throat, unfolding his arms long enough to rub tired eyes.

'Everything the merchants have told you is true, concerning the passage of the sea. My aide confirmed my estimate that the journey from here to the nearest land is a little over thirty miles. It sounds like a stone's throw, but this channel is like a giant version of the Pillars of Hercules. The currents that run beneath the surface are strong, while the winds whip the surface into large, ship-threatening waves. It bears no resemblance to the Mare Nostrum.'

He scanned the crowd of officers and picked out Brutus. 'You will know the western ocean from the naval campaign against the Veneti last year. I'm sure you will know how roiling and treacherous the surface can be and how the weather can change it from glass to deep furrows in a matter of moments?'

Brutus nodded seriously. The weather and the sea had almost brought disaster last year, preventing the naval force from performing its assigned tasks until the last moment.

'Imagine the power and unpredictability of that, forced into a channel only twenty-some miles wide. The locals have a knack with it, but even *they* avoid crossing any later in the year than this.'

Caesar waved the concern aside as though it mattered little. 'What else, Tribune?'

'Our ships will be pretty much useless. My bireme was thrown about like a child's leaf-boat on a full drain. We are exceedingly lucky to be here, and I vowed three altars and a dozen offerings to Fortuna, Neptune and Salacia just to make it back. An attempt to cross that in a bireme in any worse weather than we had is nothing short of suicidal. Even the triremes we have will be woefully inadequate.'

'Fortunately' Caesar interjected with a steady tone and a reassuring smile, 'I anticipated the unworthiness of our fleet and have already put out the order to commandeer or purchase as many suitable vessels from the Morini and the other local tribes as we can manage. The fleet will consist of at least half Gallic vessels by the time we are ready to leave. As for your worries over the weather, I intend to embark as soon as the fleet is assembled, hopefully this very week, so fear not too much over a few breezes and squalls.'

Volusenus gave his commander a look that conveyed every ounce of his uncertainty and fear as he waited to be sure that he should go on. Caesar gave him an encouraging nod.

'I have seen little of the tribes of Britannia, for in all five days of my journey, I never once set foot upon the land.'

Caesar frowned and the tribune anticipated the next question. 'With respect, general, the bireme was unsuitable for approaching the land and even the local sailors we had on board to advise and guide us advised against any attempt to make landfall. Almost the entire length of the coast consists of cliffs of a magnificent height or of dips, shingle beaches or bays that, while looking like pleasant anchorages, also appeared to my military mind to be the absolutely perfect place for an ambush or attack. In all that time, I saw little of the people of the land, only a few fishermen in their boats or farmers and riders on the shoreline and cliff tops.'

'So your grand sum of intelligence from five days aboard ship is the shape and height of the coastline and a confirmation that the locals fish and farm. Am I correct?'

Volusenus lowered his gaze. 'There was little else we could achieve, Caesar.'

The general straightened.

'Very well. Due to the restriction in fleet size and the number of troops we must move, combined with the swift and punitive nature of the campaign, I will be committing only two legions to Britannia, along with a little cavalry support and my own command group.'

As a palpable wave of relief swept through the tent, Caesar eyed his officers, each of whom was busy throwing up small silent prayers that they would not be required.

'The Seventh will take part under Cicero.' The legate of the Seventh nodded wearily, clearly having expected this. Fronto's mind raced back to what Priscus had told him of the Seventh at the start of the year. All Caesar's bad eggs in one basket, led by a man of uncertain loyalty. Caesar had told him that he had something in mind for them: an isle of monsters full of cannibals, blood-crazed druids and treacherous swamps, apparently. Despite that the Seventh consisted almost entirely of people Fronto did not know or did not like, he could not help but feel a little sorry for them.

'And the Tenth; my equestrian veterans, will accompany them.'

The bottom fell out of Fronto's world. The very idea of trying to cross that thirty mile stretch of dangerous water brought a small involuntary mouthful of bile that he had to swallow while nodding seriously.

Shit! Shit, shit, shit, shit, shit! Clearly Caesar was committing the Tenth to babysit the Seventh and make sure they did what they were supposed to. Fronto was in no doubt that he would be called back at the end of the meeting and of what that private conversation would consist. The Seventh were to be committed first to any engagement with the Tenth at their rear to keep them in line – it was plain to him. He wondered whether it was as plain to Cicero. A quick glance at the Seventh's legate left him in no doubt as to Cicero's feelings on the matter. The man looked like he'd tasted a little bile himself.

'Gentlemen,' Caesar continued, 'study this map carefully. Over the next few days the ships of our Gallic allies will be arriving in port to bolster our fleet. As soon as the ships are judged adequate, we will be sailing with the first good tide. Have your commands on constant alert and ready to move. When the order is given I want those two legions decamped in less than an hour. Varus, I want one wing of the cavalry committed too.'

Caesar leaned forward and turned the map upside down so that the coastline, marked in black smudges and looking, to Fronto, particularly craggy and unforgiving, faced the officers.

'We will be taking only the barest supplies, with rations for the journey and only three days' extra. No siege equipment and no support train. This will be a fast and extremely mobile assault force. I intend to rely on pillage and forage to support the army in the field. Brutus? You have the most experience in these matters, so I am placing you and Volusenus in charge of preparing the fleet and arranging the crews, route and so on.'

One of the other officers cleared his throat meaningfully, though Fronto now kept his fretful gaze downcast.

'Speak.'

'What of the other legions, Caesar?'

'Rufus and the Ninth will remain in Gesoriacum to control the port and secure our point of return. The remaining five legions will be sent out into the surrounding tribes: just a subtle reminder of our presence. I have noted a certain reluctance in our 'allies' desire to supply information and guides. We wouldn't wish them to start thinking too independently and undervaluing their Roman allies. Sabinus and Cotta? Split the force as you see fit. I will speak to you later about the tribes that I am concerned over.'

Once again, Fronto looked up in surprise. That task was the sort that Caesar traditionally passed on to Labienus. Throughout their time in Gaul, the tall staff officer had been Caesar's senior lieutenant who took charge of multi-legion forces in the general's absence. This sudden shift in policy would not have gone unnoticed and cast Labienus in a distinctly unfavourable light.

'Very well, gentlemen; you all have work to do: I suggest you get to it. Standard briefing at first light. Dismissed.'

* * * * *

Fronto sighed and leaned back in the chair, rubbing his knee.

'Is that it, general?'

'I think so, Marcus. You're fully briefed, and I'll be with you anyway. Just be aware of the Seventh at all times and make sure you

238

don't commit the Tenth to dangerous action when the Seventh could do the job for you.'

Fronto nodded, trying not to resent the general's dismissive attitude to a whole legion of men.

'Then...' he was interrupted by a rapping on the wooden tent frame.

'Come' barked Caesar.

The cavalry trooper on guard ducked in through the tent's entrance, bearing a wax-sealed scroll case.

'This just arrived from Rome by fast courier for you, general.'

Caesar nodded and the man strode forward and delivered the ivory cylinder. Waving the trooper away, Caesar glanced at the seal, frowning at something he saw, and then broke it, tipping out the parchment sheet and unrolling it, discarding the case on the desk. Fronto watched with interest as Caesar's expression underwent a number of blink-of-an-eye changes, despite his trying to maintain a straight face. Surprise, annoyance, anger, disappointment, decision, resignation.

'News from home, Caesar?'

The general glanced up in surprise, apparently having entirely forgotten Fronto's presence in his studious attention to the letter.

'Mmh? Oh. Yes.'

'From your pet slug, Clodius, perchance?'

The veneer completely cracked for a moment, though Fronto was puzzled to see not anger on the general's face, but almost panic.

'Yes, Fronto' he snapped, 'from Clodius.'

'You'd do well to cut that one off, Caesar.'

'Dictating terms to your commander?' There was a dangerous edge to the general's voice, but Fronto ignored it pointedly.

'We spent half a year cleansing Rome of his infection. The piece of shit tried to kill me and my family. Hell, he tried to kill you! And now you *use* him? Have you even the faintest idea how dangerous that is?'

Caesar's gaze had strayed once more to the letter in his hands and he seemed to take control of himself with visible effort, rolling up the parchment and dropping it on the desk in front of him.

'Do not presume to lecture me on dangers, Fronto. Who was it who embraced his capture and then chastised the Cilician pirates? Who marched with Crassus against that slave-filth Spartacus? Who survived Sulla's proscriptions? Who was hailed 'Imperator' in

Hispania? I recognise that you will probably serve in the military until you die or are too old and feeble to do so, and will then likely retire to an easy life back in Puteoli. But should you ever dabble in the cess pool and viper pit all-in-one that is Rome, you will come to understand that even the most odious and untrustworthy of people can be a useful tool for some tasks.'

'So what has the sewer rat been up to this time?'

Again, Fronto was somewhat surprised to notice a flash of uncertainty – even panic? – flash across the general's eyes.

'Nothing of consequence, Marcus. Nothing of consequence.'

An inexplicable shiver ran down Fronto's spine and he sat silently for a moment until Caesar waved him away in dismissal. Standing, he turned and left the tent, pausing at the doorway to glance back at the general, only to see him tearing the parchment into small pieces and dropping them in one of the braziers.

Something peculiar and dangerous was going on with the evasive, taciturn Caesar, and Fronto had a horrible gut feeling that it somehow involved him.

Chapter 13

(Gesoriacum, on the Gaulish coast, opposite Britannia)

Word of the impending campaign had already spread beyond the Roman forces and the civilian town; of that there could be absolutely no doubt. Only two days after the decision to sail had been confirmed, ambassadors from the tribes of Britannia had begun to appear. Caesar had greeted their arrival with his traditional grave expression, though Fronto could not help noticing a lightening of the general's mood with each new advocate.

Eight tribes had sent deputations, promising hostages, support, supplies and money to the Romans. Some had even gone so far as to submit themselves to Caesar's governance. It appeared that the fate of the Belgae in previous years was still fresh in the mind of the tribes of Britannia, many of whom were related to the Belgae by blood and tradition. Rather than face the inevitable iron-shod boot of the Roman republic pressing down on their necks, it seemed that several of the nearer tribes were willing to submit.

Moreover, and much to Caesar's pleasure, their arrival had supplied him with eight new, heavy Celtic ships with which to brave the crossing – ships that were designed for these waters and were capable of withstanding the tremendous pressures and strains.

After a few days, when it became apparent that no further ambassadors were likely, Caesar had taken the hostages offered and quartered them in Gesoriacum's fort. He had then set the eight groups of men on board a single ship and released them to go back to their own land, along with promises of Roman support and peaceful relations, encouraging them to spread the word and their particular brand of 'Pax Britannia' among the more reticent tribes.

Now, only three days after the ambassadors' ship had sailed off from Gesoriacum on a sea as calm as the impluvium pool of a Roman villa, the men of the Seventh and Tenth legions sat or stood on the decks of the motley collection of ships that made up the Gallo-Roman fleet in the town's harbour, staring out at what appeared to be distinctly unfriendly waters.

Only an hour before the troops had begun to board on Caesar's orders, a wind had whipped up the water's surface and changed its appearance utterly. Moreover, dark grey clouds started to roll in from the northeast as the evening sky began to darken, threatening heavy rain and worse. Brutus and Volusenus had conferred with three of the captains, two native guides and even with Caesar but, much to Fronto's dismay, had pronounced conditions acceptable.

Even the pure white lamb that had displayed a healthy liver and kidneys and clearly shown Neptune's favour had not put his fears to rest. He'd spent a small fortune on food, wine and trinkets merely to leave them reverentially on any altar he could find – Roman or native – to try and appease whoever controlled that particular stretch of water and his passage over it. He'd become increasingly convinced that his bandy-legged amulet was an image of some fat Gallic fishwife with as much divine connection to Fortuna as a dead herring.

All in all, everything pointed to a complete disaster as far as Fronto was concerned.

Then there had been the news that the eighteen ships destined to convey the cavalry across the water had been trapped in the next port down the coast, due to the weather. That was hardly encouraging and Fronto had watched with bitter dismay as Varus and his cavalry wing had ridden off south to find their vessels. The senior cavalry commander still sported his splinted arm and a pained look, but had recently taken to riding again as often as possible. Fronto had wondered with idle depression whether he'd seen the last of his brave cavalry officer friend.

The only bright spark had been the surprise addition to the fleet of Galronus and a single turma of thirty Gallic riders, their horses crammed in with the men and spread across the fleet. Caesar had apparently given the Remi officer permission to accompany the legions on the basis that he and his men shared a common heritage with the island's inhabitants – a bond that could prove useful.

The cavalry officer grinned at him and tucked into a platter of bread, cheese and pilchards. Fronto fought the urge to stand at the rail and empty his stomach contents again. He'd already done so twice since boarding, and the ship had not even slipped the mooring yet. He'd glared at the men nearby, but the smirks had continued nonetheless, increasing with every colour change his face had undergone.

'Remember, whatever happens while we're over there – on the assumption we even make the crossing – not to get yourself in a position where you're alone and anywhere near those two centurions from the Seventh. They've found it easy enough to attack people even with the whole army present. Over there, you could easily find yourself cut off and surrounded by the Seventh. Be alert at all times.'

'Marcus, stop fussing over us like a mother hen' Galronus grinned. 'We're all grown men and warriors.'

'Aye' Carbo laughed, looking up from his cup of watered wine. 'And stop worritting about the journey, sir. It's only thirty miles. Two more cups of this and I could *piss* that far!'

Again, Fronto looked around the deck of the high-sided Gallic beast in which they would cross. Such was its size that the officers had managed to secure themselves a fairly private area of deck toward the stern some distance from the groups of men sitting cross legged, rolling dice, singing songs and telling ribald jokes. They had even managed to obtain a shelter of leather tent sections that could hold off the rain that Fronto felt sure was coming.

Even as he glanced across at the steersman and the ship's captain, the hooded lamp with which they had been signalling the other ships in the fleet caught the wind from the wrong direction and went black with a hiss, plummeting the entire stern of the ship into stygian gloom.

'Whose genius idea was it to sail at night?'

'Apparently it was the best choice' Carbo chattered conversationally. 'The tide is right, the omens are good, and all the locals are predicting inclement weather in the next day or two. If we don't go on this tide, we might not go at all.'

'Sounds just fine to me' grumbled Fronto, feeling another heave of his churning guts on the way.

'Did you have any of that ginger and mint?' Galronus asked lightly.

'Like I could keep it down if I did' snapped Fronto.

'Your sister said it was the only real remedy. You should at least try it.'

'Piss off. And could you all stop eating stinking fish near me. Can't you naff off down the bow with the grunts to eat that muck?'

'This?' enquired Galronus with a grin, waving a lightly-cooked headless fish at Fronto, who immediately leapt to the rail to empty his stomach yet again.

'Anyway' Carbo said in his light, happy tone, 'if I've got my timings right, setting off now means we should arrive at dawn. We'll surprise the goat-humpers and give 'em no time to prepare.'

Fronto wiped his mouth with the back of his wrist and heaved in half a dozen deep breaths before turning and collapsing to the deck again with his friends. As well as Galronus and Carbo, Petrosidius, the chief standard bearer of the Tenth, and Atenos, the huge training centurion, sat in the small circle, wrapped in their cloaks against the chilling wind.

Glancing around to make sure they had as much privacy as the ship's deck allowed, Fronto leaned forward conspiratorially and spoke in a low voice. The rest of the ship's occupants were native Gauls or members of the trusted Tenth, but some things needed to be kept quiet, regardless of company.

'I've been thinking about our two centurion friends in the Seventh.'

'You do surprise me' muttered Galronus.

'No, I mean I think I see a way to bring something good out of this situation.'

Carbo and Atenos leaned forward. Petrosidius continued to listen, with his head up, watching the other men nearby. 'Go on' Galronus grinned.

'Well until now I've been thinking we need to be wary of Furius and Fabius; to keep ourselves away from them and not get caught where we can find ourselves in trouble. Problem is: if we keep doing that, we're never going to be able to nail them for anything. Perhaps it would be better to play this entirely the other way.'

'Draw them out, you mean?'

'Precisely. With only the Tenth and the Seventh present, they might get bold enough to do something stupid. We should be encouraging that, rather than preventing it.'

'What have you in mind?' Atenos asked, frowning.

'We need to goad them… to push them to breaking point so that they snap and go for it.'

'But how?'

Galronus grinned. 'Just be yourself, Marcus. It appears that your very existence annoys them deeply.'

The legate shot the cavalry officer a sour look, but he found himself nodding anyway.

'Irritatingly, you might be right. I am the only one who could maybe wind them up enough to break them; and they already have it in for me anyway. I'm fairly sure they'll relish the chance to get another crack at me. So the question remains: just how do I wind them up to that extent?'

'That's easy' Petrosidius shrugged. The signifer, sitting bareheaded with his wolf pelt on his knees, had been so quiet that Fronto had almost forgotten he was there.

'Go on.'

'Well the Seventh's eagle bearer, Sepunius, happens to be an old friend of mine, and he tells me that Furius and Fabius have pretty much taken it upon themselves to act as Cicero's personal guard and escort. Apparently his tribunes are a bit put out that two centurions seem to have more influence than them, but the pair have such a brutal reputation that no one'll confront them about it.'

'I've noticed this.'

'Well, Cicero is fairly outspoken against Caesar at times. A clever man shouldn't find it too hard to start an argument between the two commanders, especially one of Caesar's top men. And once you have the two commanders at each other, Cicero's pet centurions will start straining at their leash and snapping. Should be a walk in the park for you.'

A slow smile spread across Fronto's face as he pictured the scene. It really would not be difficult. Hell, he'd already seen it happen several times over the summer.

'It'll have to be when we land at the other side, of course.'

'So you have long enough to argue between hurling over the rail, you mean?' Galronus needled with a grin.

'Oh piss off.'

'You're right though' Carbo said quietly. 'But that's only half the battle, as it were. Once you've wound them up far enough to make them want to take you down again, you'll have to give them the opportunity. But play it carefully. Remember that these two are both veterans with as long a record as you or I; both strong and fearless, and they've managed several sneaky attacks so far. How do you plan to play it?'

Again, Fronto lapsed into silence for a few moments, before nodding to himself a couple of times.

'Like what happened across the Rhenus, I think. I can let myself fall behind and get separated – perhaps because of my knee. Everyone knows about that now, so no one will be surprised if I have to stop and tend to it. We'll be very unlikely to have the chance to prepare any trap in advance, so we'll just have to be ready to spring it whenever the opportunity occurs. We'll work out some signal. Then, at some point when I find myself near enough the pair of them, I'll give the signal and stop to deal with my knee or whatever I need to do to get myself alone. At the signal, you lot need to disappear, but shadow Fabius and Furius wherever they go. As soon as they come at me, you can reveal yourselves and we'll have them red-handed in the act of attempting to kill a senior officer.'

'We need an impartial witness' Carbo said quietly.

'No we don't. The word of a legate, a signifer, two centurions and a cavalry commander carries enough weight to execute a man on the spot.'

'Not in the current circumstances' Atenos cautioned. 'Bear in mind how well known your enmity toward them is. Whatever the truth, most of the army will think it was simply a setup by us. Legate Brutus and tribune Volusenus will both be present across the water. If either of them was to witness the attempt there could be no doubt over the truth, and no comeback.'

'Think we can arrange that?' asked Fronto quietly.

'I think we'll manage.'

'Alright' the legate said, clapping his hands together purposefully and then pulling out his 'Fortuna' amulet and rubbing it between his fingers. 'Now all we need to do is make it across thirty miles of Styx-water in an unfamiliar ship, at night, in a storm, with only the divine protection of a small Gaulish trout-woman with bandy legs.'

* * * * *

The sun had been up for perhaps a quarter of an hour when the call issued from the bow of the ship. Fronto heaved himself up from his sodden blankets, crusty salt deposits giving a white sheen to the grey wool. The night had been the worst Fronto could remember. Fortunately, his memories of it were blurred, scant and confused, given the amount of time he'd spent wrapped in his blanket, shivering and trying to shut out the world.

Despite Carbo and Galronus' assurance that the conditions, while foul, were not enough to capsize or wreck the ship, the legate had remained unconvinced and had shut himself away from all the horror around him.

246

There had been two rainstorms during the crossing, neither of which had apparently been particularly disastrous; not enough to cause concern among the sailors anyway. The officers had their leather shelter to retire to, but to Fronto it merely appeared to funnel the wet, salty wind into a bone-chilling draft that left the blankets almost as wet and cold as those of the troops laying wrapped up on the open deck.

The weather had seemingly broken sometime after Fronto had collapsed into a worried, exhausted sleep, and the shout of sighted land roused the legate to a world of bright skies, scudding clouds and calm sea, though the chill in the air and the faint aroma of damp belied the image of a summer morning. Gulls whirled overhead, shrieking and crying their welcome to this, the island of the druids.

Galronus was already standing at the rail with Carbo and Atenos when Fronto staggered toward them, his legs weak and finding trouble with the rolling of the ship.

'For the love of Juno!'

Galronus turned to the approaching legate and nodded. 'Impressive isn't it? My father visited Britannia when I was a young boy and told us of this coast. I always thought he must have embellished a little. It would appear not.'

Fronto dropped his elbow to the rail in a space between the others and goggled at the white line approaching them. The cliffs must be three hundred feet or more in height for, even at this distance, more than a mile out, they could be seen to tower over the water, rising and falling as small bays opened up along the line. The morning sun caught the white chalky surface straight on, creating a blinding ribbon of white.

'I think I can see why Volusenus stayed on his ship.'

The three men around him nodded sagely.

'I take it we're at the front of the fleet, then? I would have thought Caesar's ship would have stayed ahead of us.'

Carbo pointed off to one side. A trireme rose and fell with the waves some quarter of a mile to their right, its shape distinctive even at that distance. Half a dozen other ships could be seen scattered across the water between and behind them. Dots on the horizon suggested that the rest of the fleet was some way back. The general had chosen to travel in one of the less stable Roman ships, rather than a Gallic trader, as befitted a praetor.

'The trireme is Caesar's I can see the red banners.'

247

'You've got better eyes than mine.'

Carbo smiled. 'I did a rough count of the ships within sight as soon as it was light enough. I could see roughly half the fleet. I'm very much hoping that the two storms separated us and slowed many vessels down. I'd hate to think that an entire legion's worth of ships ended up turning back or, worse still, at the bottom of the sea.'

Fronto shuddered. He had trouble imagining a worse fate.

'We'll be there in about a quarter hour according to the sailor I spoke to' confirmed Galronus. 'Caesar's ship seems to be angling toward us. I suspect we're heading for that dip there.' Fronto followed Galronus' pointing finger and spotted a bay, slightly wider than the others, nestled between two particularly high sections of cliff.

The legate leaned over the rail and smiled faintly. They were almost across. He'd not been sick since the previous evening, but then it was difficult to see how there could be anything left inside to bring up. A quick probe of his torso confirmed his suspicion: that he had eaten so little since arriving at Gesoriacum that his ribs were now quite prominent through his tunic. He resolved to eat like a horse – possibly even to eat a horse – once they were safely on land.

The calm water raced by along the hull of the strong Gallic ship, the low waves picking up a little in intensity as they neared the cliffs, though nothing compared to those they had experienced during the night. Looking up and ahead once more, Fronto could not help but be impressed by the wall-like cliffs that protected the druids' isle from the clutches of their enemies. Already, while contemplating his weight loss and the intensity of the waves, the ship had covered half the distance toward the sheltered bay and the cliffs that loomed ever higher.

'Well. Time for me to get to work' muttered Carbo, pushing himself back and smacking his vine staff against his bronze greaves. His face shone almost luminously pink, the morning cold and the sea air accentuating his already ruddy complexion. Turning, he began to bellow out orders to the other centurions, optios, signifers and men of the Tenth, calling the present centuries of the legion to stand to ready for disembarkation.

Fronto smiled at the efficiency of his men and then turned again, resting his chin on his folded arms upon the rail until the rocking motion threatened to set off his guts again. Caesar's trireme was closing on them now, keeping pace, as was another Celtic ship to the far side. Those behind were doing their best to put on an extra turn of speed and catch up with the vanguard of the fleet.

Atenos grinned at him and left to attend to his duties. Galronus, on the other hand, *had* no duties yet; his cavalry turma was scattered around the fleet wherever there was room.

The cliffs rose sharply from the bay with a flat landing area not more than five hundred paces across between the slopes. Trees crowded in the dip and a wide expanse of woodland was visible stretching back behind, the forest starting only a few hundred paces from the edge of the water. As he watched, Fronto began to discern the trails of wood smoke from at least a dozen buildings somewhere close within the woodland. Clearly this bay housed a settlement, shrouded by the trees.

The heights, by comparison, seemed denuded, the white walls topped by a narrow line of green that suggested rolling grass above, dotted with only the occasional struggling, wind-blown tree.

'Stand to. All hands stand to.'

Without need for the issuing of commands, the Gallic sailors began to haul on ropes and busy themselves with the sail. Calls were put out in the language of the Gauls, and the ship burst into a bustle of life. Fronto turned back to face their destination, ignoring the activity. He could hardly care less about the details that were required to make a ship work.

Something ahead drew his attention, though.

'Did you see that?'

Galronus frowned at him. 'What?'

'On the cliff. Movement on the top. There it is again.'

The Belgic officer turned his furrowed brow to the coast and squinted. 'I see it. On the right hand cliff: scattered movement.'

'*And* on the left.'

Now the ships were coming close enough to land that Fronto found his head beginning to crane upwards gradually to see the occasional movement at the cliff tops.

'Shepherds?' muttered Galronus.

'Too many. And at this time of the morning, that many people up there can only have something to do with us. I think Carbo was wrong about us surprising them.'

As if to confirm his suspicions his attention was drawn back to their immediate surroundings as the water nearby made a 'plopping' sound.

'What was that?'

His question was answered instantly as an arrow disappeared into the water only twenty paces from the bow with another plop. Glancing up, Fronto could now see dozens of figures standing perilously close to the cliff's edge. Even as he watched, more arrows began to arc out from the land and plummet toward the advancing ships. His eyes followed one of the shafts down and into the waves just off to the right. A moment later something small and heavy that could only be a sling shot plopped into the water.

'Back!' he yelled. 'Err... reverse! Back! Retreat.'

Turning from the rail, he began to wave his arms, motioning the ship's crew to pull the vessel back out of range.

'Get us out of range of those missiles. They could kill half of us before we land.'

The sailors were now rushing in a panic, trying to slow the momentum of the vessel, while turning her, ponderously. Fronto watched, his nerves twanging, aware with some irritation that Caesar's trireme, which had encountered the same reception and had decided on the same course of action, simply reversed their stroke. It was a difficult task and took master sailors to pull it off as smoothly as they were doing, but the effect was to move the trireme out of danger considerably faster than the slow arc taken by this great cow of a ship.

A scream echoed across the morning water from the left. The other Gallic ship had begun to turn and slow a little later and had already come within range, some poor sod becoming the first casualty of Britannia before even touching its soil.

As if to remind Fronto of the more immediate danger to himself, another arrow scratched a line across the timber at the prow of the ship as it whizzed past and into the water.

'Faster, damnit! They've got our range.'

But the ship had slowed considerably now and even as Fronto held his breath the prow began to come round, angling toward Caesar's vessel and then away, bringing them out of range of the arrows.

A horn blast rang out from the trireme, calling the fleet to converge on the general's position. Slowly, the Gallic vessel closed on Caesar's ship, others turning as they approached. Fronto's gaze slid back to the cliffs that were now slipping away on his left hand side. He would be willing to swear that the number of small figures on the cliff tops had doubled since they had arrived only a few moments earlier.

Waiting patiently, Fronto watched the trireme as they closed on it, and finally identified Caesar standing at the rail, gesturing to him. As soon as he judged he was within shouting distance, Fronto cleared his throat and took a cold, deep and salty breath.

'A warm reception, general.'

He could not quite make out the expression on the general's face.

'What.... landing.... bay..... think?' called Caesar. Fronto waggled his finger in his ear, cupped his hand around it meaningfully and shrugged. Behind him, the ship's crew slowed the vessel as it approached the trireme, careful to avoid interfering with the oars that drove it.

'I said' yelled the general, 'what are our chances of landing in that bay intact, do you think, Fronto?'

'Virtually nil!' he shouted back. 'If they could hit us out at sea with those arrows, they could just as easily hit us on the beach. We'd be cut down like wheat before we could move inland.'

'Agreed!' Caesar bellowed as the figure of Brutus appeared alongside him.

'We have time to decide, sir' the legate of the Eighth called. 'It will be a few hours yet before all the stragglers reach us. Besides, we could do with waiting for the afternoon tide, to avoid falling foul of rocks on the coast.'

The general paused thoughtfully for a moment. 'Very well. Can you still hear me Fronto?'

'Yes.'

'We'll gather here and let the fleet assemble out of missile range. Then we'll move up the coast to the northeast, looking for a better landing spot. We need somewhere gentle enough to land safely, and wide enough that we cannot be prey for archers as we are here.'

Fronto gave the general a sour look. 'Or we could just turn around. Volusenus sailed this coast for five days and found it inhospitable enough to not even try to land.'

He could sense the general's irritation, even without being close enough to make out his expression. 'If you'd studied the map, Fronto, you would have seen that there are long stretches of lower coastline in both directions. We will find a suitable spot this afternoon.'

251

'I only hope half of Britannia isn't waiting for us by then' Fronto yelled. 'The population up on those cliffs is growing all the time, and I think I can see horsemen up there now.'

'The entire population of Britannia would hardly be a worry for my veteran Tenth, eh, Fronto?'

Grimacing at the general, Fronto reached up and caressed the bandy-legged figure hanging around his neck, his eyes straying to the growing force arrayed on the cliff top and awaiting them.

* * * * *

The fleet had gradually assembled over the morning and into the early afternoon and by the time the cool sun had passed an hour beyond its zenith the sea to the south was clear of shapes. Shouted reports and commands from ship to ship had come up with a roll-call figure that was only four ships short of the fleet that had left Gesoriacum, though whether those four were safely back in port or decorating Neptune's triclinium remained to be seen. The very thought sent a chilly shudder through Fronto every time he considered it.

At some time part way through the afternoon, Brutus and his captains had announced that the tide was suitable and would remain so for a while, and the fleet began to move again, calls going out from musicians aboard Caesar's vessel. The mass flotilla turned slowly and proceeded up the channel, keeping the forbidding cliffs on their left and staying safely out of arrow shot. Fronto had lost count of the number of times he'd thanked the gods that the Celts seemed to have no interest in the development of artillery. The idea of a stone-throwing onager up there just did not bear thinking about.

Regardless, the mass of Britons at the top of the cliffs had grown constantly during the wait, to the point where it could now only be considered an army. As well as the large number of horsemen that had slowly gathered, there were also fast moving shapes that could only be chariots. It looked to Fronto as though the tribes of Britannia were gathering to prevent the Roman ships landing, as was almost certainly the case. So much for Caesar's allies, hostages and so on.

Though the weather remained dry and relatively bright, the sky was still scattered with scudding and drifting grey cloud, the sun providing little heat to take the chill from the sea air. A nervous tension had begun to set in among the men that Fronto could feel

252

without seeing or hearing anything specific. The men were growing increasingly unhappy.

Nervous eyes had fallen on the cliff as the ships ploughed their way up the channel in search of a safe harbour in which to land. The force of barbarians moved swiftly and easily along the coastline, following the cliff tops and dipping down into each narrow bay, keeping pace with the Roman fleet with little difficulty, a worryingly large force of cavalry and chariots leading the way.

No matter how easy the landing place Caesar chose, the Roman forces would encounter strong resistance in setting up a beach head.

Fronto's own nervousness began to increase alongside his men as the miles slipped by until, after perhaps two hours further sailing, shadowed by the growing army of Celts, a call went out from Caesar's trireme and the fleet began to converge again.

The cliffs had been gradually falling away for the last quarter hour and ahead they finally descended to a low, flat beachy area. Beyond, nothing but dunes and low hillocks marred the easy ground as far as the eye could see. Even Fronto, whose nerves were beginning to twang they were so taut, could see the sense in reaching this terrain before attempting a landing.

Another call rang out: the order to beach and, as the ships of the fleet angled toward land, Fronto's eyes flicked repeatedly to the shore, as did those of many of the ship's occupants. A large force of native warriors had begun to assemble at the rear of the wide beach, with more arriving on the scene all the time.

The Tenth's legate leaned on the rail at the bow and watched as the land came ever closer, Caesar's trireme closing up on their right as another big merchant vessel moved into position on their left. The noise became cacophonous: a crescendo of shouting, horn calls, whistles, cries of alarm and more. The sailors of every ship bellowed their commands, keeping the fleet in line as it approached. The commanders of the troops aboard shouted orders to their men, falling in each century ready to make landing. Somewhere below, Galronus' horse neighed and cried nervously.

On land, the chariots had come forward and were now racing up and down the beach, daring the Roman invaders to land. Each vehicle was drawn by a pair of horses, harnessed with sturdy leathers to a lightweight chariot that was little more than a wood-and-wicker wheeled fighting platform. Each chariot was driven by a half-naked warrior, his body painted with whorls and designs, his wild hair whipping about in the wind as he rode the traces, reins clutched tightly in each hand. The sheer skill and dexterity of these men as they leapt about between the horses while controlling the chariot would put to shame any professional at the circus in Rome. But despite the phenomenal sight of such activity, Fronto's eyes were drawn to the figures on the chariots themselves. Each vehicle carried but one man alongside the driver and each man was clearly a leader or a powerful warrior. They were all fully clothed, mostly armoured with mail shirts or bronze plated chest-pieces, and helmeted in the most elaborate way, with plumes atop many. Some warriors carried a shield visibly similar to those held by the legionaries – if a little smaller – painted with bright designs and sometimes the images of wild animals. Most carried a long, gleaming sword, held aloft in a triumphant fashion, and all gripped spears in their off-or-shield hand.

There were enough of them to fill the beach and endanger each other as they passed and turned, churning up the sand and throwing sheets of it into the air to the whoops of the crowd of warriors and cavalry behind them.

More and more detail became visible as the ships of the Roman fleet closed on the sand.

Fronto gritted his teeth and watched.

The legate's first indication that there was a problem was when he received a dazing blow to the forehead from the heavy timber hull at the ship's bow. Shaking his head in confusion, he untangled his legs and hauled himself back to his feet to a background of calls of alarm and the crash of dozens of mailed men in chaos.

The ship had come to a dead halt, the sudden loss of momentum catapulting those at the rail into the solid timbers and sweeping almost every other man on board from his feet. Hauling himself up and ignoring all the shouts and hollers around him, Fronto peered over the rail. Concentrating hard, occasionally, though the foam and the distortions of the waves, he could see pebbles.

'We've run aground!' he shouted, immediately aware of how obvious the statement was. The triremes around them were still ghosting forward, but the Celtic ships, with their deep hulls were all falling foul of the gentle submerged slope, slamming to a sudden halt and throwing the centuries of men to the deck in a tangle.

Whoops of delight and derision rose from the beach. A few enterprising archers among the Briton tribesmen rushed forward and released a shot over the heads of the charioteers. While none of the missiles actually reached the ships, odd ones hissed into the water close enough to cause alarm.

With the swift reactions one would expect from the experienced commanders of the Roman vessels, the triremes slowed their advance toward land and began back-oaring to the same distance as the beached Celtic vessels. Galronus frowned at the manoeuver and looked across at Fronto next to him.

'Why are they pulling back?'

'Two thirds of the fleet are these big bastards that won't get to the beach. If Caesar lands he'll only have a third of his troops with him. It'd be suicide.'

Galronus shook his head in disbelief. 'A landing thwarted by four feet of water? Someone's going to lose their balls for misjudging the slope of the beach.'

'I don't think so' Fronto shook his head. 'It will have been Brutus and the trireme's captain, but Caesar will have made the decision. The big question is: what do we do next?'

Almost as if to answer his question calls began to issue from the trireme, from the general's personal cornicen, calls that were relayed by other musicians until the sequence of notes rang out across the fleet.

'That sounds like the advance!' Galronus blinked. 'But not quite.'

'That' Fronto said flatly 'is the order for the *Seventh* to advance.'

'But the Seventh are mostly in the same position as your Tenth.'

'Yes.'

The legate was suddenly aware of the presence of his primus pilus by his elbow. 'Is the general losing his wits, sir?'

'No. He's ordering the Seventh to attack the beach.'

'But there's four or five feet of water down there if not more. And why not us? The Tenth are more damn use than the Seventh any day.'

'But the Seventh are dispensable as far as he's concerned. He won't risk losing the Tenth, but the Seventh are full of the former Pompeians, dissidents and anyone who rings a warning bell. That's why they were chosen for this campaign. The Seventh are here to take the shit thrown at us and the Tenth are here to mop it all up and support the general.'

Galronus lowered his voice and leaned closer to Fronto. 'You realise this is the perfect trigger to kick off a row between Cicero and Caesar?'

'If Cicero's nearby, yes. But look at the circumstances. The wrong call here could cost us hundreds of lives; thousands even. Hardly worth the risk, I'd say.'

'Oh crap.' Though the shout came from one of the soldiers back across the deck, and was immediately followed by the crack of an officer's stick across him for speaking out of turn, the call drew Fronto's eyes inexorably back to the beach and the waiting Celtic horde.

The archers among the force were moving between the chariots and toward the edge of the water, nocking arrows as they ran.

'If they start to loose and we're still beached, we're in real trouble.'

'Where are the Seventh then?' asked Galronus, his eyes playing across the many vessels drawn up opposite the beach. 'I can't see anyone advancing.'

'They're not' said Carbo. 'It looks like their officers and men are refusing the order to advance.'

'Someone's got to do something' Galronus frowned. 'If we just sit here the archers will start killing people any moment.'

A series of notes issued from a ship two vessels to their left and, glancing across, Fronto could see a trireme flying the vexillum of the Seventh legion. Cicero's ship.

'That's the rally call. What the hell is he up to?'

Rushing across the deck, Fronto leaned over the port rail. He could only just see Cicero's trireme over the bulk of the Gallic ship between them. Certainly the likelihood of anyone hearing him was negligible.

'Cicero! You have to advance! Screw the general's call; the Tenth will go with you!'

There was no acknowledgement of the call for a long moment and then suddenly a figure appeared at the rail of the ship between them. The transverse crest of his helmet marked him as a centurion.

'Legate Fronto?'

A cold stone sank into the pit of Fronto's stomach as he recognised the voice of Furius.

'What?'

'Half the damn officers are encouraging their men to refuse the order!'

Fronto shook his head in disbelief. This was what came of an 'all the bad eggs in one basket' policy. 'What about you?' he called, narrowing his eyes. There was something urgent and angry about the centurion's manner.

'I'm not prepared to stay here and get shot at.'

'Good. All together, then?'

'Our eagle won't go. He's cowering on the command ship. Bad luck to charge without the eagle. You know that!'

Fronto looked around his own vessel urgently. Julius Pictor, the eagle bearer of the Tenth crouched by the rail, keeping his head down as he watched the approaching archers.

'Sound the advance! Pictor... I want you first in the water. Make sure that eagle's held high so that everyone can see it.'

The aquilifer turned and stared at him wide-eyed. Though he said nothing, his head began to shake almost involuntarily. Fronto glared at him. 'In the water, Pictor. You're one of the Tenth, not a street urchin!'

'Oh for the love of Mars!' snapped Petrosidius, the first century's standard bearer, stepping away from his unit. Reaching down, he grasped Pictor by the crossed-and-tied paws of the wolf skin that covered his helmet and hauled him to his feet, and indeed almost off the ground. The eagle lurched in the man's hand and nearly went overboard.

'Consider yourself demoted, piss-britches!' Petrosidius growled, ripping the shining silver eagle staff from the cowering man's hand and thrusting his own bulky standard into the open grasp. 'Follow on and try not to soil yourself.'

The standard bearer turned to Fronto and raised his brows in question. Fronto nodded.

'Tenth legion: on me!'

Without another word, Petrosidius placed a hand on the rail and vaulted over the side with the strength and agility of a man half his age, plummeting into the waves beside the ship.

With an audible moan of dismay, the men of the Tenth rushed over to the rail, where there was no sign of Petrosidius but the churning water where he had entered. There was a horrible pause and then suddenly, with an explosion of foam, the head and shoulders of the big standard bearer rose from the sea, followed by the silver eagle that glittered and shone.

'Come on in, ladies. The water's fine.'

Grinning, the wolf pelt over his helmet plastered down to the metal, Petrosidius began to move laboriously toward the beach with the difficulty of a man in chest-deep water. There was a splash nearby and Fronto glanced up to see centurion Furius rise from the sea's surface, yelling encouragement to his men.

The dam broke.

With a roar, the men of the Tenth and the Seventh began to hurl themselves from the ships into the chest-deep water, many throwing their shields ahead and trying to jump on to them. Fronto turned to Galronus and grinned.

'I'm guessing the cavalry won't be taking part!'

The Remi officer laughed. 'I think not. The general will be irritated that you took the Tenth in, you know that?'

'Not as irritated as he'd be if we all stayed here and died on deck. 'Scuse me. I've a battle to fight.' With a wicked grin, Fronto grasped the rail and threw himself over.

Chapter 14

(South-east coast of Britannia)

Fronto's world was an explosion of baffling sensory input as he burst through the water's surface and heaved in a deep breath. His ears had filled with water and, though he was aware of the din going on around him, it was all buried beneath a sloshing sound that made him feel dangerously unbalanced. His eyes stung with the brine and all he could see were occasional flashes of red or silver ahead of him as he continually blinked, trying to bring his sight back into line.

Slowly his eyes adjusted and he was aware of dozens and dozens of men around him, only their heads and shoulders above the waves, heaving toward the beach, their swords and shields held aloft as high as possible to prevent too much drag.

There was a wet pop and one of his ears suddenly cleared, shocking him with the sheer scale of the noise that suddenly assailed his eardrum.

'What are you doing?' called a voice. Fronto looked around in confusion to see Carbo addressing a legionary who was turning slowly in confusion.

'Looking for my standard, sir!'

'Don't be bloody stupid. Just get to the beach and form up with anyone you can find, even if they're not from the Tenth!'

As the man turned and struggled back toward the beach, Carbo took the time to give him a clout on the back of his helmet for his idiocy.

A mass of helmeted shapes were ploughing toward the beach. Fronto frowned as his brain told him he should be remembering something – something urgent.

'Shit!' he dropped into the water again as the arrow hissed past him and disappeared with a splash. But as he rose from the surface once more, he realised that the arrow had been a single pot-luck shot and not part of an organised attack.

'Why aren't the archers shooting us?'

'Hello sir' Carbo said, grinning as he turned.

'I said: why aren't they shooting us anymore?'

In response, the centurion cupped his hand to his ear dramatically. Fronto frowned, but after a moment, he heard the twang of the ballista on board Caesar's trireme. Ahead, there were screams on the beach.

'Ah... got you.'

Another dramatic ear cup at the other side, and Fronto smiled as he heard the thud of the catapult on Cicero's trireme release its heavy stone burden. A moment later, on the beach, one of the chariots suddenly spun upwards, the terrified horses still attached as the stone smashed the vehicle into the air, the warrior aboard dead before he fell back to the sand, crushed and broken.

'This can't hold. Let's get to the beach before they decide to do something clever.'

Carbo turned away and made for the sand, the water level now just above his waist.

On the beach, something was already happening, though. The chariots had drawn up in two lines to the rear at both ends of the long beach while the cavalry, so very reminiscent of the Gallic horsemen of Caesar's, drew up facing the sea.

'Looks like we're about to have company.'

Even above the sloshing of the waves, the shouts of men and the din of ship-borne artillery, Fronto could hear the drumming thunder as the cavalry started to move, then picked up the pace, charging toward the invading force.

Another random pot-shot arrow appeared from nowhere and glanced off Fronto's crest-holder with a clang, disappearing into the water in a cloud of severed red horsehair.

Heaving a sigh of relief, the legate concentrated once more on what was happening across the open expanse of beaching waves. A wall of horseflesh, hair, skin and bronze approached as the massed ranks of the tribal riders raced across the sand and into the shallows. The barbarians, aware now of the dangers of the artillery, had kept the noble and easily-targeted chariots out of ballista reach, as well as the archers and the bulk of their warriors. But the cavalry had the speed to reach the Roman forces in the water with the minimal risk of being taken out by artillery. Moreover, their advantage in the water was clear, and the Roman artillery would cease loosing at close quarters for fear of hitting their own people.

Fronto watched with growing dismay as the native cavalry ploughed into the water, splitting into groups and making for any legionary or small number of them who had become separated and looked like easy pickings. Even as he struggled toward the nearest such group, the ballista on Caesar's ship loosed one last time, smashing into one of the horses and throwing both it and its rider back into the shallow surf; it then fell silent.

Two legionaries and an optio were swiftly surrounded by half a dozen horsemen, their long swords rising and falling as they battered at the three men, jostling to maintain a position where they could reach. The Romans had moved back to back and their shields were raised to take the blows but their strength was ebbing fast with the sheer effort of fighting in waist deep water.

Snarling imprecations, Fronto laboured toward them, his sword slipping from its sheath beneath the water. The three men would not last long surrounded by cavalrymen with the advantage of both height and numbers.

The silent, oppressive void of the submarine world closed over him again as he slipped on a rock, his bad knee giving way and plunging him down into the salty, choking sea. Desperation grasped him and he let go of the shield he'd been gripping to free him a little from the weight and bulk. Despite the salty discomfort, his eyes remained open and he looked up to see his discarded shield bob to the surface, creating an oblong shadow above him.

A memory of muttered conversations with an angry Varus over too many drinks to be truly healthy flashed into his head as he looked up from his submarine world, and his face split into a hard smile.

He knew how to turn the tables.

Bursting from the surface with the renewed vigour that comes with certainty of purpose, Fronto began to push and fight his way through the water toward the fracas. One of the legionaries had already taken a sword blow from the horsemen and his shield was being split into kindling with the repeated hammering as he desperately clung onto life, failing to find an opportunity to use his gladius.

Closing on them, Fronto grinned, aware that they had not seen him. At a distance of perhaps ten feet, he took a deep breath and plunged beneath the surface, scrambling along in a half-crawl, half-swim in just over three feet of water.

A shadow fell across his strange, ethereal world just as he saw the injured legionary succumb to another blow and drop beneath the waves, clouds of dirty brown indicating the horrible extent of his wounds as the blood bloomed out of his chest and tainted the water.

There was plenty more of that to come.

Crouching, Fronto used the combination of his bunched muscles and the hard pebbled seabed to launch himself through the surface and straight into the horse's underbelly. Germanic tactics. It was horrible – a dirty way to fight a war – but needs must when Caesar drives...

His gladius plunged into the horse's gut and ripped this way and that. Urgently, Fronto ducked to one side to avoid the writhing of the agonised animal.

The beast screamed and tried to leap, the Celtic rider suddenly bucking from the saddle and being thrown into the water. It would have been nice to finish the bastard off, but that could come later. With gritted teeth, Fronto plunged beneath the surface, through the glowing slick of horse's blood and sought out the next equine shadow that blotted out the sun.

Quickly, efficiently, and with a rising distaste, Fronto located another of the Celtic riders and, aware that the swinging swords and danger of battle was taking place just above the surface, concluded he was better off remaining hidden. Closing his eyes and sending a mental apology to the poor beast, Fronto lifted his hand to just below the water's surface and drove his gladius into the horse's upper leg, feeling it grate off the central bone as it pushed through and out the other side.

The horse crumpled on its bad leg and Fronto barely managed to push himself out of the way as the beast collapsed into the water almost on top of him, slipping sideways. He felt the tug as the sword was almost wrenched from his grasp with the movement and it was only through a superhuman effort that he managed to maintain his grip on the hilt as it tore free of the leg.

Half-swimming backward, he watched with sick fascination as the rider, tipped unceremoniously from his blanket seat by the screaming horse, found himself suddenly beneath both the waves and his crippled mount, pinned to the pebbles as the horse thrashed, grinding him to a pulp.

Turning from the grisly scene, Fronto moved along to the next horse, repeating the unpleasant 'gutting' tactic of the Germanic warriors, ducking back into the water as the slick of the beast's blood drenched him from above.

Moving out away from all the action for a moment's breather, he stood again, aware that the quantity of blood churning in the water was now making it almost impossible to see and that he was in as much danger of bumping into the beleaguered soldiers as he was of finding another horse to deal with.

Two of the beasts that he'd attacked were dying already, thrashing in the water, part bleeding out and part drowning, while another was desperately trying to reach the 'safety' of the beach, a constant rain of blood falling from its undercarriage to the surface of the sea. Of their unfortunate riders he could see no sign, though the pair of legionaries who had recently been fighting to preserve their own skins had now taken the initiative and were battering native warriors down into the surf with their shields as their swords rose and fell in rhythmic butchery; likely the fate of the men Fronto had unhorsed.

The legionaries had no time to thank him for the relief, though. Two of the riders who had been attacking them had wheeled their mounts and pounded away through the waist deep water in search of easier targets, while the last rider, now unhorsed, floundered in the waves, trying to fight off the revenging legionaries. The fight was far from over.

The small pockets of combat had begun to spread and increase, melding together to form one great half-submerged melee, stretching from the very edge of the water, where Petrosidius fought like a man possessed, to the waist deep area, where the last men from the two Gallic vessels struggled to catch up. Two ships' worth? Where was everyone else?

Horses screamed as the legionaries attacked them viciously, unable to reach their riders. Soldiers hacked and battered with sword and shield, sloshing this way and that, taking advantage of the blood-tinted sea to drop beneath the surface and disappear whenever danger loomed, rising out of the water like some avenging spirit once the trouble had passed and moving on to the next likely target.

A quick glance around the beach revealed a sickening truth: the number of legionaries committed in the water was barely enough to hold their own against the native cavalry. If the rest of the horde decided to brave the artillery and move into the fray, all would be lost. Frowning, Fronto peered past the two nearest ships, their high-sided Gallic hulls rising majestically from the water. To his dismay, he could see soldiers lining the rails of the two triremes. Caesar had held back the men of the Tenth on his ship, and Cicero had done the same with the Seventh on his.

Unbelievable: both officers so stubborn, even in these circumstances! Despite Fronto's leading of two centuries from the Tenth, the general had clearly put out the call to hold the rest of the legion back, expecting the Seventh to carry out his initial orders. Cicero, equally, had either refused to commit his men, or possibly had found it impossible to force his reticent officers to lead them into the fight. Either way, the entire struggle for the beach was being carried out by two centuries from each legion.

Insane!

His wandering gaze took in the numerous scuffles in the water and settled on a musician with a wolf pelt over his helmet, struggling to free himself from the bronze hoop of a bent 'cornu' horn in which he had somehow become tangled as a Briton rider bore down on him, bloodied long sword raised and ready to land the blow. He was almost on the unfortunate soldier.

'Over here!' Fronto bellowed to the endangered musician, waving his sword arm. The man turned and began to wade desperately toward him, the sodden wolf fur half obscuring his vision, the horn almost comically constricting him. The legate's brow furrowed in concentration even as he began to move to intercept. With his shield gone he would stand about as much chance against the horseman as the entangled musician did if he tried to wade out and take him in a fair fight.

Luckily fair fighting to Fronto was a luxury, rather than a necessity.

Hoping he would have clear enough vision, Fronto took a deep breath and dropped beneath the surface of the water again. The salty brine had taken on the distinctive tinny tang of blood and Fronto could taste it even on his closed lips as he opened his eyes and looked up.

The water was stained dark pink and currents of blood flowed through it sickeningly, creating darker patches here and there, but he could just make out the shapes of clouds above – it would be good enough. Praying to Fortuna that his sense of direction had held, he half-swam, half-waded onwards toward the struggling cornicen, making sure to keep his head beneath the surface.

The musician was easy enough to spot as he passed by. The man pushed his way wearily and desperately through the deepening water toward where Fronto had been. Even through the murk of blood,

Fronto could see the panic on the soldier's face as he tried to find the officer who had shouted him.

And then he was past and the horse and rider were almost on him. Fronto watched the powerful equine legs pound though the water, stirring sand and pebbles into the already gloomy mix. Judging the time to be right, he stood.

* * * * *

Gaius Figulus, cornicen for the second century of the first cohort in the Seventh legion lost his footing and it was then that he knew it was all over. The native horseman chasing him down had been gaining on him as he ran and the officer that had called him had somehow vanished. Panic had gripped him then. He was not a man prone to excessive fear, and he was certainly no coward, but the simple knowledge that he was out of chances had finally fought its way into his beleaguered mind and unmanned him.

After landing in the water, following centurion Furius despite the shouted orders to the contrary, he had drawn his sword, his cornu over the other shoulder and held tight in his grip – to lose his cornu would be to suffer beatings from his centurion later, as well as a substantial loss of pay.

In a matter of moments he'd found himself in a melee, surrounded by two enemy horsemen. With no shield, he'd managed to repeatedly block their powerful, hammering sword blows with only his gladius for a hundred speedy heartbeats. He'd even eventually managed to stab one of the horses so that the rider pulled back and retreated. Unfortunately, his cornu had taken half a dozen heavy sword blows and, at some point as he'd ducked a swipe, it had bobbed on the water and managed to slip over his head and shoulder and now pinned his left arm to his side, the slightly buckled metal digging painfully into his neck. He would have no trouble untangling himself given the opportunity, but for the fact that the remaining rider was still swinging at him, and finally a heavy blow that landed broke several fingers on his sword hand and weakened his wrist, his gladius tumbling away into the water, lost.

Miraculously, another legionary had appeared and distracted the rider long enough for him to flee the scene, struggling with the horn, trying to lift it off himself as he retreated. But he'd failed, his hands trapped and bloodied, and the horseman had come after him.

And then the officer had called.

And then disappeared.

Figulus made one last effort to try and haul the cornu off him, but his left arm was hopelessly pinned in the circle of bronze, while his right hand throbbed painfully with broken blackened fingers and was too weak to help.

Turning, he observed his doom thundering through the water, bearing down on him.

And then something unexpected happened.

A figure rose from the water like the very embodiment of Neptune, armour glinting silver with a faint sheen of watery crimson, face a contorted grimace of anger, fingers of its left hand grasping, reaching, a gladius glittering in the right.

Figulus boggled as the free hand grasped the passing rider's ankle, almost hauling the apparition out of the water, but allowing the other arm to come round in a powerful swing that hacked deep into the Briton's shin.

The cavalryman screamed and, the tip of the gladius having pricked the horse's side enough to draw blood, the mount also bellowed and reared up, mid-run. The rider recovered his wits quickly enough, somehow managing to hold on to the horse's reins, but he had lost control of his steed and the beast bolted through the surf back toward the beach. Figulus stared at the officer in the expensive, if dented, helmet and muscle-shaped beaten bronze cuirass, his horsehair crest bedraggled and sagging slightly.

'I... Uh.'

The officer turned his gaze on Figulus and the cornicen took a tiny involuntary step back at the sheer anger in the man's face. The officer clearly seemed to have momentarily forgotten he was there in the thrill of battle.

'You. Can you still play that thing?'

'I think so sir. It's a bit bent and it might not sound quite right, though.'

'Don't care' the officer said flatly as he waded through the water and began to help him remove the misshapen horn from around his neck and arm. 'Do you know *all* the army's calls?'

'I think so, sir.'

'Right then. Sound the advance for both legions.'

Figulus nodded and reached his lips toward the mouthpiece, his good hand gripping the curve.

'And the command call for all ships to beach.'

'Sir? That order can only be given by the general or his staff.'

The officer's expression suggested heavily that a lot of Figulus' future rode on the next moment and he swallowed nervously, observing the officer's dented, stained armour, his grizzled features and the very plain, utilitarian blade in his hand, slightly nicked from extended use. He *could* be one of the staff, if he was one who did not pander to appearance, or care what his peers thought.

Then he caught the officer's eyes again and reached for the mouthpiece of the horn, blowing the call for the ships to beach as though his life depended on it.

* * * * *

Fronto patted the young musician condescendingly on the head as the last few notes rang out across the beach, his hand sinking into the saturated wolf fur. As he'd hoped, the other musicians across the ships had picked up and echoed the call, assuming the order had come from the nearby command trireme.

Grinning, the legate could only picture Caesar's face as he stomped around the trireme's deck, demanding to know who had given the order. But already every remaining ship was moving gracefully through the water toward the beach, the men on their decks straining, ready to leap into the fray.

Even by the time Fronto had turned away and started taking stock of the situation, the first men of the Tenth and Seventh were dropping into the water, sloshing forward to help their comrades. The sleek, speedy Roman triremes had taken just moments to move far enough forward to beach and deposit their troops, the men plunging into water that was only two feet deep, still holding their shields and swords ready, and running straight for any of the enemy they could see.

The attack had finally begun in earnest, despite the reticence and stupidity of the senior officers.

In response to this new threat, several discordant cacophonic blasts issued from the rear of the beach and the innumerable infantry of the native horde began to race toward the water to join the fray.

Fronto peered around to see where he could be best used and selected a knot of small fights in the shallows where the Celtic horsemen seemed to be getting the best of the legionaries. He

267

sloshed through the water, grateful when the glistening pink frothy surface passed his midriff and lapped around his thighs as he neared land.

'Marcus!'

Glancing over his shoulder, Fronto grinned at the sight of Galronus heaving his way through the water to catch up, his long Celtic cavalry blade unsheathed in his hand, no shield visible.

'Decided to join in then?'

'Contrary to common Roman belief, we Belgae are surprisingly adaptable' he grinned. 'I can fight, piss, and even sleep without a horse between my knees.'

'We need to force them back on to the beach where we can form up into lines. Then we've got 'em'

Galronus nodded and grinned as he caught sight of Petrosidius, only ankle deep in the water's edge, mercilessly beating a cringing, disarmed native to death with the gleaming silver eagle of the Tenth.

'I fear the general would have a fit if he saw your standard bearer doing that.'

'So long as he doesn't break the bloody thing. He's not the carefullest of men.'

Fronto baulked for a moment as he bumped into something soft and malleable and glanced down to see a bloodied, sightless eye staring up at him from a smashed head. The sea was becoming a sight to sicken even the hardiest of soldiers.

Accustomed to fighting on land, Fronto was used to the unpleasant aftermath of battle: the slick of blood and organs that covered every inch of the field; the bodies lying in gruesome, twisted positions, sometimes four deep.

The pieces of head and limb that you could not avoid treading on.

The stench.

What he was not used to, and was wholly unprepared for, was that such an action fought in waist deep water resulted in the same carnage, except that there it flowed around you as you walked, occasionally bumping into you. A hand here; half a head there.

If he'd had anything to bring up, he would have done it as he surveyed the scene.

Galronus seemed to be judiciously ignoring the grisly sea, the tidal currents dragging floating detritus back out from the areas of more intense battle in the shallows.

Closing on the knot of more intense fighting, Fronto yelled at the top of his voice to be heard over the din. 'The horses! Take out the horses!'

The focus of the struggling men changed as they began to attack the steeds while using their shields to protect themselves from the constant hammering blows from above. Pausing, he once more took stock of the situation, the water's surface now tickling the back of his knees. The enemy warriors had only partially committed to the attack. A fresh volley of missiles from the ships had strafed the screaming, advancing horde and many had drawn up short at the sudden threat and run back to their comrades beyond the beach.

Others, however, had made it to the sea, where the ballistae would not loose for fear of hitting their own, and had joined the horsemen in the desperate struggle to prevent the Romans reaching solid land. But the numbers were tilted in the favour of the invaders now and every moment saw fresh legionaries arriving from the ships that had been at the rear of the fleet against a diminishing number of natives.

'Come on, let's finish this.'

Galronus grinned by his side and the two men sloshed through the knee-deep water, racing toward a small group of howling, half-naked men wielding spears.

* * * * *

Galronus found himself running lightly, almost enjoying himself as he left the last lapping wave and crunched onto fine gravel. He barely paused in his run to pull back his heavy long sword to his right and bring it round in a wide swing that took the leg clean off the nearest Briton. The man's screaming turned from that of rage to that of agony as he fell to the shingle in two separate pieces.

This was what every Remi son was born for.

Life was the gift. Battle was the method. Blood was the price.

There would be some, especially the druids, who would condemn or chastise him for this: for running with an army of Rome and bringing blood and death to fellow tribesmen – fellow worshippers of Belenus. But the history of the Belgae was a history of tribal warfare – of brother against brother. Had not the Belgae fought among themselves for centuries before the coming of Rome? And now, simply because a new force had entered the arena, the secretive druids expected the tribes to band together against Rome? To deny a thousand years of warfare and enmity?

Galronus shook his head to discard the thought and the subject entire as a screaming, moustached face beneath a shock of spiked white hair rose up in front of him. The projected spittle of the warrior's yelled invective had hardly touched his cheek before the blood spatter joined it. Galronus paused for only a moment to heave his sword back out of the man's neck and push him to the ground with his foot, leaving him shaking out his life spasmodically on the pebbles.

The thing was that Galronus had fought with the legions for more than two years now, and in those long months he had not once visited his tribe. Truth be told, he rarely thought of them. Oh, he knew of them, for he had sent and received word these past two winters while they endured the bitter wet cold and he sheltered in warm, cosy Rome. They had thrived, despite the supposed loss of their freedoms. He had heard that they had begun to re-road the oppidum of his birth with flag stones and drainage ditches after the Roman fashion. He could only imagine the relief the children and women would feel not having to slop through half a foot of muck as they left their house.

The druids had abandoned them, of course. Most of the strange, powerful cult had crossed the water to the believed safety of Britannia and their sacred isle of Ynis Mon, while others had stayed in Gaul, but retreated from the open world to carry out their own little hate campaigns against Rome.

Galronus was not stupid. Far from it. He would never delude himself and suggest that the Belgic tribes were anything other than subjects of Rome now, or that he was still a chief of the Remi, for all that he held the title. He was now an officer of Rome. He had learned their language to the extent that people were often unaware of his origins. He had taken a liking to their wine, though not watered as they would drink it – a habit he shared with Fronto. He liked their chariot racing and their taverns. He liked their culture – apart from the dreadful theatre. He liked…

He liked Faleria.

A quick glance to one side confirmed that Fronto was still beside him, fighting with all the fury and strength of a battle-crazed Remi warrior, with the energy and agility of a man half his age. With the certainty and sureness of a man whose life is panning out exactly as he had planned it.

With the blessings of Sucellus and Nantosuelta, Galronus would bind hands with Faleria this year and the man fighting furiously by his side would become his brother.

He grinned and casually beheaded a yelling youth with a sharp spear but absolutely no ability to use it.

Strange, really. He was suddenly aware for the first time that he appeared to be thinking in Latin, with all its idioms and intricacies. When had that started?

He was so blood-tied to the inhabitants of this island that he shared not only gods, names and culture, but even language. Despite the oddities of their regional dialects, if he concentrated, he could follow three quarters of all the shouting going on around him. The swords that were being raised against him bore so much more resemblance to his own than did the short stabbing weapons of the legions. He could very easily discard his Roman-style helmet and slip among the Britons and they would not even know him for an enemy.

But Rome was the future. Better to embrace the future than to fight it and disappear without trace, such as the Aduatuci, executed or enslaved entire after Caesar's conquest.

Again, Galronus shook his head and pushed the thoughts aside. Such reflection was best saved for the dark of the night after battle's end.

'Galronus!' yelled an insistent voice.

Looking around in surprise, the Remi officer realised that the Roman forces had stopped advancing, cornu and buccina calls going out to mass the troops, standards waving, circling and dipping, whistles blowing, centurions' voices carrying across it all. In his reverie, Galronus had not stopped with the rest and was standing in a strange twenty-pace no-man's-land between the assembling legions and the expectant Britons who had drawn back up the beach. Fronto was desperately beckoning him.

'Get back here before one of their archers decides to stick you!'

With a smile, Galronus nodded and, turning, jogged back to the ranks of his new, uniformed, steel-armoured brothers.

* * * * *

Fronto took the opportunity to step out of the line and look along the assembled forces with a sense of immense satisfaction. Despite the debacle that had been the landing, the beachhead had been successfully established and the Britons had been forced to withdraw far enough to allow room to form up properly.

It did not do to look back into the surf, as he'd quickly discovered. The swirling red tint from the blood had quickly diffused and disappeared with fresh waves, but the shapes of men and horses still stood proud of the water – ugly mounds that were an equally ugly testament to the brutality of the assault. The men did not bother him so much, but the horses...

He'd half expected the Britons to keep retreating in view of the army now forming up opposite them but, to the credit of their courage, they had merely rearranged their forces, the remaining cavalry formed up at the rear, archers nowhere to be seen, infantry in a huge mass at the centre and the leaders in their chariots off to both sides.

If Fronto craned his neck, Cicero could just be seen newly arrived and bustling around at the rear of the formed up Seventh. That man would get the benefit of Fronto's personal and celebrated selection of curses later, when the entire army was not listening, though there was also the coming confrontation with Caesar that would likely be much the same, only in the other direction. Although the general could have no proof that it was Fronto who had defied him and ordered the advance and disembarkation, he would suspect, and he knew for a fact that Fronto had been one of the first over the side with two centuries of the Tenth in further contradiction of orders.

Caesar's bile was hardly new though, and he knew how to weather that storm easily enough.

In response to a demand, a shield was being passed through the ranks to the front, where the legionary behind Fronto respectfully handed it over. With satisfaction of the reassuring weight, Fronto hefted the grip, the callouses of his hand fitting harmoniously to the shape of the wood and leather. Cicero, Caesar and the other staff could stand at the back and wave their arms; he would stay here, in the front line. It was common knowledge in the army that a senior officer was as much use in the heat of combat as a knitted shield, and it was the centurionate that commanded the battle. Not so in the

Tenth, and Fronto soured to think of what his men would think of him if he stood at the rear picking his nails with his knife like Cicero.

'Ready!'

Carbo's voice cut through the general murmur and din of the assembled centuries and was repeated by the other fifty nine centurions of the Tenth and soon after by the officers of the Seventh. Across the front line, shields clacked against one another and the men planted their front feet, ready for the advance. The rattling, clanging and conversation died away to an expectant silence that was broken a moment later by the 'musical' instruments of the Britons, howling and wailing like a cat with its tail trapped in a door. With an exultant roar, the native army charged.

'I don't believe it.' Carbo muttered. On the other side of the legate, Galronus grinned behind his borrowed infantry shield. 'Believe it. It's the way they fight. To attack with the blood up is noble. To sit tight and wait for an advancing enemy is cowardly in their eyes.'

'They must know they'll never punch through this line' Fronto said quietly.

'But they will try it anyway. They would rather die hopelessly and nobly than live in the knowledge that they had not tried.'

'You mean they won't run at all?'

'Oh they'll run, when they're broken. But they'll not retreat by design.'

'Then we'd better break them.'

Carbo laughed lightly and raised his sword. 'Brace!'

Along the line, the men of the Tenth hunched behind their shields, changing their stance so that, rather than preparing to march, they had all their weight ready to push forward into the wood and leather. The entire line of shields dropped slightly to cover exposed shins and heads were pulled down to leave only the eyes exposed between the metal helmet brow and the edge of the shield.

A Roman shieldwall could withstand most attacks.

Fronto was surprised as his eyes flicked across the ranks of the enemy to see that not only were the foot warriors of the native army charging forward en masse with no formation or organisation, but the chariots at the periphery had swept forward only long enough to drop their noble passengers close enough to join the attack.

He had a mind to enquire of Galronus as to this strange tactic, but now was not the time. He counted off his heartbeats.

273

One… Two… Three…

Four more and the lines would meet.

Four…

'Mark your men.'

Three…

Shame we didn't have pila, Fronto thought, imagining all the stacks of the weighted javelins that were stored on board the ships and would have to be brought out later.

Two…

A man directly opposite Fronto with a strange bronze plate strapped over his bare chest, designs inked on his arms, his hair spiked and coated with white mud, and what he probably laughingly called his teeth bared, snarled something at Fronto.

One…

'I think he likes you' laughed Galronus to his left, as all hell broke loose.

The power and voracity of the native charge took Fronto by surprise, and all along the shield wall there were curses and shouts in Latin as the legionaries of the Tenth and Seventh fought to maintain their position, their feet driving into the scattering pebbles, teeth grinding as they heaved with all their strength into the shields on their arms.

Here and there the line buckled a little, but it held.

'One' yelled Carbo, and the legion's front line leaned back fractionally to gain a tiny fragment of room, only to smash forward with their shields half a heartbeat later. All along the line of combat, bronze shield bosses smashed into the poorly-armoured Britons, smashing bones, shattering teeth, pulverising noses and generally wrecking the momentum of their attack.

'Two' called the primus pilus, and the shields were all angled slightly, opening up gaps half a foot wide all along the front, safe in the knowledge that the shield-barge had knocked the enemy back enough to make it extremely unlikely that any of them would take advantage of the gap. Every legionary's blade jabbed out of the line, plunging into the enemy, twisting and then withdrawing. The shields clacked back together with a monstrous din.

The majority of the front men in the Celtic army collapsed to the ground screaming and bleeding, leaving a momentary space before the next set of Britons could move in over their comrades and reach their enemy.

'Three!' barked Carbo, and the legion took two uniform steps forward over the bodies of the fallen. As the front line settled back into position and made sure their shields were locked, the second rank of men stamped down with their hobnailed boots and smashed their bronze-edged shield rims into the bodies of the wounded and dying Britons, preventing them from causing any damage within the formation.

Now, the atmosphere across the army of Britons had changed from exultant, angry excitement to desperate, uncertain urging. The men back in the press pushed their comrades forward, dying to reach their enemy, pushing between their fellows where they could. Here and there a richly-armoured noble managed to elbow his way to the front. Before Carbo could repeat the process, several legionaries along the line succumbed to the brutal attacks of the warriors, their swords or axes coming down at just the right angle to miss shields and plunge into faces beneath helmet brows or smash into mailed shoulders. Even as those legionaries collapsed, screaming, from the line, the men in the second rank stepped forward to take their place, locking their shields smoothly. Of the fallen wounded there was no time or opportunity to help. They would just have to hope they were not trampled to death by their fellow legionaries in the press.

Most were.

'One' Carbo bellowed, and the manoeuvre began again. Shield-barge... shield-turn... gladius blow, twist, withdraw... step forward... lock shields.

It was simple; mechanical. Bred into the men of the legions through years of training and putting it into practice. Regardless of any selection of favourable ground, of legion formation, of enemy tactics or numbers, any centurion or veteran would stand by the fact that it was the simple three-stage manoeuvre of the front line that won the battle. It was those three stages that allowed Rome to conquer the world.

Fronto found himself humming a ditty, lost in the almost monotonous regularity of it, and his attention was only focused back on the real world when someone yelled something about fleeing. Two centurions' whistles rang out and then the entire beach echoed to shouted commands and the calls of the musicians to draw up in formation.

Peering over his shield rim, Fronto watched with weary satisfaction as the Britons broke for the treeline behind the beach, the remaining nobles mounting their chariots and hurling incomprehensible abuse at the invaders as their drivers took them away from the fight.

With a smile, Fronto felt the long scrubby grass brushing his shins and realised that the legions had pushed the enemy all the way across the beach, past the lower, pebbled part, across the sand, and finally to the grass.

And now they were running.

And if the cavalry – of whom no sign had been discerned since departure from Gesoriacum – had been here, they could chase down the fleeing warriors and deal with them. But with only thirty or so horsemen under Galronus, and their mounts still aboard the ships, such closure was merely a dream.

Hardening himself, Fronto took a deep breath. Now to face the wrath of Caesar before he got to break a few heads himself.

ROME

Lucilia took a deep breath.

'I hear him coming.'

Faleria nodded in the faint light that issued through the grille in the door at the top of the stairs and shuffled back against the wall, the blanket and pallet she had been given for comfort barely keeping away the chill of the cold stone floor.

'I wish you'd let me help.'

Faleria smiled wanly at her young friend. 'You will be helping, but the first move has to be mine.' She sighed. 'We'll only get one chance at this and, I'm sorry to have to say it, but you're too delicate and slight for it. I am – in my brother's words when I've stopped him making a fool of himself – a 'tough old bitch'. And we'll never be more prepared. Just be ready to move.'

Lucilia shuffled nervously.

'Stop fidgeting. The smallest thing could give the whole game away. Act normally.'

That's easy for you to say, thought Lucilia, eying the single door to the cellar room as the light disappeared, blotted out by the figure of the guard, Papirius. It would be Papirius. It was always Papirius. In the days they had languished in this dingy pit – enough of them that she had now lost count – only two guards had put in an appearance.

Sextius brought their breakfast in the morning – a luke-warm barley gruel that put her in mind of the muck the legions had eaten when she had lived at the Genava camp with her father. The man was a humourless ex-legionary who appeared to have been dismissed from service with six lashes for his trouble, though she had not dared to ask why. In the days and weeks of imprisonment she could count on her fingers the number of times he had spoken to them, and even that usually monosyllabic. After breakfast the man disappeared, never to be seen again that day, though his voice occasionally issued in muffled tones from beyond the door, confirming his presence in the building.

The only other voice they had heard was Papirius. The other ex-legionary was a more genial man, given their circumstances. He it was who had taken away, cleaned and replaced the hellish slop-bucket, while Sextius seemed willing to let them wallow in their own filth. Indeed, Papirius had even cleaned the cell and replaced their bedding three or four times, though he had taken the precaution of chaining them to the wall rings each time.

Papirius it was who also brought the other two meals each day: a snack of bread, cheese and olives at noon and a warm meat stew in the evening. If it was he who prepared the meals, he could be said to be a more than passable cook.

She hardened her heart. These were their guards if not their captors. For all she saw in Papirius something familiar from her time living in the proximity of the Eighth Legion, the man was still holding her against her will.

Papirius, it seemed, was overly fond of wine and therefore took the late meal shifts so that in the morning he could sleep off the skinful he inevitably had each night. It seemed likely that the man's dismissal from the legions was connected to his drinking habits.

It was partially that habit that had decided on their timing.

It had to be the noon meal. Papirius would be the least expecting of the pair and very much the least careful. He would still be a little tired and blurred from the alcohol. At noon he was less chatty than in the evening due to his bone-weariness.

To this end, the two women had deliberately played up to Papirius throughout the long days of captivity. They had been model prisoners, never even breathing out of turn. They had cooperated, even with Sextius leering at them hungrily from time to time.

And they had waited.

And they had planned.

The map they had drawn on the wall with a sharp stone they had rubbed clear only an hour later, having committed it firmly to memory.

Lucilia had begun to wonder whether Faleria would ever be ready. For the last week she had been needling the older woman, urging her to put the plan into action, but each time the situation had apparently not been quite right.

And then, last night, Papirius had confided with a wink that he was bound for the Opiconsivia festival with its ritual chariot race and then a celebratory night of feasting and drinking with a cousin who owned a farm not far along the Via Flaminia and who had brought the last of his harvest to the city markets.

Faleria had smiled as he left and the door closed with a rattle of keys. Papirius would be less alert than usual when he arose the next morning, and their time had come.

The door at the top of the stairs opened.

Lucilia bit her lip and drew blood.

Sextius!

It had not occurred to her that perhaps Papirius would have been so inebriated that his companion would have to step in and cover his shift. Damn!

'Faleria!' she hissed quietly.

'I know.'

'What do we do?'

'We go anyway.'

Sextius, his usual sour face taking on that leer at the sight of the captive women, began to move slowly down the stairs, two wooden plates balanced in his left hand, the right on the pommel of his sword.

Lucilia shuddered. Sextius was a whole different proposition to Papirius. Faleria had been planning to overwhelm the guard as he brought the food and then pin him to the floor while Lucilia tied his hands with the twine they had unthreaded from the pallet's edge. Papirius would have tried to fight them off, but Faleria was sure she could cope, especially if he was suffering. Sextius, on the other hand, was bright and alert. He would be tough to simply overwhelm.

What was Faleria thinking? They had to abort and try another day.

'Food!' Sextius announced somewhat unnecessarily as he reached the flagged floor and strode across. Lucilia looked up hungrily. Whatever her friend had planned, she had to keep up the pretence that all was normal. Faleria sat cross legged, hunched over, her head hanging down.

'What's wrong with her?' Sextius glanced across at Lucilia as he slowly approached.

'I have no idea' replied the younger of the captive women, with a distinct ring of truth.

Unceremoniously, Sextius slung the two wooden platters on the floor at the foot of their pallets, the bread rolling off onto the dirty, cold stone flags. Narrowing his eyes suspiciously, the former legionary crouched in front of Faleria, though Lucilia noted how his fingers curled around the sword hilt at his side, ready to draw at a heartbeat's notice.

'You look pale' he announced and grasped Faleria's hair roughly with his left hand, yanking it upwards and lifting her head to see her face. His attention locked on her visage, he noticed all too late the finger coming up that jammed into his eye, her nail sharp from weeks of rough treatment.

Lucilia stared as the man's left eye exploded with a popping noise, goo and blood spurting out over Faleria. He screamed, though his reactions were sharp even in his agony, the sword coming free of the sheath with a metallic rasp. Even as Lucilia goggled in horror, Faleria stepped up her vicious attack. As the wounded man let go of her hair, she smashed her forehead into his face. Nothing broke, but she felt the impact with dizzying pain and knew she had dealt him a stunning blow.

'Run!'

By the time Lucilia had reached the stairs and was bounding up them, Faleria was at her heel, the wounded captor's sword in her hand. Back in the gloom of the cell, the howling of pain was now infused with cries of rage and the sounds of scuffling as Sextius struggled to his feet.

'Come on!'

The pair ran through the cellar's door and past the small cubicle that served as a guard chamber with its little table and rickety wooden chair, out along the corridor, around two corners, past two doors, and to the stairs that led to the ground floor, up which they pounded.

Somewhere behind them issued the most animal shriek of pained rage, and the sound of hobnailed boots on stone echoed through the corridors.

'Sextius?'

Lucilia's heart skipped a beat at the sound of Papirius' voice ahead. Were they trapped? It mattered not how reasonable the genial ex-soldier had been. If he discovered they had escaped he would be merciless; of this she was certain.

'Sextius?' the call came again.

'Faleria!' she shouted in a panic, her courage draining away rapidly.

'He's off to the right. We go left at the end. Just run!'

Obeying the instructions of her forthright friend, the young woman pounded along the corridor, ignoring the doors to the various rooms on either side, nearing the end, where the left turn would take her toward the street and freedom.

She almost collapsed in panic as she sped round the corner and Papirius' hand reached out of the shadowed opening to the far side, grasping for her and tearing a rip across the shoulder of her stola as she narrowly evaded his grip.

And then she was running again. The door to the street was around the next corner and at the end of that corridor. She could see the glow of daylight at the bend. Her heart lurched again and, with a plummeting feeling of dismay, she glanced back over her shoulder as she ran.

Papirius stood in the corridor, blocking it, his sword dancing in his hand, ready to strike. Beyond him, in the gloomier reaches, Lucilia could see Faleria, an expression of grim determination on her face, raising her stolen blade. She looked up to see Lucilia watching in horror.

'Run, girl!'

Her soul crying in anguish, Lucilia turned her back on her friend and ran on, around the corner and down the short passage, bursting out through the half-open door into the bright daylight of the Subura. Behind her, now invisible in the building's gloom, she heard the faint but distinctive ring of steel striking steel.

Tears streaming down her cheeks, she grasped her filthy, soiled stola around her and ran, barefoot, for the family home on the Cispian hill.

Clodius would pay for this.

Chapter 15
(Roman beachhead, south-east coast of Britannia)

'Returning to Gaul is out of the question.' Caesar's voice was flat and quiet – that particular flat and quiet that Fronto knew all too well to be a final word on any matter. Whether Cicero was not aware of that or whether he did not care, Fronto could not say, but the man slapped a hand angrily down on the table.

'We have no cavalry. We have only two legions and no idea quite how many of the natives there are out there who will resist us. We have no supplies and not enough intelligence as to where the areas of farmland and settlements are. We can't even chase down the army that we pushed back due to the lack of cavalry support. It's a futile gesture, Caesar!'

Fronto smiled. The commander of the Seventh had begun to rant about the idiocy of the entire campaign the moment he had stepped into Caesar's tent and the argument had not let up yet, despite the increasingly dangerous edge to the general's tone. Brutus, Galronus and Volusenus stood quiet, staying clear of the matter. For his part, Fronto could not wait to get started on Cicero, but for the time being it was too much fun just watching Caesar nearing his breaking point.

All in all, it would work nicely for him. Caesar would, at some point, draw Fronto up for his actions at the beach, but Cicero had nicely diverted the general's anger onto himself. It would be ever so easy now to fall onto Caesar's side and launch his own argument at his fellow legate. That, in turn, should nicely incense Furius and Fabius enough to get their blood up. The two centurions were standing not far from the general's tent, as were Carbo and Atenos, and they would quickly become aware of the division and argument. Especially when Fronto carried the bile right to them.

'No, Cicero. Push me no further.' The general's voice sounded like a blade being drawn.

To his credit, Cicero seemed to realise that he'd walked to the edge of a precipice, and fell silent for a moment. Fronto almost laughed when, rather than stopping, the legate of the Seventh simply changed tack.

'Then I have an alternative suggestion, Caesar.'

The general's eyes became flinty, daring the man to continue speaking.

'Perhaps we can send back the fleet and collect the Ninth legion from Gesoriacum? Possibly even one of the other legions as well, if Cotta and Sabinus are still local enough? Then we could check on the cavalry and find out what happened to them? Four legions with cavalry support and we could take proper control of the island.'

'No.'

'But…'

'No, Cicero.'

The legate of the Seventh subsided into silence, though his face was an interesting puce colour, and he almost vibrated with the urge to go on.

The general turned his withering glare on Fronto and the Tenth's legate could feel Caesar forcing himself to stay calm as he prepared to deal with his other wayward legate. Fronto took a deep breath.

Now was his chance.

'I am aware that by leading two centuries of the Tenth into the water, I went against the general orders during the landing, Cicero' he said, deliberately avoiding Caesar's eyes and instead locking his gaze on his fellow legate. 'But I have to make it absolutely clear that I wouldn't have had to take such drastic action had you not flagrantly disobeyed your own orders and kept your legion back. Even those men of the Seventh who wanted to fight wouldn't do so without an eagle to follow. I hope it burns in your gut that I had to provide that eagle because yours cowered on that trireme.'

His face was coloured with fury, though inside, Fronto could not help but feel a warm glow of satisfaction as the general turned his angry gaze on Cicero once more.

Nicely deflected, if I say so myself.

'You have no idea what you're talking about, Fronto' Cicero snapped in return. 'I tried to commit my men, but the Seventh is no longer a proper legion. It's a joke. Whatever the general asked of him, your old friend Priscus saddled the Seventh with every coward, rebel, idiot and disobedient fool in the army. My legion refused to disembark into the face of Hades without the Tenth being equally committed.'

Somewhere deep inside, Fronto could see a certain sympathetic logic to that plight. Had he been in command, both legions would have been in the water together instantly. Still, the fool had just made his predicament that much worse by trying to kick the blame downwards. One of the perils of command was that, no matter how the legion acted, its commander took the ultimate brunt of any retribution for troubles caused.

'Don't bad-mouth your men, Cicero; it's unprofessional. What do they say? 'It's a poor workman who blames his tools for failure'. I fought alongside your 'cowards, rebels and idiots' in the water, and they did the eagle proud. And I heard only Caesar's call committing the Seventh. Not once did I hear your musicians sound the advance until we were already wading ashore.'

'Fronto…'

'Don't make me laugh. You're supposed to be a senior officer. Caesar may not agree with my call, but I did what I had to do to take control of the field, and the general will tell you that's just what any officer worth his salt does in that situation. If my eagle hadn't dragged your boys into the water, we'd all have died on the ships.'

'So taking control of the army out from under the general – an act of mutiny to my mind – is preferable to taking your chances against a few enemy archers?'

'Don't be a prick, Cicero.'

The legate of the Seventh rolled his eyes. 'Ever the gutter snipe, eh Fronto. If you can't answer the question sensibly, you have to resort to name-calling. You'd do well as a senate back-seater.'

'Stick it up your arse. It doesn't matter how you dress your actions up, even in a broad striped toga, failure is still failure. You disobeyed your orders, endangering the whole army, and I was forced to disobey mine just to clear up your mess. Doesn't matter what you say, I know that, and you know that.' He pointed a finger at the general, an act that raised a disapproving eyebrow. 'Caesar knows it too, as well as these others.'

Fronto grinned.

'Hell, even your pet apes know it. One of your precious psychopath centurions came with me into the water. How's that suit you?'

Cicero sank into silent glaring anger.

Got him, Fronto thought with deep satisfaction. *That* hit a nerve.

Caesar was looking back and forth between his two legates as though trying to decide who to berate first as Brutus finally stepped forward into the middle of the seething fracas.

'If I may interject, this meeting was intended to decide how best we proceed from here, not as an arena to hurl insults and air our dirty undergarments. I would humbly suggest, Caesar, that we finish for now and reconvene in a few hours when frayed tempers have healed and we are all calmer and more reasonable. I cannot see this turning out any useful conclusions as it is.'

For a moment, Caesar's gaze fell on the speaker and it looked as though he might unleash his pent-up rage on the young officer. Finally, though, he subsided with a sigh and sank into his chair.

'Agreed. Cicero? Go and think about what you want from your command. Fronto? Just go away. Reconvene here at the dusk watch and we will decide what to do. Commander Galronus? I would appreciate it if you could arrange some scout patrols from your turma of cavalry to see if we can locate farms or settlements within, say, a five mile radius?'

Galronus saluted as Fronto and Cicero continued to glare at one another.

'Very well. Dismissed, gentlemen.'

Fronto stood and glowered for a moment as Cicero tore away his gaze and, saluting briefly to the general, turned and strode from the tent. Preparing himself for the next barrage, Fronto followed on, Brutus, Volusenus and Galronus immediately behind. As they strode out into the fresh, cool air, Fronto turned and made small, subtle gestures to the three behind him to make themselves absent. As they did so, peeling off and going about their business, Fronto sped off to catch up with Cicero, who had paused next to his two veteran centurions, both of whom stood with scowls on their bristly faces. Carbo and Atenos fell in behind Fronto like bodyguards and the six men came together at the bottom of the hill, away from Caesar's tent and close to the command quarters of the Seventh.

'That was damned unprofessional, Fronto!' Cicero snapped.

'It needed to be said.'

'If you have a personal issue with me, you should take it up with me in private, not in front of the general and fellow officers.'

Fronto only partially had to fake his wide-eyed expression of disbelief.

'You dick! This isn't personal! I expect a bit of fear in a senior officer!' As Cicero went purple in colour, Fronto shrugged. 'You're not a career soldier, but a politician doing this job as a step on the ladder. It's nothing new, and it's nothing to be ashamed of. We're not all cut out to be fighters.'

Cicero was starting to splutter angrily and Fronto was having a great deal of trouble not bursting out into a wide grin.

'No. Not fear. And it's not even disobedience. Hell, I've had to flaunt the rules a few times as you're well aware, in order to get the right results. Better to be shouted at by the general for disobeying orders than to be wandering around the broken remnants of a dead army, wondering how it got to this.'

Still, Cicero seemed unable to find voice through his rising fury.

'I never had issue with you over these past years. I've never had a reason to shout at you. It's not personal. That's why I brought it up in the headquarters in front of everyone. Because what you do personally is of no interest to me. And what you think of me doesn't concern me. What concerns me is when your actions – or lack of them – directly endanger the entire army, including *my* legion. I take very great exception to that. And I will *not* back down from confrontation over something so serious. When you do things like that it makes you a bad commander and a dangerous one. So you can take your righteous indignation and you can stick it so far up your cushioned, senatorial behind that you can feel it in the back of your throat.'

Cicero wheezed out a whispered invective – the best his throat seemed able to manage.

'What?' asked Fronto, cupping an ear dramatically.

His fellow legate's mouth clamped shut and Fronto could hear the teeth grinding even then.

'Well here's a suggestion. When you can think of something to say that doesn't just confirm that you're a dick and a bad officer, come and find me and tell me. I'm going for a walk to cool down.'

Leaving the spluttering Cicero, Fronto turned and marched off toward the west gate in the temporary camp's ramparts that were still being constructed.

The last thing he noticed, with some satisfaction, was the looks of silent anger on the faces of Fabius and Furius.

By the time he was past the first two rows of legionary tents, Carbo and Atenos were at his shoulders again.

'Jove's arse, sir. I thought he was going to explode. You might have pushed him a bit *too* far there.'

'Knock off the *sirs*. No one's listening.'

'Not while we're in open camp, sir.'

Fronto shrugged. 'Are they following?'

Carbo 'accidentally' let slip his vine staff and had to crouch to pick it up. A subtle glance around and he caught up with the other two.

'No, but they're watching where we're going.'

'Good. Galronus says there's a clearing in the wood to the west. Just about every path into the trees leads to it. I'm going there. The ground's muddy and soft and even a dunce should be able to track me there. You two had best slip off back to the tents. Find Brutus. Tell him I need his help and then wait till those two leave. Follow them and make sure you're there when they find me.'

Carbo nodded and grinned.

'Let's nail the bastards, sir.'

'Yup. Now go. They won't follow if they see you two going with me.'

As Fronto strode on ahead toward the gate, his two centurions dipped to the side, into the ranks of the Tenth's temporary camp. Keeping his eyes straight ahead, he fought the urge to turn and look at Cicero and his men.

Near the command section, Cicero snapped a few commands at his centurions and Furius and Fabius exchanged hurried, urgent words before separating, the former strolling slowly down the road toward the west gate, the latter rushing off toward their tents.

* * * * *

Fronto kept his face forward as he strode into the woods, following a beaten path – presumably a hunter's trail. Despite the fact that Galronus and his men had briefly scouted the immediate surroundings of the Roman camp, they had only had time for a quick scan and it now occurred to Fronto how potentially dangerous it was to stride off into the woodland where native warriors or hunters could be lurking in the bushes, even watching their enemy.

In the safe knowledge that, if he was being followed as he hoped, the pursuers were far enough behind to be out of earshot, he slowed so as not to blunder into any unfortunate situation. His hand reached down for the gladius at his side and he drew it, just in case, pacing along the path into the heart of the unknown forest.

Still, a thrill ran through him.

At last.

After months of watching friends and acquaintances fall prey to the murderers' blades, he would have a chance to confront them. And if things went just right there would be no need for protracted trial and interrogation. They would prove their guilt in front of an independent witness. Execution would be guaranteed after that. Knowing that, of course, the pair would probably try and fight. But with Fronto, Carbo, Atenos and Brutus present, he really did not fancy their chances, no matter how good they were with a blade.

With very little warning, Fronto rounded the bole of a birch cluttered about the base with bushes and undergrowth and found himself looking into a clearing some twenty paces wide. All across it, the scattered stumps of trees in varying degrees of decay told of the reason for the clearing's size. A dark, charred patch marked where the unnecessary foliage and thinner branches had been disposed of.

Nodding to himself in satisfaction, he began to pick his way among the stumps toward the centre. He could not guarantee that Fabius and Furius would take exactly the same path and there was the possibility they could come across the clearing from any angle, so for safety he would need to be at the centre.

Finding a particularly large tree stump – a sycamore by the look of the remnants – he took a quick look around and sank gratefully to the time-and-weather-smoothed surface, taking care to fold his cloak beneath him first to keep the dampness away.

Reaching down, he began to rub his knee. While such an act was probably unnecessary in terms of explanation for his pause, the joint was still weak and giving him some difficulty after a long walk, so the massaging felt good.

A silence descended on the woodland, broken only by the occasional cawing of a crow or the faint rustling of a ground-dwelling forest creature, the latter making Fronto peer into the gloomy eaves each time. And in the background: muffled by distance and flora, the noise of ten thousand men making camp and settling in for the day.

It was so inordinately peaceful that he found himself involuntarily relaxing and almost forgetting why he was here. For some reason life was so busy and fraught that he never seemed to find the time to simply sit in the country and enjoy the peace. A rare image of his father flashed into his mind as the two of them had made the laborious climb up Vesuvius when he was eight years old.

'Life is not worth living if you can't make time occasionally to appreciate the bounty of what's around you, Marcus' his father had said. Good words to live by which he'd not even thought about in years.

'You'd probably like it here, father' he said to the sky in general. 'It's a bit colder and wetter than home, but everything's so green and lush. You'd have worn your gardening hat a lot more here.'

Another image flashed into his head: this time of his good friend Balbus, wearing just such a gardening hat, his face ruddy and healthy with an outdoor glow.

'Am I getting too old for this stuff? Oh, Quintus, you may have been right about Caesar, but you have no idea what the army has descended into since you left.'

'Talking to yourself, Fronto?'

He looked up at the interruption to see two figures at the edge of the clearing, beginning to move toward the centre. Fabius and Furius wore voluminous wool cloaks that billowed around them as they moved, their heads bare to the air. No sign of crested helmets. No obvious sign of vine staffs either. They had come without the trappings of office.

Of course. All the easier to disappear or slip by without being recognised. He wondered how they had left the camp without recognition, but remembered how easily he had crossed the half-built rampart without being questioned. Going out was always easier than getting back in.

Furius, the owner of the voice, was scratching his chin as he walked. Fabius kept both hands within the folds of his cloak.

'I have to say I'm not entirely surprised to see you' Fronto said lightly.

'I'm sure' Furius rumbled.

'Very dangerous business' Fabius added menacingly, 'coming off into the woodland all on your own. Not even a shield, I see.'

'Nor you.'

Fabius shrugged and Fronto could see with the movement how something solid and held tightly within his hidden grip lifted the cloak slightly.

Casually, so as not to make it obvious, Fronto lifted his eyes to the clearing's edge behind them. It took a moment for him to spot Carbo and Atenos in the undergrowth by the path from which they had all entered. Beside and just behind them he could just make out the shape of Brutus and even from here, he got the feeling that the young officer was distinctly unimpressed and unhappy with the situation.

With irritation, it occurred to him that if the three of them were going to lurk in the scrub, he could very well be dead by the time they managed to get involved in any fight.

He would have to string things out so they could get close enough to help.

Ever closer Furius and Fabius moved. Finally, only five paces away, Furius removed his cloak and draped it over his shoulder, his hand falling to the pommel of his gladius where it sat comfortably.

'I'm not an easy target' Fronto said levelly.

'I imagine not' Furius shrugged, his face twisting into what he might have believed was a smile.

'*And* not an easy kill' the legate went on. 'I'm no wounded officer on a medical bed or drunken fop in an inn.'

The two centurions came to a halt some seven or eight feet from Fronto and his hand dropped to the pommel of his own sword.

'Plainly' Furius replied, his eyebrow raising slightly.

Behind him, Fabius threw back his cloak, his hand lancing out with lightning speed. Fronto had drawn his gladius a finger-width from the scabbard before his racing, confused brain registered that the long, narrow object in Fabius' hand and which he'd been concealing beneath his cloak was actually a long, narrow terracotta jar – a mini amphora.

'What...?'

'Call it a salute to the only man who would jump in the water with me' Furius shrugged. 'The time has come, legate, to bury the hatchet, so to speak. A peace offering? What you did at the beach... well let's just say I seem to have misjudged you.'

Fronto was suddenly aware that he had his sword partially drawn while Furius was unhooking a leather wine bag from his belt and Fabius began to heave the stopper out of the jar. With a frown, he slid the sword back as unobtrusively as he could manage.

The two centurions heard the rasp and caught the movement, sharing a tense look.

'I hope that the division between us has not widened to the extent that we're unable to repair it' Furius said, leaning against a tall stump. 'It would appear that we have thrown our weight and support behind a fool, while allowing rumour and hearsay to blind us to the real soldiers in this army.' As Fronto shook his head in confusion and eyed the wine suspiciously, Furius glanced at the leather container and shrugged. 'I fear I may have been a little short-sighted in my accusations. Serving under some of these lunatics would drive *anyone* to dip into a jar every now and then.'

With a sigh of relief, Fabius sank to one of the nearby stumps and, gripping the jar's handle and laying it across his forearm, he tilted the container and supped deeply of the wine within.

'I thought...' Fronto floundered for a moment.

'What?'

'I assumed you two would be...' he frowned. 'You're not pissed at me?'

'What for?'

'I called your legate a coward and a prick.'

'And in a very forthright and timely fashion, I'd say. We've done our damn best to keep him on the right path – it's part of the job of a centurion to keep their senior officers out of trouble – but the man has the leadership skills of an Illyrian goat herd and will not listen to reason. He seems intent on leading his men to the very brink of destruction in his desire to defy Caesar.' Fabius made an exasperated sound, proffering the jar to Fronto as he wiped his mouth with his scarf.

'This is a whole different army from Pompey's you know, Fronto.'

'Yes, I'm sure' Fronto replied weakly, wondering what in the name of Fortuna was going on.

'In Pompey's legions there was no argument among the officers. What Pompey said was law and his officers just jumped about trying to please him. Of course, all the work was done by the centurions. The legates and tribunes were really just there to make up the numbers and to look impressive to the natives.'

Furius laughed. 'You remember that knob from Antium? What was his name, Lucius?'

'Postumius Albinus. Cocked things up so often that, in the end, he stayed in his tent most of the time and just let us get on with it.'

Fronto could not help but smile at the image. So many of the men who had served on Caesar's staff fell into a similar mould. An image of Plancus surfaced in his mind.

'Until the bastard turned on us' Furius added darkly.

291

Fronto frowned and the two centurions exchanged a look. With a shrug, Furius tugged his scarf aside to show the white scar above his collar bone. Fronto had entirely forgotten about the strange wound, but his curiosity swelled anew.

'Albinus had us up in front of the senior officers for 'overstepping our authority' and sentenced us without trial. I'd be under a mound in Anatolia with half a dozen others if Pompey hadn't ordered the bloody disgrace stopped. I was about two beats away from the blade going through my heart. It's a reminder never to step too far outside the boundaries when stylus-pushers are watching.'

Fabius nodded. 'Pompey always had to keep a tight rein on his men.'

'But the thing is' Furius said, wagging a finger, 'this army is different. Caesar's a brilliant general, but he's also bright enough to appreciate the opinions of his officers while not giving them enough room to cock it all up. I didn't see that at first. All I saw was people arguing with him in a way that would have had Pompey calling for the executioner's sword. But it works here. It actually works. When people like *you* disobey, you pull the old man's chestnuts out of the fire when he'd have made a bloody awful mistake otherwise. Like at the beach.'

'At the beach…' repeated Fronto, still trying to wrap his mind around this unexpectedly convivial conversation.

'Caesar was foolish to commit only one legion. I know why he did it, mind: I'm not daft. But in the circumstances it was stupid and short-sighted. And then Cicero – who we've tried to push into actually commanding his legion – well he compounds things by sitting back and refusing to act. If you and I hadn't dropped into the water we'd all have been screwed over.'

Fronto nodded slowly.

'That,' Furius grinned, 'was the most reckless, insubordinate, and almost unbelievably sensible thing I've seen in a long time. You're an odd bugger as a legate, but you actually do the work, instead of relying on your centurions.'

Fronto's eyes flicked up to the treeline and he realised that his centurions and Brutus had vanished. Perhaps they had decided the situation was safe, or perhaps they had moved to better overhear the conversation. He could not help hoping they were still there somewhere, though.

'But your loyalty to Caesar...' Fronto blurted. He'd been thinking it, but had had no intention of actually voicing his thoughts. He bit down on the words, but it was too late.

Furius shook his head sadly. 'Is unquestionable. I'm a centurion, legate Fronto. Once I've taken the oath, I'm the general's man. The soldier's oath is sacred, you know that.' He grinned slyly. 'I'm afraid you'll have to look elsewhere for the solution to your problem.'

With a sigh, Fronto sagged. 'Half a dozen times these past months people have been telling me I'm letting my prejudices cloud my judgement. Sorry, but Pompey's been a real arsehole in Rome, right down to putting my family in danger. I never used to have anything against him, but when his men set fire to my house, things changed. When I see a Pompeian shield, it gets my blood up.'

'All I can say is that he's a good man to serve under in war' Fabius shrugged. 'What he's like in Rome I couldn't guess, other than to state for the record that I've yet to find a straight politician. They're all bent and dodgy. Comes with the territory.'

Fronto took another swig from the jar and then passed it over to the centurion, scratching his chin reflectively.

'It would appear that I'm back to square one with whoever killed Tetricus and the others, then.'

'He was a good man, your tribune?' Furius asked, taking another slug.

'One of the best. A promising career officer, I'd say.'

'Bad way to go. When you find out who did it, make sure to let us know and we'll give you a hand peeling the bastard's skin from his bones, eh?'

Fronto shook his head, not in rejection, but in confusion at the strange turns life had taken in Britannia.

'It'd be just my luck if half a dozen druids popped up out the undergrowth now and set fire to me.'

Furius laughed.

'Come on, legate. Let's get back to the safety of camp.'

* * * * *

Publius Sulpicius Rufus, de facto commander of Gesoriacum port, rubbed his eyes wearily and looked down at the scattered reports on the desk.

'What's holding up the supply train then?'

293

Casco, the cavalry prefect of the attached auxiliary unit, shrugged. 'Without sending out a proper scout force we can't be sure, sir. We're running patrols for a three mile radius around the settlement and there's no sign of anything. Whatever the hold-up is, it must be further back than that.

'We're running out of time, gentlemen. The supplies we have may *look* impressive, and Cita informs me that the food stores will keep the Ninth for a month, but we need to bear in mind that Caesar will be bringing two hungry legions back from Britannia before winter, and that Cotta and Sabinus will be returning here to resupply at some point. We need to have a full granary and storehouse before they're needed. Three days late is starting to become worrying.'

There were murmurs of agreement around the tent. Rufus looked across the faces of the six tribunes, single cavalry prefect, and the primus pilus of the Ninth and felt a nervousness he was not used to. Three years ago he had been appointed to the high position of legate for the first time and he'd retained command of the veteran Ninth throughout Caesar's campaign. He'd had little experience of war or of command before then, but had very quickly found his feet and carved out a niche for himself in the general's army.

He was comfortable in charge of a legion, in or out of a combat situation.

What he was *not* used to, or comfortable with, was the awesome responsibility of being given a 'carte-blanche' command. Not only did he have responsibility for the Ninth now, but also for the wellbeing and safety of the Morini tribe in and around Gesoriacum, the port – to which Caesar would return, and the supply base upon which the entire army depended...

It was a mind-boggling nightmare of organisation. Cita, the army's chief quartermaster, was if anything an impediment to the smooth running of the command and, while Priscus had remained here as camp prefect, he seemed to spend most of his time stomping around and complaining or arguing with Cita.

'Alright gentlemen. We cannot afford to go on like this. Tribune Acilius: I want you to take the third cohort, along with prefect Casco and half his cavalry. Follow the river road toward Nemetocenna and find that supply train. Caesar is still unconvinced of the absolute loyalty of some of the local tribes. It is possible that they've waylaid our supplies, and I'm not willing to risk a small cavalry scout unit out among them without solid infantry support.'

Taking his eyes from the senior tribune, he regarded the other five junior ones. All of them, unlike the competent Acilius, were hungry young politicians fresh from Rome, hoping to win Caesar's praise before returning to the city in the winter. Not one of them could be trusted to do much more than tie his boots.

'Nautius and Rubellius: I want you to take the fourth and fifth cohorts and start constructing some defences around Gesoriacum itself and its harbour. You can link them up with this fort to save time. Something smells wrong to me. The supplies not turning up worries me, so let's be prepared for any eventuality. When Caesar returns, I want him to be able to land safely in the harbour, even if the whole Belgae nation is hammering at the door.'

He breathed deeply. The pair would have no clue as to how to set up effective defences, but the legion's chief engineer was in the fourth cohort and many of the best veterans in the fifth. A placebo command to keep the tribunes busy. He smiled in satisfaction as he pondered the remaining three tribunes and his eyes fell on a young, serious looking man with sandy hair, whose family had risen to prominence through their shrewdness as traders and negotiators.

'Cilo: I want you to take just a small bodyguard and head into the native settlement. Speak to every merchant you can find and secure us whatever supplies you can for the best price you can, in case our own train never arrives. We don't have the funds here and now, though, so you'll have to work it all on promises.'

The young man nodded, smiling at his assigned task.

'That leaves Murgus and Purpurio. You'll be staying in camp with me. Murgus, I want you to get on to the readiness of the men. Make sure their centurions are on task. I want all drill and training doubled. Exercises and marches, though, are to be limited to a one mile radius. I don't want a whole column of men out there in the wilds right now. Purpurio: Get on to manufacturing. I want the workshops turning out arms and armour, not pots and pans. I want extra scorpions constructed and then positioned on the defences.'

He leaned back.

'I think that covers everything.'

'Sir, do you really expect that much trouble? Isn't it possible that the wagons have just been delayed by weather?'

Rufus' eyes flicked to Murgus. 'It *is* possible, but it's also worth noting that at no time this year has a supply train been more than twenty four hours late. Three days is therefore a bit of an anomaly, especially given that we're currently rooted in one very easy-to-find place. I'll be happier when I hear from Sabinus or Cotta and we know they've encountered no trouble, but until we have an indication that everything is normal, we're on a war footing just in case.'

He glanced once more around the camp. 'Is that it? No more questions?'

Murgus opened his mouth again, but was interrupted by a respectful rap on the tent's door frame.

'Come!'

One of the praetorian legionaries on guard outside stepped in and saluted. 'Sir. Word from the south gate. A huge cavalry force is on the way in.'

Rufus frowned and, nodding, waved the legionary out.

'Get to work, gentlemen.'

The tribunes saluted, filed out of the tent and disappeared into the camp as Rufus fastened his cloak about his shoulders with the Mars Victor brooch his brother had given him last name-day and then strode out into the chilly morning air. Catching sight of Priscus hurrying across the open space before the command quarters, he made a course to intercept, falling in beside him.

'You heard, then?'

'Cavalry. Let's just hope they're allied ones. It's bloody hard to tell the difference when they're all Gauls anyway.'

Rufus smiled as the pair bore down on the south gate. The portals were firmly closed, a detachment of legionaries on guard above and beside it. The dust cloud and black massed shapes of an exceedingly large cavalry force were plainly visible on the flat grassy land only five or six hundred paces away. Rufus sagged with relief as he spotted a Roman cavalry flag among them.

'It's Varus. What the hell is he doing here? I thought he was in Britannia with the general.'

The two officers stood pensively, watching the senior cavalry commander and his entire wing of cavalry approach, filling the open grassland. 'Open the gate' Rufus shouted as the force closed on them. The veteran officer was riding out front, the reins of his horse gripped tightly in his good arm, the other still splinted and bound tightly to his torso.

As the column neared the gate, Varus gave a number of commands and the cavalry split into three groups, heading to the west and east gates, and the last, with the commander himself, slowing as they approached the south.

'What in the name of Juno's flabby arse are you doing here?' Priscus demanded as Varus came to a stop and slid awkwardly down from the saddle, his slung arm and wounded hip more than a small hindrance. His men continued to ride past him and into camp.

'Bit of a change of plan, lads, I'm afraid. Looks like you've had reasonable weather here, but it's been appalling down the coast. Time and again I gave the order to embark and the sailors told me the weather was too dangerous for any attempt at crossing. In their defence, it's been stormy as all hell down there. But that's not why we're here. I think you might have trouble.'

Rufus felt a knot form in his stomach. 'I've been suspecting as much. The supply train's three days late. What else, then?'

'This morning the weather had cleared and we went down to the harbour in the hope that we might actually be able to board, but all the ships had gone. Rather than try and find out what was going on, I thought it prudent to return here and consolidate the forces.'

'I'm glad you did. Something is definitely wrong.'

Varus nodded and patted his horse's sweaty flank. 'Let's get in the warm and you can tell me what's happening here.'

The three men turned and strode back into the camp as a heavy black cloud rolled over from the east, threatening further storms.

Chapter 16

(Roman beachhead, south-east coast of Britannia)

'So you're all pally with the pair of them now?'

'Don't make it sound so stupid, Galronus.'

'But you *are* on good terms with them?'

'I wouldn't say I'd invite them to dine with my family, if that's what you're implying, but the simple fact is that I've been wrong about them. Gods, when did it become so hard to admit you were wrong about something? I was wrong, alright. They're maybe a little harsh as centurions go, and I certainly wouldn't want to serve under them and forget to polish my mail, that's for sure, but they're solid centurions. They clearly don't harbour any anti-Caesarean designs like I thought. And they're starting to despise the failings in their own legate. They may very well be the only thing currently keeping the Seventh together as a military unit.'

'So,' Galronus glanced around to make sure they were not in easy earshot of anyone, 'I assume that means that you've removed them from the picture in respect of the deaths?'

Fronto's pace faltered as they strode across the grass for just a moment as he nodded slowly. 'To be honest, I'd not given that much thought yet. The dangerous situation we're in at the moment has sort of pushed it from the front of my mind. Well, it *had*, anyway.' He took a deep breath and rubbed a tired eye. 'I still won't rule them out until I can prove it either way, but I really can't see it now. I think I was trying to make it all fit with them because I'd already decided they'd done it. Oh, they had the opportunity, but I have the suspicion that a knife in the dark isn't really their way.'

'You know what that means though, Marcus?'

'That we're back to square one?'

Galronus shook his head and rolled his eyes. 'Hardly. It leaves you with an inescapable conclusion.'

Fronto frowned as they approached their destination. 'Hang on.' Caesar's command tent stood some forty paces ahead, two guards standing by the open flap and checking on the officers as they filed inside. 'What conclusion?' he said sharply as they came to a halt still safely out of audible distance.

Galronus sighed and tapped his temple. 'Think, Marcus. Who passed through Massilia?'

'Us. And the centurions, and Caesar's nephew. Oh, and...' The frown on the legate's face creased deeper. 'Surely you don't think...'

'Barring the discovery that someone else with a grudge was travelling north into the war-zone from Massilia, if you rule out us, and Furius and Fabius, what other conclusion can you draw?'

Fronto shook his head in disbelief. 'But those two tribunes are as wet as a duck's ringpiece! They could no more...' but his mind was already furnishing him with a mental image of Menenius standing by a farm house, his sword running with blood as he issued orders like a man born to the task. He'd saved a tough centurion's life!

'Fast as a bloody snake.'

'What?'

'When Menenius saved Cantorix across the Rhenus, he claimed he'd been lucky, but the centurion thought otherwise. And then he saved me from three...' Fronto felt his spine tingle.

'He didn't, did he?'

'Marcus, you're not finishing sentences. I may *sound* like a native Latin speaker, but you're becoming hard for me to follow.'

'Menenius!' Fronto said quietly. 'They found him wounded. He'd beaten off three barbarians and saved me, they said. You were there in the hospital. But that's not what happened, was it? Bloody Menenius didn't run and hide like a coward, did he? He lurked like a murderer. And as soon as he saw his opportunity, he tried to do for me, but three barbarians interrupted him.'

Fronto shook his head in amazement. 'Three bloody Germanic thugs saved my life. Saved me from a pissing Roman tribune!'

Galronus nodded slowly. 'Then Menenius has done an exceptional job of making himself appear ineffective and effeminate. The guise fooled everyone.'

'Even Caesar.'

'So he had the opportunity and the ability? He could certainly have been in Vienna when Caesar's nephew was there. The Fourteenth were in the front lines of the battle in the Germanic camp when Tetricus was attacked. And they were in our camp at the time he was murdered, and when Caesar's courier was done away with. The opportunity was there.'

'And that brings Hortius into the equation too' muttered Fronto. 'The pair of them are as thick as thieves. I doubt Menenius could pull any of this off without Hortius knowing about it. Besides, the medicus reckoned it would have taken two people to do what was done in the hospital.'

'But, the motive?'

Fronto shrugged. 'The same, I guess. What connection Menenius and Hortius could have to Pompey I don't know, but it still seems likely that they're trying to remove Caesar's supporters. At the first opportunity I'm going to have to have a little word with Caesar and, when we get back to Gaul, I'm going to have another quiet word with a pair of tribunes while they're held down and at the tip of my sword.'

Galronus gestured toward the tent, where the last of the officers had disappeared. 'Best get inside before they begin.'

'I'm sure Caesar will forgive me later when I explain my reasons to him, but you're right. It's starting to rain and I'd rather be under leather when that happens.'

As the first patter of drizzle scattered into the hard earth and springy grass, the two officers picked up the pace and strode hurriedly across the path and into the general's tent, the praetorian cavalry guards nodding their recognition and approval as they passed.

The tent was warm and smelled slightly of the charcoal braziers but mostly of sweat and armour oil. The legates and tribunes of both legions as well as Brutus and Volusenus stood patiently as Caesar ran a finger down a list on a wood sheet on the table before him. Fronto and Galronus fell in by the entrance and the guards closed the tent flap behind them. The dim interior gradually resolved itself in the absence of the damp morning light.

'You're late' Caesar said flatly, his eyes not even rising from the list.

'Yes, general. Apologies, but the delay was unavoidable.'

'Is it a matter of urgency?'

'Not urgency, as such, Caesar.'

'Then it should not preclude your punctual attendance, Fronto. Or yours, commander. You are learning bad habits from the Tenth's legate, I fear.'

Fronto bridled impotently. The general had not even looked at him yet. 'I will take the opportunity to explain in due course, Caesar.'

'You overstep sometimes, Fronto. I fear that I have allowed you to rush to the gate and snap and bark at passers-by too often. Legates and officers serve in this army at my convenience. You have been with me since the early days and I indulge you perhaps more than I should, but if you continue to treat this command as though *you* were the praetor and I your adjutant I may have to haul on your leash from time to time.'

Fronto's angry step forward was rendered impossible as Galronus trod heavily on his foot, the hobnails in the Remi officer's own boot digging painfully into Fronto's foot and causing him to take an involuntary sharp breath. Caesar still had not looked up and Fronto glanced angrily at his friend to see a warning glint in Galronus' eye. Slowly, he let his rage out with a measured breath.

He glanced around the tent to see every other officer's gaze lowered carefully except for Cicero. He half expected to see the man grinning, but instead, the legate of the Seventh was giving him a speculative, even slightly sympathetic look. For some reason that angered him almost as much as being spoken to in this way by the general.

'Good. At least you know when to stay silent' the general said, looking up. Galronus' hobnails pressed into Fronto's foot again as he opened his mouth to reply. Wincing at the pain, the legate clamped his lips shut.

'We have had visitors, gentlemen. A number of the local tribes have sent their ambassadors to offer me hostages and treaties. I have unilaterally accepted their offers, placing the hostages aboard one of the Gallic ships for safekeeping at this time.'

'Are these the same tribes who tried to stop us landing, general?' Cicero took a step forward. 'Because if they are, I'm not really sure how far our hospitality should extend.'

Caesar nodded. 'For once I agree with you, Cicero. We have no confirmation of the identity of those who attacked us. Quite simply our intelligence on the tribes of Britannia is not complete enough for us to make any solid guess as to who we were dealing with. Barring a few coins with unfamiliar names found upon the bodies, they could easily be from any tribe. All those who have entreated me claim to have had nothing to do with the clash at the beach, though it seems unlikely that they are all quite innocent. We have accepted their offerings, but I want this encampment fortified, regardless. I want the army on constant, full alert, and the ships under guard.'

'They're probably trying to buy time' Fronto said, trying to keep the anger and resentment from his tone.

'Possibly' the general acknowledged. 'Without a sizeable cavalry force we are effectively blind and relying on the few patrols commander Galronus can manage, and otherwise on the word of potentially treacherous natives and simple hearsay. The entire island of Britannia could be forming into an army over the next hill with a thousand druids for all we know. Thus I want the alert high and maintained.'

Cicero swallowed and took a deep breath. 'Forgive me for reiterating, Caesar, but I can still only advise that we return to Gaul. You said it yourself: we're effectively blind. We have no idea what's coming. And while we sit here and wish the cavalry would arrive, the weather is turning inclement. I can appreciate that a chastisement of the tribes that supported the Veneti against us would be a good way to instil a respect for Rome, but we can hardly punish the wayward tribes of Britannia in these conditions. Returning is the only sensible course of action.'

The general's gaze rose slowly to Cicero and came to rest there, carrying the full force of Caesar's scorn.

'For the very last time, Cicero, there will be no return to Gaul until I am satisfied that we have achieved what we came to do. If you so much as mention this again, I will consider confining you to the ships with the Briton hostages. Am I understood?'

Fronto glanced across at his fellow legate to see Cicero's speculative look being flashed back at him again. Damn it! He's still sounding me out against the general and... Fronto ground his teeth, horribly aware that he was starting to find Cicero's stand somewhat seductive.

'Very well' the general said quietly. 'The two legions will set about fortifying the camp. We have rations with us for today and tomorrow only. So tomorrow we will have to examine the situation and look at foraging for more supplies. For now, though, we concentrate on consolidation and defence.'

Caesar's eyes passed around the tent and fell upon Galronus.

'All with the exception of your good self, commander.'

The Remi officer remained silent as the general leaned over the table before him, unrolling the map that had been amended by Volusenus. Further detail had recently been added, charcoal marks and text scribbled across it. Pinning the rolled edges down with wax tablets, Caesar pointed to a place deep in the heart of the island, almost at the far edge of the map from the marked landing site.

The officers all took a few steps forward to peer at the map.

'This chart has been given some extra detail by our hostages. We appear to be largely surrounded by tribes that I consider untrustworthy and that historically have links with the Veneti and other Gallic troublemakers. There are one or two tribes in the island that have long been supporters of Rome, at least since the subjugation of the Belgae.'

Fronto noticed Galronus' hands clench irritably at that last phrase and felt sympathy for his friend. Now was not the time for confrontation, however, and Galronus clearly recognised it.

'With respect, Caesar, I have become very familiar with your language, but I am still a relative novice with your written words.'

Caesar nodded and tapped his finger on the word 'ATREBATE'.

'These are the Atrebates. They are a Belgic tribe within the heart of Britannia, closely tied with their namesake around Nemetocenna. They are one of the very few peoples on this island in whom I have any confidence of support and this is the supposed site of their main oppidum, called Calleva. They will supply us with the cavalry that we are lacking, I am certain.'

'That's a hundred miles away, Caesar' Brutus said quietly.

'Yes. A long way, and through potentially dangerous lands. No Roman would make it there, I'm sure. Perhaps one of the Belgae, though...'

Galronus nodded slowly.

'It is possible, Caesar. We would have to travel fast and light.'

'Agreed. How long do you think it would take?'

Galronus tapped his lip, glancing across the map. 'Four days each way. Plus allow a day for errors. We are entirely unfamiliar with this land and could easily find ourselves off course.'

'And that is catering for the safety and wellbeing of your horses?'

'Yes, general. Four days and the horses will be comfortable.'

'Then push them a little. Make it three days each way. And I will allow the Atrebates two days to assemble their forces for me. That is a week in total. Can you do that?'

'The horses will be strained, but it is possible, Caesar.'

'Do it. As soon as we adjourn here, I want you to take most of your turma of cavalry and bring me the Atrebates. Leave us only half a dozen horsemen for scouting duties.'

Galronus saluted and stepped back. Fronto could see the strain in his friend's face as the Remi officer had bitten off his argument over the safety of the horses.

'Alright, gentlemen. Let us get down to the detailed planning.'

* * * * *

Fronto started awake at the call for the dawn watch, his uncomfortable cot almost folding up beneath him as he rolled across to sit on the edge and rub his knee, blinking bleary eyes. Four days had passed since Galronus had taken his riders and disappeared to the west to track down the Atrebates. In that time he'd spent most of his free time alone. Carbo and Atenos were almost constantly busy with their duties and, despite recent revelations and attitude changes, he still felt uncomfortable with the idea of inviting Furius and Fabius to socialise with him. Besides, they would likely be as busy as his own centurions. And Brutus was the almost continual companion of the general.

The next morning he'd geared up to visit Caesar and discuss the matter of the tribunes with him, but had come to the conclusion that he really did not feel well enough disposed toward the general at the moment to visit his on personal terms.

And so he'd busied himself with the daily routine of a legate, such as it was in a time of tense uncertainty. The Seventh had been given the task of foraging for food in the area and were not making a bad job of it, while the Tenth had been tasked with the cutting and retrieval of timber and the construction of extra defences and a few timber buildings.

The drumming of heavy rain on the leather roof of the tent soured his mood as it had done each of the past three mornings.

The weather had gradually worsened since the rains began. There had been but a few hours of dry here and there; not even long enough for the ground to dry out. The sun had hardly shown its face at all and when it had, it had been a pale white watery thing behind a veil of grey.

Yesterday, though, had seen a turn for the worse. A storm had hit in the late afternoon and had continued to ravage the coast into the night as Fronto had wrapped up tight in his wool blankets and eventually fallen into an uncomfortable sleep, dreaming of warm afternoons in the lush vineyards near the family's estate at Puteoli.

This morning sounded little different from last night's unpleasantness, apart from the notable absence of the thunder.

While the half dozen timber and wattle structures that had been hastily constructed had been put aside for the food, wool and linen supplies, and for the armoury, Fronto was starting to consider moving his cot in there and sleeping among the grain or the armour.

Yawning, he stood and stretched, crossing to the tent flap, his bare feet cold on the rush mat that served as a floor and kept away the worst of the moisture. It was only as he neared the doorway, fastened with ties, that he became aware of another noise behind the constant hammering of the rain.

Shouting.

Panicked shouting.

Fronto felt his pulse quicken. Battle? Had the Britons come again? No. It could not be that. He'd heard the multitude of horns blowing the first watch, but no call to arms or any such message. So what was going on?

Quickly, he undid three of the door ties and ducked out into the pale, unpleasant dawn. The sun was barely up and the morning still had a faint purple look to it. Men were rushing around the camp, their centurions bellowing, the optios hurrying the men along with an occasional wallop of their stick. The sheets of diagonal rain were so heavy and fast that it was difficult to see more than half a dozen tents away through the camp.

Aware that he was already getting drenched with only his top half poking out of the tent, Fronto spotted the transverse crest of a centurion and shouted at him, waving an arm. The man, commander of one of the centuries in the fifth cohort if Fronto remembered correctly, hurried over as soon as he heard the yelling above the insistent rain.

'What's happening?'

'It's the ships, sir.'

'What about them?'

'They're sinking, sir.'

'Piss!'

The centurion paused for only a moment after Fronto disappeared inside again, dropping the tent flap, and then turned and ran on, back to his business. Inside, Fronto hurriedly pulled on his socks – doubling them over and wishing they were not still cold and soggy from the previous day – and slipped on his soft leather boots, noting with irritation the discolouration where the expensive leather had been ruined by the water. No matter how many times he'd intended to speak to Cita about new boots, for some reason he'd never got round to it. Damn Lucilia and her need to rearrange him! His old boots would have kept him nice and dry.

Deciding against armour, he quickly threw his baldric over his shoulder, letting the gladius fall into place at his side, and grabbed his cloak, wincing at the chilly dampness of the wet wool. Choosing not to enfold himself too tightly in the unpleasant garment, he held it over his head to shield the worst of the downpour and, taking a deep breath, ducked through the entrance again and out into the pelting rain.

Now, parties of men had been organised, running down toward the beach and the landing site with tools or carrying armfuls of pre-planed timber. Having crossed the water with only the lightest of supplies, there were far fewer tools and nails among the legions than would normally be the case.

Centurions were yelling at their men and Fronto spotted Brutus in the downpour also making for the beach.

'Trouble with the ships?'

Brutus glanced around in the rain, finally recognising the figure of Fronto cowled beneath the sodden cloak. The young legate of the Eighth shook the excess water from his hair and ran a hand down his face and neck in a futile attempt to dry them a little.

'So I hear. Come on.'

The two officers jogged down the grassy path toward the beach, out through the gate of the twin-legion fort that had been constructed, across the short no-man's land, and then in through the separate fortified enclosure that surrounded the fleet's landing site.

Such was the limited visibility in the torrents of water that it was not until they had reached the pebbled surface of the beach that the two men began to make out the shadowy bulks of the ships protruding from the seething waters. Legionaries were hard at work, waist deep in the sea, while centurions and optios bellowed orders from the beach. A contubernium of eight men held a huge leather sheet up as a shelter while others crouched beneath with tinder, kindling and the least soaked wood they could find, totally failing to start a fire over which they could melt tar for the caulking of seams.

It took Fronto only a moment to spot Furius and Fabius standing close together on the shingle. The former was bellowing at a soldier so loudly and so close that it looked as though the legionary might fall over under the blast of abuse. Fabius was frowning and scratching his head. As Fronto gestured to Brutus and strode over to them, the legionary scurried off to correct whatever he'd done.

'What's happening?'

The centurions looked up in unison and saluted the two senior officers.

'Problems with the ships.'

'Like what?'

'All sorts. A lot of those Gallic ships that hit ground first have sprung a few leaks. They must have been damaged when they hit, but we've only found out about it now because the storm's wrenched them free and they've started to fill with water.' Furius shook his head in exasperation. 'Should have seen that coming.'

Fabius pointed out to the north and Fronto could just make out a mess that looked like a ship-collision. 'Several of the triremes were also damaged in the storm. They were ripped free of their anchors and smashed into each other.'

Brutus pinched the bridge of his nose. 'Sounds like a disaster. Will we salvage everything?'

'Too soon to tell yet, sir. Maybe half the ships in total are letting in water to some extent, though some are worse than others, of course. We're working to secure the better ones first in case we have to cut our losses.'

'Bloody wonderful' Fronto raged. 'That's our ride home compromised. I'm really beginning to side with Cicero on this. The man might be defying Caesar at every turn but on this matter, I think he's right. This entire campaign was a fool's errand.'

Brutus turned to his fellow legate. 'How cramped would you say we were on the way over?'

'I wouldn't have wanted many more on our ship...' he caught Brutus' serious and worried gaze and thought hard. 'Space-wise we could probably fit half as many again, though it would be very cramped.'

Brutus nodded. 'I was picturing a similar figure. And we can bear in mind that on the return journey we won't be carrying the supplies we did on the way here. Also, and I know it sounds callous, but we lost about sixty men in the landing. That's almost half a ship's worth of passengers. So by my reckoning we could just about manage to ship the whole army back with two thirds of the vessels.'

'I suppose so' Fronto admitted unhappily, remembering the unpleasant crossing and trying to imagine how it would feel with crowded conditions added. 'Don't like it, though.'

'Would you prefer to winter in Britannia?'

'Shit, no. I'll *swim* back if I have to.'

Brutus cast a glance up and down the beach, trying to take stock of the grey bulks rising from the waves, some of which were clearly moving far too freely for comfort. Wiping the dripping water from the end of his nose, he turned to the two centurions.

'Find Marcinus. He's a centurion in your legion who served with Pompey against the pirates. I've spoken to him and he's got a remarkable grasp of naval matters. Get him to survey the ships as quickly as he can with some help and separate out those that can be saved and those that can't. Then get to work tearing apart those that are lost and use their timbers, pegs and caulking to repair the rest. It'll be ten times as fast as cutting and planing the timber to fit and manufacturing the caulk. We sacrifice the bad to save the good, like a surgeon.'

Furius and Fabius saluted and turned to go about the work as the young legate smiled at Fronto, rubbing the back of his neck and shuddering at the cold rivulets of water running down inside his tunic.

'That ought to save enough to carry the army at a push.'

Fronto nodded unhappily, unable to shake the image of two hundred men pressed almost back to back in a small vessel among the buffeting waves – horrible.

This campaign was rapidly turning into Fronto's least favourite military action of all time. He was willing to face any human or even animal enemy in the world, but when their enemy appeared to be a combination of the elements, the gods and their own leaders' bad decisions, what army stood a chance?

'Let me know what happens. I will be in my tent.' Glancing back at the roiling, heaving waves and the broken ribs of some of the ships he shuddered.

'And drunk' he added.

* * * * *

Rufus peered out from the timber-floored walkway above the gate in the new defences that surrounded Gesoriacum. The legion had done itself proud, digging a good ditch and raising a mound and palisade, clearing the woodland for almost half a mile around the settlement to provide the necessary timber. Despite the unpleasant conditions, visibility was reasonable now. No enemy could easily get near the defences without plenty of warning.

Not for the first time in the past few days he wished word would arrive from the other legions out there under the command of Sabinus and Cotta. It was almost as if that unpleasant ground mist that had resulted from the inclement weather had swallowed whole anything that left Gesoriacum. Not only had there been no word from the other legions, but the cohort he'd sent off to track down the missing supply train had now been gone long enough to be worrying. At a forced march, which was what they were intending, they should have reached Nemetocenna and returned by now with news.

So no sister legions. No news of the supplies and now no news from a vanished cohort. Add to that the mysterious disappearance of the cavalry's fleet and it was starting to feel very nerve-wracking indeed. Moreover, two days ago, Varus had ridden east with half of his cavalry wing in an attempt to locate and bring back the missing legions.

It had reached a point where Rufus was baulking at the thought of even sending out short patrols in case they disappeared into the mist and never returned.

The optio commanding the gate's guard gave him a nervous look and he had not the heart to admonish the man for showing his worry in front of the men. Every man in Gesoriacum felt the same, and Rufus was very aware of the fact. A wary, nervous silence covered the entire town, including the civilian settlement, as though they knew something was coming. Rarely was a local face even to be seen in the streets now.

'Carry on. Send word the instant there's any news' he commanded, somewhat redundantly – there was little doubt that word would come at a run if anything changed. The men patrolling the walls were a little too thinly-spread around the civilian town's defences for Rufus' liking, but it could not be helped. He had committed as many men to that line as he was willing to spare. The harbour was slightly better defended, with men in tall timber watchtowers with signal fires to warn of any seaborne trouble. But most of the troops, including a large number of dismounted cavalry, were concentrated in the fort on the hill above Gesoriacum.

Nodding to the legionaries by the gate, he strode down the slope of the embankment on the wooden log steps, alighting on the muddy thoroughfare that had somehow – perhaps mistakenly – been termed a street rather than merely a muddy stream. Sighing and wishing that the locals had adopted a good flagged-or-cobbled road surface, he sloshed and squelched back toward the main 'road' that led through the town from the harbour up to the fort on the hill.

His boots began to leak almost instantly, and he felt the cold, wet muck oozing into the holes in the leather, gritting his teeth against the unpleasantness. What he wouldn't give for a bath house, rather than a horse trough of cold water and a wool blanket.

Miserably, he trudged back into the centre of the town, pausing at the junction and wondering whether he should visit the harbour before returning to the fort. He glanced to his left, up the slope, trying not to notice the slurry slipping down the incline with the water that still seemed to be flowing from last night's torrential downpour. He shuddered, but welcomed the sight of the burning torches on the timber walls of the fort – mere spots of light at this distance; fireflies in the mist. For all its discomfort, the fort was essentially home at the moment. His gaze then turned the other way, down the main street, also filled with running brown and lumpy water. Behind and above the squat stone and timber shops and houses of the natives he could just make out the tops of the harbour watchtowers, their torches also burning in the grey.

No. The harbour could wait until tomorrow. Now it was time to get indoors and warm up if such a thing were remotely possible.

His gaze swept around again to face up the slope to his destination, but lingered for a moment on the side street that ran down into the backwaters of the native settlement directly opposite. Three figures had rounded a corner at the far end and were making their way toward the junction. The very presence of human life in the street was now a rare enough occurrence as to attract attention, but there was something about the figures that somehow caught his gaze and held it.

Squinting into the dismal grey, he could just discern that the three were wearing heavy wool cloaks and it took only a moment before he realised they were *military* cloaks. The three men were soldiers.

Blinking, he strained to see better and was suddenly rewarded with a flash of white. The man in the middle was a tribune. Cilo, then: still trying to squeeze supplies out of an uncooperative and reticent town. His results had been poor, though Rufus was under no illusions that anyone else would have fared any better. For some reason the townsfolk were less willing to help than he'd even expected.

He tutted to himself at the man's short-sightedness. He'd told Cilo to just take a small bodyguard, but he'd really meant more than two men. A contubernium of eight would have been more sensible. He would have to have a word with the man.

His heart skipped a beat.

While the three men moved hurriedly up the street toward the junction, another cloaked soldier had just rounded the corner from whence they had just come.

'What the hell?'

His heart began to hammer out an urgent tattoo in his chest as he watched the newly-visible legionary stumble out across the street, a sword glinting in his hand, before falling face first into the murk, shaking with agony. Rufus' heart sank as his gaze refocused on the three men approaching and he realised for the first time that the two legionaries were not just escorting the tribune up the street – they were carrying him, dragging him by the shoulders, his toes bouncing off jutting stones among the muck. One of the soldiers was also limping badly, and the other had a naked blade in his hand.

'Oh, shit!'

As if to confirm his worst fears, a sudden roar split the silent miasma as a huge crowd of natives rounded that same corner at a run, brandishing weapons and bellowing war cries.

Rufus felt the first wave of panic wrenching at his mind as he turned to check the other streets. Though he could see no further sign of an uprising, a distant roar echoed up the main street just as two beacons sprang to life atop the harbour watch towers. Cold fear gripping him, Rufus spun again at the sound of a scream and then the clash of steel at the east gate that he had just left.

Cursing under his breath, he turned back to the three men rushing toward him and beckoned desperately.

Damn it! He'd known something was wrong and he'd taken every precaution he could think of to protect Gesoriacum. No officer would have done it better, and few would have managed what he had, given his resources. But he'd been wrong-footed in the worst possible way. He'd given Gesoriacum adequate protection against anything except its own citizens.

A local uprising had not even occurred to him.

The Morini had risen.

As the three soldiers reached him, the legionaries turned the corner, dragging the limp figure of Cilo. Rufus' heart jumped again as he realised how close the mob was. The four of them would quite clearly never make it back to the fort in time like this.

Falling in next to them, he glanced at the tribune. Now that he was closer he could see the extent of the officer's wound between the flapping folds of cloak. The man's white tunic was soaked crimson with his blood, centred around a wide slash that had cut the man's gut almost from side to side. Even as he moved, Rufus saw a hint of purple intestine through the blood-soaked tunic.

Reaching across, he put two of his fingers to Cilo's neck just beneath the jaw line. The pulse was hardly there at all.

'Leave him!'

'Sir?' One of the legionaries stared at him in disbelief.

'He's a dead man; as *we'll* be if we don't leave him.'

'He's alive, sir.'

Rufus reached across and jerked Cilo's arm from the legionary's shoulder. The dying tribune slumped between them.

'He'll be dead before we reach the gate. Leave him; that's an order!'

The other legionary released his grip on the tribune's right arm and the officer collapsed to the floor, too far gone to even groan at the agony. The body slapped into the mud and shit, one leg shaking involuntarily.

'Come on!' Rufus bellowed, already breaking into a run. Next to him, the two legionaries sprang to life, racing after him. A count of five heartbeats later, half the population of Gesoriacum rounded the corner, yelling and waving swords, spears, axes and even tree branches.

'We're in the shit, sir!'

'Not if we can reach the fort. We can last a siege for at least a month there.'

Up the slope they pounded, trying not to lose their footing in the slippery muck that flowed down the hill into the town. With a cry in familiar Latin, three legionaries suddenly dropped over a side wall from a garden to their left – some of the defenders of the town's new walls, no doubt. From their urgency and curses it was clear that they also ran from pursuing natives.

'Report!' he bellowed between laboured breaths as they came alongside the new arrivals, one of whom was clutching a wounded, bloody arm, all three held swords, their shields abandoned in the rush to clamber over the walls.

The legionary glanced at the speaker in surprise and realised that it was his senior commander. Between wheezing breaths, he shouted as they ran.

'The wall's over... overrun, sir. Dozens of 'em... they... they came from every... everywhere inside the town... The lads on the... wall and down at the port.... are screwed, sir.'

'They control... the town now.... then?'

'Yessir. And... and I think there's... more coming out... of the woods.'

'The whole... damned tribe, then!'

Rufus fell silent, saving his breath for the run, grateful for the fact that his military boots with their hobnailed soles gave him a better grip on the mucky slope than civilian wear would. It also gave them the edge over the mob that chased them up the hill who were struggling to keep their feet at speed, several going over in the mud and crap.

Ahead, the fort walls loomed ever closer and finally, in the murky grey, the shapes of individual men resolved themselves on the parapet. Finally the alarm went up inside; the poor visibility must have prevented the fort's soldiers from spotting the warning beacons at the harbour.

It was a disaster all round.

'Open the damn gate' Rufus bellowed at the top of his voice. Figures were moving around the gate now, and more and more heads and torches began to appear along the wall, backed by the bellow of numerous buccinae and cornu.

The din was growing detestable as the six men closed on the fort, the cacophony of a legion preparing itself for action mixing with the unintelligible cries and curses of the Morini mob behind them.

A loud tortured groan arose from the walls ahead of them and, despite expecting it, Rufus flinched as the scorpion released with a 'crack', sending a foot-long bolt down the slope. Despite the skills of the artillerists, the bolt whipped over the heads of the mob and disappeared down into the town harmlessly.

'Angle it down more, you idiots!' Rufus snapped as he bore down on the gate, whose left hand leaf was now swinging open.

In response a second scorpion from the other side of the gate released with a 'crack', the bolt whistling over the heads of the six soldiers with only two or three feet to spare. Rufus felt his bowels clench involuntarily at the shot as the passage of the bolt actually ruffled his hair. He was about to snap out a curse at the man responsible when a shriek of pain and the sound of falling behind them confirmed the perfect accuracy of the shot.

Rufus clamped his mouth shut and hurtled through the gate, the others close at his heel.

'Close it!' he cried, somewhat unnecessarily, given the fact that the portal had already begun to swing shut as they passed through it.

Above, an unseen centurion bellowed out the order for pilum casting and there was the distinctive noise of dozens of missiles arcing out into the air, followed by the thud and rip of the pila falling into a mass of men, then the screams of the wounded and dying.

The duty centurion stomped toward the six men as they variously bent double, clutching their knees and spitting or leaned heavily against timber and coughed painfully, heaving in breaths.

'Anyone else likely to come back, sir?'

Rufus blinked away the sweat and focused on the centurion.

'I very much doubt it. They've got the town's defences under their control, as well as the port. Watch those two points where the walls meet the fort very carefully and get a good force there. As soon as you're sure it's safe enough, get some men out there and tear down a five pace section of the new town walls. I want plenty of open ground around the fort. We don't know how many of them there are or what they want.'

He straightened. 'But they've clearly planned this for a while, and there are other Morini coming from nearby to their aid, so I think we have to assume we're here for a while. I'm hoping it's just a small rabble of local civilians that we can draw out into open battle and flatten, but I have the horrible feeling that we're looking at a sizeable uprising that we're woefully ill-equipped to deal with until one of the other legions makes contact.'

The centurion nodded professionally.

'Then we'd best settle in and hope we can get control of the situation before the general returns, sir.'

Rufus felt his heart sink again. They had lost the port and there was no way to warn Caesar. Where was Fortuna when she was really needed?

Chapter 17

(South-east Britannia)

Lucius Fabius, centurion of the third century, first cohort of the Seventh legion, gestured at a chattering legionary with his vine stick.

'I'm watching you, Statilius. Shut your trap and concentrate on your job. We need to be back in the camp by nightfall and you are without a doubt, the laziest, slowest, most pointless dullard I've ever seen don a tunic. How in Hades you manage to get it on the right way round every morning is beyond me. You must have helpful tent-mates.'

The legionary flushed and the half dozen men scything the wheat awkwardly with their swords laughed.

'And the rest of you shower of shit are little better. Shut up and work.'

Turning his back on the labouring soldiers, the centurion spotted his colleague and old friend, Tullus Furius striding through the unevenly cut stubble, staff jammed under his arm and a look of irritation on his face.

'We'll never make it back to camp before dark with this lot. We might as well make the decision now. Do we leave some of the harvest, hope it survives the night well and come back in the morning, or keep working into the dark and hope we find our way back without too much trouble?'

'I say we keep working. It's only three miles and pretty much a straight line. We can – Legionary Macrobius, if I see you put that sword down or take that helmet off, you will be emptying latrines with your remaining hand for the next month, while I use the other as a back-scratcher. You got that?'

The legionary saluted, almost concussing himself with the hilt of his gladius. Furius rolled his eyes as he turned back to his companion.

'This legion is a shambles. At least if Caesar had left it as he found it, they'd have been a proper unit, and not just a patchwork collection of misfits. Half the bloody centurions don't seem to have a clue. Did you know that Lutorius has half of his men loading the grain into the wagons without wearing their armour or helmets? The prat's even got their swords lying in a heap while they work. I swear I had to clench my fists to prevent myself beating the idiot.'

'Similar story all round. Look at the amount of tunics you can see without armour. Pompey would have had half of them strung up by now. This army's soft.'

'This *legion's* soft. Since the beach escapade I've been keeping an eye on Fronto's Tenth. They're actually pretty well organised and drilled. And Brutus' Eighth when we were back in Gaul were in top condition. It's just *this* legion, mate. I tell you, by next spring I'm going to have the top spot – be primus pilus – and I'll spend the winter kicking this shower of shit into shape.'

'With any luck we'll both be able to move up and sort this lot out. Fronto's a good enough lad, but he's still a bit lax and disorganised. It irks me that his legion should be so much better than ours.'

'Here's to that. And to the Seventh being the best in the army by next spring.'

The pair fell silent, taking in the scene around them. Existing rations had run out in the morning, after breaking their fast, and replenishing the stocks had been the first priority of the day. Early in the day, the Seventh had split into four groups of fifteen centuries apiece who had left the camp all with the same assignment: Find food. It did not matter what it was – animal, wheat, vegetables. So long as it would go in a pot or bake loaves, it was required. It had taken only two hours for the first section to come across a nicely hidden wide bowl of a valley, surrounded by woodland and filled with ripening white-gold wheat waiting for the harvest, which would be due at any time.

Lutorius, the primus pilus of the legion and the senior centurion of their party had almost rubbed his hands with glee at the sight of enough grain to keep the two legions for the best part of a month. Another hour of searching the tracks that radiated into the woods had turned up the farms that cultivated the area, which supplied them with plenty of commandeered carts along with what could have been termed 'nags' if the speaker were being kind, as well as a few mangy oxen.

Now, after four hours of cutting, binding, stacking and loading, the carts were laden with towering piles of wheat. The sun was already hovering over the tops of the trees in its ever swiftening descent to evening, and though much of the wheat had been harvested, still almost a quarter of the fields remained intact.

The two centurions' gaze both fell on Lutorius, standing among a collection of sheaves, snapping out orders. Each of the four legion vexillations had its nominal command. Cicero and one of the tribunes had taken their group north, the senior tribune Terrasidius and one of the others had taken a group south. The three remaining junior tribunes had gone northwest – and were probably hopelessly lost, given the general abilities of their kind – while Lutorius had brought his command southwest.

'Who's going to persuade 'blue eyes' to stay after dark?'

'I'll do it. You've been pissing him off all day, so he won't listen to you.'

Furius nodded and Fabius turned to make his way over to the primus pilus, just in time to see an arrow whip out from the woodland that surrounded the golden field-bowl, smashing into Lutorius' eye and driving into his brain, killing him instantly.

The air suddenly filled with the thrum of arrows as men screamed and fell all around the clearing. Even as Furius turned to address the cornicen standing close by with his horn on his arm, Fabius bellowed 'Shields! To arms!'

'Cornicen: Sound the alarm!'

The musician put the horn to his lips, but all that came out of his mouth was a gobbet of blood as a thrown spear suddenly burst through his neck. His eyes went wide and he clutched at the crimson spear head sticking a foot from his front before toppling over forward, making a bubbling noise. Furius cursed.

'Testudo! Form testudos!'

The field was alive now with desperate legionaries. Furius and Fabius' two centuries were already falling into formation, their shields coming up to form the missile-proof tortoise. The two centurions jogged across to their men, well aware that most of the centuries in the clearing were doomed, having dropped their shields and weapons and some even their armour while they worked. Men were being scythed down like the wheat they had been harvesting.

'Get to the centre! Collect your gear and get out of missile range!'

It was all he could really do, and he hoped the other soldiers' centurions would follow the lead and try to protect their commands. In the meantime, he and Fabius moved outside missile range, behind their centuries.

'Prepare yourselves for the next move!'

They did not have long to wait. Having lost, at Fabius' estimation, some two hundred men just to an initial volley, the remaining legionaries had pulled back to the centre of the clearing, out of the reach of the arrows and spears, where many were hurriedly arming themselves and jamming on helmets. Only half of them wore their mail shirts, though, and a number were missing shields. Furius and Fabius shook their heads in disbelief as their two centuries, the only two in the Seventh to be fully equipped and fighting fit, backed up to join their comrades.

'Drop testudo. Form a defensive circle!' Furius shouted. 'Everyone! Form a circle. Three lines deep, those with armour and shields on the outer line!'

Warriors were now beginning to step out of the woods, spears, axes and swords raised, some with shields or helmets, even some with mail shirts. Many of them were decorated with blue designs, and their hair was spiked long and white with dried mud. It hardly came as a surprise to note that the legion was completely surrounded, though it was with some dismay that the centurions recognised the shape and sound of both cavalry and chariots thundering down the numerous pathways and tracks into the wide bowl-shaped clearing.

They were trapped.

Having secured their prey and being wary of the shieldwall that had caused so much havoc at the beach, the native warriors advanced slowly, moving cautiously out into the open.

'Why didn't they just keep peppering us with arrows?' shouted an optio nearby. Furius ground his teeth angrily. The men were nervous enough without officers giving them extra reasons to panic.

'Because, shit-streak, they've got us where they want us now. Their 'noble' warriors want a chance to carve us up themselves. It's only noble to a Celt if they can look into your eyes when you die.'

Fabius forced a grin. 'But that's not going to happen. We're going to give these native piss stains something to think about. For Rome!' he bellowed and started to smack his gladius blade against the shield edge of the man next to him, lacking one himself.

The battle cry had the desired effect, building the courage of the trapped men rapidly, and the crash of swords on shield rims slowly rose to a deafening crescendo.

Fabius was focusing on the warriors opposite him who blocked the track that led back toward the camp where the Tenth would be busy cutting timber and constructing buildings and palisades around the new annexe for the storehouses.

'Silence!' he bellowed, as he squinted at the mass of warriors. A slow, grim smile spread across his face. In the wide, grassy, rutted track, stood one of the carts of wheat, already fully laden. Two legionaries were waving from the top of the cart, as yet unseen by the Briton army that lay between them and their fellow legionaries.

'Get to camp' Fabius bellowed. 'Go. Get help!'

For a moment, he worried that the cart was too far away for the men to hear, despite the fact that the legion had silenced immediately at his call, stilling their swords. He watched anxiously as the two figures apparently conferred. Taking the risk, Fabius waved his arms away, gesturing for them to leave.

One or two of the natives seemed to catch on to what the centurion was saying and turned, spotting the cart several hundred paces down the track and shouting to their friends. To Fabius' relief, the cart suddenly lurched and started to move, the two men on top almost falling with the sudden jerk.

With a roar, a sizeable group from the army of Celts raced after the cart and Fabius watched tensely as the vehicle built up speed slowly. They would never make it. Why didn't...

Even as the notion occurred to him, it seemed to have struck the men on the cart, who were hurling the sheaves of wheat from the vehicle to lose some weight and give it an extra turn of speed. The warriors closed on them, regardless, and the two desperate legionaries began to actually hurl the sheaves at the pursuers themselves, knocking aside the nearest of them.

Fabius' gut soured as a thrown spear caught one of the cart-riders dead centre in the chest, impaling him and throwing him from the bouncing vehicle. The scene was becoming difficult to make out now, the retreating cart and pursuers shrinking with distance, but he was fairly certain he saw the vehicle continue to bounce off down the track as the warriors came to a tired halt, pushing and shoving each other as they tried to assign the blame for letting some legionaries escape.

Fabius nodded to himself.

'That's it lads. Help will be coming soon enough. We've just got to hold them for a bit.'

Even as he said it, he wondered how many of the other officers and men of the Seventh realised that the 'bit' he was talking about would in all likelihood be an hour. It would take probably quarter of an hour for the cart to reach camp – at even a dangerous speed. It would take the same again for the Tenth to come to their aid, even at a run. And there would be at least that of getting the army ready in between, calling back the workers from the woods and so on. It was distinctly possible that this vexillation of the Seventh legion would be corpses picked over by crows by the time the Tenth came to relieve them.

But it was a chance; a hope. Moreover, it was something for the men to believe in; to cling on to.

'Every man that makes it out today will go down in my book and when we get back to Gaul, you'll all get a bonus, an extra acetum ration, and a week off duties in rotation.'

From somewhere to the right, out of sight, he heard Furius' raised voice. 'Any man who distinguishes himself in the next hour earns himself 'immune' status!'

There was a roar of approval from the men of the Seventh and Fabius grinned. A dead man's boots had just given his friend a field promotion and made him effective primus pilus and commander of the vexillation. And that made Fabius the second centurion of the legion.

'Alright men. I've just had a 'blood promotion' and I'm bollocksed if I'm going to die now and give it up straight away. Lock shields and ready yourself to kill as many of these blue-skinned goat-humpers you can. Any man who kills more of them than me gets an amphora of good wine.'

Another roar of approval from the men was almost drowned out by the matching roar of the Britons who burst into a charge.

'Come on, then. Time to die!'

* * * * *

Fronto stood on the raised parapet of the camp's wall next to the west gate, watching the men of the first to fourth cohorts gradually widening the killing ground around the camp by reducing the treeline into the distance. They were bringing back an almost constant supply of good heavy, solid timber that had had the bark and any extraneous branches or nubs removed and had often also been cut down to rough planks. Behind him, in the main camp and in the new supplies annexe, the men of the Seventh to Tenth cohorts were busy planing the new timber and trimming it to shape, carrying it around the camp and using it to continue the construction of the buildings.

While the legions did not expect to be staying here longer than another month at the most – even the general had been insistent that this punitive campaign had to be complete before the dangers of winter crossings were upon them – the construction of timber buildings had been considered not only preferable, but even necessary.

Many of the men's tents had become rickety and leaky. Normally, these would be patched and repaired, or even replaced from the supply train. Such was not possible with the ocean between them, and a good timber building would keep the inclement weather away from the men and give them the blessed opportunity to dry out and warm up overnight.

Trying not to swear, Fronto felt yet another spot of rain 'plip' onto his forehead. What was it with this island? How could the druids hold this place sacred? Were they part duck? Italia was hardly free from storms, but at least the place had the decency to give its population a break in between, and when the storms came they were often noteworthy.

But *this* place? This place was the physical incarnation of a bad mood. Not a single day since they had struck the beach had passed without at least a short shower to remind them that they were outsiders. Some days it never *stopped* raining from one dawn watch to the next. Most often it came in fits and starts, just giving the ground enough time to almost dry and deceptively clear away enough clouds to look hopeful. Then, as soon as you stepped outside, the next drizzle would begin. It was as though the Gods of Britannia were urinating on them from a great height. That was it, too: it was not *proper* rain. Not like the torrents they'd had at the Rhenus, or the thunderstorms of Gaul or Hispania. Most of the time it was just a depressing, gentle, insistent, cloak-soaking drizzle.

It was the most disheartening climate he'd ever spent time in. For the first day or two, he'd revelled in how green and fresh everything was. But that was before he became truly aware of the price for the lush greenery. What he *couldn't* understand is how it didn't all drown!

Hopefully this would just be a short shower again and he would not have to give the order to down tools and get inside. It was not that the men couldn't work in the rain, but morale was already low enough on this side of the ocean, and making the soldiers plane wood in the pouring rain would hardly give it a welcome boost.

'Work proceeds apace.'

Fronto turned in a mixture of surprise and gloom. Caesar's voice was very familiar and unwelcome; he'd managed to spend many days in a row now without exchanging a single word with the general. Ever since the man had launched into him concerning his perceived insubordination, Fronto had been harbouring a deep-felt grudge and avoiding the risk of pushing the beak-nosed old bastard's face through the back of his head.

Fronto forced a smile that barely reached his face.

'We'll have the food and cloth stores complete by the end of the day, if we work through twilight. If it's straight down to the Tenth, two more days will see good timber accommodation for everyone. If the Seventh are done with their forays and can join in tomorrow, we should all be under a solid roof by tomorrow night.'

'Good.'

The two men fell silent and Fronto still resisted glancing at his commander. He could feel him though; feel the eyes boring into the side of his head; hear the click of the general's knuckles as his hands rubbed and gripped one another behind his back. He'd been with Caesar long enough now to know every sign and every mood. The general was uncomfortable. Good. So he should be.

'Marcus?'

'Yes, sir.'

'Let us not stay on such terms. I am aware you've been avoiding me. I may have gone beyond the pale in dressing you down the way I did in front of your peers.'

Fronto's jawline hardened. 'You think I care about it being in front of the others? You know me better than that, Caesar. You shouldn't have done it *at all*. I was fractionally late for a non-time sensitive meeting.'

'I know, and...'

'And,' Fronto snapped, rounding on him with flashing eyes, 'you should bear in mind that for four years in Gaul and before that in Spain and Rome I have supported you when others you relied on turned against you. You know damn well that the only times I have ever stood in opposition to you is when you were wrong, plain and simple. I know the world thinks you're infallible, but you and I know that *no man* is infallible. You were in a bad mood, plain and simple, and you took it out on me, because you knew I'd take it, when it might break others.'

Caesar sighed and smiled weakly.

'I'd had another episode.'

'What?'

'You know exactly what I'm talking about, Marcus. I thought I was done with it. I'd not had trouble since Saturnalia, when I'd given a huge offering to Venus to try and stop it for good. All year I'd been clear and happy. And now: twice since we crossed the sea. Twice! The first time, I failed to clamp on the leather in time and took a piece out of the corner of my tongue.'

Fronto's brow lowered and his nostrils flared.

'You have my sympathy, Caesar, but only children take it out on other people when they're sick. And as you've pointed out before, you're hardly a child. Neither of us is.'

'Can we not draw a line beneath this, Marcus? I've admitted I was in error. I offered not an excuse, but an explanation. I need my good officers around me.'

The legate took a deep breath and fought back every curse and argument that rose to mind, of which there were many. 'I would like to think so, but I'm starting to become concerned with your judgement, Caesar.'

'How so?'

'Clodius?' Fronto raised an eyebrow in challenge, turning to face the woods again.

'Clodius is just a tool.'

'He certainly is. A great big, throbbing one. But I cannot condone you using him for any reason. Were I you, that man would be caught in the eddies and reeds at the side of the Tiber, fat faced and blue. Feeding the fishes, which would be about the most useful and positive thing he's ever done.'

'Clodius' usefulness will come to an end soon, and I'm convinced that so will he soon after. Can you not be satisfied with that?'

'Not really, no. And your re-formation of the Seventh using only people you don't trust has shattered what was a veteran legion with pride and ability and turned it into a mess. If they can pull their pride out of the gutter – which will be partially served by shifting Cicero the hell out of there – then they could train back up into a good legion, given time. But it was a waste.'

'I had to be sure of where my opposition were.'

'They're everywhere. And the more you use thugs and villains to further your political goals, the more enemies you'll create.'

He frowned. 'What was that *look* about?'

'I beg your pardon, Fronto?'

'That look. I *know* that look. That's the guilty recollection of something I won't like and that you're not telling me. In my book of 'Caesar's facial tells' that's in my top ten warning signs. What is it?'

'You read too much into nothing, Marcus.' Caesar gave him an easy smile. You said, that day at the meeting, that your delay was unavoidable. I never asked why, and you don't usually bother with an excuse, so it must have been important.'

'It was, but I'm not sure whether discussing it here or now is a good idea.' Fronto narrowed his eyes at the attempt to deflect the subject.

'If it's important, Fronto, then it's important. Tell me.'

'The murders.'

'Yes?'

'All of them. Pinarius, Tetricus, Pleuratus, and an attempt on me. I have reasonable suspicions as to the culprits now.'

Caesar rolled his shoulders, his cloak falling back down behind him. Several more spots of rain fell.

'I believe that your suspicions were centred on two centurions from the Seventh?'

'You're apparently well informed, Caesar. And yes, for a time, I was sure Furius and Fabius were behind them. But I am now more or less convinced that they're innocent of the attacks.'

'Really?' The general tapped his lip, an upward curl of humour twisting one side of his mouth in a manner that really annoyed Fronto.

'Yes. I haven't the proof yet, but I suspect the tribunes Menenius and Hortius of the Fourteenth.'

Caesar burst into a short, explosive laugh. 'I think you must have been eating the strange fungi from the forest. Neither of those men could effectively swat a fly.'

'Nevertheless, it was them. I'm fairly sure.'

'And their motive?'

'Removing your supporters: your courier, your nephew, me and Tetricus – two of your more loyal officers. And Tetricus threatened the pair of them once in a briefing, so there's an additional motive.'

'Menenius is a client of mine, who owes me a great deal. He is hardly likely to be troubling me. He would be 'biting the hand that feeds him' so to speak. And Hortius? Hortius is in a similar situation. He's expecting a position as an aedile next year, which he can only get with my support. No, Marcus; the two would have too much to lose by kicking my legs out from under me. You should look elsewhere for your pro-Pompeian traitors.'

The legate continued to stare ahead, though his eyes flicked to Caesar again and he just caught another flash of that look. There was definitely something going on here that Caesar knew about and was keeping to himself.

'What on earth is that commotion?'

Fronto glanced across at Caesar's exclamation and then followed his gaze to see that a number of the men of the Tenth had downed tools and were running toward a cart that was hurtling out from the woodland path to the west.

'Looks like a grain cart. One of Cicero's I wonder?' the general mused.

'Looks like trouble, more like.'

Without waiting for further information, Fronto turned around and spotted the nearest centurion.

'Have your cornicen call the duty cohorts to order. Get 'em lined up before the ramparts. We're about to need them.'

As the centurion ran off, shouting for his musician and standard bearer, Fronto turned back to the approaching cart. It was now bouncing across the short, well-trodden grass beyond the multitude of stumps, only a hundred paces from the camp. Already a number of Caesar's praetorian cavalry officers had fallen in behind him from where they had been lurking at a respectful distance.

The general stepped down the slope, with Fronto at his shoulder and passed through the gate toward the cart, which slewed to a halt some thirty feet from the rampart. Two men slid down from it. The driver looked harried and panicked, while the man who had been clinging to the top of the load was clutching a wound in his side and staggered as his feet hit the ground.

'It would appear that you were correct, Fronto. Trouble it is.'

'Sir!' The legionary driver, wearing just his tunic, unarmed and unarmoured apart from the gladius at his waist, came to a sudden halt and saluted, his wounded mate attempting the same a few paces back, but failing as he slumped to the ground.

'Report, man.'

'Natives, sir. Thousands of 'em. They came out of the trees...'

'Where?' Fronto said, holding his gaze.

'About three miles west. It's on main paths. I can take you.'

'Are the men still... it wasn't a massacre?'

'No sir. When we left they was in a circle, holdin' 'em back. But they won't last long, sir. They're outnumbered.'

Fronto glanced across at Caesar, who nodded.

'Then get ready for a run. You can take me and two cohorts back there, fast as we can.'

The man saluted wearily and the legate turned to his general.

'Can you-?' Fronto began, but Caesar was already shooing him. 'Go, Marcus. I'll bring the other cohorts as soon as we can get them armed up.' He turned to one of his cavalrymen. 'Have this wounded soldier taken to a medic, and put out the call for the first, the second and the Seventh to Tenth cohorts to down tools, retrieve their kit and form up. The third and fourth can remain to garrison the camp under Brutus and Volusenus.'

Turning, the general was about to offer a word of encouragement to Fronto, but the Tenth's legate was already moving across the grass bellowing commands to the assembling men, pausing only to collect an unattended shield from the ground where its owner had left it and would rue his action later when his centurion found him unequipped.

The general watched him go and shook his head. While an ambush of the foraging troops was never a good thing, at least it had finally brought the opposition out into the open and provided a timely interruption from Fronto's probing and uncomfortable questions.

* * * * *

Fronto blinked away tears of pain and willed the gap in the trees that opened out into the clearing and signalled the end of their journey nearer. He was, he knew, still fitter than most men his age, and many of the soldiers – carrying much the same load and a great deal younger – were struggling at least as much as he. The rushing of the blood pounding in his ears and the hot rasp of the heaving breaths racing in and out of his lungs were not the main issue though, for all their discomfort. Three times in three miles he had been forced to drop out of the run and rub his knee, turning his leg and re-tying the supportive wrap he'd used on the advice of Florus the capsarius. Each time he'd had to put in that much extra effort to regain his place in the force that charged to the relief of the Seventh.

He tried to guess how many wounds he'd taken in one form or another throughout his life of service, but could only take a stab at two-to-three dozen. And of everything that had happened, it seemed only fitting of Fortuna's strange sense of humour that the one thing that could trouble him in battle was the result of an unfortunate and purely random twisted knee. Florus had told him that if he rested it properly for a few weeks it would strengthen, which had simply led to an argument in semantics over the meaning of the word 'rest'.

The sounds of desperate fighting issuing from the clearing were welcome, for all the horror they indicated. At least they stated clearly that the Seventh were still there and had not been wiped out.

Panting with the effort, the legate pushed out to the front, putting on an extra turn of speed, the energy for which he seemed to pull in out of the very desperation in the air. A moment later, he was running alongside Carbo, who had proved time and again that his strength and fitness really did belie his less than svelte shape. The centurion was more pink faced than usual, but ran with a steady, enduring gait, the breaths coming out measured and rhythmically.

The forest path was clearly used by local farmers with their carts and oxen, wide enough to admit a wagon with plenty of room to spare on either side. It was enough to permit a column of legionaries eight men wide without the danger of entanglements, and the two cohorts of the Tenth ran in perfect formation, in the manner drilled into them over the years by first Priscus and then Carbo.

Ahead, the path opened into the huge clearing and though Fronto could see little for certain, he had the impression of wide, golden fields of grain trampled by screaming men. His view was somewhat impeded by the chariots and the cavalry. It appeared – at least from this angle – as though the Britons had blocked the exits from the clearing with their cavalry and empty chariots while the bulk of their force, on foot, including the chiefs and nobles from the vehicles, had charged the Roman circle, trying to batter them into submission.

'Chariots' Fronto barked out between heaving breaths.

'We'll take them down first' Carbo acknowledged, apparently – and irritatingly – not even short of breath.

'And... cavalry.'

'We'll try, but they'll be too fast and manoeuvrable for us, I fear. So long as we can cut a path through to the main force we'll be fine.'

'Surprise?'

'Unlikely. Even over the noise, these hairies at the back will hear us coming. The Tenth are a fearsome force, but we're hardly subtle.'

Fronto smiled at the wide grin on the centurion's ruddy face. He knew for a fact that Carbo actively encouraged the making of noise and the use of war cries in the Tenth to put the fear of Hades into whoever they faced. As often as not it worked.

'I just wish we had time to deploy and surround them. We could wipe them out' Carbo sighed.

'Carbo... there are several... thousand of them. There's less... than a thousand of us! *Surround* them?'

'You know what I mean, sir. I hate to think of them escaping again.'

Another couple of spots of rain pattered off the rim of Fronto's helmet, reminding him that yet another rainstorm was imminent, the clouds darkening by the moment. Reaching up, he fondled the bow-legged fishwife amulet at his neck and hoped it was not insulting to Fortuna, praying that the full extent of the rain held off for another hour or so. A battle in the pouring rain was high up on Fronto's list of hateful things. Letting go of the figurine, he dropped his hand to his side and drew his gladius, steadying his grip on the heavy shield he'd borrowed.

A strange, guttural cry went up ahead and the few Briton horsemen they could see at the clearing's entrance wheeled their mounts. The cohorts had been seen and suddenly all hell broke loose among the enemy.

'Ready, lads!' Carbo bellowed. 'First five centuries punch straight through and make for the back of the infantry. Next four split off to either side and take care of the cavalry and chariots. Centurions mark your position and prepare your signals.'

Back along the running column, the officers identified their century's number and prepared to either push forward or file off to the side. Beyond the first nine, the other centurions would appraise the situation as they reached the clearing and deploy as required.

The horsemen were now wheeling away from them again, riding off into the clearing, bellowing warnings. Clearly Carbo was right: the cavalry could easily remain out of reach unless they chose to commit – an unlikely option. The chariots were even now turning to move away from the arriving legionaries, trundling along the forest's edge, their athletic drivers leaping about on the traces and yoke and manoeuvring the horses.

Fronto had heard enough Celtic shouting in the past four years to begin to separate the meanings by tone alone. The shouts now going up all across the clearing were not the ordered calls of warning or redeployment, but the panicked calls of men wrong-footed and in fear of their lives. Clearly they had not expected reinforcements. The legate grinned – fear was almost as powerful a weapon as the gladius.

'Give 'em a shout, Carbo.'

The centurion nodded. 'For Rome!' he bellowed. Behind him, the cry was echoed at the top of almost a thousand voices, protracted so that it was still ringing out when he shouted 'For Caesar!' beginning a second cry that was instantly taken up. By the time of the third cry – a standard call for the legion – the men were pre-empting him. 'For the Tenth!'

The shouts, as intended, devolved quickly to a general din and tumult of bellowing, shouting legionaries, the noise of which was enough to almost drown out the sounds of fighting in the clearing.

One of the chariots had been unlucky enough that, as it turned, a wheel had caught on something among the stubble, and the vehicle had almost overturned. The driver was manoeuvring desperately, trying to free the wheel, when he and his chariot were completely engulfed in a river of crimson and steel.

Despite being in prime position at the front of the cohort, Fronto forewent the opportunity to negotiate the vehicle and attack the driver, recognising the very real chance that his knee would give and he would plunge embarrassingly to the ground beneath the chariot. Instead, he contented himself with a quick glance at the Briton's unpleasant demise as one of the legionaries swarming round the vehicle lifted his shield and drove the bronze edging into the man's chest without even stopping. As the soldier ran on, heedless, the chariot driver disappeared with a squeal below the running feet of the cohort, where he failed even to bring a weapon to bear before he was trampled to death by hundreds of hobnailed boots, smashing his face and chest and snapping his limbs.

Fronto afforded himself a quick glance around as the century raced on toward the mass of the enemy pressing on the defensive circle of Roman steel. In the manner so reminiscent of Celts everywhere their army was fighting as a thousand individuals rather than a homogenous whole. Gods help the world if these bloodthirsty lunatics ever managed to achieve discipline under a capable tactician. It would be like the sack of Rome by Brennus all over again.

Fortunately, these Britons were no tacticians.

The cavalry were already fleeing the scene, racing away down other paths into the forest. The chariots rushed away around the edge, keeping out of the reach of the pursuing cohorts while remaining close enough to be available for their masters when required.

Even the infantry, where they were involved in deep and desperate combat with the men of the Seventh, were now starting to break away at the rear and race for the safety of the trees.

The disposition of spent bodies told the story eloquently enough for Fronto. Hardly anywhere around the enormous clearing's periphery could a native figure be seen, while in places the glassy-eyed corpses of legionaries lay so close as to be touching. The Britons had come out of the forest with a hail of spears and arrows, routing the Romans and driving them back to the centre of the clearing where they were trapped and formed a circle that had been steadily diminishing for almost an hour.

'They're getting away' a legionary shouted angrily, watching a sizeable chunk of the native force peel away and race for the woodland.

'Forget them!' Carbo cried. 'Concentrate on saving the Seventh!'

With the exception of the four centuries securing the clearing's edge and driving the chariots before them, the entire force of the two cohorts bore down on the main army at the centre, paying no heed to the fleeing Britons, intent on breaking the throng pinning the Seventh down.

The paces passed in a blur of discomfort, the sharp stubble of the field scratching Fronto's shins and calves as he ran, keeping pace with the men of the first century, hoping he did not fall or collapse with shortness of breath.

And suddenly the old familiar battle calm fell over him. Despite the lack of a disciplined Roman shield wall – the Tenth discarding conventional tactics in favour of speed and terror-inducing fury – it was familiar and simple. As always the worries of the world – of the rightness of their campaign, of the intrigues within the army and the nobles, of his own ageing and deteriorating stamina, even of Lucilia back in that nest of vipers that was Rome – they all went away, pushed down and sealed into a casket as the immediacy of battle took over.

A warrior who had turned to flee with a couple of his friends found himself staring into the advancing visage of an ageing Roman demon with fiery eyes. Desperately he raised his axe, haft sideways. Fronto feinted with his gladius, causing the man to sweep the axe handle to the side to stop a blow that would never come. As he was overbalanced and leaning to his left, Fronto slammed into him with the large, curved shield, smashing his arm and several ribs and driving the startled barbarian back into the press of his compatriots.

Beside Fronto, a legionary helpfully put half a foot of sword into the falling Briton's armpit before moving on to another of the fleeing men. Fronto had lost sight of Carbo, but could hear his reassuring voice denouncing the man he faced as a cross-breed of a number of unlikely animals.

The native force was now breaking up all across the rapidly widening front of legionaries, groups of men some twenty or thirty strong taking to their heels and racing for the treeline. A man who had likely arrived on a chariot suddenly pushed his way through the throng, spotting Fronto and recognising the crest and cuirass as indicative of a commander. He bellowed something that sounded as though it was probably a challenge. The warrior wore a mail shirt that looked as though it might have been of Gallic manufacture, a decorative helmet with a stylised rearing boar on the crown, a shield, oval in shape, and a sword that was probably the pride of a whole family.

The only good thing that could be said about his personal appearance, however, was that his straggly and bulky moustache at least hid half his grotesque pig-like features, though the hare-lip even marred *that*.

Fronto grinned at him.

'Come on then, pretty boy.'

The man swung the sword with surprising speed, though little cunning, over his shoulder and down. Fronto neatly sidestepped, almost falling into the press of men in the attempt. The warrior made a strange surprised sound as his heavy long sword cleaved only empty air and dug deep into the body of an already fallen warrior below. Fronto shook his head in mock dismay as he stepped forward and jabbed the man in the throat with his gladius.

Too easy; just too easy.

A spray of crimson erupted from the shocked noble's neck, spraying Fronto in the face and forcing him to look away for a moment. The warrior released his grip on the jammed sword and clutched at his throat, temporarily stemming the spray so that the blood merely ran in torrents between his fingers.

'Sweet Venus you are an ugly bugger aren't you?' Fronto grinned as he knocked the dying noble aside with his shield.

'That you, legate Fronto?'

Looking up in surprise, Fronto could just see Fabius over the heads of half a dozen natives, his helmet gone and blood streaming down his head, giving him the look of a red-painted man.

'Got yourself in a bit of trouble, I see!'

'Nothing we can't handle, of course, but thanks for the timely assistance.'

Fronto laughed.

'Looks like they've broken.'

Indeed, even as Fronto cut another man down, the press between the two speakers was thinning out. The attacking force at the far side of the circle had taken the opportunity to flee the field before the Roman cohorts could get to them, freeing up much of the Seventh to reform and start pushing back. Already, the number of barbarians still committed in the clearing had fallen from perhaps three thousand to four or five hundred, those now being trapped between the men of the two legions. No longer even attempting to fight, the Britons were pushing bodily through the attacking Romans, heedless of wounds, in an attempt to escape the field and melt into the woodland.

'They're running' a legionary bellowed. 'Come on!'

'Leave them!' Fronto shouted at him, simultaneous with Carbo's cry of 'Let them go!'

The field was theirs.

The remaining five hundred or so men of the Seventh were safe, and the Roman force lacked the manpower and horses to chase down the fleeing Britons. Besides, no sensible commander would ever commit to pursuing them in unfamiliar territory that the Britons would know as well as their own hand.

'Come on' Fronto sighed, leaning down to rub his knee as he watched a few of the fleeing men fall to careful parting strikes. 'Let's get this grain back to the camp and settle in. It's about to piss down.'

ROME

Quintus Lucilius Balbus strode across the Via Nova and began to ascend the slope toward the Palatine and the ancient piers of the ruined Porta Mugonia, a look of cold, calm and collected determination written into his features. In defiance of Rome's most ancient laws and his own personal codes, the polished, decorative-hilted gladius that had graced his uniform for years as legate of the Eighth Legion was gripped so tightly in his right hand that his knuckles were white and the veins stood out purple like a map of unknown rivers.

An elderly man with a broad stripe on his expensive and high quality toga paused in the street off to one side; his brow furrowed, his nostrils flaring and eyes flashing with righteous indignation as he realised that the similarly togate muscular man was wielding a naked military blade in the hallowed ancient city centre.

'How dare you!'

Balbus barely acknowledge the man, turning his head slightly and delivering a withering glare of pure malice that had the elderly man stepping back down the street nervously.

Three men hurried along behind the former officer, each of them wearing their own toga, and each bearing a well-kept military blade. Two nephews and a cousin of Balbus' who resided in the city and owed him a favour had brushed aside any need for persuasion to the task once Balbus had explained what he was about.

After all, Clodius had the reputation of a poisonous snake among all good citizens of breeding, and Gaius Lucilius Brocchus, former tribune in the Eighth, had already encountered the man's venom in business circles. To discover that they also held a noble Roman lady of a good house against her will and had kidnapped their dear Lucilia – despite her daring escape – was too much for the three young men to countenance and they had been reaching for their blades before Balbus had even tried to persuade them to join him.

The crowd that invariably filled the Via Nova surged back in to occupy the street in the wake of the small armed party for whom they had made way. Armed gangs were far from unusual in the city these days, but they were almost always base thugs with concealed knives or cudgels. To see four noblemen in fine togas with naked military blades was a new and worrying sight in broad daylight in the urban centre.

The privately-hired guards who stood outside the street-front entrances to a few of the more exclusive houses in the area took a quick look at the group and studiously averted their gaze. Such was not their concern unless the four men should descend on their door.

The crowd thinned out as they climbed the narrower street to the hill where the houses of many of the wealthier families stood. Not here the hawkers of products of dubious meat, the beggars and pickpockets, the stallholders or lurkers. The presence of so many private forces of guards kept the streets here clear of the lower rungs of society. Indeed, by the time Balbus reached the small square with the benches and the apple tree, the only life to be seen was a small family group hurrying to some event in their best clothes. They and an incongruous single young man in a dusty tunic collecting the fallen as-yet-unripe apples and bagging them in large sacks.

Paying no heed to anyone, Balbus led his three companions to the right and along the narrow side street, the four men lowering their blades but not sheathing them as they came to a halt in front of the residence of Atia – niece of Julius Caesar.

Reaching up, Balbus rapped three times on the studded wooden door and then clattered the bell to the side for good measure. There was only the briefest of pauses before a small hatch opened in the door at eye height, protected by an iron grille.

'Yes?'

'Be so good as to ask the lady of the house to attend.'

The slave frowned, taken aback by this breach of etiquette. 'I will most certainly do nothing of the sort, sir. If you state your name and business, I will consult my mistress.'

Balbus leaned sharply forward so that his eye was suddenly only a few finger-widths from that of the slave, separated by a thin iron strip. The man instinctively ducked back nervously.

'I am Quintus Lucilius Balbus. Former legatus of the Eighth Legion. I have brought the fortresses of countless Celtic tribes down to rubble and enslaved their people. If you think for one moment I will be inconvenienced by a simple door, you are sadly mistaken. Open this door and fetch lady Atia.'

The hatch slammed shut and the three younger men behind Balbus all lunged forward.

'The swine!'

'We can break the door!'

'For Jove's sake...'

Balbus, his face still stony cold, reached out an arm and held them back. 'Wait.'

As he stood, the three men impatiently straining to move against the house, Balbus took a deep breath. The number of thugs within the building could determine the course of the next quarter hour. At least Lucilia was safe, having been delivered to the temple of Vesta by Balbus and half a dozen of his most trusted slaves and servants that morning. The priestesses would watch over her until he collected her, and even the city's most depraved thugs would refuse to enter Vesta's compound.

After a long moment there was a click and the door swung open wide. Lady Atia Balba Caesaonia – a relation of his, incidentally, though by the most distant and tortuous route imaginable – stood in the corridor that led to the atrium, her porphyry-toned stola hanging licentiously from one shoulder, her makeup perfect in every way and her smile as manufactured and calculated as every other facet of her appearance.

'Dear Quintus, you must excuse my fool of a doorkeeper. He's new and from Lusitania. They're all inbred and backward there, you know?'

Her eyes flicked momentarily to the blades in his and his companions' hands, but her smile and composure never faltered. She was clearly cut of the same cloth as her uncle. Balbus felt his resolve harden, rather than weaken as she probably intended. He also noted with professional interest the four men busily cleaning the hallway behind her. Dressed as common house slaves and servants but there was no disguising the wiry muscles beneath their tunics or the bulge at each waist where a knife hung. Atia was not a woman to take chances, despite appearances.

'Where is Clodius Pulcher?' he said sharply.

The lady of the house simply stepped back and allowed her smile to fall slightly and her brow to furrow in surprise. She's so calculating she should be in the theatre, Balbus thought absently.

'Clodius? Oh he no longer stays here. Despite my uncle's request, I simply cannot abide the thugs who accompany him in and out, slamming doors day and night, drinking and whoring in my beautiful domus. I suggest you look for him at his own townhouse. I'm sure he will be there. In fact, I recall him saying as much before I had to eject him – somewhat unceremoniously, I'm afraid.'

'You won't mind if we come in and have a look, then?' snarled Brocchus behind him, the gladius in his hand rising in a threatening manner.

'By all means. Perhaps you will all join me for a repast? I have good Falernian wine and honeyed dormice prepared? You will, of course, leave those barbarous blades at the door shelves as is customary?'

Brocchus opened his mouth to snap out a reply but Balbus placed a restraining hand on his shoulder and nodded respectfully at the lady, his blade slipping beneath his toga and into the sheath at his side.

'That will not be necessary, Gaius, and I must respectfully decline your invitation, my lady. We have pressing business with Clodius the rat. Should he put in an appearance, I would take it kindly if you would warn him that we are looking for him?'

'Of course, Quintus, of course. You must call again when you have more time.'

As the former legate stepped back and bowed, an unseen doorman swung the portal closed with a very final click. Brocchus opened his mouth angrily, but Balbus put a finger to his lips in warning and strode off toward the square. As they reached the corner and were finally long out of sight and hearing of the house, Balbus cleared his throat.

'It was not the right time.'

'Why not?'

'Either Clodius was not there, as Atia said, in which case we would have drawn a blank and made ourselves look to be the rudest of fools, or he *was* there and so well prepared that Atia felt safe inviting us in and it would have been tantamount to falling on our swords to even try. No. It was not the right time.'

'So what now?'

Balbus took a steadying breath and strolled across the square to the boy collecting the windfalls, flipping three copper coins to him.

'Ossus? Tell me.'

'The posh one left yesterday with two patrician types' the boy said, scratching his chin. 'He's not been back since, but nobody's moved out all the personal stuff he moved in yet, so I reckon he's still based there. He's got this friend, who looks like an old soldier, but he's so tall he looks like he'll bang his head on the city gates. Talks with a weird accent; Greek, I think. That fella comes and goes quite often and he's been around today. In fact, he came out of the back gate while you were at the front, with a couple of other thugs.'

Balbus nodded in satisfaction and tossed him two more coins.

'Where did they go and did you hear them say anything?'

Ossus grinned at his new acquisition. 'They went that way – toward the circus' he pointed south. 'His accent's really weird, but I heard the Aventine mentioned. That's about it.'

'Sounds like they *did* head to Clodius' house' he confirmed to the other three. 'The rat has a large residence in the shadow of the circus. Like so many he considers the Aventine unlucky, so he carefully lives just *below* the hill, rather than *on* it. Cheap property, so he can live like a king for a low cost – gives him extra cash to spend on thugs and gladiators. If he's taken Faleria there we'll need a small army to dig her out.'

With a friendly smile, he turned back to the young lad.

'I've a new job for you, Ossus. It's more dangerous, so I'll double your pay. Find the house with the Bacchanal mural opposite the circus and near the Neptune's chariot street fountain. Keep an eye on the place and take note of all comings and goings again. If you see, or hear of, a lady in her thirties who looks like she might be there against her will... No – this is Clodius. If you see any lady at all – other than slaves – come and find me immediately. You got that?'

'Got it, sir.'

Balbus breathed deep again.

'We must move carefully, gentlemen.'

And yet time may well be running out for Faleria.

Chapter 18

(Caesar's camp on the coast of Britannia)

Fronto stood on the rampart and peered out into the torrential rain as the winds battered him, threatening to knock him from the parapet and driving the downpour at an almost horizontal angle. The soldiers on the walls had taken to moving considerably slower than usual due to the extremely slippery nature of the timber walkway, which had already caused a number of minor accidents. Back down in the camp, what had begun as puddles a day and a half ago were now small lakes that reached up above men's ankles and the grass across much of the site had now become a thick, cloying mud.

'There's going to be too many of them. You know that?'

Caesar, standing beside him, tapped his chin thoughtfully with a finger. 'How many was the estimate?'

'The scouts came up with various figures, but I'd safely average it out to about twenty thousand.'

'And we have less than ten thousand.'

'Precisely. And those men are undernourished, cold, tired and have the lowest morale I've seen in years. When the Tenth start to mutter and complain you know there's something wrong.'

'Indeed, Marcus. But this could be our moment. We came here to chastise the Britons for their interference in Gallic campaigns and to make them think twice about doing so again. If we can smash their force here, we could perhaps break their spirit and consider our task complete. Then we could return to Gaul and think about wintering the troops.'

The legate of the Tenth nodded with little enthusiasm. 'That's reliant upon us actually winning, though, and I'd be dubious about wagering money even on a one-to-one basis right now, with the legions in the condition they're in. Certainly two-to-one worries me.'

'We could still leave' Cicero muttered on the other side of Fronto, quietly enough that only his fellow legate could hear before the wind whipped the words away. Fronto ignored him, despite the sense he spoke. The two men had shared a strained relationship ever since the aftermath of the beach assault.

'We need an edge. We need to pull something out of our helmets to even the odds.'

Caesar nodded and tapped his foot irritably. 'If we had the cavalry we could harry them from behind. That would make all the difference.'

'No use pondering on the 'could-haves', Caesar. Unless...'

A smile crept across Fronto's face.

'What?'

'Maybe we could use their tactics against them?'

'What do you mean?' Cicero asked interestedly, leaning closer.

'These Britons are the same as the Germanic tribes we fought, and the Belgae and so on. All these Celtic peoples favour ambushes. The worst battles we've fought are the ones where they've fallen on us from the woods. Remember the Nervii at the Sabis River? They very nearly put an end to your whole Gallic campaign. And only days ago the locals came out of the trees and surrounded a vexillation of the Seventh. But they feel safe attacking us, because word gets around. Everyone knows that Romans fight in the open ground. We like an empty field.'

'Go on' Caesar said thoughtfully.

'Horns of the bull. We array most of the army in the open before the camp, exactly as the Britons will be expecting. But they won't notice two cohorts missing. Cicero can take his veteran first cohort out to the south, through the trees, and I'll take mine north. We'll get ourselves lined up in the cover of the woods to either side of the open fields and as soon as they engage your force, we'll come out of the woods and fall on their flanks. We can do them so much damage it might even the odds for us.'

Cicero shrugged. 'Why not two cohorts each? Why not come right round behind them and seal them in? After all, we need to stop them escaping like they have every time.'

'No' Fronto shook his head. 'More than two cohorts makes enough of a difference in the army's size that they might notice and suspect a trick. On top of that, on the off-chance we run into trouble in the woods, we only lose Caesar two cohorts and he can still make a try for victory with the remaining eighteen. If we risk four cohorts we risk leaving too few to succeed.'

Caesar nodded. 'And while I would love nothing more than to stop them fleeing the field, it's stupifyingly risky to trap a force twice your size with no means of egress. They are then forced to fight to the death and that makes any army twice as dangerous. If we

341

wish to survive it ourselves, we have to leave them a way out when they break.'

He glanced around Fronto at the legate of the Seventh.

'Are your men up to it? The Seventh have had a difficult time of it so far. Perhaps Brutus can take Fronto's second cohort?'

Cicero opened his mouth, a look of sheer disbelief on his face being quickly overcome by one of anger, but Fronto stepped forward to block the view between them and addressed the general.

'Caesar, Cicero is an able commander and his first cohort fought like lions the other day. They have a number of good veteran centurions. This is the way we need to move. We'll be taking the primus pilus of each legion with us, so Brutus will need to take charge of the Seventh, on the assumption that you will command the Tenth, Caesar?'

He stepped back and allowed the air to crackle between the other two officers for a moment. Caesar seemed to be weighing up the situation in his head and finally nodded.

'Very well. Good luck to you both. You had best move now, before they arrive. They must be close.'

With a quick salute, Fronto gestured to Cicero and the pair slipped and clambered down the logs that formed the stairs to the ramparts, leaving Caesar to watch the tree line pensively.

'The old bastard goads me deliberately' Cicero snarled as the two legates strode through the siling rain and sloshed through the muddy pools. It was the first time he'd spoken to Fronto in many days without issuing a threat, an accusation or a curse of some kind. Perhaps it was time to bury the hatchet. If Fabius and Furius could do it for him, surely he could do it for Cicero. The army needed to pull closer together; not to continue fragmenting.

'You have to understand a certain level of uncertainty, though' Fronto said with a sigh. 'Your brother is the general's most outspoken opponent. He denounces Caesar at every turn of the wheel. The general's bound to level a certain amount of mistrust at you.'

'I have been his loyal legate throughout the campaign!'

'And one of the most forthright in opposition to his decisions' Fronto declared, biting down on a reminder that this 'loyal legate' refused Caesar's orders at the beach. 'You do yourself no favours.'

Cicero looked around to discern just how alone they might be, but every man in camp was busy making preparations, waiting for the call, or huddling beneath their cloaks against the driving rain. None were paying any attention to the small talk of senior officers.

'Marcus, you have no idea. I am Caesar's loyal man; always have been. But because I will not distance myself from my brother, and because I advocate a path of calm and sense, I am tarred with the brush of a traitor. And I'm not alone, either. Labienus cannot fall much further from favour without having to look *up* at the turf! Remember that you are not that far behind us, either.'

Fronto turned, ready to proclaim himself Caesar's man, but a plethora of thoughts battered at him in that briefest moment. Just how much *was* he Caesar's man? Certainly his allegiance to his general had waned throughout the campaign. And given the vehemence of Cicero's statement, it was more than possible that his fellow legate had, at a deep level, a more solid and anchored support for Caesar than he himself. Quailing at even the thought, he swallowed and broached a new subject – almost new, anyway.

'What of Menenius and Hortius? Why are they not in the Seventh with you if Caesar's lumping all his potential dissidents in one legion?' It was blunt. Much blunter than he intended, but the conversation had taken a difficult turn that had hit him unexpectedly, and he felt ill-equipped to attempt subtlety.

'I'm sorry, Marcus?'

'The two tribunes from the Fourteenth. Make no mistake: whether they're tied to you and Labienus or not – or whether they're tied to your brother or even Pompey, I *will* deal with them for what they've done. But how did they escape the policy of 'all Caesar's opposition in one legion'?'

Cicero actually stopped walking for a moment in surprise, standing in a muddy puddle and apparently not even noticing as his boots started to saturate.

'*Tied to me*? What are you talking about, Fronto? What *have* they done?'

'They've been undermining the general, removing those with close links to him. I can appreciate a bit of opposition, such as you and Labienus – that's healthy and keeps the general grounded, but taking action and killing officers is tantamount to treason and murder and I won't have it – especially not with my friends.'

Cicero frowned as he started walking again. 'I thought you landed that blame squarely with my centurions. Hell, you only started speaking to *me* civilly again since we found out we were in danger.'

'Fabius and Furius are innocent – martinets, but innocent. It's the two tribunes, Menenius and Hortius.'

'You're mistaken, Fronto.'

The legate of the Tenth glared at his counterpart.

'Don't protect them, Cicero. I will have my time with them.'

'I'm not protecting them, you idiot.' Cicero grasped Fronto by the shoulders. 'I've avoided every contact with those two. They're Caesar's pets.'

'Oh, please...'

'They are, Marcus. I've seen them in the general's tent late at night when most of the army is asleep. They creep around and fawn to the general. I don't know what they're up to, but they're certainly not killing Caesar's favourites.' He lowered his tone, despite the fact that no one was remotely interested. 'Menenius is so far into Caesar's purse he would clean the general's arse with his tongue if he asked. The Menenii were once consuls but they've fallen so far, and now they're living on farms in Illyricum. They're but a spit from being plebs these days, Marcus, and Caesar's the only thing upholding their ancient noble name. And as for Hortius – well the man may play a noble fop but his mother served in a brothel on the Esquiline and his father was... let's say a regular visitor with solid mercantile wealth. He owes his current high position to the general.'

Fronto shook his head. 'It's them. I know it's them.'

'I fear you're mistaken, Marcus. The men would return to relative obscurity without Caesar. They're his creatures. It's why they're assigned to the Fourteenth that's always on supply train duty and safely out of the danger of combat. Speaking of which...'

Cicero gestured to Carbo, who stood beside Fronto's neat little room at the end of a timber building. In the wide space beyond, his men were formed up ready for action.

The legate of the Tenth came to a stop. Cicero paused on his way to the Seventh and clasped hands with him. 'Now is not the time for such talk or thoughts – we go to fight. Forget about your conspiracies, Fronto, and concentrate on the Britons.'

Fronto nodded and clasped the other legate's hand. 'Mars be your strength and Fortuna your protector. Come back safe, Cicero.'

'You too. I'll meet you half way through the Celt army.'

Turning from his fellow legate, Fronto found the somewhat serious face of Carbo grimacing at him, pink and somewhat unhappy as the torrents poured down his face and soaked his tunic and armour.

'I know that look, sir. What sort of cockeyed insane plan have you cooked up now? With respect, the boys are near breaking point.'

Fronto nodded to him and strode on past to where the legion was assembled.

'Men of the Tenth' he shouted in his most inspiring voice, loud enough to be heard over the incessant roar of the rain battering on armour and helmets. 'In order to give us an unfair advantage over the enemy, I am forced to split our legion.'

There was a groan from the men, though from no easily identifiable individual source.

'I and Carbo will be taking the first cohort into the woods to pounce on the enemy's flanks. Cicero and his legion are pulling the same manoeuvre on the other side of the field. The rest of you…' he grinned. 'The rest of you will create an impregnable wall. You'll be serving under the direct command of the general.' He paused to let the fact sink in, during which there was silence, though whether a happy or a troubled one, he could not tell.

'The general will allow the looting of the tribesmen when the battle is over and all the local settlements will be ours to pick over.' He grinned wickedly. 'And despite your Roman origins, I know you've all grown quite fond of the native beers of Gaul. Well, guess what? These Celts brew the same stuff, though this beer is apparently strong enough to make the hairs on your chest stand up straight. And it'll be ours for the taking when we finish. Just make sure you hold the line and stay alive long enough to enjoy it.'

A roar of approval greeted the statement.

'Now let's get ready to kick them so hard they don't wake up 'til three weeks after they're dead.'

* * * * *

'Shit shit shit shit shit!' Fronto hissed as he collapsed in an awkward heap, trying to remain as quiet as possible despite the agony that tore through his knee, having entangled his foot in a thick gnarled tree root and twisted his leg on the way down.

'You alright sir?'

'Fine!' he snapped at Carbo. 'Don't worry about me.'

The primus pilus gave him a look that hovered somewhere between concern and disapproval and wiped the rain from his face. Here in the depths of the woodland, the rain was no longer a hail of watery shards, but a constant battering of heavy, bulbous droplets that formed on leaves and deposited themselves unerringly down the necks of the men.

'You sure you know where we are?' Fronto barked at his senior centurion.

'With respect, legate, finding north in a forest is a very easy task. We've already turned back south and we're heading toward the field.'

'I hope you're right' Fronto grumbled, using the rough surface of the tree to haul himself to his feet. 'I'm remembering now why no famous general has ever led a campaign in a forest.' He glanced around to see the four hundred and twenty seven men who currently comprised the slightly under-strength first cohort, spread out in the woods, glinting in the sunlight between the trees, unable to hold to a formation. 'If they anticipate this and come at us in...'

'Shh!' Fronto blinked as Carbo stopped dead and put the finger to his lips. Behind Fronto, the entire cohort came to a halt, the noise of the battering raindrops once more taking the place of the steady movement of soldiers.

'What?' He hissed.

In reply, and frowning at Fronto's volume, Carbo cupped a hand around his ear. Fronto fell silent, trying to hear over his own laboured breathing and the downpour. As the thumping of his pulse and the wheezing of his lungs died down, he could now just make out the sounds of fighting.

'They're already engaged!' Fronto hissed in surprise. Carbo nodded and Fronto shook his head in disbelief. The cohort had been ready to move by the time Fronto and Cicero had returned from their wall meeting with Caesar and they had been heading out of camp toward the forest's edge before the encamped legions had even put out the call for assembly. How long had they been in this damned dripping sylvan nightmare?

'*Fully* engaged, too' whispered Carbo. 'That's not the opening roar of two lines; that's the sound of ongoing fighting. We'd best move.'

Fronto nodded as his centurion made several hand gestures that began the cohort moving again, as quietly as they could through the woods, trying not to spook wildlife or snap large twigs. Inevitably, the noise level was louder than any officer would wish it – and certainly a different matter entirely to the surprisingly stealthy Celts – but with the din of battle growing louder with every cautious step and the background roar of the rain, there was little chance of the cohort being heard on the battlefield.

Carefully, slowly, Fronto approached the growing white-green ribbon of light that heralded the tree line and the field of battle. It would be overestimating their contribution to things to say that everything rode on their little manoeuvre, but certainly it would make a vast difference to the way the fight went, and might mean the saving of – or the death of – a great many men. Fronto found himself seething that they had not thought of this earlier. He could have been moving through the forest with his men as soon as the scouts had even finished estimating their numbers. *Then* they would have been ready. Now...

The whole plan had been based on the notion that both his and Cicero's cohorts would be in position at the forest's edge and ready to pounce when the Britons arrived. Now they were playing 'catch-up' and had to commit as soon as they were reasonably able. Would Cicero be there? Had he already arrived and committed his men, cursing Fronto for his absence? Was he still wandering around these cursed Britannic forests getting wet and angry and unaware that the fight was already on? Or was he too creeping through the undergrowth worrying about what might happen?

Finally, he began to see the movement of a vast seething army of men, largely naked or dressed in those curious long trousers such as the Gauls wore, painted and adorned with bronze or even gold where their status warranted. Every man seemed to be armed with a different weapon, like an unruly mob hastily dragged from their beds to save their land. Even in the haze of the downpour it was hard not to be chilled at the number of them.

They would be no match for a Roman legion in top fighting condition, even at two-to-one odds. But at the moment it was at best touch and go as to which side would gain the advantage and Fronto knew as well as any experienced commander that morale was half the battle. The army that thirsted for blood would push all the harder and an army that broke was lost in that instant. It was sadly a little too obvious which force had all the morale on that field.

The Roman lines, invisible somewhere behind the mass of warriors, were making only the noises of a group of men fighting for their life: grunting, yelling, screaming, occasional horn calls or bellowed commands. There was no roar of defiance; of the might of Rome, nor the silence that was sometimes called by a commander to frighten the enemy – a totally noiseless armoured advance was a disturbing sight for anyone.

The Britons, on the other hand, were in full spirit, bellowing their war cries and howling their blood lust, exhorting their strange gods to help them drive these hated invaders from their island, heedless of the rain battering their oft-naked skin. Likely the inhabitants of this accursed island viewed heavy rain as the normal weather for any time of the year. Fronto found himself wondering whether there were druids among them. It seemed that any Celtic force gained a dangerous amount of heart when they knew they were in the presence, and had the support, of that bunch of weird blood-drinking goat-humpers.

Closer now they crept, passing the boles of trees only ten or twelve paces from the edge. The field was becoming clearer all the time, the denser foliage at the periphery returning the roar of driving rain on green leaf.

Fronto felt a slow smile creep across his face as he took in the situation. The Britons had held nothing back in this, their apparently last ditch attempt to drive Rome from their shores. The bulk of the men – nobles and warriors alike – pushed and struggled to get to the Roman lines, formed in a mass. Their cavalry had apparently charged en masse on this flank at the north side of the field, expecting to break the Roman ranks. Whether it had been Caesar's decision or that of the senior centurion among the Tenth's ranks there, the Roman lines had pulled the age-old 'fake flight' manoeuvre, apparently breaking under the cavalry's charge, but then consolidating again to slow their advance and enveloping them, wrapping them in a circle of steel. A small reserve cavalry force remained at the rear, on the far – southern – edge of the fight, but not enough to swing the battle. The nobles had all joined the throng, leaving their chariots in the hands of the drivers who, unaware of the approaching danger, had brought them toward the forest's edge to watch the battle progress and wait for the call from their masters.

There was a chance, then. As long as the centre, a joint command of the Tenth and the Seventh, could hold against the much greater numbers of their enemy, there was a chance.

Glancing across at Carbo, Fronto tried to use his hands to mime the shape of a chariot, drew a line across his throat, pointed to himself and held up two fingers. Carbo nodded his understanding and turned, gesturing for the centurion of the second century to follow their legate. Like a flowing river of shining steel through the forest, the cohort separated, nine centuries forming on Carbo near the forest's edge. The remaining century moved to Fronto's location, where he repeated his mime until they all nodded.

With a last motion to Carbo, urging him to wait, Fronto gestured to his century and they spread out along the line of the trees in their eight man contubernia, each group opposite one of the waiting chariots. As soon as he could look along the line and see that they were in place and all movement appeared to have ceased, he made the motion to attack.

The chariot drivers were oblivious; all their attention locked on the battle before them, they were hopelessly unprepared for a sudden attack from behind. By the time Fronto and his eight man unit reached the nearest chariot, the man was only just turning in alarm at the sound of jingling metal above the driving rain. His yell of panicked warning was cut short and became the gurgle of a man with an opened throat as a particularly energetic legionary bounded up onto the yoke, his shield hardly inconveniencing him as he plunged his gladius into the Briton's neck, wrenched it free, and dropped down the far side without pause into a puddle of mud churned up by the vehicle's wheels and horses' hooves. For good measure, a second legionary put his blade in the driver's ribs just to be sure, dragging him down from the traces to die on the sodden turf.

Two more men from the contubernium hurriedly cut the horses free of the vehicle and smacked them on the rump, sending them running from the field in panic. This last was, strictly speaking, unnecessary, the chariots having been rendered ineffective with the loss of the driver, but the wanton destruction emboldened the legionaries and gave them much needed heart.

A quick glance left and right told much the same story all along the forest's edge. Of the ten parties that had sortied from the trees, only two had been forced to make a fight of it, their targets more alert than the others, and three of the contubernia had already moved on to take other chariots out. One or two of the vehicles that stood to the western edge of the field were making a run for it, and Fronto briefly considered ordering that they be chased down, but reminded himself that this was about a quick win, not a thorough trouncing – let them go.

Now, Carbo's men were moving out of the tree line, filtering between the useless chariots and forming up into shield walls one century at a time, twenty men wide and four deep. Already Fronto's contubernium was moving on to a chariot that was busy wheeling and making to leave, but which had neither the time nor the space to evade the onslaught.

Glancing around, Fronto tried to see what was happening elsewhere. The enemy's reserve cavalry had apparently noticed the sudden danger from the wing and were forming up to come and meet them but behind them he could see the shapes of armoured legionaries emerging from the forest to the south: Cicero had arrived.

Calls were now going up among the horde of Britons, warning of the danger from the flanks. The warriors began to turn at the edge of the mass and form a front against this new threat. The reserve cavalry, preparing to charge Fronto's cohort, was suddenly warned of the newly arrived force behind them and dissolved into chaos, some of the riders turning to attack this fresh army, while others kicked their steeds into life and continued their original charge.

Such it always was with a disorganised army. The reserve cavalry had still been a strong enough force to punch through either new cohort, but having become divided and without the advantage of a system of officers and signallers, the force had neatly split into two groups, neither of which would have the strength to break a Roman advance.

With a wave at the centurion of the second century, Fronto signalled him to pull the men back into formation, but the well-trained soldiers were already finishing off the last of the chariots within reach and moving toward their standard, the glinting silver decorated with sprigs of greenery from its difficult passage through the woodland.

Cornu blasts and the cries of officers from the far side of the field revealed that Cicero's cohort were moving against the far flank at a run. Carbo, ever the long-sighted officer, had slowed his own men so that all the advancing centuries could fall into step, allowing time for Fronto and his men to catch up and join them and, above all, letting their comrades beyond the enemy horde know that they had arrived.

Even as Fronto listened, he could hear the rhythmic battering of gladius on shield from all along his cohort's line. There would be no surprise to this attack; the enemy had had sufficient warning from the chariots' destruction to turn and face them, and so Carbo was sending a strong signal to the beleaguered centre of the Roman lines that help had arrived.

Sure enough, even as Fronto and his century began to form up and move at a jog to plug the gap Carbo had left them, an answering roar arose from the Roman force as they fought with renewed vigour, aware that they were no longer on the defensive.

The tone in the enemy also changed, though not enough. There were cries of dismay, but as many cries of defiance as the mass of warriors turned almost inside out to present three faces, leaving a clear way only to the west.

Fronto met up with the line only ten paces from the waiting Britons and shuffled along to find a spot between his century and the next where he was not ruining a centurion's formation.

'Respectfully, sir' an optio called from behind his men, where he was busy using his stick to prod them into a straighter line, 'but you need to fall in at the rear, sir.'

Fronto stared at the junior officer in disbelief.

'You *what*, soldier?'

The optio did not even bend under the malice of Fronto's gaze.

'Orders of the primus pilus, sir. On account of your knee, sir.'

The legate's glare simply hardened as he struggled to come up with a spiteful enough reply, but already the line had closed in front of him. Fronto was closer to his legion than most legates, but he was still a world apart, while their primus pilus might as well be Mars himself wielding a thunderbolt and no legionary would be about to defy the man.

Fronto realised he was standing glaring at a man who had already moved his attention back to his own men, and determined to have this out with Carbo the moment they were in private. His thoughts were interrupted a moment later by the tremendous crash of two armies meeting in a line of bloody violence.

* * * * *

Galronus, chieftain among the Remi tribe and commander of an entire wing of Caesar's auxiliary cavalry force rubbed his hair to rid it of the excess water as his horse danced impatiently. 'How far?'

'Not far' his best scout shrugged the rain from his shoulders as his horse came to a halt and it took Galronus a moment in the torrential downpour to see the grin on the man's face.

'What?'

'You don't recognise the ground, sir?'

'Don't try my patience, Senocondos. I am tired, saddle sore, and now I find we're on the trail of a damned war band!'

It had been two and a half days since he and the small cavalry command had left the lands of the Atrebates, riding as fast as they dared for the south-east coastline. The local chieftain had taken some persuading and the promise of very heavy future concessions, but had not been averse to dealing with Roman commanders. Now, four hundred horsemen travelled with eight hundred mounts, changing beasts regularly to see them arrive fresh and capable for action.

Better than that, the Atrebate nobles' sons who led the contingent under his command knew the land well enough that their return journey had been a lot shorter and more comfortable than the horrible ride into the unknown west over a week ago.

And only half an hour ago, weary and becoming aggravated with the incessant bad weather, the riders had happened upon the unmistakable trail of a large force that had recently passed by in the direction of the Roman landing site.

'Apologies, lord. This is land we scouted when first we landed. Caesar's camp is less than half a mile distant. We can follow the trail and it will lead us there.'

Galronus' jaw hardened. The freshness of the trail suggested that any meeting between this force and the Roman expeditionary legions was likely still in progress. If it was already over, then it would have to have been a massacre one way or the other. Those possibilities did not bear thinking about.

'Keep to your tired mounts!' he called to the men gathered around him. 'As soon as we are close enough to hear the battle, change mounts and set the worn horses to graze. Then we muster and charge.'

One of the young Atrebate nobles shook his head. 'If we do not tether the horses, they may bolt. These are strong, noble and *costly* beasts.'

'And your fathers and their chieftain have donated their services to our cause. You will follow my orders, or you will dishonour the lord of the Atrebates in your defiance.'

Satisfied with the look of sullen and grudging acceptance in the young man's features, Galronus squared his shoulders and sat straighter.

'Quickly now. To the coast and battle!'

* * * * *

Fronto stormed along the line of fighting men. Despite having apparently issued the order to his men to make sure their legate stayed safely out of trouble, Carbo was inaccessible, fighting somewhere in the front line where Fronto could hear his bellowed commands even though he could not see him.

The men of the cohort might have effectively locked him out of their fight, but there would come a point where the line of legionaries came to an end, where the way had been left for the Britons to escape the field.

For a while Fronto had wondered whether that would truly be likely. The enemy had fought them with unending vigour and seemed undaunted by this 'boxing in' of their army. But in the last few moments the atmosphere had changed subtly. That breaking point had almost been reached. He could feel it crackling in the air like the promise of lightning.

Sure enough, there, a few paces ahead, the last century in the cohort had been fielded at double the density and only half the width, providing extra protection for their own flank – it was not unknown for a surrounded enemy to outflank their own attackers. Had the Britons worked it out, it could have been easy enough for them to send out a large enough force to break around the edge of the Roman line and start smashing them to pieces.

Fortunately, a combination of two elements kept the flank safe. Firstly: the enemy's chaotic nature where, rather than thinking on the grand scale of how to win a battle, the Britons were simply falling over each other to get at the nearest Roman, while their cavalry flittered uselessly among them and around the edge – scattered and ineffective. Secondly: years of drilling and practising under first Priscus and then Carbo had kept the Tenth not only strong and disciplined, but also adaptable and able to think for themselves when required. On the very flank, the primus pilus had placed his most trusted veterans, interspaced with his biggest and strongest men. Behind them, in the subsequent rows were fast men capable of responding to threats speedily and efficiently. Every time the enemy tried to break the end of the Roman line through brute force they encountered only the mean and brutal response of Carbo's bear-like veterans. Every time a small group attempted to move around them to turn the flank, a highly mobile force of legionaries appeared as if from nowhere to deal with them.

It was working.

It was also where Fronto would be able to join the fight without being pushed out.

'Cavalry!'

Even as he'd started to pick up the pace to reach a fighting position, nearing the end of the line, Fronto looked up at the shout from a nearby legionary and saw a force of hundreds of Celtic horse bearing down on them from the woodlands. It appeared the Britons were not alone.

'Hold the line. Don't worry about that cavalry' Fronto bellowed. 'Just hold the line!'

Yet despite his command, the legate was no longer sure about making a fight of it at the line's end. If that cavalry came in at a charge and chose to hit this particular position, he would be trampled before he even had a chance to bloody his blade.

Tucking his gladius under his shield arm and stepping back away from the fight, Fronto reached up to the amulet supposedly representing Fortuna and gave it a little caress for luck as his eyes roved this way and that, trying to take it all in. A groan was rising from the Roman ranks as they realised that Celtic reinforcements meant it was almost certainly over, though the officers back at the main legion force were still pushing their men as the buccina and cornu blasts confirmed.

And then the strangest thing happened.

Even as the Roman force began to sag with the dire expectation of death, a bellow of something unintelligible arose from somewhere in the crowd of Britons and was echoed back and forth until it became a moan of despair. The few horsemen who were still free at the periphery of the fight made to escape, running not for the relief force, but obliquely, into the woods.

Fronto stared as the mass of footmen broke in an instant and began to flee as best they could. His eyes followed them and paused for a moment on the newly arrived cavalry. Blinking, he focused on the force once more. No, his eyes had not deceived him: that was a Roman banner among them.

Galronus!

Even as the allied cavalry slammed into the fleeing Britons driving them into a frenzy of fear, Fronto straightened with a grin – the tables had just turned unexpectedly.

Determinedly, he collected his sword from beneath his armpit once more and took a step forward. Was he being stupid? Though Galronus' cavalry had almost sealed in the enemy within a neat box, there were still gaps where the Britons leaked out making for safety as best they could like water bursting from holes in a dam, and he'd made his way to a position directly between them and their objective.

Most of the Britons, however, were now purely intent on escape, fleeing past him, heedless of this lone Roman officer and flowing around him like a stream around a rock as he kept his shield forward to ward off any stray blades while he slashed and struck at the figures running to either side of him.

A blow struck his back and he wondered for a moment whether it would be mortal. It would be a truly awful fate to die and be buried in this wet, forbidding, sickening land.

'Watch your back, sir.'

Blinking, he realised that the blow had not been an enemy weapon, but rather a legionary falling in at his side, protecting him. Even as he nodded at the man, a similar thump announced the presence of a soldier at his other side, effectively forming a small shield wall on his position. Did Carbo's interference know no bounds? Now men were being sent from the cohort to protect him? Somewhere deep in his soul, Fronto started to seethe.

Safer than he had any intention of being, the legate moved his shield slightly to gain a better idea of what was going on amid the chaos of fleeing Britons, hefting it sharply back into position just in time to take the blow of the sword he'd fleetingly seen coming. The point of the long, Celtic sword slammed through the layered boards and leather of the shield, stopping alarmingly close to his sternum and then ripping back out, tearing pieces of shield with it.

Concerned, Fronto risked rising momentarily to peer over the very top of the shield.

He blinked in shock.

The man before him was a druid!

There could be no doubting it. The grey-white robe and the feathers and bones braided into his hair and long beard that tapered to twin forks spoke volumes about the man's status. What surprised Fronto more, though, was the martial aspect of this druid. While he'd seen their kin in Gaul bearing swords, he'd never imagined them as true warriors. This one, though, looked thoroughly at home with his heavy sword as he drew it back with a muscular arm for another blow. His other hand held no shield, but a short stabbing spear, which he was raising for a thrust over the top of Fronto's shield. The big man's hair was held back by that appeared to be a plain iron crown.

Like all druids, he was arrogant and sure of himself. Like all Celts, he fought as though attack was all. Like all their kind, he overextended and opened himself up to quick attack by a trained soldier of Rome. Fronto raised his shield and angled it slightly to ward off the spear thrust as he lunged with his gladius. The tip tore through the dirty robe of the druid but to Fronto's surprise met the unyielding metal of a finely-forged mail shirt beneath, striking sparks as it skittered across and past the man's ribs, becoming lost in the voluminous folds of the man's robe.

Almost in a panic, Fronto felt himself overbalanced and falling forward with the momentum. Just as surprised, the druid tried to step back to allow this Roman room to fall gracelessly forward where he could easily deliver the killing blow, but the press of his fleeing countrymen around him prevented the move. Desperately, Fronto toppled like a falling tree – his soft, useless boots unable to find purchase in the soaking mud – and was suddenly jerked straight as some unseen hand grasped the back of his cuirass and hauled him upright.

The druid had already recovered and had both spear and sword raised and pulled back ready to strike. That bubbling seething feeling in the pit of Fronto's stomach began to boil. Anger coursed through him, vying with embarrassment.

He had been effectively babysat by his own legion, prevented from getting himself into trouble and, determined to do his part like a spoiled child – something he was beginning to recognise in himself, much to his irritation, he had found a way to involve himself in the fight only to seriously underestimate his opposition and have to have his arse hauled out of the fire by the same damn babysitters, proving them, beyond a shadow of a doubt, right!

Furious at himself, his men, this damn druid and his irritating people, this drizzly, wet and hopeless island, the endless bickering, backstabbing and uncertainty of Caesar's army, his own limitations and even his apparent abandonment by Fortuna, Fronto snarled, his ire and anger forging a white hot spear in his brain.

He snapped.

* * * * *

Two hours later, lying propped up on a raised bench with a relatively soft pallet beneath him as the medical staff worked on him, he talked to Atenos, who, it turned out, was the man who had grabbed him and hauled him back up.

The huge man shook his head with a disbelieving grin.

'I've never seen anything quite like it!'

'What happened? I seem to remember punching that druid a few times.'

Atenos laughed out loud as the medicus stitched the cut on Fronto's shoulder. 'You really don't remember? I honestly thought you might take them all on yourself!'

Fronto could feel himself flushing and knew he should be angry, but somehow there was not enough anger left in him. He just felt exhausted.

'It was like the great berserk rages of the heroes of our legends. You actually threw your shield at him.'

'You should have stopped me then. That's stupid enough in itself. If a legionary did that, you'd have him beaten for his negligence.'

'I *did* try to stop you, legate. How d'you think I got this black eye? A Briton?'

Again, Fronto flushed.

'By the time I'd recovered,' the centurion grinned 'so had the druid. You'd confused him a bit, I think, when you threw your shield at him, but that was nothing to his expression when you kicked him between the legs.'

'I did what?'

'Went down like a sack of grain, he did. I swear his eyes even crossed. I think you beat him about half a mile past the point of death. He looked more like a lamb stew than a man by the time you'd finished with him. All we could do was put a shield wall around you and stop you getting trampled as they fled.'

'Oh for the love of Juno!'

'Legionary Palentius tried to haul you off him. The other medicus is looking at him now to see if you broke his jaw.'

Fronto rubbed his head in a mix of embarrassment and tiredness.

'Anything else I need to know?'

'Not really, sir. After that you just sort of started laying about you among the fleeing Britons. I hate to think how many of them you sent to Elysium this afternoon. They only got you four times, and none of them bad – miraculous, really. Of course the men were around you as best they could manage, but it wasn't easy. You were like a damned hedge-pig with that sword.'

'I honestly remember very little. I think I saw Galronus, but the first thing I really recall with any clarity was when you hauled me up off the floor. I think the enemy had gone.'

'It was over. I think you'd blacked out.'

Fronto leaned close to the huge Gallic centurion. 'I'd take it as a personal favour if you tried to stamp on this before it becomes common knowledge?'

Atenos grinned. 'I'll do my best, legate, but you were in the middle of the army, and a bit of a sight. I suspect the story's already spreading round the campfires.'

Fronto leaned back and winced as the suture the medicus was tying off pulled tight.

'Sit up, legate.'

Fronto looked across at the surgeon. 'I'm trying. So tired. Sorry. Atenos, I think I'll stay in the hospital for the night. You know... just in case.'

The big centurion nodded sympathetically.

'I'll leave you in peace, sir. Get some sleep.'

Fronto was unconscious before the centurion had reached the door.

Chapter 19
(Beachhead on the coast of Britannia)

The ships looked distinctly unseaworthy to Fronto. He sat on a folding campaign stool on the beach under the shelter of a large leather awning watching the relentless driving rain batter the sea, the pebbles, the ships and everything in sight – which was not a great distance in these conditions. The sky was a leaden grey and the weather had not let up for more than an hour at a time in the three days since the battle had ended.

Kicking a pebble down the beach in irritation, he realised he was brooding on his actions in that conflict yet again, in spite of himself.

In the aftermath of the fight, Fronto's reputation seemed quickly to have reached almost legendary status. Every time he heard the story of his frenzy the tale grew in magnificence and by rights he should probably be deified by now. Gradually, pieces of the struggle had returned to him, and the medicus had confirmed, much to his relief, that he'd received a blow to the head during the fight that was the most likely cause of his fragmentary memories of the attack rather than a simple complete loss of control and wit.

Still, despite Atenos and Carbo swearing to try and suppress the tale, it had exploded, and the legate had the sneaking, though unprovable, feeling that the two centurions may well be at the heart of its speedy spread.

By the end of that first day, he'd taken to closeting himself away, and by the afternoon of the second he'd been forced to go in search of new places to hide from people. If anyone had ever suggested that he might spend days hiding from people who wanted to buy him a drink, Fronto would have laughed in their face, but that time had somehow come.

In the end, this cold and blustery location was one of the few where he was almost guaranteed peace. Due to the value of the ships, the fortified beachhead was under constant guard, and only those with business here were allowed through the gate, meaning that the only soldiers the legate stood any chance of bumping into on the beach were sailors, engineers or other officers, all of whom had their own business to attend to.

It was not the most comfortable of places, though. The shelter had been erected days ago for the duty officer and his staff to oversee the repair and loading of the ships and, while it held off the rain from above, it did not keep the ground below dry or prevent the biting winds from along the beach or off the sea from whipping at him.

Irritably, he pulled the cloak tighter around him, shivering into the damp, cold wool.

Soon.

Soon, they would return to Gaul, and then the legions could be settled into winter quarters if Caesar meant to continue this madness, or settled if not.

Despite his earlier concerns, the legate would have to admit now that he was almost past caring about Caesar's motivations and future plans. This constant search for a new war was fraying him round the edges, and every place the army moved seemed to be less inviting and less worthwhile than the one before. All he wanted to do now was get back to Rome and to Puteoli; to see Balbus, Faleria, Lucilia.

With a sigh and another sickened glance around at the rain falling like rods from a lead sky, he took a swig of the wine in his clay beaker and huddled tighter still.

'Wishing yourself thirty miles south, legate?'

Glancing up in surprise, Fronto was relieved to see the hard, bristly face of Fabius looking down at him from beneath the awning. Furius appeared at the other side. Without further comment or requesting permission, the two centurions unfolded camp stools and sat to either side. Fabius produced two cups from his sodden cloak and a small jar of watered wine, while Furius withdrew a bowl of steaming stew that he must have carried extremely carefully to avoid spilling it down his front.

'You need this. You've been on this beach for two hours now without warmth or food. If you're trying to make yourself ill, you're going about it the right way.'

Fronto eyed the bowl of warm, appetising food uncertainly for a moment and then accepted it with a nod and took a mouthful, blowing round the hot meat to cool his mouth. Strange how things turn out, he thought to himself. Never, since that journey from Ostia, could he have imagined himself actually grateful to see the two former Pompeian officers, let alone for them to be trying to look after him.

'Actually I'm wishing myself several hundred miles south. I know you two are new to this campaign, but I'm starting to get quite sick of it, myself.' He cocked his head curiously. 'You two got no pithy remarks about my conduct the other day? No one else seems able to stay quiet.'

Fabius shrugged. 'You lost it. You were damn lucky not to be cut down. I've seen legionaries do it when they've been pushed far enough to snap. We keep our men drilled under the harshest conditions to inure them to anything so their breaking point is considerably higher than most, but when it does happen, it endangers every man near them. If you'd been one of my men, legate, I'd have put you down myself.'

'Good.'

'I suspect there's a little more pressure on you than on the average soldier, though?' Furius hazarded. 'Carbo's a little concerned.'

Fronto turned a sour, angry look on the centurion. 'What's that shiny pink bastard been saying now?'

'Oh nothing like that, legate. He still worries that there will be attempts on your life, and yet you take every opportunity that comes along to stay outside his protection. He's trying to keep you intact. It's one of the jobs of the chief centurion. He thinks you're stuck in a turbulent position, between Labienus' liberal dissidents and Caesar's die-hard supporters, too. He seems to think that somehow you're a bit of both. I'm not sure I disagree.'

'It's so gratifying to know how much people discuss me when I'm not there.'

'Take it as a complement, Fronto. Your men value you too highly to risk you. That's an uncommon thing for a legate.'

The three men lapsed into a silence that was instantly filled with the insistent hiss of heavy rain on the shale of the beach.

'Well the season is almost over' Fabius finally said with a sigh and took a swig of his wine.

'If we don't sail soon' Fronto muttered, eyeing the ships, 'the weather will trap us on this shithole island for the winter. Don't know about you but I really don't fancy that.'

Furius nodded, but with a smile. 'Of course, you weren't there this morning. It's been decided. We sail the day after tomorrow on the first tide. We've taken all the hostages from the local tribes that Caesar realistically feels we can safely fit aboard the ships, even with the four ships we've 'obtained' from the Cantiaci. There's enough impounded goods and loot that every soldier's going to board his ship weighing twice what he did when we arrived. I hope the vessels can take it. He's even planning to take the new Atrebate cavalry back with us.'

'It's been a lucrative campaign' Fronto sighed bitterly.

'And that's bad? The men don't think so.'

'If it's lucrative enough it'll just push the general into trying something similar as soon as the seasons grant the opportunity. Where will he go next, d'you think? Back here? Back to Germania? Maybe off past Illyricum and into the wilds of the Pannonii? Conquest breeds conquest.'

He sagged in the chair and spooned some of the hot stew into his mouth, talking between chews. 'It's not that which is driving me mad, though. It's the damn politics. If it was just the army campaigning for the senate and the republic I'd be happy with it, but you just can't separate the politics from the army these days. After all that business with Sulla, Marius and Sertorius, I really thought that the republic would settle under the guidance of men like Caesar, Pompey and Crassus, but if anything it just gets worse.'

'That's why men like us serve in the army, legate, rather than trying to serve in Rome. Better to be given a sword and pointed at a barbarian than to get involved.'

'But we *are* involved, Fabius' Fronto snapped, spitting meaty juice onto the pebbles. 'In the early days, when we marched out against the Helvetii, I could easily tell myself that Caesar was campaigning for the good of the republic. And then the Belgae revolted, and then the coastal tribes and others. And we put them down, because they'd revolted against us. It needed doing. You see? There was a reason for everything – until now! Germania, even. I could just about delude myself that our little jaunt across the river was a necessity.'

'But this?' he swept a hand angrily around at the beach. 'This is a publicity stunt, pure and simple. This is his way of saying to Pompey and Crassus: 'I'm better than you and stronger than you and more important than you'. And saying it to Rome, too. To strengthen his support among the mob, along with the added loot that will help him maintain a stranglehold on the weaker senators and raise new troops, despite the injunctions against him doing just that.'

'Legate, that's very dangerous talk. You sound like certain other officers who…'

'But they're *right*! Don't you see that? I've argued against it, but they're right. Don't get me wrong: I'm not saying Caesar's anything

362

unusual in that. Crassus is doing exactly the same thing. Rumour has it that he's going to invade Parthia. Do you think he's spending all that money raising new legions and disappearing into an endless desert for the good of Rome? No! He's trying to beat Caesar at his own game: popularity and loot. And Pompey? Well he's just sitting in Rome, tugging strings and building webs and trying to undermine them both.'

'Fronto...' Furius hissed his warning, his eyes strafing the beach to make sure they were all out of earshot.

'It's true, though. I know that you served with Pompey and that he's a great general. And now you serve Caesar and he is, too. But it's not their military prowess I'm condemning. It's their dabbling in the control of Rome itself. This is a damn dangerous time to be a citizen, I can tell you.'

With a sigh, he ate another spoonful of stew. 'It won't bother you, I suppose. You've been given a sword and pointed at a barbarian. And you're the top two centurions now in the Seventh. You effectively run the legion, so you'll have your work cut out turning them into a proper fighting force again over the winter.'

Furius and Fabius exchanged a strange glance and the latter shrugged. 'Hopefully. We're on detached duty for a while, though, so it might have to wait. The men will need to settle into their winter quarters anyway and our training officers can get the work started.'

Fronto frowned and glanced back and forth between the two men. For a moment some of his earlier fears for the two centurions returned. They were clearly hiding something, but he knew now from experience that with these two, confrontation over anything was hardly likely to be productive.

It was another added worry, though. In a brief flash he remembered Caesar's face as they stood talking on the rampart of the nearby camp around a fortnight ago, the general wearing a look of guilty secretiveness as he neatly evaded and parried all Fronto's more important questions.

'This whole thing is pissing me off. All this politics.'

'Then concentrate on what's important.'

'Getting home' Fronto said flatly, and then clenched his teeth. 'And dealing with Hortius and Menenius.'

'What?' Furius said, frowning.

'The two tribunes from the Fourteenth. I'm pretty sure they're the ones who've been murdering Caesar's supporters. Your legate thinks I'm wrong. He says they're too loyal to Caesar for that. But I'm still convinced.'

Fabius stood up and pulled his stool round so that he was sitting in front of the other two, creating an almost conspiratorial huddle.

'Then you must find a way to be sure, legate; draw them out and extract a confession. Who are the injured parties again? We are not tied to you and may be able to unearth facts that you cannot.'

Fronto pursed his lips. 'Caesar's nephew – You remember him from Ostia? He was killed at Vienna on the journey north. Pugio strike to the heart from behind. Then there was Tetricus, my tribune. Took both pugio and pilum blows at the battle in the Germanic camp, and was then finished with a gladius blow in the hospital. Pleuratus, Caesar's personal courier. Drowned in the Rhenus, tied to a boulder. And they tried to take me out with a slingshot, too.'

'And that's all?'

'All I know of. There may well be more. Given the number of casualties on a campaign like this there could be a dozen more deaths that have gone unnoticed.'

Fabius nodded. 'Then let us pry into the matter, too. And when we return to Gaul and you confront them, you may call upon us to aid you if you wish. I can assure you that we are very capable in such a situation.'

'I'm not yet sure what I'll do, but I'll let you know when I decide. On the assumption we make it back across, that is.'

Across the beach, they all watched the ships bucking and diving amid the rolling waves.

* * * * *

'Fronto! Get over here and help me hold this thing steady!'

The legate of the Tenth, ashen faced and shaking like a leaf, wrenched his head around, peering into the driving rain, trying to identify the source of the voice. It took only a moment to recognise Brutus, grasping the steering oar of the trireme and desperately straining to hold it in position. Taking a quick glance over the side at the rhythmic rise and fall of the oars, Fronto quickly wished he had not and pulled away from the rail, though his whitened fingers appeared reluctant to let go.

'Fronto!' Brutus bellowed again.

The legate looked up at the boiling black and purple sky, lit by occasional sheets of blinding white that cast the entire fleet into an eerie stark monochrome. A fresh flash of lightning temporarily blinded him and he shook his head, blinking away yellow-green blobs until he could see the huge, frightening waves rising and falling again.

'For the love of Venus, Fronto, I can't hold it on my own!'

Another quick glance told him that Brutus was not exaggerating. The swinging steering oar was sliding sideways and despite all Brutus' efforts, his boots' nails were leaving score marks across the timber as he was steadily pushed away.

He quickly glanced about to see whether anyone else could help, but every man on board had his tasks, most of them rowing or trying to hold pieces of the ship together.

He *could* have been on one of the big Gallic ships, but he'd decided to risk a trireme just to avoid being closeted with anyone that would either annoy him or bother him. He was regretting his decision about now, only three or four miles from their destination and yet caught in a storm the likes of which could easily dash them to pieces.

'Pissing Caesar' he snarled as he let go of the rail with some difficulty and staggered along the boards, slipping left and right with the lurching of the ship and the wet timber. 'He could have left earlier and not bothered with the damn hostages.'

Brutus had his teeth gritted in the gale, pushing the steering oar with all his might. Some five feet from him, the trierarch who actually captained the ship lay sprawled against the rail, blood washing down from his head in torrents as Florus – the young capsarius from the Tenth who had treated Fronto more times than he cared to remember – busily tried to mend a too-large hole in the man's head caused by a splintered oar that had snapped and shot upwards, catching the commander a blow on the way past.

Staggering across the deck, Fronto fell in with Brutus, grasping the steering oar and pushing it straight once more, trying not to pay too much attention to the sight of a wave that suddenly reared up higher than the ship's rail.

'Thank you' the young legate yelled. 'We were veering toward that!'

Fronto glanced off to the side, where he could make out nothing in the roiling blackness until another sudden flash lit up a rearing spur of land, menacing and pale grey in the light.

'Maybe we *should*! Can we not land there? Beach the ship?'

Brutus shook his head. 'Rocks. Too many rocks. We wouldn't so much beach it as sink it. We have to press on for Gesoriacum. We're nearly there!'

Fronto reached up to brush the plastered hair from his forehead and then quickly slapped the hand back to the beam as it began to move again. Five miles might as well be fifty as far as he was concerned.

Despite missing the morning tide due to trouble loading the nervous native horses, Caesar had persevered, pushing the fleet to prepare for the evening tide. They had managed most of the crossing in reasonable weather – driving rain had now become so commonplace as to be considered reasonable. But then, as the sailors were beginning to feel happier at the approach of the Gaulish coast, the storm had broken.

The fleet, having been fairly close throughout the journey, was now scattered by the wrath of Neptune, and no sign of any other vessel had been noted for more than half an hour now.

'We'll be damn lucky if we hit the right bloody nation, let alone the right port!' yelled Fronto, eying the coastline with distaste.

'It's alright, Fronto. This is the land of the Morini. I've done extensive charting and research, and I remember these cliffs from our first sailing. Not much longer and we'll see the lights of Gesoriacum.'

'Not much longer and we'll be pinned to the seabed under a hundred tons of timber' grumbled Fronto.

'Help me!'

The two men turned at the sudden panicked call, to see Florus the capsarius desperately trying to hold down the figure of the ship's captain who was bucking and shaking.

Fronto looked back at Brutus helplessly.

'Go on. I can hold it for a moment now, but don't be long.'

Nodding, Fronto gingerly let go of the steering oar and, once he was certain that Brutus still had it, skittered across the deck to the site of medical aid. As he dropped to wobbly knees next to the two, he felt his gorge rise and had to swallow down the bile. What looked like a simple head wound with a lot of blood through the rain and distance was considerably more unpleasant up close. A large piece of the trierarch's skull was missing at the crown and through the white-fringed bloody hole, Fronto could clearly see the pulsing grey mass of the man's brain, leaking blood. The bile rose again and had to be swallowed back.

'He's a goner, Florus.'

The capsarius shook his head, pushing the captain down hard. 'Not yet, sir. If you can hold him, I can get him padded and bound and covered. Men have survived worse. I removed the splinter from his brain, after all.'

This time nothing could stop the vomit as Fronto failed to prevent the image of that quick surgery surfacing. Wiping his mouth, Fronto reached down and grasped the captain's arms, pushing him back hard to the now vomit coated deck to stop him leaping about and shaking. Florus nodded his thanks and stood, rocking this way and that with the motion of the deck as he began to rummage in his leather bag.

'You really think he can survive? The man's a heap of shaking blubber.'

'You'd be surprised at the resilience of the human body, legate Fronto. I've seen *you* take a few wounds in my time.'

Fronto could not help but smile at the optimism in the young man. Ever since his first action against the Helvetii three years ago on a hilltop near Bibracte – after which he had transferred into the medical service – the boy had grown confident and capable.

'Get on with it, then. I need to get back to the steering oar soon.'

Florus nodded and tipped acetum onto the wadding in his hand. Staggering across, he dropped to a crouch again and began to gently push the pad into the hole in the man's skull. Fronto, for all his years of causing such wounds, found that he had to look away, and closed his eyes, gritting his teeth as he strained against the thrashing officer beneath him.

'Look out!' someone called from further down the deck, but Fronto could not see what it was from here and just had to continue gritting his teeth and pray to Neptune and Fortuna that it was not the cliffs and rocks getting too close.

'Oh, shit' yelled Brutus and this time Fronto opened his eyes and looked up, just in time to see a wall of black, glittering water looming over the side of the ship before it crashed down over the rail and across the deck, shaking the entire trireme as though it were a child's toy in a bath tub. The sound of shearing oars was just about audible in the roar of the water and Fronto felt the captain's body being torn from him. Desperately, he hooked his elbow round the rail and gripped the wounded officer with all his might.

It felt like hours that the wave pulled at him, for all its brevity, and when it finally released its hold on the trierarch, Fronto was so surprised that he actually fell back and let go for a moment.

The flash of white light illuminated the deck for a moment and revealed a scene of chaos and devastation. The rowers were in disorder, trying to even out the remaining oars as the boat bucked back and slapped back down level to the water. Men were hauling each other back to their seats and some were even pulling each other back over the side rail. Shattered pieces of timber and oars were being washed across the ship.

Fronto's eyes, however, were locked on where Florus had been a few moments earlier. A wad of bloodied padding plastered to an upright of the rail was the only sign that the young medic had ever existed.

'That was too close' yelled Brutus.

Fronto ignored him, painfully aware that the man he'd tried so hard to save had stopped thrashing during the wave and was now dead, as was the man who had been so positive about healing him.

Almost blinded by the lightning flashes and the pounding rain, inured to the cold and the wet and heedless of the shaking and tipping of the deck, Fronto stood, staggered and slipped across to the side rail, collecting the bloodied wadding and staring out at the boiling, rolling sea.

For the briefest moment he fancied he saw a figure carried off by one of the waves, but it could as easily have been a trick of the light or his own vision. A voice from further down the deck called out 'Man overboard!'

He wondered for a moment how the oarsman knew, but then realised they were looking over at one of the other rowers. Torn between the need to try and help and the knowledge that there was little he could do anyway, Fronto watched as the hapless, screaming sailor rose over the crest of a wave and disappeared from both sight and hearing.

Turning, he shuffled across to Brutus and the steering oar once more, grasping the end as he had a few moments earlier.

'Even the damn gods have turned their back on this campaign, Decimus.'

'Didn't think you were that pious, Fronto.'

'I try not to actively defy them.'

'Well rub that bow-legged Goddess of yours, Fronto. Look.'

The legate peered off in the direction of Brutus' pointing finger. It took him a moment to spot two flickering fires.

'That'll be the beacons they were going to set up at Gesoriacum. They must have lit them to guide ships in through the storm. We're nearly there; closer than I thought. A mile at most.'

Fronto gripped the beam tight, his eyes locked on the twin fires that twinkled in the darkness, intermittently vanishing as the waves reared or a particular gusting cloud obscured them. Suddenly another white flash lit the scene and Fronto finally felt relief wash over him at the regular shapes of a harbour and buildings, with the unmistakable outline of a Roman fortification on the hill behind.

Gesoriacum.

They'd made it.

* * * * *

The 'Demeter' bounced against the jetty of the Gesoriacum harbour and Fronto silently thanked every god and Goddess that rose to the surface of his mind. He'd almost swallowed his tongue in fright as Brutus steered them through the surprisingly narrow entrance to the river-mouth harbour, but the young man had proved more than equal to the task.

An even more welcome sight as they had entered was that of another of the fleet's triremes already in the harbour and scooting lazily toward the dock on their few remaining oars.

There was no sign of life down by the docks, though Fronto could hardly blame anyone for that, given the weather. He glanced across from the rail at the sister ship that was just docking at the far side of the jetty. The 'Fides' looked in worse shape than their own ship, but its crew and complement of troops were moving toward the rail gratefully.

Brutus had left the steering now to one of the sailors and strode across to where Fronto stood.

'Best get everyone disembarked and get up to the headquarters to report in.'

Fronto gestured to the beacons blazing on the towers and the new ramparts around the port's periphery, barely visible in the dark and the rain, except when lit starkly by the lightning.

'Rufus has been busy in our absence. Look at those works. Think he was bored or expecting trouble?'

'Let's go find out.'

Fronto nodded and called to the centurions of the two centuries on board.

'Get your men formed up on the jetty. Arms and armour only. We'll come back and unload everything else in the morning when it's light and hopefully drier.'

The centurions saluted and Fronto looked across to where the men were now disembarking from the Fides opposite. Two more centurions were bellowing at their men who were filing off and into tent-groups.

'Come on.'

As soon as the sailors had run out a plank, Fronto hurried down to the jetty with a profound sense of relief, Brutus hot on his heels. A few steps on the stable jetty were almost enough to allow him to adjust, though he still felt as though he was swaying gently. The two centurions on the wooden jetty were unknown to him, and apparently men of the Seventh, though they saluted him and his fellow legate readily as they approached.

'Have your men in two single lines on the jetty. I'll form the other two up the same.That way all four centuries can march together back up to the fort.'

'Yes sir. What of the cargo, sir?'

'Leave it till morning.'

'But sir, we've got four of the cavalry horses – one of them may have to be put out of its misery, mind – and if we leave any of the loot here, it might be pillaged by the locals.'

Fronto shook his head. 'Have the ship's officer and men lead the horses ashore when we've left and take them to the nearest stable. No one's going to steal your treasure, though, centurion. Look at those ramparts. The port's under Roman control.'

The centurion managed to remain apparently unconvinced, but saluted and went about his business.

Having made the arrangements, Fronto stepped forward a few paces, giving the four officers the space to muster their men. Brutus followed him and stood tapping his lip thoughtfully.

'Have you noticed the lack of people?'

'It's pissing down, Brutus.'

'Yes, but even on the walls.'

'Come on. Rufus only has one legion and he's got the port, the town, the fort and who knows what else to deal with. There'll only be a few of them down here and they'll be keeping out of the rain. After all, who else would have lit the beacons?'

Brutus nodded uncertainly and glanced up at the town, with smoke rising from numerous roofs. The thought of getting somewhere he could huddle by a fire in the dry was overwhelmingly attractive.

It took a few moments to get the four centuries lined up, the men moving as fast and efficiently as possible, each one feeling the urge to reach somewhere dry, warm and stable. As soon as the four centurions confirmed that their units were ready, Fronto issued the command and the small force marched out proudly into the heart of Gesoriacum.

Across the cobbled quay they strode, toward the main thoroughfare that ran up the hill to the looming shape of the fort, almost obscured behind the clouds of smoke rising from the cosy fires of the Morini townsfolk.

A constant river of brown liquid ran from the slope of the street, across the quay and down into the harbour. The men eyed it with distaste and a certain amount of unhappiness as they moved into it, preparing to slog up the street toward their objective.

At commands from the centurions, the four lines of men doubled out, splitting into eight columns of forty – give or take the few fallen in Britannia – and they began the trudge up the slope with the two legates out front.

Brutus turned to Fronto with a nervous frown.

'Can you feel it?'

'What?'

'Something's wrong. The hair on the back of my neck's standing up.'

Fronto glanced around and then ahead again and felt a chill run down his spine, terminating in his coccyx and causing him to shudder.

'No one. Not a sentry, not a guard, not a local. There's no one.'

'Not quite' Brutus shook his head and pointed at a house as they passed. Fronto followed his gesture and saw the shutter on a window close hurriedly, leaving only the faint glow of firelight around the edge, but not before he saw the face of a young girl glaring at him.

'I think you're right. Trouble.'

'What do we do?'

'Nothing yet. Any move we make to ready the men is going to be seen by dozens of people and we don't know what's happening yet. We might make it up to the fort without trouble. Let's not rock the boat, so to speak.'

Brutus nodded. 'All the same...'

Turning to the centurion behind him as he walked, he hissed as quietly as he could 'Be ready. Have your men on the alert as quietly as you can. No weapons drawn as yet.'

The centurion, clearly relieved that the two officers had also noticed the eerie emptiness, nodded and turned to pass on the word.

'What the hell's happened here? We've been away, what, a month you think?'

'About that. I think Rufus might be in trouble.'

'Not just Rufus.'

'Maybe we should just get back down to the ships and head down the coast a way? At least wait until the rest of the fleet gets here?'

Fronto shook his head. 'Quite apart from the fact that I don't think they're all that safe or seaworthy now, I'm not at all convinced what'll happen if we turn around and start to walk away.'

Brutus nodded unhappily.

'Come on.'

Slowly they climbed the slope, the liquid mud running into boots and making the thoroughfare treacherous. They had almost reached the main crossroads when Brutus grabbed Fronto's arm.

'Look!'

'What?' Fronto peered up the street into the pouring rain.

'The smoke.'

'It's making it quite hard to make out the fort.'

'Fronto, it's coming *from* the fort.'

'Oh shit.'

Fronto fought the rising alarm and resisted the urge to start shouting. Smoke could mean several things, even in those amounts. It could mean a larger force of men inside than the fort was designed for, sharing outdoor fires. It could mean the place had been ransacked. But it could also mean an ongoing siege. There was no way to tell without seeing it close to hand.

'We've got to pick up the pace.'

'You want to *go* there?' Brutus said incredulously.

'We've got to. Rufus could still be up there with his men.'

'Then let's move.'

Fronto glanced back at the centurions behind him.

'Subtlety over, lads. Swords out. Double time to the fort.'

The officers saluted, shouting out the commands to their men, who drew their gladii with an enormous, collective rasp.

The shape of the fort was starting to resolve better now in the gloom as Fronto squinted ahead. His heart skipped a beat when he realised that the smoke was rising from the front gate, and apparently outside rather than inside.

'They haven't fallen yet. We have to get inside!'

Without the need for a command, the four centuries put a little extra speed into their ascent.

'Fronto!'

The legate glanced across at Brutus' shout just in time to see the opening shutters of windows all around them, silhouettes of men formed by the warm firelight within.

'Testudo!' he bellowed, dropping back several steps and grasping Brutus by the upper arm, yanking him back down the street. The legionaries raised their shields, moving into formation better than Fronto could have hoped, given the incline and the fact that they comprised men of two different legions unused to working together. Here and there were gaps that quickly closed up, while others lifted their shields to create a roof. The four centurions joined the two legates as they disappeared inside the relative protection of the 'tortoise' formation just as the first arrows, stones and spears started to strike.

The regular drum of the heavy rain on the shields joined the falling missiles to create an almost deafening noise.

'Piss!' shouted Fronto with feeling.

'Move forward' Brutus commanded. 'We have to get to the fort.'

The testudo started to stumble up the slope under a constant hail of missiles and Fronto shared a look with his fellow legate. They were both horribly aware of the shrieks from further back down the testudo where gaps opened due to the near impossibility of holding to formation while climbing an uneven, slippery slope.

'This is going to fall apart soon' Brutus said.

'I wouldn't worry too much about that' replied Fronto with a grim expression. 'Listen.'

Above the drumming of rain and missiles and the occasional yells of wounded men, they could now hear the roar of the natives rushing them from the side streets and the slope behind.

'Bollocks.'

Chapter 20

(Gesoriacum)

Fronto glanced left and right in the almost claustrophobic press of the testudo, his vision filled with mail-shirted torsos, dirt-streaked arms, sweat and dripping water. Brutus gave him an equally helpless look.

'We've got to take control of the street or we're done for!' Fronto shouted.

'On the bright side, they'll stop firing things at us once they're carving us up!'

'We'll have to break the testudo – get the men at the front to split off and deal with the ambushers. They can block the windows with their shields and maybe kill the bastards while they're at it.'

Brutus nodded, taking a deep breath. 'Then we can form a defensive retreat up the hill. You take the lead and I'll form the rearguard.'

The two men held one another's gaze for a moment and then Fronto returned the nod.

'At my command,' he bellowed 'the front tent party in each line will break formation. Pick a target from the men shooting at us. Get to his window, take him out and block off any further attack with your shield. Hold that window until further orders.'

Pausing, he could hear the war cries of the Morini closing on their rear and steeled himself.

'Break!'

The men of the Tenth and Seventh legions that led the advancing 'tortoise' immediately scattered at the command, eight contubernia splitting off, their shields coming up directly in front as they ran to protect them from the inevitable missiles pouring out of the open shutters of the low, squat Gaulish buildings, their swords gripped ready for action.

It was obvious to Fronto's professional eye which legion was which even when scattered. The Tenth had been a proud unit with a strong bond among its men, well-trained and constantly drilled over years by some of the best officers the republic had to offer. The Seventh was a recent hotchpotch of men from different legions as yet new to working together as a unit, lacking the focused training of a veteran legion. Almost every man in the Tenth marked a window and ran for it, a contubernium of eight men held back for a moment, ready to take the place of any man who fell on the way. The men of the Seventh, however, moved in sporadic groups, often two or three men marking the same window.

Fabius and Furius would have their work cut out over winter if they survived all this.

An archer at one of the nearest windows managed to pick off his attacker as the legionary pelted across the street, the arrow taking him in the chest and knocking him back to the slippery, muddy road, tripping the next legionary so that they rolled down the gentle, messy slope in a tangle. Before Fronto could shout the order, two of the reserve party were moving. While one ran off up the street after a different target, the other raised his shield and charged the window where the archer was busy nocking another arrow as fast as he could. The legionary, two broken shafts already protruding from his shield from his time in the testudo, angled his shield slightly to lessen the chance of the arrow punching straight through as he ran. The archer proved to be both quick and surprisingly accurate as the arrow thrummed out of the window and punched into the wood and leather. A look of wide-eyed desperation fell across his face as he desperately fumbled another arrow from the sheaf on the timber in front of him and tried to bring it up in time to loose again at the legionary.

There was clearly no time and the Roman was upon him before he could draw the string back. As the soldier swatted the bow aside with an almost contemptuous and amazingly dextrous flick of his shield, the archer screamed, his arm broken by the bronze edging strip. He floundered, dropping the bow from useless fingers, and reached down for the hilt of the sword at his side. The legionary leapt up, leaning in through the window and driving his gladius though the man's throat before twisting it and ripping it back out.

The archer fell away, gurgling and clutching his neck with his good hand, blood spraying up and around the window, while somewhere back in the dim interior lit only by the glow of the warming fire a woman screamed and threw a red clay bowl that skimmed the legionary's helmet and crashed out into the street. A quick glance inside confirmed for the soldier that no other missile wielders occupied the room and he set his shield to block the aperture, keeping only enough space free to peer over the top and keep watch on the woman.

Similar stories were playing out along both sides of the street. Here and there a legionary had fallen foul of a well-aimed arrow or slingshot, or a sword or spear thrust from a better prepared defender. It seemed, though, that the ambushers had not expected such an efficient and organised reaction, and only one Gaul had taken position at each window. With only seven men down, the small Roman force had quickly taken control of the street's edges, nullifying the dangerous crossfire. The last few stones and arrows bounced down to the ground and allowed the hiss of the rain and the roar of the pursuing Morini to fill the air once more.

Brutus had pushed his way through the centre of the mass of legionaries, most of whom were still holding to an almost testudo formation until further orders came. Arriving at the rear of the small force, he strained his ears, listening out. After a few tense heartbeats, during which the Morini began to rain blows down upon the shields of the rearmost legionaries, he finally heard Fronto's call that the missiles had been nullified.

Taking a deep breath, he gripped his sword tight in his hand and looked about.

'On my command, everyone but the rear four ranks will turn and break toward the fort, taking further orders from legate Fronto when you reach him. The rest of you will hold with me until we have room to manoeuvre.'

Fixing his thoughts arbitrarily on a number that would give Fronto plenty of time to consolidate further up the hill, Brutus counted to ten and bellowed 'Now!'

Almost two thirds of the force in the street, some two hundred men, broke from the party and began to hurtle up the incline toward the looming shape of the fort walls, their passage now safe, legionaries from Fronto's vanguard holding the windows against further assaults.

'Right!' Brutus yelled. 'On my next command, the entire force will take three quick steps back and reform as a solid shield wall three men deep that fills the street. Mark your position in advance. There cannot be any gaps!'

Even as he prepared to give the order, the legionary in front of him suddenly exploded like a ripe melon, a Morini axe finding its way over the top of the unfortunate soldier's shield and cleaving both helmet and skull in its descent. Brutus spluttered for a moment,

377

stunned and coated in blood and brain matter as he saw the axe man withdraw his weapon with the grating of bone and a slopping sound, pulling it back for another blow. There was little room in the press to react with the sword which was held down by his side and he bore no shield.

'Reform!' he bellowed, bracing himself.

As the axe reached its apex and began its extended descent toward the Roman officer, Brutus felt the press of men around him suddenly give as they shifted into position and he found himself almost manhandled back out of the way as a legionary stepped in front of him and brought his shield up high. The axe buried itself in the wood, becoming lodged only half a foot from the boss. Grimly, the legionary heaved the heavy, cumbersome shield and trapped weapon to the side a touch – enough to drive his gladius into the pit beneath the man's extended arm.

Not even waiting to see him die, the soldier pulled the blade back and closed the gap. Some of the weight on his shield fell away as the warrior expired and released his grip on the axe, though the weapon itself remained wedged.

Brutus, his heart pounding a tattoo in his chest, stepped back a few paces and took stock. The seething mass of the Morini tribe were now held back by a thin shield wall. It would do for a while, but not for long.

'On my command, the line will begin to withdraw in good order up the street toward the fort.'

He took a deep breath and raised his voice enough to double as a signal for Fronto back up the street.

'On the count of five, strike and then take two paces back and reform.'

'One... two... three... four... five!'

En masse the thirty men angled their shields and stabbed out into the mass of howling Gauls, took two steps back and locked shields again.

'Good!' Brutus bellowed. 'Now we repeat the move until we reach the fort. And I can't afford to lose the line, so any man who dies will get docked a week's pay!'

A laugh rippled through the desperate defence despite the situation, and Brutus straightened.

'Here we go... One!'

Further up the street, Fronto heard Brutus' shouted commands and sighed with relief. They might pull themselves out of this after all. Watching the approaching men who had broken from Brutus' force, he felt a lurch of worry again as he realised how few soldiers his fellow legate had left himself to bar the way to the enemy.

'You men' he addressed the legionaries guarding the windows. 'You will hold position until the rearguard reaches you and then fall in and join their line as they pull back.'

Pinching his nose, he looked down at the blade hanging from his hand. He'd not even drawn blood yet. Was this what it felt like to be a normal commander? Ordering men around with no personal involvement? Blinking, he refocused on the large force of soldiers slowing as they reached him. No time to muse on the nature of command now.

'You men come with me. I want you formed into an advancing shield wall. The bulk of the enemy may be behind us, but there could yet be Gauls between us and safety. Someone was trying to burn the gate, after all. Form up and prepare to advance in good order.'

The legionaries, a confused mix of the Seventh and Tenth, quickly formed into a column ten men wide, the front line holding their shields up ready to meet any resistance.

'Advance at the steady march.'

With the slow, determined tramp of a marching legion, the column of protected and armed legionaries began to stomp up the road toward the camp. Up here, the houses of the Morini townsfolk – rebels? – petered out with no archers in windows threatening them, and were replaced by small orchards, vegetable gardens, animal pens and patches of waste ground.

Closer they moved until finally the path curved slightly and gave them their first clear view of the fort. Fronto grinned. Rufus had really gone to work on his fortifications. An extra ditch had been dug around the fort, and the joins between it and the new settlement ramparts had been severed and cleared, the ditches extended through them.

The smoke that had appeared to be from an attempted burning of the gate proved instead to be the charring, smouldering remains of the Morini's attempt at creating a vinea – a protective mobile shelter – that they had apparently used to cover a battering ram. The ram itself was now a huge, black cinder in the centre of the smoking pile, hissing in the rain.

379

The fort had held and held well. The amount of churned mud and destruction around the outer ditch and the bodies piled within it suggested that the siege was probably in its second or even third day now.

'Come on, lads. We're clear' he shouted to the legionaries.

A few figures appeared at the top of the gate, on the parapet. A man with a transverse crest on his helmet, visible in the light of a guttering torch, turned and bellowed out commands. Fronto could not quite hear what the man had said, but the words 'Roman' and 'relief' were definitely among them.

The fort's gate began to swing open and the duty centurion and his men issued out in full battle array, looking about as relieved as Fronto had ever seen a man. The advancing force came to a halt and Fronto strode out ahead.

The centurion saluted and grinned. His face was streaked black with soot and dark circles hung under his eyes.

'It's very good to see you, sir. Can I ask what legions you bring?'

Fronto sheathed his sword and coughed quietly.

'Just four centuries of the Seventh and Tenth returned from Britannia, I'm afraid. We're not so much a relief force as fellow prisoners.'

The centurion tried to hide his disappointment, his face hardening. 'Then it's good to see you back, sir. Legate Rufus is in the headquarters building. I assume you'll want to see him straight away?'

'I will. Legate Brutus is on his way up the hill with the rearguard, followed by a sizeable force of Gauls. Get these men fell in with your own and prepared in case they decide the night can stand another attack yet.'

The centurion nodded as Fronto strode in through the gates.

* * * * *

'Legate Rufus sends these with his compliments, sir.'

Fronto turned, taking some care on the slimy timbers of the rampart walkway, to see an optio from the Ninth saluting him, two legionaries behind him carrying a bundle of pila some twenty-odd in number, bound into a sheaf with leather ties.

'Thank you. I suspect we'll need them. Looks like they'll coming back for another try any time now.'

The two soldiers struggled up the ramp to the parapet with their burden and then upended it to rest against the palisade wall, saluting as they caught their breath before turning and jogging back the way they had come. The junior officer threw out another salute and marched back to his duties.

Geminius, a hard-bitten ginger haired centurion with a flat nose and a hare-lip that showed failed stitch-marks, grinned his ugly grin along the palisade.

'Shall I distribute them, sir.'

'Go ahead.'

Fronto watched Geminius as he began the task. The centurion was one of the two from the Tenth who had disembarked with him last night, the other having fallen foul of a particularly vicious sword wound in the retreat up the street from the port, and currently waiting to greet Hades in person in the makeshift hospital. The wounded centurion's optio had only been made up in Britannia and was, as yet, not ready to take full command and so Geminius had combined the survivors of the two centuries into one outsized unit that had been given the northeast sector of wall.

'Lounging about again?'

Fronto turned at Priscus' voice, too tired to anger – he'd found that since his explosion of untamed rage in Britannia anger was slow to come and less common, or possibly he was deliberately making it so. He'd had less than an hour's sleep since leaving Britannia and the fatigue was beginning to wear him down. The rain had stopped at dawn to the great relief of the men, clearing the sky and bringing a cold wind and pale sun that totally failed to dry up any of the standing water. For the thousandth time, Fronto wished he was in Puteoli with a bunch of grapes and the timetable for the races. It seemed so far away in both distance and probability.

'Haven't you got to be annoying somewhere else, Gnaeus?'

'I am free of duties for a grand total of quarter of an hour in order to halt my steady descent into starvation.'

The prefect produced a cloth-wrapped bundle and opened it to reveal two small loaves of freshly-baked bread, half a cheese, and a small bowl of meat chunks the origin of which Fronto was not about to question. It was common knowledge that cheese was in ridiculously short supply and that meat had run out before they had even arrived.

'I hope you shaved the rat first.'

Ignoring the meat, he gratefully tore off a piece of bread and a chunk of cheese, only realising as he bit down on them how hungry he was and how much his stomach was growling.

'All quiet?' Priscus enquired lightly

'Sort of…'

The Morini had given them a period of grace after the column had reached the fort, pulling back out of range of the walls to change tactic. The new arrivals had had little time to rest, though. After an hour's meeting with Rufus, Brutus and Priscus, Fronto had managed maybe three quarters of an hour of shut-eye before the alarm sounded and the army rushed to the defences to prepare for the next onslaught. Rufus had explained unhappily that this routine had been going on now for days, the locals never giving them more than four or five hours of rest.

'They're not going to rest until they have the fort.'

Fronto shook his head. 'They know there are still several Roman legions out there, as well as the cavalry. It's a matter of time. They need to wipe out this garrison and then disappear into the woods before another army appears. I can see what they're planning; I just can't see why they've gone this far. I just can't figure what triggered it?'

Priscus swallowed his mouthful and cleared his throat. 'I talked to Rufus about it. I gather the Morini were never truly under Caesar's thumb by the end of last year. To expect them to sit by and let us use their main settlements as a campaign base was maybe a little short-sighted.' He leaned closer. 'Personally, I think they were expecting you to come back from campaign rich and loaded down with slaves. I think it was an ill-conceived and opportunistic attempt to essentially rob the victors of their spoils. It's all gone wrong for them though, as only two ships made it back to harbour. I expect they've looted your ships and are still hungry for more.'

'I can only assume that Sabinus is doing his job well, though' Fronto countered. 'I don't know how many there are in the town, but I wouldn't estimate more than six thousand. Rufus reckoned there were probably three times that number when the Ninth were first attacked. If it weren't for Sabinus and Cotta out there standing on various necks, the number besieging us here would be growing, not shrinking.'

'There *are* more. They're just hidden in the woods in a cordon, keeping us trapped here. We tried sallying out to get provisions after the first assault and it was a bloody massacre. Lost three centuries of the Ninth and they never even reached the tree line. Don't underestimate them, Marcus. They reduced the Ninth by about a third of their manpower and sealed them up in this fort in a matter of hours.'

Fronto turned to his friend. 'They're not going to keep me pinned here until Hades reaches out for me. I've a longstanding arrangement with the bookmakers at Rome and Puteoli; I've half a cellar of good quality wine; and I've a very attractive, if controlling, young lady waiting for me to make her officially betrothed.'

'Then you'd best tell *them* that' Priscus said quietly, casting aside his bread uneaten and pointing over the palisade. Fronto did not need to look. He could hear the roar.

'Geminius? Time to use those new pila.'

The centurion nodded and turned to the men lined up along the wooden wall, tapping his vine stick on his greaves impatiently.

'Pilum at the ready. Mark your man and check the soldier on each side to make sure you've not doubled up.'

Priscus and Fronto drew their blades and strode over to the wall. 'You staying for the show?' Fronto asked, reaching down and collecting the shield leaning against it, settling it into place.

'Why not? I was getting sick of riding my desk into battle. Got a spare shield?'

Fronto nodded to a stack of five slightly damaged spares and, as Priscus collected one and gripped it ready, he crossed to the wall and looked over. The slope from this corner of the fort – the northeast – descended quite gently through a large apple orchard. Beyond the ditches, the ramparts of the town sloped away to the north on his left, the settlement itself only visible beyond as a jumble of roofs interspersed with trees. The view here was excellent; despite the apple trees that obscured the slope, the fields beyond opened up and were clear and visible for at least two miles, where they met the edge of the forest.

What was of more urgent interest, however, were the scattered forms of the Morini rebels scrabbling up the slope beneath the trees.

'They look a touch desperate?' Priscus noted.

'I thought that' Fronto replied with a frown. 'They're coming up dangerously fast and not at all carefully.'

'Release' bellowed Geminius. The legionaries along the wall, each having selected an approaching Gaul, cast their pilum with an expert arm, the twenty four missiles arcing out over the palisade and descending into the trees. Fronto watched with a sense of pride in his legion as the pila punched into torsos, heads and limbs, tearing through them and inflicting horrible injuries, often killing outright. In several cases the plummeting, screaming bodies of the warriors knocked their fellows from their feet and brought them down in a jumble, coming to rest against tree trunks. Others were pinned to trees or the ground, transfixed in agony. One particularly brave warrior, affixed to a tree with a pilum through his middle, was hauling himself painfully forward off the weapon, leaving a trail of gore along its length.

'Get ready!' the centurion shouted. The legionaries who had cast the pila were already drawing their swords and stepping forward to protect the wall. Moments later, the first of the Morini reached the outer ditch, which had been rendered somewhat ineffective now by the large quantities of brush and rubbish that had been tipped into it over the past few days to grant access to the walls. Leaping forward, the warriors pushed across the unstable and difficult infill. The second, inner, ditch was now of little more use then the first. Originally filled with pointed stakes to maim those crossing it, the lowest portion was now blocked with scattered bodies that obscured the stakes and lowered the gradient enough that the warriors hardly slowed to pass it.

And suddenly battle was joined. The majority of the pila, arrows and other missiles had been used up over the first day of attacks and the scorpions had fallen silent since then. The workshops had slowed their production – their manpower being reassigned to help hold the walls – and were largely given over now to the repair of mail, helmets and shields, rather than the production of helpful missiles.

Fronto was surprised not only at the desperate speed and ferocity of the attack, but also at their numbers. Over the past half day, each push had been several hours apart, carefully planned and often executed at a new position on the walls; usually two or three places at once. Moreover, the attacking forces had clearly been rotated each time, allowing many of the tribe to rest while the freshest warriors took their turn reducing the defending garrison. This attack was different: the mass of men storming up from the orchard, combined with the shouts of alarm from all around the fort, suggested that the Morini were committing every last man to this assault.

Two warriors, each with arm rings of bronze and mail shirts denoting their high status, rushed at Fronto's position, charging up the slope of the inner ditch and continuing at speed to the bank of the rampart and the palisade. One had a long spear with a wicked blade, which he thrust up at Fronto from the flat between the rampart and the ditch, forcing the legate to raise his shield and knock the point aside; the spear clearly had enough reach to cause him trouble above the wooden palisade. The second warrior had thrown himself at the timber and managed to hook an arm over the top, his other hand bringing the long sword slowly up to a position where he could strike. Fronto, continually batting away the jabbing, probing spear, looked across quickly at Priscus, but the camp prefect was fighting his own spear-battle.

Just as the legate was trying to decide how best to deal with the two men, a third tribesman – a young man with no armour and a muddy face – leapt up from the ditch and threw a rope with a looped end with heart-stopping accuracy. The loop fell around the point of one of the wall timbers and slid downwards, tightening as it went.

He hardly had time to register the move, though, as the spear was there again, lunging for his face. Glancing across, he could see the second noble warrior almost pulled up to his chest, ready to throw himself over the defences and come at them from inside. One of Rufus' reserve legionaries appeared as if from nowhere and ran at the man, smashing his shield boss into the climbing Morini noble and sending him back over the parapet with a shout of pain and alarm.

'Good man!' Fronto barked as he finally noticed an opening in the spearman's attack. The warrior continually jabbed in a three-move sequence, after which he drew back for a moment, gaining position to begin once more. Smashing the heavy shield around and panting with the exertion, Fronto knocked the point aside; and again, and again. As the man took a single step back, the spear waggling in an ungainly manner, Fronto swung sword and shield toward one another, the shield sideways and rim-out. The two edges connected on the spear about two feet below the head and smashed through the ash shaft, neatly trimming off the dangerous part.

There was a sudden crack and a creak as one of the wall timbers began to move outwards and separate from the rest. Alarmed, Fronto ducked forward to see four burly men hauling on the rope, pulling in an attempt to destroy a section of the wall. Almost contemptuously, Fronto leaned over and cut the rope with his gladius, trying not to grin as the four men fell back into the ditch, holding the severed rope.

His attention was neatly returned to the current dangers as the broken haft of the spear smashed into the side of his helmet, ringing it like a bell.

'Right, you little turd!' Fronto snarled, his eyes blurring slightly with the impact and his ears filled with the metallic ringing. Gripping his sword, he resettled the shield and prepared to deal with the attacker.

'Look!' bellowed Priscus as he smashed a man in the face with the bronze edging of his shield and then pulled back to point with his blood-soaked gladius. Fronto followed his gesture and grinned at the sight.

Two columns of gleaming silver and crimson were emerging from the trees to the northeast, with a large force of cavalry on their flank.

'That's why they were so damn desperate!'

Reaching down, Fronto tried to stab at the man with the broken spear, but the noble had turned and was already scrambling back down the hill. All around the fort cheers were rising from the defenders, as the discordant shrieks of the carnyx – the strange Gaulish horns – called the rebels to flee the field.

'Must be Sabinus and Cotta both, looking at the size of that army!' Priscus said with a grin. Fronto squinted and peered into the distance at the column, trying to hear over the ringing in his ears.

'I can't make the banners out yet, but I'm willing to bet Caesar's with them. That looks like the Tenth in formation to me, and the show-off in red on the white horse has to be the general.' Lowering the tip of his blade, he stepped back and blew out a relieved breath. 'Looks like we're saved.'

'I only hope the old man brought several tons of beef stew with him' Priscus grumbled. 'I can't feed the three thousand men we've got here, let alone the rest of the army!'

'That's right,' grinned Fronto, 'find the gloomy side to it.'

* * * * *

The general gave Fronto a curious look as he rode through the gate and the Tenth's legate grinned back at him, blood-soaked and dirty.

'I would ask what happened to you and Brutus, but I haven't the energy now, Fronto. Come and see me at the headquarters once I'm out of my armour and have a bite to eat.'

Fronto nodded, his attention already locked on something else further down the column.

'You alright?' Priscus asked quietly next to him.

'That's the banner of the Fourteenth. I've words to have and a score to settle with a certain pair of tribunes.'

'Don't cause me extra work. I don't want to have to organise your flogging.'

'Don't worry. I won't get caught doing anything wrong.'

'Very reassuring' Priscus replied sourly. 'I'd best run. Caesar will no doubt have questions and endless requests for me and I have a few things to do first.'

Fronto half-heartedly waved him away, his eyes still on the flag of the Fourteenth. Plancus rode at the front as usual, his armour gleaming and not a spot of dirt on him. Fronto was staring in concern at the Fourteenth's tribunes, who seemed to number but four with two conspicuously empty saddles, when he felt someone slap him on the shoulder. Turning in surprise, he saw Sabinus standing next to him.

'You took your time.'

'You're welcome' the staff officer replied with a weary smile. 'I'll catch up with you properly after a debrief, but we visited Nemetocenna on our circuit and there was a courier there looking for you. I told him I'd pass the message on.'

Fronto looked down at Sabinus' outstretched hand, in which lay a small ivory scroll case. The seal of Balbus was clearly recognisable in the wax.

'Thanks. I'll have a read as soon as I get a moment's peace. I'm looking for two of Plancus' tribunes. Did you lose them in battle?'

Sabinus glanced up at the empty horses as they passed.

'Those two? Hardly! I don't think Menenius or Hortius would last ten heeartbeats in a real fight. They requested to be released of their commission in Nemetocenna so they could use the courier

387

system to head home quickly. Plancus nearly spat teeth but I overrode him. The army will be better off without them, don't you think?'

Fronto turned a slow, disbelieving gaze on Sabinus.

'You did *what*?'

'Well they're hardly a blessing to a military unit, are they? I'd say they can be less harm in Rome. So I let them go.'

'You idiot!'

Sabinus blinked at the venom in Fronto's voice, but already the legate of the Tenth was stomping away angrily. His thoughts in turmoil, Fronto strode purposefully though without true purpose until he reached the empty granary at the centre of the fort, where he slowed and leaned against the timber wall, breathing heavily.

The pair had gone.

He'd blamed Sabinus, but somewhat unfairly. From a command perspective, it really did make sense, and it certainly removed a threat to Caesar that he was not even aware of. But where did it leave Fronto? He'd been determined to deal with the pair for what they had done, and military life would probably have presented him with half a dozen opportunities. Would he have those chances in Rome? Would he even be able to find them and get to them?

Angrily, he ground his teeth and finally looked down at the message in his hands. What did Balbus have to say? Perhaps he'd finally agreed the arrangements with Faleria. Despite the reluctance he'd once felt to think of the coming betrothal, he now found himself almost eagerly awaiting news. His thoughts slid happily to Lucilia and he felt himself beginning to calm and relax. Perhaps this was for the best. He would bring the vengeance of Nemesis down on the two tribunes in good time, but there were more important things in life...

He snapped the wax seal and was about to remove the contents when he spotted Fabius and Furius striding toward him, grinning like devils.

'Tullus here worried that Neptune had dragged you to his depths when you got separated from the fleet' Fabius laughed. 'I personally doubt that even Neptune has the patience to deal with you!'

Fronto sighed and smiled weakly.

'Sorry. Caught me at a bad time.'

'So I see' Furius frowned, gesturing at the liberal coating of grime and blood across Fronto's armour.

'No. It's not that. Menenius and Hortius have left for Rome. Sabinus released them from duty.'

'They won't hide from you there. You're a native of the place, right?'

'Puteoli actually, but I know Rome well.'

'Then track them down and let us know when you're ready. I daresay we'll be due a furlough.'

Fronto smiled again, this time more genuinely.

'First thing's first, though: Caesar wants to see me.'

Furius and Fabius nodded and turned to their own business, leaving Fronto staring into space again. With a deep breath, he pushed himself away from the granary wall and began to stroll toward the headquarters, tipping the contents of the scroll case into his free hand as he walked. Trying not to get the expensive parchment too grubby with the mess from his blood-and-mud-stained hands, he gingerly unrolled it and began to read, making sure he was on a clear course across the grass to prevent embarrassing falls while not paying attention.

He was only four paces from the granary when he came to a complete halt.

Three heartbeats later his fingers punched through the delicate parchment as his hand tightened in response to his clenching jaw.

His eyes burning, he was suddenly striding with furious gait toward the command tent, damaged parchment hanging from his hand.

To Marcus Falerius Fronto

I hope this finds you in good health and in a position to hand your command to another and return to us with all possible speed. I shall not waste words with too much periphery.

The villain Clodius has had the audacity to abduct both your sister and my daughter from the streets of Rome in broad daylight. Through the unbelievable bravery and resourcefulness of Faleria, Lucilia managed to escape her imprisonment and has returned to me to deliver the news. I have to admit to having almost broken at the disappearance of my daughter, though my joy at her return was soured by the knowledge that your sister bought Lucilia's freedom with her own return to captivity.

From her description, it appears that Clodius' actions were entirely his own. Whether or not he has spoken to Caesar about the matter I cannot confirm, though I doubt it. Despite my opinion of the general's motives, I do not believe he would order harm to our womenfolk. I have attempted to speak to Clodius, but he is no longer at the house of the Julii woman. I believe him to be secure and walled up inside his veritable fortress of a house with a small army. I too have arranged a private force and would like nothing more than to reduce his residence to rubble and pick over the corpses, but I fear for the safety of Faleria if I try and so I bide my time, fretting about her safety.

I know that your first thought will be to come to Rome and help, and I pray that you do, but I also urge you to visit Caesar first and secure his aid in bringing the beast Clodius to heel. Only his master's command will likely speed our cause.

Know that I continue to watch the house and as soon as anything happens I and my men will be on the bastard's back.

Hurry home and do not tarry.

Good travels.

Quintus Lucilius Balbus.

Fronto burst into the headquarters building, the door slamming against the wall and shaking dust from the rafters, two of the cavalry guard of Aulus Ingenuus trying to restrain him.

'Caesar!'

Rounding the corner to the main room of the headquarters, the chapel next door glinting with the eagles, flags and standards of eight legions, Fronto came to a halt, the two cavalrymen still grasping his arms.

'Caesar, call these pricks off!'

The general, his eyebrow raised in surprise, waved the two guards away nonchalantly. He had removed his cloak, cuirass, helmet and sword, and slouched back gratefully in his chair wearing only his tunic and breeches, a slave unfastening his boots. Brutus and Rufus stood to one side, Cotta and Varus the other, the latter leaning against the wall and rubbing his splinted arm.

'You seem fraught, Marcus. I realise you've had a bad...'

'What have you got your weasel Clodius doing?' Fronto demanded.

'I'm sorry?' replied the general, a dangerous edge entering his voice.

'Clodius. You'll no doubt be interested to hear that Lucilia Balba escaped and told her father all about it. But not so my sister. Oh, no. Faleria's still missing. But then you know that, don't you?'

'Marcus, calm yourself and breathe. I have no idea what you're talking about.'

'Yes you do' snarled Fronto, storming across the room and slamming a blood-stained fist on the table, letting the parchment skitter across the surface to the general, who picked it up with a frown. 'I knew when I was talking to you in Britannia that you were holding something back from me; something you knew I wouldn't like. Were you ever planning to release her? I mean, surely it would have been better to just cut her throat and bury her, so that I never found out about it?'

'Fronto...'

'No, no, no, no, no. You delayed didn't you. Because you hate to waste a commodity that might be of use later. And you waited too long, because Lucilia escaped and now she's a liability rather than a prize. You cocked up, Caesar, and I heard about it. *I found out!*'

Caesar stood slowly and slid the parchment across to him.

'I will state again, Marcus, and swear to Venus Genetrix herself that I was not aware of her captivity, as your friend seems to suggest in his letter. I hold both your sister and the family of Quintus Balbus in very high esteem. Had I been aware of their abduction, I would have released them and been the one to break the news to you myself.'

Fronto was shaking his head. 'You can't hide your secrets from me. I knew you were up to something. I can read your expressions, Caesar; I've known you a long time.'

The general gestured to the others to leave, and Varus, Rufus and Brutus filed out of the room, their faces a mix of shock and embarrassment. As soon as the door clicked shut, Caesar sat once more and picked up a tablet and stylus, beginning to write furiously.

'What are you doing?'

'I'm writing you three messages. The first is to Publius Clodius Pulcher ordering him to release your sister and warning him that I will be returning to Rome very soon to deal with him. The second is an authorisation that will give you access to every resource in my army's supply and courier train between here and Massilia, so that you can use as many horses as you need to travel home at speed and have the best accommodation en route. The last is to the captain of my trireme in the port of Massilia, granting you full use. Get home, Fronto and sort this out.'

Fronto stood for a moment, wreathed in anger, concern, confusion and gratitude, hardly able to figure which way to turn.

'But you're not telling me something!'

'Marcus, there's a *lot* I'm not telling you. Some of it is for your own good, and some of it is for mine. Rest assured though that I am not party to this abhorrent act. Now stop wasting time spitting in my face and go and help your sister. I will be a week behind you at most.'

Fronto stood staring helplessly at the general for a moment, not quite sure what to believe, and finally nodded, grasping the three tablets carefully as Caesar sealed them one by one, wiped his signet ring clean and then sat back.

'What the hell was *that* about?' Brutus said quietly as Fronto emerged from the building. Varus and Rufus had moved off, but the young legate stood with his arms crossed, waiting.

'I need to get back to Rome. Make sure the Tenth is looked after; they've fought hard this autumn.'

Brutus nodded and turned as his fellow legate strode on past. 'Good luck, Marcus.'

Fronto, barely hearing him, fixed his eyes on the dirty figure of Galronus staggering wearily across the road toward the building that served as a mess hall, a gesticulating Priscus at his side. The cavalryman dragged his feet and looked like he had not slept for several days and was waving away the busy figure of the camp prefect as he walked.

'Galronus?'

The two men paused at the sound and sight of Fronto and the Remi noble broke into an exhausted smile.

'Marcus! I'm so pleased to see you.'

'No time to rest. Get back to your horse; we need to be in Rome before I even have time to shit.'

Galronus blinked at him in surprise.

'Marcus?'

'Clodius has abducted Faleria. Come on!'

Instantly, the cavalryman shook off his fatigue, his eyes flashing with the same anger present in Fronto's. The two men nodded at Priscus and ran off toward the stables of the cavalry as though freshly awoken.

Priscus stood silent for a moment. Should he go with them? There was nothing he'd prefer, and certainly Marcus would welcome his help. But the camp prefect's place was here, particularly at this stage of the year's campaigning.

Scratching his head irritably, he caught a legionary running past and hauled him to a stop.

'Sir?' the legionary saluted in a panic.

'I have a job for you lad. I want you to find someone for me.'

Chapter 21

(Vienna, on the Rhodanus, 160 miles north of Massilia)

Galronus dropped heavily from his horse and almost staggered with fatigue as he led the beast toward the stable area of the Sweeping Eagle, their first stop within the traditional borders of the republic. Fronto slid down with equal lack of grace from his own mount and grasped the reins to lead the beast on. He'd have felt more confident riding Bucephalus back home, but had decided to leave the magnificent black in the care of Varus, opting for the speed to be gained from a constant change of courier horses on the road south.

'I'm for an unhealthy quantity of wine tonight' Fronto said without humour. 'I need a proper sleep for a change.'

Galronus inclined his head in agreement. 'Once we stow the gear. A good hot meal is high on my agenda too.'

Nodding, Fronto strode toward the door into the courtyard and stable area. The groom appeared as if from nowhere as the two men neared the entrance and reached up to take the reins, leading the beasts into their stalls for the night.

Leaving the young man to his work, the two officers hoisted their bags over their shoulders. It had only occurred to Fronto almost a hundred miles from Gesoriacum that he'd not arranged the transport of the rest of his gear, but figured that half of it would stay with the Tenth as usual and that Priscus would find a way to ship the more immediate and personal kit to Puteoli for him. For what he had in mind at the moment, all he required was clothes, a horse, a sword and a bad temper.

The interior of the Eagle was heaving with drinkers, diners and gamers intent on their dice and various miscellaneous competitions. Fronto looked around for the familiar figure of the proprietor, Lucius Silvanus, but could not spot the large ex-soldier among the press. Every table appeared to be full, but he felt fairly sure that someone would respectfully make room for them to sit and eat once they were ready.

Gesturing to Galronus, he shoved his way through the throng to the bar, surprised at the lack of shown deference until he remembered that he was wearing only his stained, battle-scarred tunic, breeches and military cloak, a utilitarian gladius at his side.

Without digging out his better kit, he looked not unlike any other off-duty soldier.

The bar was being tended by a bulky Gaul with hands like hams and arm-hair like a bear, and by a young woman who would have been stunningly attractive were it not for the pox scars and the missing ear that was just visible occasionally as her hair moved.

'Innkeep?'

The huge Gaul handed a local his change and shoved a clay cup toward him before sidling down the bar. Fronto thought he caught a hint of recognition in the man's expression as he suddenly moved from the sullen keeper of drinks to the helpful attendant of the bar.

'Good evenin' officers. What can 'us do fer yer?'

'Where is Silvanus?' Fronto enquired quietly. 'He normally looks after visiting officers himself.'

'The master's gone to Nemausus to secure a supply of oil an' garum from 'ispania, sirs. Can us 'elp yer?'

Fronto shrugged. 'About time Silvanus got some good food in here. The beer and 'wine' I'm getting used to, but I was getting sick of roast pig.'

The Gaul grinned. 'Then y'ain't gonna like the menu tonight, sir!'

Fronto sighed and pointed at one of the amphorae stacked against the wall behind the bar, still sealed and with the seal facing him.

'We need a good, quiet room for the night, two full dinners... no, make it three but split it between two plates, and that amphora of Sicilian wine that I don't even care how you got.'

The Gaul laughed. 'Find yerself a table, then, master officer, an' us'll get things ready fer yer. Citizen officers can settle up in the morn. 'Tis house rule.'

Fronto smiled gratefully.

'If it's all the same, we'll go to the room first and dump our kit, wash, and then be back down in about half an hour for food?'

'If'n yer please, sir.'

'And don't sell that wine to anyone else while I'm gone!'

Again the Gaul gave a deep belly laugh and collected a good iron key of Roman design from the counter at the rear of the bar, tossing it over to Fronto.

'Top o' the stairs, end o' the corridor on the right. It's over the stables, so's the noise is low.'

'And smells of horse shit. Still an improvement over this lot' Fronto grinned wearily. 'Cheers. See you in half an hour or so.'

Galronus frowned as they turned and pushed back across the room to the stairs that led up to the second floor where the rooms were.

'I don't think I like Sicilian wine. Too heavy.'

Fronto shook his head in mock disbelief. 'For a man whose people brew something that tastes like foot fungus and old boots I'm not sure your viniculture opinion holds much weight. Silvanus has cocked up. There's no way that amphora should be on public display. He'd normally keep something like that hidden in the cellars in case major dignitaries happen to stop by.'

'Maybe while he's away your big barman friend is running the place?'

They reached the foot of the wooden staircase and Fronto cast a glance across the heaving main room of the inn.

'If that's the case, Silvanus has chosen well. The place is packed. He must be raking it in!'

With tired, straining leg muscles, the two officers climbed the stairs and turned down the corridor, strolling along the length of it until they reached the far end, where a window stood, the shutters open. Fronto glanced out interestedly across the roof of the annexe that had been only half-constructed the last time they were here and which lay just below the window. To the right was the courtyard, the stables below them.

'It certainly is quieter along here' Fronto muttered. Galronus simply nodded and peered out of the window himself as Fronto reached up with the key and unlocked the door. Shouldering his kit bag again, the legate pushed open the portal and strode into the room.

Galronus turned back to the doorway and looked into the room, lit by the early evening sunlight shining in through the window.

His hand went to his sword immediately as his eyes focused on the thing between them and the window.

The body of Lucius Silvanus, former cornicen in the Eighth Legion, veteran officer and proprietor of the Sweeping Eagle, swung back and forth, rhythmically blotting out the sunlight, his face contorted, swollen purple tongue extended and neck at an uncomfortable angle with the noose knotted around it. A patch of detritus marred the floorboards below the swinging corpse.

As Galronus drew his long, Gaulish cavalry blade with a rasp, he shouted the warning to Fronto, who had entered the room without looking ahead, his attention locked on trying to remove the stiff key from the door.

In the event, he was too late. As his sword came free and his mouth opened, a shadowed figure appeared from behind the door, throwing an arm round Fronto's neck and yanking him out of sight.

Fronto squawked in surprise, somewhere unseen behind the door.

Desperately, Galronus pulled back his heavy-duty blade and, squinting and making an educated guess as to the relative positions of Fronto and his assailant, slammed the blade through the hairline crack between planks in the door, smashing the boards aside as the blade punched easily through.

He was rewarded with an unearthly scream and, as he withdrew the sword with some difficulty from between the planks, he noted with great satisfaction the dark oily blood coating the blade.

'Shit!' shouted a voice from behind the door.

'The bastard's killed me!' added a second voice

'Shit!' repeated the first.

Neither was the voice of Fronto, both speaking in a southern Gallic dialect, confirming to Galronus that at least two murderers were waiting for them.

Suddenly, Fronto staggered out into view again, one hand clutching his throat where he'd been momentarily strangled, the other reaching down for his sword as he backed toward the swinging body.

Without waiting for Fronto, Galronus stepped into the room, turning to face the men behind the door. One was clutching his belly, blood pouring between his fingers and down to the floor just as it drained from his face. In his other hand, he held a hunting and skinning knife, clean-bladed and unused. A few feet from him a second man held a similar blade, but was edging away toward the window.

'No you don't.' The Remi officer turned with the man's movement and sprang like a wildcat, his sword coming back up as he leapt. The would-be assassin made a momentary decision between fleeing for the window and trying to protect himself from this madman. Figuring that he would never reach the window in time, he turned and lashed out with the knife as the cavalryman came down on him, sword descending in time with his body.

Fronto watched in horrified fascination as the world seemed to slow to a crawl.

Galronus hit the assassin feet first, both heels slamming into the man's knee and smashing his leg beyond hope. At the same time, his blade came down and even as the knee turned backward the heavy blade bit deep into the man's torso at the angle between neck and shoulder, cleaving a foot deep into him.

Simultaneously, the hopelessly outclassed assassin had struck with the knife. Galronus' arm had come up protectively to save his face from the blow at the last moment and the knife hammered home into his forearm, neatly slipping between the two bones and driving straight through his arm up to the hilt.

The would-be-murderer was dead before his body settled to the ground. Fronto stared as Galronus stood, gritting his teeth and, wincing, drew the blade out of his arm with a splash of blood.

'I could have done with questioning him.'

'What about the other one' Galronus asked casually, but realised as he looked across the room that the man had driven his heavy knife deep into his own heart to end the torment of the belly wound that would take perhaps a day to kill him.

'Now we have no idea why all this.'

Galronus shrugged. 'It occurs to me that your friend the barman will know; he must have been in on this. Perhaps we should ask him?'

'I think not' Fronto said quietly, sheathing his sword and hoisting his kit back onto his shoulder. 'If *he* knows, probably half the people down there do. No one looks too concerned with Silvanus' absence, and he's only been dangling there less than a day. *Half* a day, I'd say. Unless we want to find ourselves facing off against every lowlife in Vienna, we'd best make a sharp exit and get somewhere way south of town for the night.'

As they peered down the corridor and confirmed no one was watching, Fronto locked the door once more and started to climb out of the window. Galronus cleaned his blade on a piece of the assassin's tunic he'd ripped off, and sheathed it.

'You think it's your tribune friends?'

'I can't really think who else it could be. This was deliberately targeted at us; not just aimed for the first Roman officer that came past. They even put an amphora of expensive Sicilian in plain view just to occupy my thoughts and stop me noticing things out of place or wondering about Silvanus. Of course he wouldn't have gone to Nemausus for stuff – he'd have *sent* someone. Come on.'

Fronto padded across the roof of the extension and slid down, dropping to the courtyard.

Galronus followed suit with more dexterity, landing easily as Fronto winced in pain and rubbed his knee.

'You've got to sort that out' Galronus scolded him.

'The first chance I get to give it a month's rest I'll do just that. Now let's get the horses and get out of Vienna before we discover that Menenius and Hortius bought every thug in the place.'

* * * * *

Fronto and Galronus slowed their tired mounts and reined in outside Poseidon's Palace, the most grandiosely named inn in Massilia. The large building with two wings of accommodation had done its Greek owner extremely well since Caesar's push into Gaul, being selected as the official stopping point for all officers and couriers passing through the independent city and boarding or disembarking ships. In fact, the Roman traffic through the inn, for which the owner was paid a healthy monthly stipend, had all but driven the free trade from its doors as few locals or merchants could afford to rent a room. Even the décor and the food and drink were now thoroughly catered to Roman tastes.

The groom, a young man with one leg slightly longer than the other, lurched from the wide gateway of the stables and greeted the two officers pleasantly, his accent that strange mix only found in the former Greek trading colonies of the west.

The two men nodded and handed their reins over to the servant, patting the steaming flanks of the beasts that had carried them the last leg from Glanum and wishing them well as they ended the horseback segment of their journey. It had been ten days of tense desperation, saddle-sores, constantly changing mounts and rough cots in the small, stockaded way-stations set up by Cita to provide the enormous supply system that flowed from Narbonensis, Massilia and Cisalpine Gaul.

Ten days of trepidation.

The incident at Vienna had pushed them to a new turn of speed, having gained them a night with no rest and therefore a further thirty miles under their belts. Neither man had spoken of the attack after they had left the Vienna area almost three days earlier, hurrying through the night to be free from the danger of assassins. That the two tribunes were prepared to take the risks and spend the money paying off local bandits and even murdering settled veterans spoke eloquently of the lengths to which the men were willing to go in removing Fronto from the picture.

Though neither man voiced it, both Fronto and Galronus had come quickly to the conclusion that the tribunes would have been successful had they themselves sprung the trap, and the fact that they did not and instead entrusted it to the unknown quantity of paid killers suggested that they were otherwise engaged in a task that was too important to delay even for that. Such a task was worrisome indeed.

His bag of personal kit slung over his shoulder, Fronto strode into the 'Palace', Galronus at his heel. The main chamber of the inn, mostly given over to tables for eating, with a fire at the more open end that warmed the room, was thriving, though here and there were spaces still available at tables.

Their eyes strayed across the occupants – more than ninety per cent of whom were Roman, and rested on the long bar with the innkeeper and his slave working like mad to tend to the custom. They had a more urgent appointment than that, though. Feeling their muscles loosen at the warm and cosy atmosphere, the two officers strode across to the table close to the fire which was stacked with tablets, sheaves of writing wood, styluses and the endless accoutrements of the bureaucracy. The man sitting on the only chair at the desk was the mirror of every mid-level administrator across the republic: well-dressed above his station and full of self-importance. And yet who could deny him deference, given the vital role he played in the support of Caesar's campaign?

Flavius Fimbria was the man with a stranglehold on all travel and goods in or out of Massilia, a man with a plethora of slaves and functionaries, to whom every Roman who passed through the city must speak if he wished to arrange sea passage, horses, a cart, or supplies.

'Master Fimbria' Fronto greeted him formally, approaching the table.

'Can I help you, soldier?'

Fronto felt Galronus stiffen at his side, bridling at the lack of deference to officers of their rank. The legate himself knew that despite their lofty positions they resembled nothing more than a travel-worn legionary or junior officer and a somewhat Romanised Gaul.

'Yes. Please arrange for the *Glory of Venus* to make ready to sail in the morning at the first available opportunity, and arrange suitable space for two officers and their personal kit only. The destination is Ostia and the ship is to make the fastest sailing possible.'

Fimbria narrowed his eyes. 'You have the authorisation for this?'

Fronto dropped one of Caesar's tablets to the table in front of him, the others having been well used, but this still fresh and sealed. The administrator examined the seal for a moment, seeming surprised to find it genuine, and then snapped it open and perused the contents.

'Very well, legate Fronto – I presume – I will send to the ship and have your arrangements made. The first sailing will be just past dawn. Could you arrange to be at the seventh jetty in the port by sun-up?'

The legate nodded and reached for the tablet just as Fimbria swept it away. 'I'm afraid I shall need to retain this to pass on to trierarch Sura to confirm your authorisation. You understand?'

Fronto shrugged. 'Just have it ready.'

Turning their back on the administrator they strode across the room to the bar and caught the attention of the innkeeper.

'Officers?'

'We need two rooms for the night, an evening meal and a morning call an hour before dawn.'

'You have the relevant documents?' The man held out a hand expectantly and Fronto handed over the well-worn travel authorisation sealed by Caesar. Every man wishing to partake of the inn's hospitality would need a stamped pass or would be required to pay upfront. The innkeeper peered at the tablet, an eyebrow raised at the seal of the proconsul of Illyricum and Cisalpine Gaul. He nodded as he snapped it shut and passed it back. 'Please find yourself a table and I will have food and drink brought to you.'

Fronto rubbed his eyes wearily and gestured to the bag on his shoulder questioningly.

'Leave your kit here and I'll have one of the boys take it up to a room for you, sir.'

Galronus glanced uncertainly at Fronto, remembering the troubles at Vienna, but Fronto simply dumped the bag gratefully on the bar and turned to stride away.

'Will they be safe?' the Remi officer asked quietly.

'Here? Nowhere safer. The place is built on Roman coins and too high-profile for anyone to buy trouble in. Come on.' They made their way to one of the tables near the open space and therefore within the reach of the fire's welcoming warm glow. The tables on the edge here were busy; legionaries and lesser officers, functionaries of Cita's supply system, occupying each bench and seat.

'Any room for two tired officers?' Fronto asked pointedly, in response to which a number of soldiers shuffled away, shifting their drinks, platters, dice and small piles of cash, leaving two stools at the end of a table, opposite one another.

The two men sank gratefully to the seats nodding their thanks to the men who had moved up to make room.

'Our pleasure, sir. You just come from the north, sir?'

Fronto pinched the bridge of his nose. He could really do without chatting to the passing soldiery at this juncture, but politeness cost nothing and the man was simply being hospitable.

'Hot-foot as it were from the north coast and bound for Rome, soldier. And you?'

'Escort for a wagon full of furnishings and other goods for the legate of the Fourteenth legion, sir. To ease the hardship of winter quarters, I suspect.' The man smiled a knowing smile and Fronto could not help but chuckle. He could only imagine what was in the wagon bound for Plancus' tent.

'Everything, sir' the soldier said as if reading his thoughts. 'Right down to a marble statue of a dancing satyr and some naked girls. Pride of place, that one.'

Fronto laughed again. 'Do me a favour and try and damage some of it in your travels.'

'More than my life's worth, sir. I'd get my arse kicked right back to Ostia, and with nailed boots, too.'

This time even the recently-dour Galronus smiled. 'Good luck on the roads north' the Belgic officer said, stretching. 'The Rhodanus valley's safe enough, but the passage across the lands from Bibracte to Nemetocenna will be difficult if the weather turns, and it will do so any day now.'

The soldier nodded gratefully. 'Thanks, sir. We're pretty well organised with goods and escort, so we should be fine. There's nothing happening on the trail upriver then, sir?'

'No' Fronto frowned. 'Why?'

'Well there's not been many come back down from the campaign yet, sir, and the ones as passed through yesterday seemed concerned and in a bit of a hurry. Wouldn't even exchange words with me.'

Fronto looked up sharply. 'Two tribunes by any chance?'

'Aye, sir. Proper posh they were, sir. Wouldn't talk to anyone but Fimbria over there.'

Galronus had turned to the man now.

'They were here yesterday?'

'Yes sir. They came in after sunset in a real hurry. Arranged passage on a fast courier ship. I expect they sailed with her this morning, sir.'

Fronto and Galronus exchanged a look.

'Thanks.' Fronto pushed a couple of denarii over the table to the soldier. 'Have a few drinks on us.'

The legionary grinned. 'Cheers, sir' he muttered, touching his forehead in salute and scurrying off to the bar to cash in his new coins for wine.

'So,' Fronto leaned across the table into an almost conspiratorial huddle, 'if we needed any confirmation, there it is. Menenius and Hortius are only a day ahead of us and bound for Rome. Mark my words, Galronus, I'm *going* to find them and deal with them.'

The Remi officer leaned across the table toward him. 'And I will help you when the time is right, but do not let your thirst for revenge cloud your judgement. The tribunes must pay for what they did to Tetricus and the others, but our first concern has to be Faleria and Clodius.'

Fronto nodded as that cold weight settled in his stomach again. He'd done everything possible on their long journey to keep his mind off the peril his sister was in and Galronus had pointedly avoided the subject, though whether to protect Fronto or for his own comfort was unclear. Suddenly it now felt as though a taboo had been lifted; a taboo that had covered them for eleven days.

'You realise there's every possibility that she's not... that she...'

'She is alive' Galronus said flatly. 'Do not allow yourself to think otherwise. Whether Clodius is working on Caesar's orders or not, the man would not dare touch Faleria.'

'He dragged her off the street and imprisoned her.'

'But without harm as far as we know. Caesar would not harm her; you know that, and so Clodius would not dare. *I*, however, will harm *him* when I find him.'

Fronto nodded emphatically.

'We need to work out a plan of action; before we get to Rome.'

'Go to Clodius' house. Kill everyone in the way' Galronus suggested without a hint of humour.

'Impossible and you know it. We would be slaughtered. Clodius has a small army at his command and a well defended house. The man is paranoid and for good reason. And if we did somehow get inside, he could simply kill her and dispose of the body before we got close.'

'Then how can we deal with him?'

'The same way he deals with everyone else' Fronto sighed. 'With fear. The only thing that will make Clodius defer and offer terms is when he knows he's outclassed, outmanoeuvred and there's no other option. He has a small army; we have to have a larger one.'

'You want to hire an army? In Rome? With the legal restrictions on openly bearing arms?'

'Screw the restrictions' Fronto snapped. 'We're dealing with a cold criminal and we have to do whatever is required. Balbus has a force already assembled and he's just waiting on my word to go for the man's throat.'

'He will not have enough.'

'No. But it's a start. When we get to Rome, you make your way to Balbus' house and let him know what's happening. Get him to ready his men for a fight. I'll go to my townhouse. It's still being repaired, but mother has a small fortune hidden in three different places under the floor. I know where they are, so I'll go collect the funds and then hire us as many gladiators, thugs and retired veterans as I can find – everyone in the city who knows what end of a sword to hold. Then I'll send them all to Balbus' place and follow on. As soon as we have a big enough force we'll go down to see Clodius and demand the release of Faleria or start to demolish his house with him still in it.'

Galronus nodded. Criminals and bullies were the same in every culture. It only took someone with a bigger stick to force them to back down.

'You will have to describe the directions to Balbus' house.'

'I've never been there myself, but I know where it is. He's described it before. Alright, from the Circus Maximus, you need to skirt the Palatine hill...'

* * * * *

The harbour of Ostia slid implacably toward them and never had Fronto been more desperate to set foot on land. The seasickness had taken a backseat during the journey, the worry over his sister's captivity continuing to gnaw at him, and worsening with every league they sailed.

'When Faleria and I are married,' Galronus said suddenly, in an attempt to smash through the oppressive cloud that covered them both, 'I would like you to be the auspex.'

Fronto blinked, his gloomy, negative reverie shattered by the sudden, bizarre request.

'What?' he said almost incredulously, turning from the rail and its view of the approaching dock.

'When Faleria and I...'

'I didn't mishear you then? You're really set on this?' For some reason, the campaign season had almost driven his friend's decision from Fronto's mind, and now it seemed peculiar to think on it, especially given his sister's predicament. And yet, he had to admit that, upon receiving the news of her captivity, he had not turned to his old friend Priscus, but had immediately reached for Galronus. Not because the ties that bound them were any stronger than with Priscus, but because at a gut level, Fronto knew how much Faleria meant to the Remi noble.'

'Of course.'

'And you're *that* sure she's interested in you?'

'She is.'

Fronto felt a smile crack through his tense shell. 'You're certainly not lacking in confidence, my friend. How do you know about the auspex? How do you know about Roman marriage at all?'

'I've made some enquiries over the summer. It sounds as though your ceremonies are not too dissimilar to ours, though they seem to involve a lot more unnecessary complications and a longer period of betrothal.'

Fronto leaned against the rail and folded his arms. 'Do I really strike you as the right man to read the auspices from the guts of a pig? Even my bandy-legged fishwife Goddess seems to have abandoned me.'

'You know as well as I, Marcus, that no one is expected to actually divine anything. It's a show. I may have trouble rounding up many of the witnesses, though. Faleria may have to choose all ten.'

Fronto shook his head and smiled. 'Witnesses are the least of your worries.'

'Then you will do it?'

'If you can get Faleria to agree to take you on, I'll do it, yes.'

'Good. And now to more immediate matters: look over there.'

Fronto frowned and followed his friend's pointing finger. Across the harbour, a sleek, low ship was making for a dock at the far side of the port.

'It's a liburna, privately owned. Nice looking thing. My best friend's uncle had one when I was a kid; used it for trade runs between Puteoli and Sardinia. Fast and light, but only useful for small cargo, 'cause the hold's not very big.'

'It was in dock in Massilia when we set off.'

Fronto shrugged. 'We've travelled fast for a trireme, but a liburna can travel faster. He probably set off after loading. We came empty.'

But Galronus' eyes remained locked on the ship. 'I don't like it.'

'I personally don't care. It's the ship with those two slimy bastards on that I'm bothered about, and that'll have docked yesterday.'

Their attention was pulled back to their destination as one of the sailors bellowed a call and men began to run around on the deck, the rowers giving a last pull and then raising their oars as the vessel coasted in toward the dock. Workers in the port ran up and down the dockside, preparing to take ropes and help the boarding ramp settle into place. Boys scurried into position to do some hopeful begging from the passengers on this clearly important ship.

Fronto gripped the rail hard and waited for the bump, steadying himself. The ship settled to the dock with very little disturbance and the two officers waited for the ramp to be run out as two of the sailors hurried up to them carrying their bags.

'Thanks. We'll take them now.'

Throwing the bags over their shoulders, they hurried down the ramp and onto the dockside. As the begging children crowded toward them, Fronto pulled half a dozen small, cheap coins from his purse and cast them to one side, drawing the gaggle of shouting boys and girls out of their path.

'Come on. Let's go find the courier station.'

Galronus nodded as he moved on through the crowded port. They had decided on the speed afforded by a horse rather than taking Caesar's trireme up the Tiber to the city. Given the river's current and the traffic upon it, they would gain at least half an hour by horse.

Polyneikes took a deep breath and concentrated on the wooden crutch beneath his right arm that clattered along the stones of the port in time with his limp.

It was one of the hardest things to do, he reflected as he peered between the heads of the crowd: to fake such an injury. Many people could affect a limp and heave themselves along on a crutch, but it was too easy to do badly. Most people ended up limping with the wrong leg to the crutch, which was a rookie mistake.

Five years of training with some of the most dangerous men in Athens had taught him tricks that most people in the business would not even know could be done. The single raised shoulder was easy enough, particularly with the crutch, but to temporarily disfigure the neck and pull in one's head so that one appeared to be a malformed half-man was a real talent, and Polyneikes would always be grateful to Crino for his expensive lessons – may the bastard rot in the pits of Hades for all eternity.

The only thing that still rankled about affecting such a disguise was the smell. To pull off the guise of a twisted beggar one really had to spend an hour or two carefully urinating oneself and saturating the clothes and even defecating and making sure the smell clung.

Still, for twenty gold aurei and the chance of many future jobs, Polyneikes was willing to live with a little shit.

His reputation was unmatched in Ostia, and even in Rome his services were sought and commanded an above-average fee. But a reputation was never too strong that it was not worth strengthening with ties to wealthy, high class patrons.

His hand reached down the wooden crutch and his fingers caressed the tip of the blade attached to it with easily breakable twine.

He'd been lucky, and he knew it. The patrons had been uncertain as to whether the target would even pass this way. It seemed there was some doubt as to whether they would reach Italia at all. Not that it would have mattered really. He'd been paid up front and if his target had not shown in a week, he would have lost the chance to improve his reputation, but he would still be living like a senator for a week or two.

But then the ship had arrived. The *Glory of Venus*; Caesar's own ship. It was hard to miss the arrival in port of such a vessel, given the fact that the entire place quickly rearranged itself to allow a clear passage to dock. And even if the ship had carried half a city's population, he'd still have been able to identify the pair of them from the description: 'A dishevelled veteran soldier, probably not dressed as an officer, but with the look of a predator, and a tall, moustachioed Gaul in the kit of an auxiliary cavalryman. They would have stood out in any crowd.

The two men were making their way toward the courier station, where two legionaries lounged by the gate, leaning casually against the wall with the look of men who expected nothing more than to watch the world go by until their shift ended.

As was always the case with crowds in places like Ostia, the currents pulled three ways. Those with legitimate business went about it heedless of the two officers, often getting in their way until asked to move. Those whose business was illegal or underhand in some way scurried away from them, avoiding any possible confrontation with authority. And those whose business it was to accost strangers pushed through the crowd to get to them: traders; whores; beggars...

Polyneikes angled his approach. His very realistic limited mobility slowed any action and made planning that much more essential. Carefully, he swung and weaved, giving the impression of a man trying to keep on his feet despite his terrible afflictions, while in fact threading a speedy and neat passage between the crowds toward the two figures with the bags slung over their shoulders. He could easily earn an extra eight aurei if he could dispatch the big Gaul too, but Polyneikes was no fool. Twenty was plenty, as he was wont to say, and escaping the scene after one perfect, deadly strike was easy enough to a well-trained man. Whereas giving in to greed and attempting a second blow was tempting the Fates, and he was not about to push Atropos into snipping his thread this early in his career.

As he estimated the distance at ten paces and mentally added a count of six for the difficulty of movement, Polyneikes the assassin began to count under his breath.

Twelve.

The Roman had turned to speak to the Gaul. The pair were completely oblivious, It was almost too easy. His fingers closed on the pommel of the knife and gave a gentle tug.

The blade, a wicked thing of Parthian origin that had been sharpened to the point where it could almost cut through sound, came loose from the twine easily, the twin severed loops falling unnoticed to the ground beneath the 'beggar'. His tattered, filthy wool cloak swung to and fro, concealing the glinting iron blade.

Six.

His hand twisted, the thumb releasing the tie carefully crafted to the inside of the cloak to keep it in position and covering the knife. The cloak billowed slightly as the knife began to rise.

'...at the Porta Trigemina' the Roman was saying. 'Then I'll make my way...'

Polyneikes' grip changed on the hilt, raising it for the blow.

'Not so fast, sonny.'

The Greek assassin's world collapsed around him as a hand clamped round his mouth and dragged him back through the crowd, a blade simultaneously sliding up between his ribs and plunging deep into his black heart. His eyes wide, he watched the dishevelled Roman and the big Gaul disappearing off through the crowd, completely unaware.

They were completely lost from sight when the hand came away from his mouth and he hit the cobbles, no longer able to scream as Atropos of the Fates snipped the thread and his eyes glazed over. By the time his death was noticed by anyone who cared in the press of bodies and the cry went up, both his targets and his assailant were gone.

Fronto and Galronus rode past the multitudinous beggars, traders, whores and bustling city folk outside the Porta Trigemina and slowed only slightly at the gate where two of the private militia raised on the orders of Pompey nominally monitored the traffic in and out of the city. The bored looking men barely glanced up, even at the unusual sight of a trouser-wearing Gaul entering the sacred bounds of Rome.

Once inside, Fronto glanced off toward the slope of the Aventine and then refocused as his mind locked onto something that had reached his ears but had not initially registered. Frowning, he tapped Galronus on the elbow.

'Go to Balbus' place. I'll see you there soon as I can.'

The Remi noble nodded and rode on toward the Forum Boarium at a steady pace, allowing the city's populace time and room to get out of the way. Watching him go for a moment, Fronto slid from the saddle, hooked the reins over his forearm, and strode over to the stall of the merchant whose cries had caught his attention. Peering up and down the trinkets on display, his eyes fell on exactly what he'd hoped to find. Picking it up, he examined it a little closer and, satisfied, held it up to the stallholder.

'How much?'

'To a soldier? Ten denarii, to help you save the republic, eh?'

Without taking his eyes from his new acquisition, Fronto fished in his purse and passed the coins across. The trader blinked in surprise at some mug paying the extremely inflated asking price without haggling down at least a third of the way. Avarice lending speed to his hands, he quickly stashed away the coins and attended to someone else before this visiting officer decided he'd been cheated.

Fronto turned away from the stall and smiled with the first hint of real satisfaction in days. Reaching up, he undid the leather thong hanging around his neck and slid the strange bow-legged Gaulish woman from it. For a long moment, he stared at the amulet in distaste, wondering just how different the season might have been if he had not insulted his patron Goddess with the horrible little image.

Teeth bared, he turned and flung the offending article out across the crowd and into the Tiber, where it disappeared from sight and the world of men. With a deep breath of relief, he slid the new, well-crafted bronze figurine of Fortuna onto the thong and retied it around his neck.

With a sudden flash of inspiration, he returned to the stall.

'Do you have Nemesis, too?'

The trader, his greed propelling him back to his new gullible best customer, nodded and reached down to the table, collecting a small ivory image of a winged Goddess with a sword in her hand.

'Just the one. Elephant ivory and good work. Very rare.' The trader narrowed his eyes. 'Not cheap.'

Reaching into his purse, Fronto withdrew a gold aureus and dropped it onto the table. The stallholder almost frothed at the mouth. 'I don't have much change' he hazarded.

'Keep what you think's fair and donate the rest to the shrine of the Goddess next time you're passing. I'm not paying *you* over the odds; I'm paying a healthy value for the favour of Nemesis.'

As the trader almost pounced on the coin, Fronto added the new amulet to the cord round his neck, a grim smile crossing his face. *Now* he was a little more prepared. The two divine ladies that he worshipped above all and who had always looked after him now dangled together over his heart: Fortuna and Nemesis; luck and vengeance,

Gripping the reins, he hauled himself back up into the saddle and trotted off in the direction of the still-ruinous, part-repaired house of his ancestors

Chapter 22

(Rome: The Aventine Hill)

The townhouse of the noble Falerii stood heartbreakingly incomplete. It saddened Fronto to see the house in which he'd spent so much of his youth in such a condition, although it was a considerable improvement on the last time he'd seen it. Gone were the protruding charred timbers and the smoke blackened walls around the windows. New doors protected it from the street and the roof of one side was already covered with newly-fired red tiles. The other side was covered with temporary protective sheeting, while the side gate into the yard stood open, revealing a scene that looked more like a workmen's store than the place where his father had taught him the rudiments of swordplay.

The house was quiet; no work going on. Likely they had finished for the day, and the partially used stacks of bricks in the yard suggested they had downed tools and left recently. For a moment, Fronto reached for the handle of the front door, his hand going to the purse at his belt, before he realised the locks had been changed and his key would be useless. Presumably the workmen kept the keys during rebuilding, as well as the keys to the locked store where all the furnishings, decorations and other goods of the house were contained until the work was complete.

Frowning for a moment, not happy with the thought of having to break down his own door, a thought struck him and he made his way into the yard, tethering his horse to the gate and sidling between stacks of bricks and tiles, saw-benches and sacks of lime and of sand brought from Puteoli; bagged mere miles from the family's estate. The side door of the house stood as he remembered, though slightly charred and as yet unreplaced.

Some small irritated part of his soul complained silently about the slow progress of the workmen, but Faleria had been insistent on choosing the men who had the best reputation for completed work rather than the fastest.

Hurrying across the yard, he was grateful to find the small plant pot with the Ceres decoration, upending it and retrieving the key to the yard door. Taking a deep breath, unsure as to what to expect from the house's interior, he scurried across and opened the door with a click, swinging it inwards. The corridor running off left and right seemed to be in a completely charred and ruinous state. Work had not yet reached this part of the house and the floor was covered with cement-stained boards, empty sacks and small piles of materials.

Resisting the urge to see what had become of the garden, he turned left. The atrium would be the first port of call for cash-gathering; then his mother's room, and finally the oecus. Mother was old-fashioned and did not like even secretly buried money to be anywhere near the slave quarters.

Shaking his head at the stained walls and ruined frescos, the cracked and broken marble floor and the general smell of cement and damp, he moved through to the atrium. The monochrome floor mosaic of a hunting scene was a uniform grey of cement dust, though it seemed to have suffered no damage. At last, as Fronto glanced toward the front door, he realised he'd reached the current point of work, and he had to admit that the refurbishment of the hall to the front door and the walls of the atrium had put them in probably better condition than he'd ever seen them. New paint was being applied to one of the walls, a sheet hung over it to prevent the dust in the air from damaging it.

A chisel and hammer and a pile of white marble sat in a corner, where a craftsman was busy re-skirting the wall's base with loving care.

It almost seemed a shame that he was about to start creating extra work for them.

Picking up the hammer and chisel, he moved across the mosaic to where an African man had speared a great cat and bore a look of amazement that had amused Fronto when he was a child. Carefully placing the chisel so as to damage the fewest tesserae possible, he tapped the top and began to deface the mosaic. The other two caches were sensibly buried beneath a single flag, but he remembered father being adamant that he wanted a hunting mosaic in the atrium because the fat and wealthy Scaurus had one. Mother had been unwilling to admit to having funds buried of which he was unaware and had watched with a straight face as the beautiful mosaic was laid over her first storage pot.

Tap. Scrape. Tap. Scrape.

A strange noise stopped him for a moment and he paused, the chisel held above the maimed African. Silence. After a moment he decided it was the sound of cats in the street outside somewhere. They were a menace in the neighbourhood.

Tap. Scrape...

There it was again. It was not cats. Definitely not cats; and it appeared to be coming from inside the building.

Suddenly alarmed, Fronto gently lowered the hammer and chisel to the floor and rose from his crouch, glancing at the kit bag that he'd dropped nearby. Crossing lightly on the balls of his feet, he bent down and withdrew his gladius from the bag, unsheathing it with a quiet hiss and dropping the scabbard back to the floor. Feeling a little more secure, he began to pad quietly into the corridor opposite the one from which he'd entered, glancing up briefly and noting the fading light in the sky. Evening was approaching and the shadows in the house were growing menacing.

There was the noise again!

Convinced now that it was coming from his mother's room, Fronto crossed toward it tensely, sword gripped tight. His mother should still be safely at the villa in Puteoli with Posco and the slaves. This area of the house had apparently been completed, and a hanging sheet separated it from the current workspace, keeping the dust and mess from contaminating the finished work.

The walls had been painted in the modern style, updated from the old look according to Faleria's designs, mimicking open arches with gardens and landscapes beyond. The work was truly excellent, if a little slow. Faleria the elder's door had been replaced with what appeared to be ebony, inlaid with a lighter wood. Even in his tense and worried state, Fronto found himself frowning with irritation at the door, wondering just how much the damned thing had cost. More than a centurion's yearly pay probably.

The strange, muffled noise was coming from behind the near-priceless ebony as he'd suspected – and he moved across, placing a hand on the bronze ring and gently pushing the door inwards. The portal swung on the hinge without a sound; no squeak or creak, oiled and balanced perfectly. His mother's room, unfurnished, but completed and gloriously decorated, sat in deep shadow and Fronto peered into the gloom, trying to make out something other than the faint shape of the room itself.

A heap on the floor caught his attention and he felt his heart skip a beat. It was a person. A body? A corpse? No, for it moved slightly and shuddered.

A dreadful anticipation creeping across him, Fronto paced quietly across the room and crouched as he neared the heap. He felt a chest-freezing mix of joy and panic to realise that it was Faleria. Was she…?

Gingerly, he dropped the sword to the perfect marble floor and reached for his sister, gently grasping her upper arms and rolling her over. His heart lurched again as her face came into stark relief in the light from the door.

Her eye was swollen and discoloured and there was a huge black-purple patch on her left temple with dried trickles of blood down the side of her face. She had been hit hard enough to kill her, yet Faleria was made of sterner stuff.

She groaned, barely conscious, and one eye flickered, unable to open fully, the other sealed shut by the beating. Grimacing and worried, he began to gently probe around her neck and shoulders, down her arms, then felt gently across her ribs, down to her hips and then her thighs, knees and ankles and feet. Other than the wound to her temple, she appeared to be intact and unharmed, for which he was grateful. The head wound may have been intended as a killing blow anyway, of course.

If Clodius thought he was going to get away with this just by leaving her body for him to find, the scum had another thing coming. Presumably the weasel had received word that Fronto was on his way and had brought her here to unburden himself of her. There would be no direct proof of his involvement now, though Faleria could still accuse him. Undoubtedly that was why he'd had her brains smashed out – or so he thought.

Leaving her, Fronto stood slowly. There were sacks and sheets here and there in the work areas. He could make up a temporary pillow and covering for her until he could speak to Balbus and arrange for a physician. Despite his initial checks, he knew enough never to move someone in her condition until a professional had confirmed she was alright.

His thoughts running rapidly through everything he was going to do to Clodius, Fronto left the room, striding back to the atrium, where he crouched and collected two sheets and a sack of used rags. Grinding his teeth, fury vying with concern for control of his brain, Fronto rose and turned to go and make Faleria comfortable.

He froze to the spot as his eyes fell on the corridor to the peristyle whence he had originally entered the building. The diminishing light from the garden cast the shadow of a man on the wall: a man moving slowly and purposefully toward the atrium, the telltale shape of a gladius held in his hands.

Still gripping the sheets, knowing that if he dropped them, he might make too much noise, Fronto began to pad almost silently back to the room where Faleria lay, grateful for the first time all year that he'd never exchanged the soft, quiet leather boots Lucilia had bought him for a pair of loud, hobnailed ones.

Carefully, he lifted aside the hanging sheet that separated the completed part of the house and slipped past, lowering it gently so that it hardly moved with his passage. Past the sheet he could just make out the shape of a man with a sword silhouetted on the wall in the atrium, moving toward the impluvium pool at its centre.

Quickly, he moved back to his mother's room and passed within, feeling the first twinges of pain in his knee and willing it to hold as long as he needed. With a fresh speed, he danced across the room, dropping the sack next to Faleria and covering her with the sheet, so that she resembled at first glance one of the piles of rubbish the workmen had left.

Her eye opened for a moment and, though he could not be sure she would see him or that she'd comprehend, he held a finger to his lips as he crouched and collected his sword.

He'd done all he could do now, other than what he'd trained for all his life.

Gripping his sword's handle, he padded back out of the room, turned toward the atrium and strode purposefully forward, throwing the sheet dramatically aside.

Tribune Menenius stood almost ghostly in the pale light

* * * * *

There was no preamble. Fronto, surprised by the tribune's presence when expecting Clodius' thugs, had faltered for a moment and Menenius was on him instantly. In a flurry of blows, Fronto was driven back through the sheet, blocking as best he could and ducking and dancing out of the way of the flickering strikes that were coming so fast he could hardly credit it. Back in Germania Cantorix had described the tribune as 'fast as a snake', and now Fronto could see what the man had meant.

Menenius was no novice with a blade; indeed, he was quite clearly the finest swordsman Fronto had ever seen, his movements

416

lithe and economical. Wherever Fronto moved, Menenius was already there, that shining blade lancing out, swiping, sweeping, descending, rising, lunging, never even needing to block; Fronto simply did not have time to try and strike back, spending every heartbeat desperately trying to prevent himself from being skewered.

His breath was coming in gasps already, while Menenius seemed to be hardly winded, a malicious grin plastered across his face.

Strangely, despite the desperate circumstances, Fronto could not help but notice the sword in the tribune's hand. No legionary sword, this. Menenius' gladius was a perfect blade. Noric steel with straight fuller running down the centre, the hilt formed of orichalcum and embossed with the images of deities. The handle, where he could see flashes of it moving, was of perfectly carved ivory. The sword was worth more than the damned ebony door. It was not the sort of sword carried by an ordinary soldier.

Who *was* this Menenius?

Back he moved again. Drawing his opponent past the open door to the room where his sister lay, Fronto kept his eyes on the man, desperately watching that dancing blade and barely reacting in time. His knee gave a warning wobble and he almost fell as he rounded the corner, heading toward the rooms where he, Priscus and Galronus had stayed the previous year.

'You're better than I thought, Fronto.'

Menenius' voice was light, as Fronto remembered, but mature and steady, lacking all the frivolity and foppishness he'd heard before.

'You too.'

'I'll end it quickly for you if you don't make me work for it. A proper soldier's death?'

Fronto sneered. 'A proper soldier dies in battle, not submitting to a murderer. Is that the blade that killed Tetricus?'

'Why yes, Fronto. It so happens it is.'

The tribune was suddenly under his reach, slashing with the razor edge of the beautiful blade. Fronto felt it skitter across his ribs and hissed with the pain as he danced to the side and almost fell on his weakened knee.

'So that will be your end, Fronto. Your knee can't hold you when you have to move sharply left. Best keep your guard to the right, then, eh?'

In a flash – a fraction of a heartbeat – the sword was withdrawn and then stabbed again, before Fronto could even bring his own gladius down in the way. The blade bounced off a rib again, only a finger-width below the previous cut, and he involuntarily moved away, his knee buckling and almost bringing him down. Panicked, he staggered a few steps away, realising with a sinking sensation that, not only was he hopelessly outclassed, he was backing into the corner, and when that happened it was all over.

'Very good, you know?' Menenius complemented him. 'Despite your weakness, you're still the best I've faced all year.'

'Not difficult' Fronto snapped, 'given that the rest of them were sleeping or unawares.'

The tribune laughed and the sound chilled Fronto to the bone.

'You have no idea, Fronto. If you only knew the scale of my year's work.'

Fronto's mind raced. Overconfidence? Perhaps he could trick Menenius into doing something foolish? The man was clearly supremely confident. No. He recognised instantly how dangerous such an attempt could be. The tribune was certainly confident, but also totally in control. Every move he made was calculated beforehand, faster than Fronto could credit. Menenius was not a man who would fall into the trap of overreaching himself.

Which left only the unexpected.

He saw the door to his room as he passed and realised he was almost at the corner and running out of time. The tribune's blade lashed out again, this time higher, scarring a line across his bicep, though not enough to wound or incapacitate. Lurching left and wobbling on his knee, Fronto realised that Menenius was playing with him like a cat with a mouse. The bastard could have killed him ten moves ago or more. He was forcing him to put his weight on his weak knee and smiling maliciously every time that leg shook.

With a sudden flash of realisation, Fronto knew what he could do; the *only* thing he could do. But it relied on Menenius moving first.

The legate gave a pained hiss and his left leg trembled slightly.

The blow came, exactly as Fronto expected, to his right hand side and high, to score across his shoulder. He allowed it to connect. If he was seen to feint, the tribune would know and counteract instantly. The man was simply that fast. Instead he had to play into Menenius' expectations.

As the blow drew blood, Fronto staggered on his bad left knee and fell. Even in the heartbeat it took, the tribune's glorious sword came back for another blow, rising to drive down at his fallen opponent.

But Fronto was not falling. His leg screaming agony at him, he pushed on his bad knee and rose again, coming up unexpectedly at the tribune's side, out of the reach of his weapon.

Swordplay forgotten, Fronto's free fist lashed out and landed a skull-fracturing blow to the side of Menenius' head. There was an audible crack and for a moment Fronto wondered whether he'd broken the man's neck. But Menenius, stunned by the blow, simply folded up and fell to his knees, his broken jaw misshapen and hanging down at one side, blood gushing from his lips and his cheek where the Falerii signet ring had imprinted the Ursus symbol into his flesh.

The tribune's sword skittered away across the marble from numb fingers as his knees cracked to the floor.

'I'd love to take the time to go through your crimes with you one by one' Fronto grunted as he stepped in front of the murdering tribune. Raising his sword, he reversed his grip and made ready to stab downwards. 'I'm not playing your games though. Say hello to Hades for me.'

The bulk-issue military gladius, pitted with marks from battles long past, a blade that had been with Fronto for two decades, descended toward the point in Menenius' neck where his collar bones met; a killing blow.

And suddenly Fronto's world exploded in agony. He'd been so intent on the strike that he'd not heard the telltale whup... whup... whup... of the sling. The lead bullet struck his hand where he gripped the hilt and he felt three fingers break under the blow, the sword almost launched from his hand to clatter across the floor, coming to rest next to the tribune's own beautiful blade, and almost parallel.

Fronto gasped with the astounding pain and stared down at his bloody, misshapen hand.

How had he not anticipated this?

Idiot!

Tribune Hortius strolled calmly from Fronto's own room, the perfectly oiled and silent door now standing open.

'What a fool. I said we should just have jumped you together from the start, but my poor, dear friend has always had such a flair for showmanship. And a total self-belief. He simply could not conceive of a way you could beat him. I argued, but what can you do? He's a friend.'

The tribune had discarded the sling, allowing it to fall to the floor, drawing his sword as he moved into the room.

'I would humbly say that I have a less inflated ego than dear Menenius. I may not be quite the swordsman he is, but I suspect you'd find that I'm still considerably better than average. And not quite so prone to showing off.'

Fronto glanced across the floor at the swords and made to rise, his knee screaming at him in pain. Energetically and with impressive speed, Hortius danced across the room, placing a foot heavily over the fallen sword.

'Oh, no. I'm not so subject to my own ego that I have to let you re-arm first. Step away from Menenius.'

Fronto did so, slowly and quietly, backing shakily toward the side corridor and its guest rooms. The tribune gestured to his friend with his free hand. 'Are you alright? Can you stand?'

Menenius nodded, wincing at the pain in his unhinged jaw, standing slowly. Hortius scooped up the fine sword with his foot and flicked it toward his fellow tribune. Menenius caught the hilt and changed to a comfortable grip, reaching up with his free hand and touching his jaw tenderly, almost crying out in pain.

'I do believe my friend would like to carve you into slices for that.'

'Why?' Fronto said as he backed into the corner.

'Because of his jaw, you fool.'

'No… why all *this*? Why Tetricus? Why me? Why Pinarius or Pleuratus?'

'Or any of the others? Are you blind, Fronto? For Caesar. All for Caesar.'

The bottom seemed to fall out of Fronto's world.

'*Caesar?*' he croaked in shock.

'Sometimes the general doesn't even know what's good for him. You yourself have said that. He needs protecting from himself. It's only right to repay people for the good they've done you and Caesar's looked after us.'

Fronto's mind raced. If the pair were not removing those close to Caesar, what was going on? The realisation struck as his mind furnished him with the image of the general when he'd received the news about his nephew. *A problem solved.* And Pleuratus? He'd carried sensitive messages about Clodius and all but revealed that to Fronto. And he and Tetricus? Well it was quite possible to see Fronto as a problem for the general. And... 'the others'? He wondered just how many corpses the tribunes had left across Gaul, Britannia, Germania and even Rome itself.

'You made a mistake with Tetricus though. You just took a dislike to him, didn't you? And if you hadn't murdered him, I'd never have bothered looking into the matter as deeply.'

Menenius made a painful mumbling noise and Hortius leaned close to his friend, nodding.

'He's right: what difference does it make? I'm afraid the time's come, but I *will* make it quick for you, since you were once one of Caesar's closest. Perhaps we'll even lie you next to your poor sister.'

Fronto realised with a shudder that whatever else he might have done, Clodius had delivered Faleria to her house unharmed, where she had come across the tribunes lurking in wait. The bastard *tribunes* had done this to her.

The two killers stepped forward, blades coming up.

'Tsk, tsk' came a voice from the corridor behind them.

Fronto blinked and peered off into the gloom. The shape of a heavy, squat man with a blade in his hand was silhouetted against the light from the atrium. As the tribunes turned to the new arrival, a taller, thinner man stepped out next to him. Fronto's heart pounded.

Fabius and Furius?

* * * * *

Fronto watched in stunned disbelief as the two centurions stepped forward, raising their swords.

'You two are a disgrace to the army of Rome' Furius growled as he stepped to the side, flexing his arm ready for the coming fight.

'Pompous fool' Hortius snapped and leapt at them, Menenius right behind him despite the broken jaw paining him.

Fronto watched the opening flurry of moves in tense silence. Menenius was slower and more deliberate than before, his cocky speed absent as his face sent waves of pain through him with every pulse of his blood. And yet, Fronto had to admit, he was still very much a match for any ordinary swordsman. Fabius and Furius were quickly driven back to the corner. Fronto glanced around and saw his sword lying unattended. Scrabbling over to it, he picked it up in his left hand, the fingers of his right still pointing off at unpleasant angles.

He would not be able to wield the damn weapon. He had long ago learned that wielding a sword with his off-hand was more of a danger to him than to the enemy, and there was no hope of him gripping it with his right. With deep regret, he dropped the blade again. This fight would have to be up to the two veteran centurions.

The four combatants were now out of sight, back around the corner toward the atrium. His skin prickled again as he realised there was every possibility the fight might range into the room where Faleria lay under her sheet. He could ill afford to let that happen, when even a stray footfall might be the end of her, weakened as she was.

Rounding the corner, he could see the two centurions being pushed back into the atrium through the hanging sheet, which was now shredded with sword cuts. His eyes fell on the door to the right hand side and he scurried across to it.

His sister was on her knees, her head held in her hands.

'Faleria!'

She looked up sharply, her one good eye wide and blood-tinted.

'Marcus?'

His heart pounding in his chest, weak knee threatening to give way any moment, Fronto ran across the room and dropped to envelop his sister in an embrace.

'Are you alright?'

'I... headache!' she said quietly.

'Come on. It's not safe here.'

Almost as if to confirm his words, the sounds of fighting increased in volume and he could see the shadows of fighting men on the corridor wall opposite the bedchamber's door. As slowly as he dared, Fronto helped his sister to her wobbly feet and crossed the room.

'Maybe we should lock ourselves in' he mused, but decided against it. Better to find somewhere to hide her than trap themselves where the tribunes already knew to look.

'The baths. Come on.'

Almost carrying her, tears running down his face at the pain in his broken fingers and from biting his lip against it, he hurried her from the room, past the ongoing fight at the edge of the atrium and back toward the house's small bath complex. A quick glance told him that things were not going so well for his would-be saviours. Furius was already moving at a lean, his free hand clutching his side as he fought, and Fabius was limping and leaning against the wall. Worse still, the fight seemed to have spun around in the atrium and the centurions were now backing toward them, retreating into the bedchamber corridors again... and the bath complex.

Desperation beginning to hound him, Fronto grasped Faleria with his good hand, his bad one held away but the arm beneath her side for support, and guided her along the corridor to the bath house, horribly aware that there was no exit anywhere on this side of the house. If the tribunes killed their opponents, they would only have to search long enough and they would find the siblings.

He would make them work for it, though, and pay for every pace of ground. He would not let them get to Faleria if he could possibly prevent it.

The door swung open under their weight and he hurried Faleria into the changing room. The complex was completely refurbished and smelled of fresh paint and tiling cement. Positioned at the edge of the house, the only light that shone into the room was from a window that opened onto the peristyle. For a moment, Fronto wondered whether he and Faleria might fit through it, but decided against an attempt. It would be touch and go at best, and with Faleria barely conscious and his hand ruined, their chances were small.

His eyes ran to the corner of the room at the house's outer wall, where the doorway led deeper into the baths toward the hot bath and the steam room. Pausing for a heartbeat, he listened. The sounds of desperate fighting were clearly getting closer. Damn it, the centurions were being driven back toward the baths.

Urgently, he made it to the doorway and looked down the dark vestibule lit only by a small aperture high in the wall. He held Faleria up and looked her in the eye.

'Can you hear me? Do you understand me?'

'Yes. I...'

'Get in there. Go to the cold room at the far end and hide in the bath. The complex is not active, so there's no water. Don't come out until I shout you.'

'What if you don't' she asked pointedly.

'I will. Go hide.'

Faleria held his gaze for a moment and then nodded painfully and scurried off down the passageway. Fronto looked around the room, taking in his options as the fight drew ever nearer. The room was virtually empty. A mosaic covering the floor and displaying Thetis and Peleus coddling the infant Achilles was a new addition, as were the multitude of fascinating fish painted on the walls. Other than that there were three niches for clothes and a single labrum bowl on a stand at waist height. Unlike the great marble dishes of the public baths or the sizeable granite one in the steam room, this one was perhaps a foot and a half across and of carrara marble. Large enough for a single person to wash their hands in.

It would offer little protection, and as yet no water flowed into it.

What was it with these baths? Last year he and Priscus had fought two gladiators in the damned complex. Now, refurbished and looking like a different place entirely, here he was waiting for swordsmen again.

There was a thump against the bath complex door and instinctively Fronto ducked behind the labrum and tried to disappear in the shadow.

The door opened with a crash and Furius almost fell into the room, staggering backward all the way across the mosaic until his back hit the wall opposite. Hortius came limping in after him, dragging a leg down which a torrent of blood flowed. As the two met again at the wall, their blood-slicked blades clashed and rang, both fighting for their lives and both badly wounded. Fronto looked from the pair to the door and back, wondering whether he would have time to get Faleria out, when Menenius backed into the room, lurching left and right, awash with blood. Fabius staggered in after him, slashing wildly and clutching his bloodied face with his free hand.

What to do?

Slowly, Fronto stood, his weak knee giving slightly and causing him to grasp the labrum and put his weight onto it. The bowl wobbled where the cement had not quite taken properly. He steadied himself and straightened in time to see a killing blow.

Furius, backed against the wall, plunged his gladius through the tribune Hortius, straight into the sternum, pushing until the blade emerged from his back in a gout of blood. The tribune staggered, spasming, the blade falling from his twitching fingers, but Furius was in no condition to stand on his own and, all his weight thrown into the strike, the two men collapsed to the floor together, where the centurion let go of his sword and rolled away onto his back, breathing in shuddering, heavy gasps as blood trickled from a dozen wounds.

Fabius, meanwhile, was having less luck. Menenius, even with his broken jaw, was easily better than him, and was driving him back across the room, inflicting cut after small cut, gradually bleeding the strength out of the centurion.

The centurion staggered back, cursing noisily, wiping the blood from his face where it ran in torrents from a vicious cut that had ruined his left eye. Fabius was almost done, and he clearly knew it. Furius would be of little help, lying on the floor and trying to hold on to his consciousness without expiring. And Fronto would hardly be able to hold a sword in his right hand or swing it convincingly with his left.

His fingers gripped the edge of the labrum with seven good fingers and his knuckles whitened with frustration.

It took him only a moment to realise that he'd actually lifted the marble dish from the stem, jagged and cracked cement hanging from the bottom.

A slow grin spread across his face as he watched Fabius being driven across the room toward the far wall, Menenius intent on the kill. Almost silently in his soft leather shoes – thank you again, Lucilia – Fronto padded around the room's edge, gripping the labrum as best he could. Once he was directly behind the tribune, he began to step slowly and silently forward, raising the bowl to strike.

His grin fell away as Menenius stabbed the centurion in the shoulder, causing him to yell and stagger away, and then turned to face Fronto and the raised labrum bowl.

The tribune tried to say something, but his jaw would not allow it, and instead he winced, his eyes flashing angrily as he readied his sword and stepped forward to lunge at Fronto.

The legate screwed his eyes tight, waiting for the blow he could do nothing about, but all that happened was a dull thud. After another heartbeat he opened his eyes to see Menenius toppling to the floor, Fabius standing behind him, sword raised and the ash pommel coated with matted hair and blood.

'Sorry we're late' the centurion managed, grinning through the blood pouring out of his face before collapsing to his knees, breathing heavily.

Fronto stared down at the two men. The centurion was rocking slightly on his knees, reaching up to his lost eye gingerly with a blood-slicked hand. Menenius was groaning as he lay on the floor, blood running from the fresh wound on his scalp.

His own eyes narrowing, Fronto dropped painfully to a crouch, casting the bowl heavily to one side where it cracked several tesserae of Achilles' shoulder, and wrapping the fingers of his left hand around the hilt of the tribune's magnificent sword. His hand closed on the ivory grip and he lifted it slowly, feeling its reassuring weight. It really was a stunning piece of work. Much too good for a murderer, however uncommon he may be.

His mouth set in a firm, unyielding line, Fronto shuffled across to the fallen tribune and turned him over. The man had his eyes closed, groaning and probably concussed from the pommel-bashing.

'Wake up, you vicious bastard!'

Menenius opened his eyes a crack, but they refused to focus.

'Come on' Fronto urged him. 'Wake up!'

Less than gently, he gave the tribune a prod in the neck with the point of the gleaming, crimson blade, drawing a bead of blood. Menenius' eyes shot open and his vision resolved itself.

'Thank you. And fuck you.'

With every ounce of strength he could muster, Fronto drove the blade down through the tribune's sternum, hearing it crack and then groan as the widening blade forced the split bone apart. He felt the blow ease as the tip found organs to tear through and then slow again at the spine – though it punched through without too much difficulty – creating a shudder-inducing sound as it screeched on the mosaic tesserae beneath.

Menenius gasped and almost bucked like a panicked horse, pinned to the floor with his own blade.

Fronto leaned over him and watched for almost a hundred heartbeats until the light went out in the tribune's eyes and he passed away. He then reached down and found a coin from his belt purse with his good hand and carefully slid it into the man's mouth.

'What the hell did you do that for?' Fabius asked quietly. 'He doesn't deserve to pay the ferrymen.'

Fronto looked up at the centurion and grinned lopsidedly. 'Well I don't want his malevolent spirit knocking about this side of the Styx. Besides, if he passes to Elysium I'll get the chance to gut the bastard again when I get there.'

Fabius laughed, a trickle of blood issuing from his mouth as he did so.

'What in the name of Juno's knockers are you two doing here?'

The centurion sighed and sagged.

'Priscus thought you might need some looking after. He's a bit busy, but he seemed to think we might be able to help.'

'You were the ones on that liburna at Ostia?'

'Mm-hmm' the centurion confirmed.

'Well I'm damn glad you came.'

Fabius struggled to get to his feet and Fronto leaned over to help. The two men aided each other to make it upright, swaying a little as they stood. As the centurion staggered over to the heaving form of Furius, Fronto bent and drew the blade from the tribune's body with some difficulty, admiring it as it came free.

'I don't normally like to loot the dead, but... well, it's not like he needs it.'

He grinned at the look on Fabius' ruined features and hurried over to help him lift Furius. He was no medicus but he'd seen plenty of wounds in his time. Fabius would live, for all the loss of his eye, but it was touch and go whether Furius would survive his belly wound. The next day or two would tell.

'Do you suppose you can make it out to the storehouse in the yard?'

'I doubt it. Why?'

'Because there should be a jar of wine out there and I'm in sore need of a drink.'

Fabius laughed painfully.

'First, I think we need to retrieve your sister and try and send for a medicus of some kind.'

Fronto shrugged and almost fell as his knee wobbled.

'I feel I might be about ready to give this knee that month or two's rest now.'

EPILOGUE

The slave opened the door and started in surprise at the gathering outside.

'Tell your master that Marcus Falerius Fronto is here to see him.'

The slave nodded and closed the door, scurrying off inside. Fronto turned to those who had accompanied him.

'Are you sure you want to do this?' Balbus said quietly.

'Positive.'

'And you don't want me there?'

Fronto shook his head. 'I'm fine, Quintus. In fact, you should go and see Faleria and tell Galronus to break the seal on that amphora. I'm certainly going to need a drink when I get back.'

Lucilia narrowed her eyes at him and squeezed his arm. 'Do you want me to stay, Marcus?'

'No. Go with your father. I'll see you all back at the house. We've got things to arrange, and I want to be there when Galronus pops his question. I will piss myself if she says no.'

Lucilia smiled warmly. 'That's not going to happen, Marcus. Get used to the idea.'

Fronto laughed quietly and watched as Balbus and his daughter turned to head back to their house on the Cispian. At the bottom of the street, a respectable distance away, half a dozen of Balbus' newly-hired guards waited for them. No longer was the older man willing to risk the ladies on the streets of Rome without a suitable escort. Things had changed in the city, and not for the better. Still, things would be better for *them* next week when they left along the Via Appia for the winter at Puteoli; Balbus, Corvinia, young Balbina and their retinue included. After all, how else would they gather the families together for the wedding ceremony that was now looming on the horizon.

'Stop smiling like a dazed girl-child' Fabius admonished him from behind. 'You'll look like an idiot.'

Furius, at his other shoulder, laughed for a moment until the pain of his belly wound stopped him.

'I don't really need you two either.'

'I think that experience suggests otherwise, don't you?' the shorter centurion grinned.

Fronto opened his mouth to deliver a suitably cutting reply that he was not sure of yet when the door opened again and the servant stepped aside.

'Please follow me, gentlemen.'

Fronto stared across the threshold. It had been almost two weeks since the death of the tribunes and he'd done little more exerting since then than stroll down to the bakery – or the circus when Lucilia was unaware – and his knee was already beginning to feel stronger and easier. Fabius had had his various wounds tended and Fronto had to admit he was impressed with the tall centurion's stamina. He was already beginning to exercise again, retraining himself with his sword in the courtyard of the villa to fight with only one eye, which altered his perception.

Furius would pull through, the Greek medicus said. After four days of monitoring the bad wound, he'd noted no putrefaction and announced that he'd succeeded in saving the centurion. It would be months before the shorter officer could take even the lightest exercise, but the man was willing himself better and refused to stay still.

And so here they were, out in the city.

The three men stepped through the door. Despite the austerity of the exterior wall, the inside of the house was well appointed. Tasteful, yes, but displaying great wealth and power.

Caesar sat in his triclinium, an untouched platter of fruit at his side, a great map laid out on the table before him. He looked up, his face betraying no surprise at the three men's arrival.

'Fronto? What can I do for you?'

The legate of the Tenth legion walked across to face his patron and folded his arms, the two centurions falling in behind him.

'First thing's first, Caesar. Tell me about Clodius.'

'Hmm?'

'Clodius. What did you do?'

The general frowned as though trying to recall the name. 'Oh yes. Clodius. I expressed my displeasure to him.'

'And that's all?'

'I am not about to smash a useful tool, Fronto, because I accidentally nicked myself with it. Yes. I expressed my displeasure. He will not overstep his bounds so again.'

'I see.'

The general scratched his chin idly. Fronto's eyes fell on the map.

'Britannia? Trying to figure out what went wrong?'

'Hardly. I am trying to decide how best to deal with them when the sailing season opens again.'

'You're going *back*?' said Fabius from Fronto's shoulder, his voice betraying his surprise.

'Indeed I am. The task is not yet complete.'

Fronto snorted. 'I hear that the senate has voted you twenty days of thanksgiving. I suspect your task *is* complete, unless twenty days isn't enough?'

Anger flashed across Caesar's eyes. 'Have a care, Fronto. You may think you command independently, but I am still the praetor of the army and you serve me.'

'Not any more.'

Caesar's brow furrowed as he sat back in his seat and reached for the fruit.

'Do tell...'

'You go too far, Caesar. I simply cannot stand there and deny everything that Cicero accuses you of, gainsaying Labienus and his supporters when I can see plainly and with my own eyes just how right they are.'

'Fronto...'

'And the thing is that I'd be willing to support you, even then, in your insane endeavours to the very edge of the world in search of glory and prestige if it weren't for the company you insist on keeping and the little regard you show for common decency.'

'I've almost had enough of this Fronto.'

'And so have I.'

Fronto stepped forward and leaned on the table, his face only two feet from the general's.

'Your man abducted and held my sister and you have the temerity to give him a mild ticking off? And your two new pet tribunes, who you may not see around as much in the future, spend the better part of a year carving their way through some of the best men in your army, and all you can muster is mild disappointment.'

He straightened again.

'I've had enough of the politics, the uncertainty and the infighting. I've had enough of bringing war to ever more distant peoples simply to gain you a little political advantage over Pompey and Crassus. I've had enough of my family living in danger because of my allegiance to you. In short, Caesar, I hereby sever all ties to the Julii. I no longer consider you my patron and you can cross me off your client list. You can keep your campaigns and you're welcome to them. Good luck in your future endeavours.'

Without even a nod, Fronto turned his back on the general and strode from the room. He felt the presence of the two centurions at his shoulders as he strode away and, though he was aware of the general demanding he turn round, he felt lighter and freer with every step toward the street. By the time he stepped from Caesar's door into the crisp, late autumn blue of the Subura he felt happier than he had in years.

'Well I think that calls for a drink. Are you too coming to share a wine with a former colleague?'

Fabius laughed. 'I don't know about 'former' yet. We're signed away by Priscus until after Saturnalia now. And after a winter in your company I'm not convinced of our fitness for service in the legions again.'

Fronto gave a slightly manufactured laugh. While he could treat such comments lightly, Fabius must be thinking hard in truth about his fitness for command now, given the impairment of his missing eye. Such a thing had been known in centurions, but it would make everything a tiny bit more difficult.

He sighed and felt the happiness flood through him..

'Have either of you two ever sampled the delights of beautiful Puteoli?'

END

Author's Note

Conspiracy of Eagles once more takes some of the focus away from the campaign in Gaul, though only in a supplementary way. Following on from the third book, clearly some further expansion on the political situation in Rome was of value, and Fronto's private life needs to be prised open like an oyster shell in the hope of finding pearls within.

This book sees two of the most famous scenes in the whole of Caesar's Gallic Wars: the landing in Britannia with the signifer leaping into the water, depicted in so many images, and the astounding piece of engineering that was the Rhine bridge. And yet it would be all too easy to see this year as the pinnacle of Roman success and power.

Conversely, I have introduced two elements to counteract that. Firstly the assassinations that form one major thread of the tale, and which illustrate the divisions among the triumvirate at this time and the effect that must have had on the army. They also help me show the most uncaring side of Caesar's nature.

Secondly, the continuing failure of Rome to settle the troubles in the region. The rising at Gesoriacum only goes to show that Gaul was far from conquered in 55bc, a fact that will continue to build as the books move toward the great revolt.

Fronto is starting to show his age. After all, he is now around forty years of age, which is not young for a member of the Roman military. And yet as his physical strengths appear to be on the wane, his social life is becoming all the more vital and active.

Book 4 may be something of a surprise to the reader after the first three, but it is far from the end, despite the events of the epilogue. In fact it informs the entire plot of book 5, which will continue to explore Fronto's personal life particularly in respect of the powerful Caesar and Pompey, the crumbling control of Gaul and the legions' return visit to Britannia in the hands of some of Fronto's old friends.

Fronto is far from done and there is yet a place for him in the final conquest of Gaul. But he has a number of demons to best before he can be the man for that job.

I hope you enjoyed Conspiracy of Eagles.

Thank you for reading.

Simon Turney - March 2013

Full Glossary of Terms

Ad aciem: military command essentially equivalent to 'Battle stations!'.

Amphora (pl. Amphorae): A large pottery storage container, generally used for wine or olive oil.

Aquilifer: a specialised standard bearer that carried a legion's eagle standard.

Aurora: Roman Goddess of the dawn, sister of Sol and Luna.

Bacchanalia: the wild and often drunken festival of Bacchus.

Buccina: A curved horn-like musical instrument used primarily by the military for relaying signals, along with the cornu.

Capsarius: Legionary soldiers trained as combat medics, whose job was to patch men up in the field until they could reach a hospital.

Civitas: Latin name given to a certain class of civil settlement, often the capital of a tribal group or a former military base.

Cloaca Maxima: The great sewer of republican Rome that drained the forum into the Tiber.

Contubernium (pl. Contubernia): the smallest division of unit in the Roman legion, numbering eight men who shared a tent.

Cornu: A G-shaped horn-like musical instrument used primarily by the military for relaying signals, along with the buccina. A trumpeter was called a cornicen.

Corona: Lit: 'Crowns'. Awards given to military officers. The Corona Muralis and Castrensis were awards for storming enemy walls, while the Aurea was for an outstanding single combat.

Curia: the meeting place of the senate in the forum of Rome.

Cursus Honorum: The ladder of political and military positions a noble Roman is expected to ascend.

Decurion: 1) The civil council of a Roman town. 2) Lesser cavalry officer, serving under a cavalry prefect, with command of thirty two men.

Dolabra: entrenching tool, carried by a legionary, which served as a shovel, pick and axe combined.

Duplicarius: A soldier on double the basic pay.

Equestrian: The often wealthier, though less noble mercantile class, known as knights.

Foederati: non-Roman states who held treaties with Rome and gained some rights under Roman law.

Gaesatus: a spearman, usually a mercenary of Gallic origin.

Gladius: the Roman army's standard short, stabbing sword, originally based on a Spanish sword design.

Groma: the chief surveying instrument of a Roman military engineer, used for marking out straight lines and calculating angles.

Haruspex (pl. Haruspices): A religious official who confirms the will of the gods through signs and by inspecting the entrails of animals.

Immunes: legionary soldiers who possessed specialist skills and were consequently excused the more onerous duties.

Kalends: the first day of the Roman month, based on the new moon with the 'nones' being the half moon around the 5th-7th of the month and the 'ides' being the full moon around the 13th-15th.

Labrum: Large dish on a pedestal filled with fresh water in the hot room of a bath house.

Laconicum: the steam room or sauna in a Roman bath house.

Laqueus: a garrotte usually used by gladiators to restrain an opponent's arm, but also occasionally used to cause death by strangulation.

Legatus: Commander of a Roman legion

Lilia (Lit. 'Lilies'): defensive pits three feet deep with a sharpened stake at the bottom, disguised with undergrowth, to hamper attackers.

Mansio and **mutatio**: stopping places on the Roman road network for officials, military staff and couriers to stay or exchange horses if necessary.

Mare Nostrum: Latin name for the Mediterranean Sea (literally 'Our Sea')

Mars Gravidus: an aspect of the Roman war god, 'he who precedes the army in battle', was the God prayed to when an army went to war.

Miles: the Roman name for a soldier, from which we derive the words military and militia among others.

Octodurus: now Martigny in Switzerland, at the Northern end of the Great Saint Bernard Pass.

Optio: A legionary centurion's second in command.

Pilum (p: Pila) : the army's standard javelin, with a wooden stock and a long, heavy lead point.

Pilus Prior: The most senior centurion of a cohort and one of the more senior in a legion.

Praetor: a title granted to the commander of an army. cf the Praetorian Cohort.

Praetorian Cohort: personal bodyguard of a General.

Primus Pilus: The chief centurion of a legion. Essentially the second in command of a legion.

Pugio: the standard broad bladed dagger of the Roman military.

Quadriga: a chariot drawn by four horses, such as seen at the great races in the circus of Rome.

Samarobriva: oppidum on the Somme River, now called Amiens.

Scorpion, Ballista & Onager: Siege engines. The Scorpion was a large crossbow on a stand, the Ballista a giant missile throwing crossbow, and the Onager a stone hurling catapult.

Signifer: A century's standard bearer, also responsible for dealing with pay, burial club and much of a unit's bureaucracy.

Subura: a lower-class area of ancient Rome, close to the forum, that was home to the red-light district'.

Testudo: Lit- Tortoise. Military formation in which a century of men closes up in a rectangle and creates four walls and a roof for the unit with their shields.

Triclinium: The dining room of a Roman house or villa

Trierarch: Commander of a Trireme or other Roman military ship.

Turma: A small detachment of a cavalry ala consisting of thirty two men led by a decurion.

Vexillum (Pl. Vexilli): The standard or flag of a legion.

Vindunum: later the Roman Civitas Cenomanorum, and now Le Mans in France.

Vineae: moveable wattle and leather wheeled shelters that covered siege works and attacking soldiers from enemy missiles.

If you enjoyed the Marius' Mules series why not also try:

The Thief's Tale by S.J.A. Turney

Istanbul, 1481. The once great city of Constantine that now forms the heart of the Ottoman empire is a strange mix of Christian, Turk and Jew. Despite the benevolent reign of the Sultan Bayezid II, the conquest is still a recent memory, and emotions run high among the inhabitants, with danger never far beneath the surface. Skiouros and Lykaion, the sons of a Greek country farmer, are conscripted into the ranks of the famous Janissary guards and taken to Istanbul where they will play a pivotal, if unsung, role in the history of the new regime. As Skiouros escapes into the Greek quarter and vanishes among its streets to survive on his wits alone, Lykaion remains with the slave chain to fulfill his destiny and become an Islamic convert and a guard of the Imperial palace. Brothers they remain, though standing to either side of an unimaginable divide. On a fateful day in late autumn 1490, Skiouros picks the wrong pocket and begins to unravel a plot that reaches to the very highest peaks of Imperial power. He and his brother are about to be left with the most difficult decision faced by a conquered Greek: whether the rule of the Ottoman Sultan is worth saving.

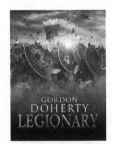

Legionary by Gordon Doherty

The Roman Empire is crumbling, and a shadow looms in the east. 376 AD: the Eastern Roman Empire is alone against the tide of barbarians swelling on her borders. Emperor Valens juggles the paltry border defences to stave off invasion from the Goths north of the Danube. Meanwhile, in Constantinople, a pact between faith and politics spawns a lethal plot that will bring the dark and massive hordes from the east crashing down on these struggling borders. The fates conspire to see Numerius Vitellius Pavo, enslaved as a boy after the death of his legionary father, thrust into the limitanei, the border legions, just before they are sent to recapture the long-lost eastern Kingdom of Bosporus. He is cast into the jaws of this plot, so twisted that the survival of the entire Roman world hangs in the balance.